Heartland

CATHRYN HEIN

HEARTLAND
First published Penguin Group (Australia) 2013
This edition published by Cathryn Hein 2016
Copyright © Cathryn Hein, 2013

Heartland is a work of fiction. All names, people, places, businesses, events or incidences are fictitious and a product of the author's imagination. Any similarities to actual people, living or dead, or actual places or events are entirely coincidental.

Cover Art by Kellie Dennis at Book Cover by Design
www.bookcoverbydesign.co.uk
Formatting by Polgarus Studio: www.polgarusstudio.com

cathrynhein.com

About The Author

 A South Australian country girl by birth, Cathryn loves nothing more than a rugged rural hero who's as good with his heart as he is with his hands, which is probably why she writes them! Her romances are warm and emotional, and feature themes that don't flinch from the tougher side of life but are often happily tempered by the antics of naughty animals. Her aim is to make you smile, sigh, and perhaps sniffle a little, but most of all feel wonderful.

Cathryn was born horse mad, which is little wonder with three generations of jockeys in the family. After scoring her first horse at age 10, upon whom she bestowed the eternally romantic name of Mysty, Cathryn spent the rest of her teenage years in equine bliss riding pony club and hunt club, and competing in eventing, dressage and showjumping until university beckoned.

Armed with a shiny Bachelor of Applied Science (Agriculture) from Roseworthy College she moved to Melbourne and later Newcastle, working in the agricultural and turf seeds industry. Her partner's posting to France took Cathryn overseas for three years in Provence where she finally gave in to her life-long desire to write.

Cathryn currently lives in New South Wales at the base of the Blue Mountains with her partner of many years, Jim. When she's not writing, she plays golf (ineptly), cooks (well), and in football season barracks (rowdily) for her beloved Sydney Swans AFL team.

Contact Cathryn via

cathryn@cathrynhein.com

or the contact form on

cathrynhein.com

You can also follow her on social media at:

Facebook:

https://www.facebook.com/cathrynhein/

Instagram:

https://www.instagram.com/cathrynheinauthor/

Twitter:

@CathrynHein

Goodreads:

www.goodreads.com/author/show/5137697.Cathryn_Hein

For Jim

One

Kingfisher beer in hand, Callie Reynolds wandered onto the tiled balcony of her shared Airlie Beach apartment. She gazed out over the glorious, island-dotted Whitsunday Coast. The sea flickered gold and silver with sunset, white boats baubling its surface. Further out, dark clouds hung bloated and ominous across the horizon. A rising breeze brushed her loose cotton singlet and ruffled her straggly surfer-girl hair. If Callie was lucky, later that evening she'd be treated to a storm show. Not the blaze, noise and spectacle of Darwin in its build-up to the wet, but a show all the same.

She hooked her bare foot around the leg of a cheap green plastic chair, dragged it forward and sank gratefully down, lifting her feet and placing them on the warm steel balcony rail. She took a swig of beer and half closed her eyes. A whole night off. Damn, she was looking forward to this. No drunks wafting alcoholic breath over her, no clothes and skin stinking of stale booze, no tinnitus from the endless doof-doof of loud music. Just peace washed down with a couple of beers, a curry from her favourite Indian takeaway and a DVD of her most cherished secret indulgence, *National Velvet*. Bliss.

The screen door scraped open, revealing Callie's housemate Anna in all her shiny, nightclub-primed glory. With perfectly straight silky blonde hair and light golden skin covering a supermodel's bone structure, Anna looked like the Nordic goddess she aspired to be. Except Anna came from Charters Towers, stood less than a metre and a half tall and possessed a voice so harsh and nasal she sounded like a flu-ridden duck. But she had a typical country girl's generosity and sense of fun, and Callie adored her, even if Anna never did pay her share of the rent on time.

'Are you sure you don't want to come out?' Anna asked, reaching down to slip on a ridiculously high platform shoe. 'Mark'll be there.'

'Positive. I've had enough of pubs for the week.'

'We're going to Bohemia afterwards.'

Callie shook her head. She hadn't set foot in a nightclub since her elder sister Hope's death—not even for work—and it wasn't a rule she was about to break. Pubs she could tolerate. Nightclubs roused too many memories.

Second shoe on, Anna tottered toward Callie, her skimpy halterneck top shimmering. 'You should come out and have some fun.'

Anna said 'fun' like Callie never had any. She did. More often and more easily with each year that passed. Fun simply came in different forms these days.

Callie glanced at the tattoo wrapping around her right wrist like an ornate bracelet. Hope's name circled her skin in hollow uppercase script, the letters outlined in black and filled with blue—the same colour as Hope's eyes. Each capital ended in a flourish decorated with exquisitely tiny leaves, flowers and birds, like the initials of an illuminated medieval manuscript. It'd hurt like crazy, especially where the bone neared the surface of her skin, but unlike the laughing, splashing dolphin on her left bum cheek, Callie never once regretted the tattoo.

'Come on, Cal,' said Anna when Callie remained mute. 'You'll have a great night.'

'Leave her alone,' said their other housemate, Rowan, as he slid open the door and wandered out with one of Callie's beers. Catching her frown, he tilted it at her. 'I'll pay you back tomorrow.'

'You could have asked first.'

He shrugged. 'I knew you wouldn't mind.'

She wouldn't, either, but that wasn't the point. Callie stared back out to sea, wondering if she'd made the right decision to stay in Airlie when Darwin was the safer option. The three of them were all so comfortable now. Nearly eighteen months of sharing a living space, pinching each other's food, enduring loud sex and drunken antics had made them close. Perhaps too close, although nothing like her parents' desperate smothering. Besides, Rowan and Anna liked her for who she was.

She turned back to Rowan. 'Aren't you working tonight?'

'Nope.'

'Going out?'

'I wish.' He made a face. 'Study.'

'Ah,' said Callie, hiding her dismay over her disrupted evening behind a smile of understanding. 'If I steam some extra rice there should be enough curry for two.'

'Thanks but I'll order a pizza.' He grinned. 'That's true brain food.'

'Then you'd best order two,' said Anna, nudging him. 'Seeing as you only have half a brain to start with.'

'Big call from a blonde.'

Anna boggled her eyes at him. 'Blonde and brains aren't mutually exclusive, you know. Anyway, blonde beats bloodnut any day.'

'Hardly. Bloodnuts are bright. In every way.'

Callie intervened before they could really start sledging. 'So what is it this time?'

Rowan screwed up his freckled nose. 'Accounting for Decision Making.'

'Urgh.'

He took another slug of beer. 'Tell me about it. The first assignment's due in a week and I've barely looked at it.'

Which was situation normal for Rowan. Despite the flexibility offered by Open Universities, and as desperate as he was to complete his Bachelor of Tourism and escape the unreliable pay and monotony of bar work, study time proved hard to come by. He, like Callie and Anna, had to take as many shifts as he could get. Thanks to an influx of Baby Boomers, Airlie Beach was no longer a sleepy coastal town. Rents on apartments like theirs had soared, and although cheaper accommodation existed away from the coast, the apartment had a great view, was within walking distance of all their workplaces, and suited their carefree lifestyles.

For all three of them to have a night off, especially a Thursday night when the town was gearing up for the weekend, was a rarity, but they'd make up for their respite over the coming days. Monday morning would find them exhausted, moaning and wondering if it was all worth it.

'I'll try to keep quiet,' said Callie, thinking of *National Velvet*.

Rowan waved her off. 'Don't bother. I'll wear my headphones.' He turned to Anna. 'But if you could keep the sex racket down for once, that'd be helpful.'

'Who said I'll be bringing anyone home?'

Callie and Rowan looked at her. Anna always brought someone home. Usually a computer repairer named Bruce.

'Jealousy's a curse, you know,' said Anna with mocking sneer.

Callie blinked. 'You think I'd be jealous of Bruce?'

Anna's sneer fell. 'Bruce is a mistake.'

'A mistake you seem to make a lot.'

'At least I have sex,' Anna countered.

'Ah,' said Callie, grinning and pointing her bottle Anna's way, 'but is it good sex?'

Rowan cast them a confused look. 'Isn't all sex good?'

The two girls rolled their eyes and laughed. Cicadas joined in with their evening whir. Lights began to blink on from the harbour's flotilla of boats, while the chatter of holidaymakers heading out for dinner wafted from the street below.

Anna glanced inside at the wall clock. 'I'd best get going. I'm meant to be meeting Mark and Donna at Magnum's about now.' She gave Callie a last look. 'Text me if you want to come down. Donna missed you last week and I know Mark'd be happy to catch up.' She winked. 'And a bit more.'

'Thanks, but I'm fine right here.'

And as appealing as Mark was, Callie wasn't interested. She reserved sex for cute backpackers who wanted no more from the encounter than she did— an emotionless but fun romp. Although, to be fair, Callie hadn't had that in a while either.

Rowan leaned his arms over the rail and stared out at the blackening sea, while Callie gazed at the sky, nostalgia for home unexpectedly pinging in her chest. Unlike her home town of Melbourne, where twilight lingered, night fell swiftly in the tropics. She missed the south's lazy close of day, where sunsets slow danced into night. At her grandparents' farm, Glenmore, on Victoria's far western coast where the land sprawled flat toward the sea, they seemed to last even longer. If she closed her eyes, she could remember Poppy's shadow on the beach, stretched reed thin over the grey sand, their fishing rods like endless strings as they cast one more line into the sea.

'She's right about Mark, you know,' said Rowan, turning to lean his back against the rail and perch his elbows on the top.

'I know.' She picked at the label on her stubby. 'And he's nice.'

'But?'

'Too nice.'

'And you prefer bad boys.'

'Maybe.'

Good boy, bad boy—it didn't matter. The truth was she didn't want anyone. No ties, no commitment, no fear of letting anyone down. As much as she liked him, Mark deserved more than she could offer.

Rowan gave her a contemplative look, the one that made her sometimes think he might understand what she'd been through. That perhaps they could talk and share. But losing your eldest brother in a car accident didn't compare. Rowan had nothing to do with Des's death, whereas Callie still struggled to shed her guilt over Hope's.

'So are you still planning on leaving?' he asked after a few moments.

Callie took a swig of beer before answering. Rowan and Anna had been left up in the air for long enough and deserved a decision. Making one, though, had proved difficult. Callie *should* leave. Airlie had been the longest she'd lived in one place since she walked out of her parents' home eight years ago. For the first time in her wanderings, Callie felt settled, as though maturity had finally dulled the edges of her pain. It would never fade, she knew that, but perhaps a kind of freedom beckoned. A freedom she could grasp if she had the courage to try.

'I don't know. I need to settle down somewhere.' Callie looked at him, thinking that maybe if she said it out loud the words would make it real.

'Maybe this might be a good place to call home.'

'There are worse places.'

'There are.'

He held her gaze, a smile in his kind, faded hazel eyes. 'I'm glad.'

Rowan wandered back inside and Callie continued her contemplation of the ocean, wrapped in the warm possibility that perhaps, for once, deep within in her heart, so was she.

***

Callie picked her way onto the marina wall, her tatty salt and sand-encrusted Dunlop Volleys scant protection against the sharp rock angles. To her surprise, she'd slept past dawn. Now she had to hurry to make the turn of the tide and the best fishing. Finally reaching her favourite spot, she laid down her tacklebox and rod and busied herself setting up.

Though still early, the hot sun scalded her skin through the fabric of her long-sleeved shirt and the tatty cotton of her daggy but beloved fishing hat. She squatted down to fix a squishy, crab-shaped lure to her line, making sure to avoid grazing the fine nylon with her sunscreen-slathered legs. One touch and she could kiss goodbye to catching anything, but Callie wasn't stupid enough to venture out without protection. The tropical sun might be beautiful but skin cancer could kill.

Like the sea. Her grandfather had passed away long ago, but she'd never forgotten his lesson: always watch. Rock fishing was one of the most dangerous sports in Australia. No matter how calm things appeared, a freak wave could build in seconds.

She stood and cast out into the open sea with an expert flick, smiling to herself at the whir of the line and the tug of the lure as the current took it. She glanced at the sky, clear but for a few clouds. Last night's storm had passed through and now the day steamed. Unless the breeze picked up the pub where she worked would be stifling tonight, although she was conditioned to the claustrophobia of it and would be too flat out to care anyway. Besides, evening shifts were worth the slog for the freedom of these glorious mornings.

The line tugged. Not hard, just a couple of taps but enough to put her on alert. Callie braced her feet, digging them into crevices, and waited. The hit came. She jerked the rod, grinning when she felt the hook embed. Bream, she guessed from the fight. Not a big one by the feel of things, but size wasn't why she fished. It was the sport, the adrenaline rush and the preservation of memories that after all she'd let go still meant so much.

She reeled the fish in, catching glimpses of it as it fought near the surface, silvery scales reflecting the sun like jewellery. Taking care not to brush it or the line against the wall, she dragged the bream to the edge of the rocks before squatting down to catch it in her landing net.

Her smile broadened. Pan sized. Perfect for lunch.

With the fish scaled and cleaned and stashed in her backpack with a cooler brick, she glanced at the sky again, noting the sun's course. Perhaps another hour, and if she caught enough she might be able to treat Rowan and Anna to a feed as well. Provided Anna was out of bed and not too hungover to eat.

Callie cast out again, thinking about her decision of the night before. She wanted to make this work. She had to, because what had running solved? Nothing. The rift Callie had forced between herself and her parents was too wide for her to ever return home, and no matter where she lived, her guilt still followed. Besides, life was easier here. Full of young transients like her. She fitted.

Rowan was up when she returned late morning, lifting weights at the bench press he'd set up in the lounge, spicing the room with his deodorant and pungent male sweat. His singlet was dark with moisture, his freckled chest heaving with each push. Even with the door open and a breeze clearing the room, the air had that closed-in, dense feeling so unique to the tropics in the wet. Callie itched to turn on the air-conditioning, but after the shock of their last power bill, she, Rowan and Anna had made a pact to use it sparingly. Without air-conditioning, the humidity was impossible to escape.

The barbell made a metallic clank as Rowan set it back in its rack. He took a few deep breaths before sitting up to wipe his sweaty face on a towel. 'Any luck?'

Callie waved her bag at him, talking as she stowed it in the fridge. 'Enough for lunch. For all of us.'

'Cool.'

His attention flicked to the hall, eyes suddenly sparkling. Callie followed his gaze, pressing her lips together as she caught Anna shuffling toward them in a short blue satin dressing gown, her blonde hair knotted and her eyes bloodshot. A lanky, dark-haired man sporting a sheepish smile followed in her wake.

Callie slid a peek at Rowan and quickly looked away before she cracked up. 'Hey, Bruce. How's things?'

'Great.' He placed a hand on Anna's shoulder, unaware of the pained expression it brought to her face.

'Do you want to stop for lunch?' asked Callie, ignoring Anna's sharp look. 'I've enough bream for four.'

Anna's gaze turned withering.

Callie swung away, still trying not to laugh. Poor Anna. She might spout that Bruce was a mistake but that didn't seem to stop her bringing him home. To be fair, Bruce was sweet in a geeky sort of way, and although she refused to recall the incident, Anna had once drunkenly admitted that he was even sweeter in bed, a quality she blamed for her lack of resistance.

'Thanks, but nah. Too much work on. I'll catch ya all later.' He nodded at Rowan and Callie before farewelling Anna with a gentle kiss on the cheek and a cute wink. 'Soon, I hope.'

When the door clicked shut, Anna sank onto the lounge, dropped her head into her hands and groaned. 'Why, why, *why* do I do this to myself?'

'I don't know, Anna,' said Callie. 'Why do you? Perhaps because you actually like Bruce?'

'He's a dork.'

Rowan stood and began wiping down the weight bench's vinyl padding. 'He's all right.'

'So he's a bit dorky,' said Callie. 'He's also sweet and likes you. A lot.'

'You could do a lot worse than Bruce,' said Rowan, tossing the towel over the bar and heading for the door. 'You need anything? I'm going for a run.'

Callie shook her head. 'Anna?'

'Amnesia pill?'

'There's always the hair of the dog,' said Rowan, laughing when Anna made a retching noise. 'Don't expect any sympathy from this end. It's your own fault.'

He left them to it. As soon as the door clicked shut, Anna issued another despairing groan and flopped to her side, wrapping hanks of tangled blonde hair over her eyes as though to shield herself from the world and all its misery.

Callie crossed to the lounge, sat down next to her and stroked her forehead. 'Poor baby.'

'Don't patronise.'

'I'm not. I've had enough regret-filled mornings after to know what it's like.'

Letting go of her hair, Anna rubbed her red eyes and focused them on Callie. 'Why do I keep going back to him?'

'Because you like him.'

'But he's so . . .' She made a face. 'He's a nerd! He fixes computers! I want a man who wrestles crocodiles and rides bulls and drives a proper car. Bruce drives a Hyundai, for god's sake.'

'So you'd trade someone who loves you for some cowboy who probably shags anything that moves?'

'He doesn't love me.'

'Why not give him a chance and find out for sure?' Callie leaned forward, smiling a challenge. 'What have you got to lose?' She glanced at the wall clock and patted Anna's shoulder. 'Are you up for lunch? Only I have to get a wriggle on. My shift starts at two.'

'I think so.' She sniffed then grabbed Callie's fingers, squeezing hard. 'Thanks.'

A choke threatened Callie's throat as she wondered if this was how things would have been with her and Hope, had her sister lived; intimate talks made cosy with friendship. Callie swallowed the roughness down. 'You're welcome.' She squeezed back, emphasising the heartfelt truth of her words. 'Always.'

Half an hour later, Rowan returned wet with sweat and with every exposed centimetre of his pale freckled skin glowing. He threw a large yellow envelope onto their pine dining table before raiding the fridge for cold water, overspill sluicing down his neck as he gulped straight from the jug.

'Stinking out there,' he said between gulps. 'Going to be filthy in the bar this arvo. Letter there for you, Callie.'

'Thanks.' Callie continued slicing cucumber for their salad, in no hurry to check the post. 'Lunch won't be too far away.'

'Good,' said Anna, leaning over the breakfast bar, almost human again after some paracetamol and a long shower. 'I'm starving. I hardly ate anything last night.'

Callie tossed the last of the cucumber into the salad bowl along with the red onion, rocket and tomato, before grabbing a bottle of French dressing from the fridge and splashing it over. The foil-wrapped fish were baking in the oven, the slices of lemon she'd inserted into their cavities already releasing enticing citrus smells. Her stomach rumbled in response. Breakfast was hours ago and salt air always made her hungry. She tossed the salad, pinching a juicy tomato quarter as she worked and wishing Rowan would hurry up in the shower so they could eat properly.

She placed the salad on the table and, for want of anything else to do, picked up the envelope Rowan left for her. She turned it over and glanced at the Alice Springs post mark. Frowning, she retrieved a knife from her place setting and slit open the pasted- down end. Another envelope slid out followed by a torn-off sheet of notepaper upon which her old flatmate, Andrea, had scribbled a cheerful 'howdy-do' followed by an apology and a 'give me a call some time'. Mail had come for Callie then been misplaced in the usual household chaos, but Andrea was forwarding it now, better late than never.

Dropping the note, Callie picked up the other envelope. A few seconds passed before her brain registered the familiar tight scrawl of the handwritten address.

Dad.

She inhaled deeply, hand fluttering to her mouth.

Over the past eight years, contact with her parents had dwindled to Christmas and birthday phone calls. Short conversations marred by hurt and confusion and too many references to the past. Even when Hope wasn't mentioned she cast a shadow, reminding Callie of what she could never escape.

The last call was eighteen months ago, to her flat in Alice Springs. An out-of-the-blue call from her father 'just to see how she was'. They'd been awkward, careful with their words, and though Callie wanted to reach out she saw that her continued withdrawal had gouged a rift too wide for them to bridge.

Straight afterwards, gripped by restlessness, she'd left the Alice and headed for the coast, wandering until Airlie claimed her. This time, whether by accident or subconscious design she wasn't sure, Callie broke her habit and failed to forward her parents a postcard advising them of her new address and phone number.

'Who's it from?' asked Anna, moving close, her voice full of concern.

'I think it's from my dad.'

Anna said nothing. Callie had carefully fobbed off any talk of her family. All her housemates knew was that she'd had a sister who died. She hadn't even wanted to reveal that except doing so was impossible with Hope's name permanently encircling her wrist.

The shower stopped. Rowan would be out any minute—they'd have lunch then head off to work. Callie had to open the envelope now or she'd never make it through her shift for anxiety about what her father had to say.

Nervous but resigned, she slit it open. A letter sat inside, along with another, folded over envelope. She pulled both out, walking toward the balcony as she did. Anna didn't follow, but Callie could feel her scrutiny as sure as she felt the scented sea breeze against her skin. She opened the letter and scanned the contents. Once, then again, as disbelief at the words jumbled their meaning. Hand over her mouth, she reached for the plastic chair and slumped down.

Nanna. Dead. Over a month ago. Alone in Glenmore's kitchen.

Tears fought with anger. How could she have been so selfish? For the sake of a postcard she'd missed Nanna's funeral, and more. She jammed the letters between her legs and covered her face. Nanna had died alone. And Callie never had the chance to say sorry. That she loved her. That she never meant for any of this to happen.

'Callie?' Anna stepped out onto the balcony, Rowan close on her heels. 'Are you okay?'

She sniffed and tried to hide her turmoil, the returning swirl of fear and guilt, and the overwhelming need to run from her friends before she let them down too.

'My grandmother died last month.'

'Oh, Callie, I'm so sorry.' Anna made to reach for her but Callie turned her shoulder and tore the other envelope open as Anna and Rowan exchanged looks.

She read this letter more slowly, absorbing each word, grief and disbelief rising like a wad of thick dry cotton in her throat. She let the letter flutter to the ground, her brow furrowed as she tried to take it all in, tried to understand. She, of all people, didn't deserve this. Surely Nanna had understood that?

A sob threatened. Callie rolled her lips together, pressing hard against its rise. Seeking calm, she stood and faced the ocean, fingers tight around the rail, attempting to think, but her mind kept skittering, emotions darting between gratitude, fear and guilt.

She snatched up the letter and read it again, bland words explaining an unfathomable legacy. The paper in her hands shook, partly from the breeze, partly from her hold.

'Callie?' It was Rowan.

Conviction settled as Callie traced the outline of her sister's name on her wrist. So Nanna's benevolence was misguided, but that didn't mean Callie couldn't correct the mistake.

She stooped to pick up her scattered papers, hair curtaining her face as she willed her stoic mask into position. It was an expression Callie had spent years perfecting, a calm normalcy behind which she hid her turmoil, showing the world that she was strong. With deliberate endeavour, she folded the letters and slid them into their envelopes before facing Rowan and Anna.

'I'm sorry, but I have to go.'

Anna's eyes widened. 'What do you mean, go?'

'I mean I have to leave. Here. I have to drive south.' Callie took a shuddery breath, forcing herself to say the words. 'I have to go home.'

Anna threw a fretful glance at Rowan. 'But why?'

Callie looked at them both, heart aching with loss—for Nanna; for her housemates; for what she was about to do.

'My grandmother, in her will, she left me Glenmore.' She swallowed hard, fingers creasing the envelopes. 'Now I have to give it back.'

Two

Matt Hawkins leaned his arms on the high, weathered, grey redgum rail of Amberton's round yard and rested his stubbled chin on his hands. Though still early morning, sweat soaked his shirt and the waistband of his work trousers. Intense January sun thudded against the crown of his broad hat, burned through his clothes and stung his already deeply tanned arms. The air held a strange hush. Most mornings bird calls added colour to the muted landscape but today they were absent, not even a magpie warble to break the heat ripple, as if the birds were too suffocated to sing. Or, as was the case with a lot of the birdlife in this far south-western corner of Victoria, screech.

The heat didn't bother Matt a scrap—not much did these days. He was back in Australia, out of the army and taking his first steps toward the life he'd coveted since a Taliban bomb had almost shredded his existence and taught him what really mattered in the world. Sure, he had a long way to go yet to reach his dream, and Amberton might not be his ideal image of home, but at least it wasn't Afghanistan.

From the far edge of the yard, his great uncle Wal clicked his tongue, making that special soft noise he reserved for horses, before breaking into a low rumble of one-sided conversation. The words were nonsense. They didn't have to mean anything, only soothe, but it never ceased to amaze Matt how loquacious Wal became in the presence of horses. Around people the old man was taciturn, often rude, whereas horses exposed the humanity and compassion he kept so well closeted.

The leggy chestnut colt Wal was breaking blinked and stepped toward him. Wal stroked Topanga's neck with his left hand. In his right he held a saddle blanket, and as he continued to talk in that low, soothing voice, he raised the blanket and rubbed it over the colt's shoulder. The horse didn't shuffle, merely turning his head to sniff at the blanket before nudging Wal.

They'd been doing this with blanket and saddle for days and the time had arrived for Wal to mount the horse. In previous sessions, Wal had laid across him bareback, letting Topanga get used to his weight and contact, before slowly introducing the saddle. But today would be the day Wal actually sat on the fully tacked colt's back properly.

'You going to check those sheep?' Wal asked suddenly.

'Thought I'd better keep an eye on you. Make sure you don't fall off and hurt yourself.'

Wal laid the blanket over Topanga's back and waited a moment. The colt did nothing except droop his eyes, bottom lip quivering slightly as though lost in a dream of lush pasture. The old man left the horse and reached for the stock saddle he'd left slung over the rail, casting Matt a look as he did.

'If anyone needs keeping an eye on, it's you.'

'Maybe,' said Matt, unfazed by his uncle's tone, 'but my bones aren't as fragile as yours.'

Wal's mouth furrowed so deeply it nearly drowned in wrinkles. Ignoring the comment, he refocused on Topanga, going through the same careful ritual with the saddle as he had with the blanket. The colt remained calm, trusting his human partner. Matt had never seen Wal use any force on a horse. He never showed anger or impatience, or harmed them in any way, understanding that, like all prey animals, fear ruled their instincts. For the horses, no matter what he did, Wal represented calm and safety. For Matt, the old man's skill engendered admiration, respect and more than a little love.

Which was why Matt had no intention of leaving his post.

Topanga shuffled a little as Wal lifted the saddle onto his back, but soon settled with a stroke of his neck and more calming words. The old man moved around the horse with a gentle grace belying his eighty-plus years. Although shrunken with age, his skull as bald and spotted as a quail's egg, and skin as corrugated, dry and nut brown as a freshly ploughed paddock, Wal still possessed his fine-boned jockey's build. The old bugger remained fit and agile too, surprising his nephew with the occasional bow-legged fence leap and handling stock with a strength Matt had assumed long faded.

As Wal secured the girth, Matt climbed up the fence and sat on the top rail, observing closely. Wal moved away to the centre of the ring and clucked at Topanga, indicating for the horse to circle him. Topanga responded as he'd been trained, quietly plodding around, chestnut coat glowing like gold in the bright sun. With a double click from Wal he broke into a trot, tossing his head and snorting, but not in agitation, in celebration. The equine equivalent of happy-to-be-alive joy.

Matt grinned. The horse reminded him of himself when he'd landed back in Townsville after his second tour. The one he'd forced himself to make to prove a point. There were times amid the endless dust and cramped conditions, the exhausting hyper-alertness, when he wondered what the fuck had got into him. First time round he'd nearly been blown to bits. Surely he had enough scars and nightmares? But by the end, Matt knew he'd done the right thing. He'd braved it and, thanks to the army psychologists, was coping okay with the trauma of war and loss. Now he could move on.

After a few laps, Wal called Topanga back to the centre and caressed his nose in approval. Maintaining his chatter, Wal moved to the colt's side and, with one hand on the saddle's pommel, sank his other into a handful of mane. Aware of what was to come, Matt's fingers tightened on the rail. The horse was big, over sixteen hands, and a well-developed two-year-old thoroughbred, bred by a local equestrienne and destined for a showjumping career. Beside the colt's muscled body, Wal appeared small, old and very breakable.

With barely a bounce, Wal leaped onto Topanga's back and settled astride. Topanga arched, his hind quarters tensing as though readying for a buck, and Matt braced himself to jump down to the rescue, but except for the move of his lips, Wal sat quietly, comfortable and relaxed in the deep saddle, unperturbed by the horse's reaction. Taking his cue from Wal, the colt unwound a little, his spine softening from its coiled hunch. Only the twitch of Topanga's ears as he concentrated on the human on his back belied his uncertainty and nerves. Matt let out his breath, his tension easing slightly.

Wal cast him a smug look before breaking back into seriousness. 'Go check those sheep.'

'Are you getting off?'

'Sheep. Now. Or you're fired.'

Matt grinned. 'So you've officially hired me then? Remind me to give you my tax file number and super details.'

Wal muttered something that sounded like 'muppet' and, dismissing his nephew with a small flick of his hand, returned his attention to Topanga.

Matt eyed the horse for a moment, but the colt seemed more curious than anything else about the weight on his back. Perhaps it was safe to leave them alone. The old boy had, after all, been doing this for years without help. And the sheep did need checking. Recent unseasonal rain had brought a deluge of flystrike, and it was cruel to leave the sheep untreated.

He slid off the fence and forced himself to walk away without looking back.

As he passed her tree-shaded run, Dolly, Wal's faithful collie, hoisted her body from her squirmy, nipple-latched pups. Shaking them off as she walked, she pressed her head against the fence, eyes pleading for attention. Matt paused to scratch her ears through the mesh, feeling sorry for the dog and wishing he could take her with him.

'Serves you right,' he told her. 'You can't go sneaking off for sex without facing the consequences.'

Although, in this case, the consequences were undeniably cute. Neither he nor Wal knew for certain who the father was, but they had their suspicions. The pups' fluffy coats and black-and-white colouring said pure collie, which narrowed the field considerably. The only other collie within sniffing range was the Baxters'—the McMansion-building hobby farmers from across the road. Much to Wal's irritation, their dog, Yoda, had a habit of wandering, and worse, stressing Wal's sheep by practising his herding instinct. Words had been exchanged, Yoda's trespassing habit constrained, but for Dolly the damage was done.

He gave Dolly a last scratch and left her to her clamouring pups, choosing to drive out to the far paddock in his ute instead of Wal's. The decrepit LandCruiser's air-con hadn't worked in years and Matt hadn't bought a new car just to let it sit in the shed. Plus he liked the way the Volkswagen Amarok handled. It might not be a traditional farm ute but if it was good enough to act as a Dakar Rally backup vehicle, it'd handle Amberton's unchallenging terrain, and then some.

He found the ewes clustered around a stand of gums, panting despite the shade. Behind them, the state forest spread in a dusty grey-green tangle of trees, shrubs and bracken. He grimaced at the built-up undergrowth. According to Wal, the district hadn't seen a proper burn in years, nor were the authorities doing their job and reducing the risk. Matt had to agree. The forest was a fire waiting to happen. He just hoped like hell it didn't.

He stepped out into the heat, observing the sheep closely. Most seemed okay, hot but normal. Two, though, showed signs of breech strike. Wal had assured him the ewes had been jetted after shearing but there were always one or two who suffered no matter what preventative treatments were used. Those sheep had to be treated and isolated fast before they attracted more blowflies or suffered too much injury.

Matt set to work with a sigh. Even as a kid he'd hated this chore—the smell, the sight of raw, maggot-infested flesh, the dumb suffering of the sheep. Fortunately, he hadn't had to endure it often. Enrolment at boarding school meant he only travelled to Amberton from Geelong during holidays, and then only when his mother decided she didn't want to see him—an occurrence that became increasingly common as he grew older and her career more high-powered and consuming. Flystrike monitoring and treatment was left to Wal or, when he bothered to leave the rural-town pleasures of nearby Dargate, Wal's grandson, Tony. Still, stomach-roiling or not, this was the life Matt intended to pursue and one day, if his plans worked out, he'd have his own place and be tending his own sheep. Until that time, he'd work, observe and suck Wal dry of knowledge.

Trouble was, the old boy wasn't in too much of a hurry to impart any.

With the sheep cleaned up and isolated, and the cut-away maggoty fleece in the back of the ute, Matt drove back to the house, checking troughs and fences as he went. Wal's small herd of Angus cattle watched him curiously as he cruised past, mouths working as they monotonously chewed, tails flicking against the swarming, ever-present flies.

The livestock were all fat, happy and, in the case of the cattle and horses, glossy coated. As far as Matt knew, things had never been any different on Amberton. Matt's aunts had always joked that Wal wasn't much of a husband, but animal husbandry? Now that was a different matter.

Which was why Wal's treatment of poor wart-infested Phantom remained so unfathomable. As Matt turned past the front house paddock and spied the horse standing forlorn and lonely near the gate, he vowed to broach the subject again. Wal would probably give him short shrift as he had every other time Matt brought Phantom up, but Matt wasn't about to let that stop him trying.

Like dreams, some things just couldn't be let go.

***

'So what's the story with Phantom?' Matt asked his uncle early that evening as he drove along Thiedeke Road toward Dargate. Tony had invited them to join him and his family for dinner at Dargate's Commercial Hotel. Wal had tried to pike out, citing tiredness and an early start the next day, but Matt had convinced him to go. It'd do them both good to get out for a night and Matt wanted to connect with his cousin.

Wal's arms tightened across his chest, eyes held straight ahead, lips tight, sealing in any reply. His whiskered chin jutted as his mouth sank inward. In a show of sulks, the old man hadn't shaved although he'd at least shown enough consideration to shower, which was something.

Matt flicked him an amused glance. The old boy hardly needed to speak anyway. His body language said it all: bugger off and mind your own business. Perhaps he should. Amberton and its animals belonged to Wal, not him. He was just a worker.

A worker with a conscience.

'Is it because he was Maggie's?' He looked back at Wal, checking his face for anguish. Maggie was Wal's near neighbour who'd passed away only a few days before Matt's arrival five weeks earlier. The two had been close. Perhaps close enough to have been more than friends. 'You wouldn't be the first person to take your grief out on an animal, you know.'

'Don't be a bloody muppet.'

'Then what?'

'None of your business.'

Irritated by his uncle's recalcitrance, Matt's fists tightened around the wheel. If Wal thought for one second his snappy tone would thwart his great nephew, he had another thing coming.

'I have to look at him every day. That makes it my business. The horse is left covered in warts and ignored while every other animal on the place is cosseted like a baby, and I want to know why.'

A good twenty seconds' silence passed before Wal relented, though his response was a begrudgingly muttered, barely audible, 'I'm waiting.'

'For what?'

'You'll see soon enough.' He waved a finger toward the road. 'Now shut up and drive.'

Matt's jaw felt like Wal's looked—rigid with anger. He considered pushing harder but decided to let it drop. He may have lost this battle but the war wasn't over. Other tactics remained. He just needed to think them through.

Besides, if he was right and Wal's behaviour toward the horse was because of grief, then Matt understood all too well. Grief was an emotion capable of turning good men cold with loss. It could make them behave in ways they didn't mean. Warp their appreciation of what mattered. Matt ought to know. He'd seen it enough.

They finished the journey in silence. As expected on a Sunday night, Dargate's streets were quiet. A few people strolled about, making the most of the cooler evening and extended southern twilight, but the pub carpark sported only a couple of cars and a single motorbike.

Matt parked next to Tony's silver BMW, easily recognisable by its custom GRANEY numberplate. He grinned at the sour expression on Wal's face as he clocked the sleek SUV. Wal had made an identical face when he'd seen

Matt's Amarok. According to his uncle, LandCruisers had built this country, which may have been true, but that didn't mean other makes couldn't continue the job.

'Things must be good in the property game,' Matt remarked as he unclipped his seatbelt.

Wal's only response was to grunt. Given the vanity plate, Matt considered that strangely apt. His cousin had changed since they were boys, and not necessarily for the better. These days he went by his full name, Anthony—as if changing your name made any difference to the man you were. He lived in an architect-designed house on a huge block surrounded by landscaped gardens, which overlooked town from a rise commonly referred to by Dargate locals as 'Snob Hill'. Even his real estate office was ostentatious—a modern, rendered brick building close to the centre of town, painted in the Graney Realty colours of blue and gold.

Tony dressed in expensive-looking men's clothes, wore designer sunglasses, conducted business via iPad and kept his dark hair slicked back like a twenties gangster. Even his speech had changed, from lazy rural broadness to a deep but clipped, slightly snotty-sounding articulation. Matt used to like his cousin but he had a suspicious feeling Tony had grown into a bit of a wanker.

Dinner progressed easily enough, with conversation ranging from the weather, to the local cricket competition, to the much-debated need for a pedestrian crossing in Dargate's main street. Determined to charm Tony's twin girls, Maddy and Flora, Matt parked himself opposite them. The four-year-olds were doll-like miniatures of their mother, Debbie—snub nosed, cupid mouthed and with unruly manes of strawberry blonde curls surrounding their cheeky-cute faces.

On first meeting they'd scuttled away from him, eyes not leaving his face as they whispered urgently to one another from behind cupped palms. Though disappointed, Matt couldn't blame them. His scar gave him a dangerous air, no matter how he tried to soften it with grins and twinkling green gazes. The doctors had done their best but the deep cicatrice extending from the left corner of his eye to his chin before curving back along his jawline toward his ear remained an ugly reminder of how close he'd come to death.

In time it would fade, become less confronting, or so they'd promised, but Matt knew that was a long way off. In the interim, he had to rely on his personality to gain the little girls' trust.

He smiled at them. 'Has Gramps promised you one of Dolly's puppies yet?'

Maddy and Flora shook their head in unison, before darting blue eyes to their mother.

Deb cast him a weary look. 'Don't encourage them, please. They already have Canute.'

'Another dog wouldn't make much difference and Canute would appreciate a bit of canine company. And the pups are seriously cute. There's one that has one ear standing straight up while the other flops straight down.' He raised his hands to his head, demonstrating with his fingers before tilting his head to the side and panting. The girls began to grin.

Head shaking, Deb turned away, distracted by baby Jarrod banging his plastic spoon on his high chair tray. Removing the spoon from his pudgy grip, she chucked him under the chin. In return, the baby blew a happy spit bubble that made his mother glow with love.

A pang of envy hit Matt's chest. The same envy he'd experienced when he visited his old nanny, Antonella, in London after the bombing and found her joyously clucking over her ever-expanding family like a broody mother hen. Until then, he'd used the army as his substitute family, just as he'd done with his old boarding school and, to a lesser extent, Amberton. Yet in those few days, she'd done what no one else had ever managed and shown him what family was really about, what really mattered in life. A life he was now determined to claim for himself, as Tony had.

Matt tamped the feeling down. No point wallowing. His time would come.

Recovered, he tuned in to his cousin's conversation with Wal.

'It makes sense,' said Tony, leaning closer to his grandfather. 'Dargate has never had a period of prosperity like it. And that offshore drilling isn't going to last forever. Prices will come down. This is a once-in-a-lifetime opportunity.'

'No.'

Catching Wal's tone, Matt eyed him. Wal's face wore the same stubbornly shuttered look as in the car, when Matt had brought up the subject of Phantom.

'Gramps, I'm not talking a few hundred thousand here. The Baxters paid over three and a half thousand dollars an acre for their block.' At the mention of the Baxters, Wal's chin jutted even further but Tony carried on. 'You wouldn't even have to organise anything. Graney's would take care of all the subdivision work. And we'd market it. Not that we'd have to do a lot of that. We have buyers clamouring for acreage and Amberton's closer to town than anything we or the other agents currently have on their books. Three and a half thousand dollars an acre, Gramps. Work it out. You're sitting on a gold mine.'

Wal lasered his rheumy eyes at Tony. 'You deaf, son? I said no.'

Tony placed his hand on his grandfather's shoulder and smiled kindly. Perhaps he thought the gesture and expression sympathetic, but for Matt the only thing it conveyed was condescension. Anger on Wal's behalf sharpened his senses.

'I know you love the place, Gramps, but you have to face facts. You're getting on. There'll come a time soon when you won't be able to manage the farm. Mum and Dad have never had any interest in it and farming isn't something I'm keen on either. And you've worked hard all your life. You deserve a break. Isn't it about time you retired, enjoyed yourself, instead of working yourself into the ground?'

With a savage jerk, Wal shrugged off Tony's hand and thrust back his chair. Lifting himself upright, eyes flashing with fury, he pointed a finger at his grandson. 'If you think for one second I'm going to let you split up my land and sell it to a bunch of blow-ins like the Baxters you've got another thing coming. As for locking me away in a nursing home, you can stick that idea fair up your arse. The only way I'm leaving Amberton is in a coffin. You hear? A coffin!'

Tony stood, his own anger leaking through his caring facade. 'You're being stupid.'

'Stupid?' Wal's chest heaved as he sucked in breaths.

Matt glanced at the girls. Their eyes were like discs. Sensing tension, Jarrod broke into a wail. His flustered mother tried to soothe him but the baby only screamed louder.

'Please, Anthony,' she pleaded, glancing at the other tables. Though only two other couples were present in the dining room, all four faces were turned their way. 'Not here.'

Her entreaty worked, at least on her husband. Alerted to the stares, Tony sat down quickly. 'I'm sorry, Gramps. I didn't mean that. Of course you're not stupid. I'm just worried about you, that's all. We all are.' He gestured to Wal's seat. 'Sit down. We'll talk about it.'

'Nothing to talk about. Conversation's over.' Wal nodded at Matt, who caught a hint of wetness in his eyes. Whatever his tough exterior, Tony had hurt him badly. 'I'll see you at the car.'

Wal walked out, leaving the table quiet behind him. Even Jarrod ceased his wails.

Tony ran his hand over his hair. 'Stubborn old fool. He's eighty-two. He should be in a nursing home.'

Placing his cutlery together, Matt shook his head. 'That's as good as putting a bullet in his head. He's doing all right. A bloke who can still break in a horse at eighty-two can't be too frail. Besides, I'm there to help out now.'

'Yes.' Though fleeting, Matt caught a narrowing in Tony's expression. 'So you are.'

'Don't even think it.'

'Who says I was thinking anything?'

'Your face does.' Matt dug out his wallet. 'Think what you like but I can tell you right now I'm not after Amberton. I'm just there to pick Wal's brains until I find a place of my own.'

Tony thought on that for a moment before turning his body toward Matt and laying an arm across the back of his chair. 'Then maybe we can help one another.'

Movements deliberate, Matt picked three twenties from his wallet and placed them under the salt shaker. It was more than enough to cover their meals but he didn't have any change and didn't want to go to the bar to fetch any. Tony had made a show of paying for their meals at the counter, whipping out a platinum credit card before Matt could hand over any cash. Matt hadn't minded then—if Tony thought it proved something, he could go to town—but he minded now. A lot.

'I don't think so.'

'Don't be so hasty. You ever heard of a finder's fee?'

'Forget it, Tony.'

'Anthony. And I won't. This is too big an opportunity.' Tony's face moderated into the same false sincerity he'd used on Wal. He leaned even closer and held Matt's gaze. 'Look, I was serious when I said I was worried about Wal. So are Mum and Dad, but they can't keep an eye on him now they've moved to Noosa. They're relying on me, and I have every intention of being a good grandson and looking after Wal's best interests.'

Though his meal was unfinished and his beer only half drunk, Matt slid his chair back, dislodging Tony's arm. The greedy, selfish atmosphere was making him sick. And he needed to escape before he did something dumb, like punch his cousin square in the mouth.

'A good grandson? You're trying to sell Wal's home from beneath him. That place—the horses, the livestock, the land and forest—keep him alive. Sell it and you'll kill him. So don't talk to me about being a good grandson. You don't even come close to the definition.'

Though Matt had more he wanted to say, he stopped. The girls didn't need to hear what he really thought of their father, and Deb was upset enough. 'I'd better chase up Wal. Thanks for dinner. I'll see you round.'

With a quick nod to Debbie and the girls, he copied Wal and stalked out.

As Matt stepped out into the summer night and spied Wal pacing furiously across the carpark like a demented gnome, his anger suddenly vanished. He shook his head in disbelief as his mouth quirked into a wry smile. So much for playing happy families. Between him and Wal they couldn't even make it through dinner.

Yet for some weird reason he didn't mind. The old boy might be a cantankerous fool but he mattered. Besides, the soldier in Matt liked a good fight. And if tonight was anything to go by, this one might prove to be a beauty.

Three

Callie parked her ute in the crushed limestone bay at the front of Glenmore's worn weatherboard house and leaned back against the seat, breathing shallowly. After too many years and 2600-plus kilometres she'd finally made it back. Even with all those hours of open road rationalising, of making plans, of telling herself this was her path to freedom, the shock of seeing Glenmore, of knowing there'd be no Nanna, no Poppy, no dogs to bark a welcome, no fat Phantom whickering his delight on seeing his mistress, left her shaky and anguished, but mostly unsure if she could endure what needed to be done.

In her shorts pocket sat the keys she'd picked up from Nanna's solicitor in Dargate. She didn't like the feel of them. Keys spoke of distrust when Glenmore had always been a place she and Hope felt safe and loved. A place where the door always stood open, like the hearts held within.

She threw a look at the single-storey house and almost choked at its forlorn loneliness. Once, in the happy past, it welcomed visitors with two polished window eyes set in identical wings extending either side of an inviting, flowerpot-dotted and swept porch. Now the porch was scattered with dried grass, twigs and leaves, the windows opaque with grime. The timber-clad walls still appeared solid but the white paint was flaking, and the green gutters and sills sagged as though weighed by silent tears.

Memories drifted through. Times when the Reynolds family would roll up at Glenmore—herself, Hope, their mum, Jacqueline, and dad, Michael— and even if Nanna was in town and Poppy out working the paddocks, the house would always be open and welcoming. Being family, and immune from formality, they'd use the back door. Mum, a born-and-bred city girl, would shake her head and tut-tut, sending Dad in to check things out before allowing Callie and Hope to set a foot inside. He'd laugh at his wife's city ways, reminding her that no one locked their house out here, but that never stopped Mum fretting.

Callie released a long breath. Thoughts of her family wouldn't help; she needed to focus. And the ute was becoming stifling.

Biting sun stung her shoulders and bare legs as she made her way around the side of the house, the fingers of her left hand tracing the wall's crackled paint. From the stand of stringybarks to the right, where the clover-infested buffalo lawn gave way to a small paddock before merging into state forest, came the rusted screech of a black cockatoo. Callie swung her head, hoping to spot the bird, a local subspecies that had been under threat for years, but all she caught was the sway of trees and heat shimmer.

Another bird sounded, but she didn't recognise the call. The lessons Poppy taught had long faded, lost along with so much else.

More memories. Glenmore pulsed with them. Hope turning cartwheels on the lawn. Little girl tea parties that Nanna dutifully supplied scones for. Hope patiently plaiting Callie's constantly unruly hair in readiness for pony club. Her sister tanned, fit and stunning in cut-off jeans and a bikini top, vibrant with youth and dawning sexuality.

Callie halted for a breath, dropping her hand from the wall and rubbing her arm as though cold, reminding herself again that this was only temporary. A few days of sorting and cleaning, a couple of trips to the dump and charity shop, and she'd be off Glenmore and driving north, leaving her painful past behind forever.

The cockatoo screeched again, and this time she spotted it soaring above the treeline, the underside of its tail flashing scarlet. For some reason, the sight made her smile. She could do this. Hope would want her to move on, and for her own heart, Callie needed it. Fortified, she continued walking round the corner of the house, concentration on the cockatoo's flight.

A streak of fast-moving white exploded in the bottom corner of her vision, followed by a loud, vicious hiss and an orange flash darting lightning fast toward her. Pain burst across her unprotected knee. Yelping and clutching her stinging leg, Callie hopped backward, only to smack her heel into the edge of a raised brick path. The impact sent her windmilling, the pressure popping the stopper from the toe-piece of her thong. She had just enough time to register that her attacker wasn't a snake but an outraged goose before the bird flapped its great wings and lunged again, beak snapping like a rubbery rat trap. Off balance, Callie tumbled flat on her back, the air knocking from her lungs in a great whoosh.

Triumphant honks filled the air. Callie stared at the sky, gulping as she tried to refill the vacuum in her chest. For a moment, a horrible churning panic threatened to overwhelm her as breath refused to come, then her lungs inflated, the ache subsided and with each grateful, shaky breath, her composure slowly returned. Delight began to buzz her insides. Callie rolled her head to the side, a broad grin stretching across her face as she watched the goose strut across the lawn with his beak in the air and his chest puffed out like a squat feathered Napoleon.

Honky-Tonk, Glenmore's little emperor. How the hell could she have forgotten about him?

'Why aren't you dead?' she asked the goose, but Honk's only reply was to release another nasal trumpet before smugly waddling off to pick at grass.

She studied the bird, still astonished and delighted to see him. Honk had been at Glenmore ever since she could remember, and given Callie was now twenty-six, that made him at least twenty, probably much older. For a bird of that great age he appeared remarkably fit—white feathers well preened, his feet and beak a healthy orange, body fat from good pick. But perhaps it wasn't a surprise at all. Nanna had always doted on Honk, and she'd only been gone five weeks.

Nanna. Callie refocused on the house. The paint peel was even worse on this side, savaged by winter weather originating straight off the Southern Ocean, less than a few kilometres away. At the far corner, where the rainwater tank sat separated from the house by a concrete path, the green Colorbond gutter drooped, its connecting downpipe bent out of shape. A loose scrap of iron curled where the other end of the pipe had pulled from the rainwater tank. The windows were dust filmed, the hinges of the rear screen door rusting. Desiccated plants—geraniums by the shape of the leaves and withered flower stalks—flopped sad and brown over the rims of the pots either side of the back door. Only the welcome mat seemed bright with newness.

Poppy would never have let things go like this. But Poppy passed away only months after Hope, condemning Nanna to lonely suffering, an accidental victim of the Reynolds' all-consuming grief. What would Callie know of her grandparents' care for Glenmore? Love hadn't stopped her abandoning them like her parents had done. Anger at herself threatened to bubble through her joy at seeing Honk. She smacked it down. That was unchangeable history; it was the future that mattered.

She raised her foot and waggled the broken thong, the split in the rubber telling her it was unsalvageable.

'Look what you did,' she said, waving her leg at Honk. 'They were only new a couple of weeks ago.'

Honk merely honked and continued grazing.

She shook her head. Flat on her back and talking to a goose. Not quite how she imagined her visit would pan out, but it would make a fun story for Anna and Rowan.

Callie sighed. Flopping about goose chatting wasn't getting any work done and she had a house to sort. She hoisted herself up, dusted off her bum and, unwilling to risk her feet on the hot concrete, half hopped, half tripped on her broken thong to the rear steps. Feet safely on the mat, she pulled the keys from her pocket, struck again by the strangeness of it. That hollow sense of loss.

The screen door opened with a rusty squeal that set Honk off again.

'Oh, shut up,' said Callie, peeling off her broken thong and frisbeeing it, then its partner, in his direction and laughing as Honk raised his snaky neck to the sky and let Callie know exactly what he thought of that impertinence.

Sobering and ignoring the goosy clamour, she turned back to the timber door. With a fortifying breath she unlocked it and pushed it open, hovering on the threshold as the years dissolved and she became an excited child once more. Except on this visit, there'd be no comforting Nanna hugs or whiskery Poppy kisses. All she had now were ghosts.

The kitchen had barely changed since the last time she sat in its homely warmth. Though the fridge and microwave seemed newish, and the faux slate vinyl flooring a vast improvement on the faded red and white lino of Callie's memory, the kitchen still looked as it always had, like something out of a seventies film set. A walnut veneered built-in kitchen occupied the eastern side of the room and anodised pink canisters sat in rows on the shelves above the cupboards. Along the western wall, to the left of the back door, stood a walnut and etched glass dresser, the mirrored back reflecting the good china and crystal stacked neatly inside. Crocheted doilies decorated the top and protected the surface from the scratchy bases of Nanna's most treasured knick-knacks—a yellow and black toreador, his scarlet cape elegantly draped at his side, and the impossibly bright red bull that was his foe.

As if placed there by Nanna only that morning, folded tea towels hung neatly over the door handle of an upright cooker that for years had baked hundreds of cakes, biscuits, pavlovas, roasts and casseroles. And still in pride of place above the kitchen sink window, its surface now confettied with fluff, hung Nanna's beloved velvet picture of Elvis, her favourite singer.

Callie smiled as images flooded her mind. Nanna washing dishes, humming 'Suspicious Minds' to herself. Nanna fussing with chocolate crackles, briefly silencing Callie's obsessive horse chatter with a chocolate-crusted spoon to lick. Poppy with his ear to the radio, listening to the race day call of the card, scribbling notes on his form guide. Hope in the corner near the stove, playing with Mitzi the bitza's ears, bright and pretty, the way she used to be before teenage rebellion made her unfathomable.

A blowfly buzzed Callie's ear, forcing her inside. She shut the screen door but kept the timber one open to let in air. The kitchen had a musty edge, the atmosphere almost cloying, and for a fanciful moment she wondered if death still clung to the dust motes. This was where her dad said they'd found Nanna, slumped at the scratched Formica table.

Callie closed her eyes. How cruel that she should die alone like that. Even crueller that her sole surviving granddaughter had received the news too late to make the funeral. Another rejection of a loving woman who was owed so much more.

Clean up, put the farm on the market and get the hell out, the faster the better, leaving all these memories and mistakes for good.

Easy.

Except it wasn't.

Because no matter how she hardened herself, each time Callie thought of letting Glenmore go, a part of her inner self cried out at the injustice, and her heart bled a bit more with loss.

She breathed in a shuddery breath, tears threatening. Nanna always knew this was where she'd been happiest. 'You're one of us,' she'd say, usually with a ruffle of Callie's hair. Even as a child Callie recognised Maggie Reynolds's subtle rebuke to her daughter-in-law, who had always found rural life alien and trying. To be fair, Jacqueline did enjoy the local equestrian fraternity, which suited Callie perfectly. All that had mattered to her back then was unfettered access to her adored second home and the love of her life, Phantom.

Callie rubbed her hand over her face. Wallowing wouldn't get the job done and hours of work lay ahead. And tears. There'd be plenty of those. Happy, nostalgic ones, she hoped.

Recalling her promise to Anna, she punched out a quick text message.

Arrived safe. Bit sad but OK. Lots 2 do. Will be in touch. x

Anna, the text message queen, shot back an almost immediate reply.

**hugs* Call if u need shoulder 2 cry on. Remember we're here 4 u. Always.*

***

Three hours later, her nose sore from blowing it on Nanna's cheap tissues and the skin of her cheeks salted and itchy from dried tears, but with the main bedroom cleared out, Callie returned to the kitchen for a rest and a cuppa. Plastic bin liners full of clothes were propped along the hall ready to be hauled to the ute and driven to the Salvation Army's collection bin in Dargate. On the kitchen table sat a box of belongings she couldn't bear to part with:

Nanna's silver brush set; a string of pearls Callie discovered slipped down the back of the dressing table; a cameo locket with *Love Tom* engraved on the back and youthful photos of her smiling grandparents inside; a silver frame containing a black-and-white photograph of Callie's great-grandparents, staring starched and sour-faced at the camera.

And on top, the item that had finally melted every ounce of stoicism she possessed—Callie's first blue ribbon.

She'd found it folded inside an envelope in Nanna's hanky and stockings drawer. Despite the years, the felt retained its cobalt blueness. Even the yellow screen-printed letters remained, cracked but vibrant, spelling out their special message: Dargate Pony Club Gymkhana. First Place.

Setting her cup of instant black coffee aside, Callie picked the ribbon up again. She remembered what it was for now—quietest mount, 14–15 hands. No surprises given Phantom's bombproofness. You could let a cracker off and he'd barely shudder. But take his feed bucket away and the stout grey gelding turned into an eye-rolling, lunging lunatic. A Honk, but with bigger teeth.

Damn, Callie had been proud. She'd even slept with the ribbon clutched tight against her undeveloped chest, wracked by the childish panic that a jealous stranger would come in the night and snatch it away. It had taken days for the novelty to wear off, but by the end of those school holidays she'd earned two more and that first ribbon seemed to lose some of its specialness. Yet Hope understood what it meant. She'd placed it in the envelope when Callie's interest had faded. Nanna must have found it and, understanding too, kept it safe.

She let the ribbon slide back to the table and stared at her right wrist. Her tattoo seemed brighter today, as though the colour responded to some unknown force in the atmosphere. Perhaps, like Nanna, an essence of Hope lingered, floating from the walls and into Callie's skin. Conveying the message that Callie's choice was the right one.

The noise of a car slowing and changing gears broke her contemplation. She listened closer, frowning as the crunch of tyres on gravel battled with the rising noise of a diesel engine. Wondering who the hell her visitor could be when no one apart from the solicitor, Anna and Rowan knew she was here,

Callie walked to the sink and peered through the window. A battered and rusty white LandCruiser towing an equally battered aluminium horse float pulled up in the potholed space that stretched between the house and Glenmore's decaying machinery shed.

The engine cut and a short elderly man alighted.

'Damn,' said Callie, recognising Wal Graney. Like Honk, she'd assumed Nanna's nearest neighbour had passed away long ago. Wal had seemed ancient even when she was a child, yet there he was, a bit stiffer and bow-legged, and a lot balder and wrinklier, but well and truly alive.

Without so much as a glance at the house, Wal jammed a faded Carlton Football Club baseball cap on his head, stalked to the rear of the float, lowered the tailgate and disappeared inside.

She glanced at the ribbon. She had Wal to thank for that. And for all the others that followed. He'd taught her to ride.

Her heart skipping with pleasure at the sight of her old mentor, Callie ducked out the door, wincing as her feet struck hot concrete and cursing her rashness in tossing her thongs at Honk. She hopped and ouched her way to the front of the house and her ute, pausing to dig into the tray for her boots and pulling out her fishing sandshoes instead. Not ideal but they'd do. Callie hooked them on as she continued her ungainly hop back round the house to the float.

'Where are you, Wal? Don't tell me you've grown shy in your old age.'

A grunt emanated from the float, making her grin. Wal may have grown older but from the sound of it he hadn't changed. Good. She liked his surface grumpiness. It made him a perfect target for teasing.

'I hope you're not here to flog me one of your dud racehorses. I'm broke enough as it is.'

Shoes fixed, she peered inside, jerking back as a bay gelding wearing a blue webbing headcollar with the lead dangling, clattered down the ramp, eyes huge and worried as it stared around. Callie's fingers shot to her mouth as she caught sight of the horse's face, pity thickening her throat and stinging her eyes.

Greyish lumps of varying diameter spattered his skin, extending like a hideous pox from his muzzle to the edge of his jowl. The infestation was worse around his mouth and eyes, making his skin appear as though it swarmed with small pale flies. Despite the lumps, the horse seemed in good health, with a bright inquisitive expression, pricked ears and a coat that, while needing a good brush, seemed glossy enough. Callie glanced at his feet, noting that they'd been recently trimmed and that the hoof walls appeared smooth and without cracks.

She ran a critical eye over his build, impressed by the straightness of his hocks, the curve of his shoulder and width of his chest. Longing tugged at her insides the way it always did when she saw a horse. The feeling never faded, no matter how hard she suppressed it. Her love for this most magnificent of creatures was part of her DNA, with her for eternity.

Wal picked his way down the float ramp, caught the lead and rubbed the animal's cheek before turning to consider Callie with rheumy brown eyes. He gave her a long look up and down, mouth working as he took in her straggly blonde hair, her low-waisted, high-cut shorts and loose tank top, the tangle of friendship bracelets around her left wrist and, finally, the tattoo around her right.

'Hmph,' he said, as though he hadn't expected much different.

'Nice to see you, too,' replied Callie, grinning and moving forward to kiss him affectionately on the cheek. 'It's been a long time.'

She pulled back to inspect him more closely. He seemed sturdy enough, though his face had sunk from what she remembered, as if it'd seen enough of the world and caved in on itself in protest.

'You've grown.' The words came out like an accusation but Wal always acted as though he disapproved of everyone and everything. Callie didn't mind. She knew from experience that gruff exterior hid a heart full of kindness.

'It's what happens, Wal. Natural human biology.' She turned her attention to the horse, drawn by her yearning and compassion. 'What's wrong with him?'

'Warts.'

She made a face, earning a sour look from Wal.

'Look at you, turning up your nose. Grown up into your mother, you have.'

Callie threw an equally sour look back. 'Hardly.'

The accusation rankled. Even before Hope died, Callie's relationship with her mother was difficult. For most of their childhood, Hope was as happy at Glenmore as her sister, but she was also very much Jacqueline Reynolds' daughter, and Callie felt their connection acutely. The way they talked fashion and make-up and celebrity gossip, and liked to go shopping together, dressed with the same sleek care. The way they'd tease Callie for her lack of fashion sense and tell her how, if she wasn't careful, she might turn into a rustic, as if that was some sort of terrible fault. Her dad used to hug her close in sympathy but it never alleviated Callie's feelings of alienation, of lacking something that Hope so obviously possessed.

Plus, no matter how adult she tried to be about it, the role her mother played in Phantom being sold still hurt.

'Acting like her.' Wal gave the horse another cheek rub as though in apology for Callie's rudeness. 'They're only grass warts. They'll be gone in a month or so.'

Determined not to let her annoyance show any further, Callie reached out to the horse, letting him sniff her fingers before tracing her hand up his nose and stroking the perfect white star in the centre of his forehead. The delicious heady scent of horse filled her nostrils. Damn, how she'd missed that smell. Nothing existed like it in the world.

'He's lovely,' she said, meaning it despite the warts.

'Glad you think so.' Wal grabbed her hand and slapped the lead rope onto her palm and closed her fingers around it. 'Cos he's all yours.'

For an unreal moment, Callie's heart surged with joy. The animal took a step forward and nudged her shoulder, hunting for more pats. She stroked his neck, feeling eight years old again, drawn to that unforgettable day when Poppy had taken her hand and led her to the paddock where her new not quite pony, not quite horse, Phantom, waited.

'Right. I'll be off then,' said Wal, bending to raise the float ramp.

With a blink and a whump, Callie landed back in the present. Her gaze flicked from Wal to the rope to the horse and back again. Still uncomprehending, she held up the lead.

'What about this?'

'Told you. He's yours.'

She threw the lead at Wal's chest as though it were on fire and took a rapid step back, palms held up as she vigorously shook her head.

'Oh, no, no, no. This is not my horse. Nanna's will mentioned nothing about a horse.' She ticked items off her fingers. 'House, land, furnishings, term deposit. No horse.'

'Well, there wouldn't be, would there? Maggie only bought him a few months ago. Name's Phantom.'

Phantom. She breathed in hard, wanting to cry. *Damn you, Nanna.*

With intense effort she brought herself under control. 'I don't care what his name is. I don't want him.'

Wal merely stared stubbornly back with his arms crossed, making no move to take the lead. She eyed Wal and then the animal, who blinked long-lashed eyes at her like a horsey come-on. A young thoroughbred, she guessed. Around sixteen hands. Probably straight off the track and as mad as a cut snake. Although he didn't look crazy, just warty, perplexed and, with his lead dangling, unfazed by the prospect of freedom. Dumb then. Too stupid to be good for anything.

When Wal still made no move, Callie snatched the lead rope and held it out like a peace offering. 'Look, Wal, you have to understand, I'm only here for a few days. Just long enough to clear out the house and put the farm on the market. Then I'm off.'

Wal sucked his lips in so hard his mouth nearly vanished in a wave of wrinkles.

'That'd be right. Go on, run and hide again. Leave poor Phantom here to rot like you did the first one.'

That stung. Badly. Callie clenched her jaw against the hurt, her words emerging like bricks. 'I didn't run and hide.'

Wal made a disgusted pfft noise. 'Yeah?'

'I was sixteen. I had no way of getting here!'

'Ever heard of a bus?'

She threw her arms up, startling Phantom, who snorted and shuffled a few steps back. 'It was too hard! I couldn't help it.'

'No, but your sister could've stopped her carry-on. Broke Maggie's and Tom's hearts, not seeing you girls.'

Callie held up the flat of her hand, indicating no more, anger fizzing at the attack on Hope. Her sister was off-limits. To everyone. 'You leave Hope out of this.'

'Bit hard when she was the cause. Bloody city people with their discos and drugs.' Ignoring Callie's narrowed eyes and barely stoppered fury, Wal turned his back and secured the tailgate. As he finished, Phantom stepped forward to nudge him in the shoulder. Wal gave the horse an affectionate pat. 'You be good for the missy now or she's likely to send you to the knackers.'

'Oh, shut up. I'd never do that and you know it.'

He pointed a stumpy finger at her. 'The only thing I know for sure is that the missy I taught to ride wouldn't have run away from what she loved, but you did.' His hand dropped. 'Don't forget to lock up Honk at night or the foxes'll get him like they did the chooks. And wash out his water bowl. Geese need clean water like any other animal.'

As the last of his words left Wal's mouth the subject in question waddled around the opposite side of the float. Spying trespassers, Honk immediately stormed into a flurry of wing flapping and outraged honking. Phantom skittered in shock before his flight instinct kicked in. Intent only on escape, he barrelled forward, knocking Wal against the end of the float and sending the old man's head crunching hard against the sharp steel corner of the tailgate.

Wal's legs collapsed, dropping him into the horse's panicked path. Callie lunged to protect him only to collide with Phantom's shoulder, the impact catapulting her to the ground. Even more frightened, Phantom surged ahead, almost falling to his knees as his front hoof caught on Wal's hip, before regaining his balance and clattering away toward the house paddock.

Callie scrabbled to her hands and knees and stared at Wal's crumpled, still body.

'Wal?'

Silence returned to the farm. Even Honk seemed shocked by the chaos he'd caused.

Stomach a frozen knot, Callie crawled to Wal's side, breathing hard as memories of that terrible night with Hope crowded in.

'Wal?' She took his hand and rubbed it, willing him to groan, to move, to do anything. 'Wal, please.'

A cockatoo screeched across the hot sky like an echoed scream from the past.

But just as in Callie's nightmare with Hope, the old man didn't respond.

Four

Matt strode down Dargate Hospital's main hall toward Wal's ward. He'd only been here once before – twelve years earlier when Tony broke his wrist falling from the flying fox they'd secretly rigged by Amberton's creek—but nothing much had changed. The walls were still a soothing pale blue, the floor well-scrubbed grey lino. Although updated, photographs of Dargate's great and good added cheerful colour to the bland interior. He even recognised the kindly voiced nurse who directed him to his great uncle. She recognised him, too, smiling secretly at Matt's surprised blinks before patting his shoulder and sending him on his way.

He wondered how she stripped time like that, taking him from mature adult to teenage boy in a glance. There were days when he stared in the mirror barely recognising himself, and it wasn't just the ugly scar zigzagging his face. Age and sun exposure had weathered his once clear, flush-cheeked boyishness. His dark hair, for so long kept buzz cut, now reached the collar of his polo shirt. Stubble decorated his formerly clean-shaven jaw. But the biggest change was in his expression. Amberton had made him smile again.

Except he wasn't smiling now.

Fucking Tony. So they'd had a bit of a row in the pub. That didn't mean his cousin could take all afternoon to alert him about Wal. Tony had his mobile number. He was just being a prick.

Matt turned the corner, glancing into the main waiting room as he passed. A tanned, athletic-looking blonde woman stood with her forehead pressed against the floor-to-ceiling window, but she wasn't admiring the room's walled garden. Her eyes were closed, her lips compressed, her arms wrapped tight around her body.

A body that turned Matt's feet leaden.

Hope.

But it couldn't be. Hope was dead, yet he'd know that jawline, those cheekbones, that small, slightly pointed nose anywhere. Sensing his scrutiny, the blonde twisted her head to the side and regarded him with red-rimmed blue eyes. Alike, but definitely not Hope.

'Supercallie,' he said without thinking.

She frowned as if she hadn't quite heard right. Fuck. Supercallie was Hope's special name for her sister. Matt shouldn't have known it. Needing to cover up, he headed toward her, hand extended.

'Callie. Good to see you.'

She took his hand, the frown turning to puzzlement. Unlike the nurse, she didn't recognise him, but that was no surprise. Their acquaintance had been limited to brief encounters at Wal's or on the sandy trail leading to the broad, seaweed-strewn sweep of MacLeans Bay. It was her sister he'd spent all his holidays with.

'It's Matt. Matthew Hawkins. Wal's great nephew.'

As soon as he mentioned Wal, her eyes widened. Grabbing the sleeve of his shirt she launched into a series of rapid fire questions.

'How is he? Is he conscious? I followed the ambulance but they wouldn't let me into emergency, and now no one will tell me what's happening. He's okay, isn't he? It's just a bump, isn't it? A bit of concussion?' Her blue eyes, so like Hope's, widened even further as she misinterpreted his slow response. 'Oh, my god.' One hand went to her mouth as the other stretched behind her for a chair. She collapsed onto the vinyl, fingers fluttering above trembling lips. 'He's dead, isn't he?'

He'd never heard anyone sound so broken. Weird, given as far as he knew neither she nor her family had set foot in Dargate in years. What would Callie Reynolds care about the old boy?

A lot, by the look of things.

Matt crouched in front of her. 'Hey, shh. It's all right. Wal's fine. Fractured hip, sore head, but fine.' He smiled reassuringly. 'He's a tough old bugger. It'd take a lot more than a knock from a horse to take him out.'

She breathed out hard and leaned her head back, blinking at the ceiling, hands gripping the chair arms, and he noticed that the bracelet around her right wrist wasn't a bracelet at all, but an ornate tattoo. He studied it, his stomach curling with sorrow as he recognised the letters. Thinking how much worse it must be for Callie. For him, Hope was a bittersweet memory from which he'd moved on—the girl who'd broken his heart and later died in shocking circumstances. But for the underage sister who'd reportedly found her dying on a nightclub floor, forgetting wasn't an option.

For several heartbeats, Callie didn't say anything, then she focused on him and it was as though a different person had slipped inside her body. Colour returned to her face. Her mouth lost its tightness. Her shoulders and arms loosened, her body easing free of tension, face settling into bland politeness, as if her previous distress had never occurred.

'I should have realised nothing could crack that hard head of his,' she said, a smile in her voice. 'Can I see him?'

He shook his head. 'The nurse said family only. He's only just come out of surgery. Tomorrow you should be right.'

She cast a wistful look toward the door. 'Tomorrow. There goes my fast getaway.'

'Short visit then?'

'Very. I wouldn't be here at all except the house needs clearing out. Once that's done and Glenmore's on the market, I'll be off. My grandmother died,' she added unnecessarily. 'She left me the farm.' Shaking her head, she gave a half laugh. 'A farm, a mad goose and a horse.'

She wanted to put Glenmore on the market? Matt didn't get it. Hope always said her sister loved the farm. That she was obsessed with the place, counting down the days between visits, phoning daily to check on her horse. Tagging Glenmore as 'home' instead of their suburban Melbourne address. Why would she want to sell a place she loved so much?

Callie's tattoo flashed vivid blue as she raised her hand to tuck a wayward tress of sun-bleached hair behind her ear, explaining everything.

'Right. It's for the foundation.'

The amusement in her eyes turned dull. 'It's for a lot of things.'

Fuck. Another stupid mistake. What was wrong with him? So she was a hot-looking blonde. Like he hadn't come across one of those before.

Rattled by the strength of his attraction, Matt straightened and tilted his head at the exit. 'I guess I'd best go check on Wal.'

The dullness eased; life returned to her expression. 'Of course. Will you tell him I'm glad he's okay and that I'll visit tomorrow? Oh, and tell him not to worry about Honk. I won't forget to lock him up.'

'Will do.' He paused, hands deep in his pockets, knowing he should walk out right now before he said something else idiotic, but caught by their connection, albeit minor and secret on his part, with Hope. 'It was good to see you again, Callie.'

'Good to see you, too, Matt.' She smiled, and for one incredible moment he was fifteen again, facing Hope in awkward teenage silence while she bounced his lovesick heart with a single look. 'Maybe I'll see you around.'

And all Matt could think as he headed back up the hall was that he hoped like hell she did.

***

'Looks like someone's been spoiling you,' Matt said to Wal the following afternoon as he spied the flowers, grapes and ginger ale lined up on Wal's bedside table. He picked up the glossy hardcover book lying next to the grapes—a biography of the previous year's Melbourne Cup winner, and the horse's unconventional rise to fame—and flicked a quick look at the photos in the centre before placing it back down again.

Wal jerked his head at the table. 'That's all the missy's doing.'

'The missy?'

'Maggie's granddaughter.'

'So she's been in already?'

'Spent most of her time trying to convince me to take back Phantom.'

Matt dragged a plastic chair to the bed and sat down. He glanced across at the ward's other patient, a shrivelled, elderly man curled up on his side with his blanket pulled up to his ears and whom Wal had identified yesterday as that 'useless alcoholic Arthur Metcalf'. Though Arthur didn't appear to be listening in, Matt kept his voice low. A man didn't have to be a local to understand what rural towns were like.

'I take it Callie's arrival was what you've been waiting for.' When Wal didn't answer he went on. 'It's no big secret any more. She told me Maggie left her the horse.'

'You been talking to her?'

'I saw her yesterday, remember?'

Wal avoided his gaze and Matt felt a pang of sympathy. Given Tony's recent treatment, his uncle probably didn't want to admit he couldn't remember much about Phantom bowling him over, or the events thereafter.

'She doesn't want him, Wal.' His uncle's mouth drew in and for a moment Matt thought he saw a glisten of tears in Wal's old eyes. He placed his hand on the bed near Wal's. 'You might have to take him back.'

'Can't.'

'Why not?'

'Because I promised Maggie, that's why not.' Wal tried to shift but the pain of his hip stilled him. He threw a filthy look at Matt, as if this were all his fault. 'When are they going to let me out of this place?'

'Not for a while yet. They get all tense about broken hips in geriatrics.'

'You watch your tongue, lad.'

'Wal, you're eighty-two. That makes you a geriatric.'

Wal turned his head away, mouth screwed up so hard his nose almost crumpled into his chin. Matt's sympathy deepened. The poor old sod couldn't accept that his body wasn't the same as it once was.

'Tony came earlier.'

'Oh yeah?' Matt didn't like the way Wal sounded. He leaned forward, watching him closely.

'Looked at me like I was about to drop off the perch. Little shit then had the nerve to ask if I had a will.'

Matt kept his expression neutral but his fingers curled in anger. Just being a good grandson, like fuck—the only thing motivating his cousin was greed.

That Amberton was worth a small fortune in the current property climate couldn't be denied but the point was it was Wal's place, not Tony's. Wal loved it and, though he had no real ties, so did Matt. The influence Wal and Amberton had on Matt's life, on his maturity, was profound. He'd learned to be a man there.

And he'd loved. Lost just as hard too.

He dragged a hand across his jaw, clean shaven for the first time in days, thinking yet again of Callie. How she reminded him of Hope but in a more knowing, adult way. So she should. He was a grown heterosexual man and Callie had developed from adolescence as much as he. Impressively so, in her case.

'You finished that fence?' asked Wal, interrupting his thoughts.

'Just about.'

Wal grunted. 'Should've had it done by now.'

'Yeah, well, believe it or not, I've been more worried about you.'

'Heifers probably need moving.'

'I'll do it this arvo.'

They lapsed back into silence, the same as they did over breakfast and dinner at Amberton. Matt picked up the book again and flipped to the title page, surprised to discover Callie had signed it. *To the best riding instructor in the country. Get well soon. Callie x.*

He studied her writing. Nothing like Hope's. Callie's script was round and loopy. Hope always used print, each letter carefully formed. He'd loved her writing, the little poems she sneaked into his pockets, the cards she sent to him at boarding school, causing him great pride and embarrassment at the same time, and making the long wait for holidays even more agonising. He'd loved everything about her. Or thought he had.

Looking back he could see it for what it was—complete teenage infatuation, made more intense by its secrecy and always destined to end in heartbreak.

'You should go check on the missy this afternoon,' Wal announced.

'What for?'

'Make sure she's looking after Honk properly. And Phantom.'

'I'm sure she remembers how to look after a horse, and Honk can take care of himself.'

Wal grunted. 'Don't trust her.'

'To look after Phantom? Come on, she loves horses.'

'Changed, she has.'

'Of course she has. She watched her sister die on a nightclub floor. What did you expect?'

Wal didn't answer.

Perplexed, Matt inspected him. The old boy fairly churned with frustration. His hands were clawed around the top of his blanket. His mouth worked as though trying to suck his teeth out of their sockets, and his eyes were narrowed in that way they did when he was fuming inside.

Matt replaced the book and leaned forward. 'All right, what's going on?'

'Nothin'.'

'Don't give me that.'

Wal's indignation won out against his natural taciturnity. 'It's that bloody missy, isn't it? Selling Glenmore. Ungrateful little wench. And after all Maggie and Tom did for her.'

Brilliant. Wal was off on another of his rants about things he had no clue about. For a man of such extreme sensitivity to animals his empathy for humans, bar the occasional insight, was almost non-existent.

'Oh, come on, Wal. You can't blame her,' Matt said, irritated. 'She spent half her childhood there with her sister. She probably sees Hope in every corner, not to mention her grandparents. It's taken courage for her to even set foot in the place.'

Wal pointed a shaky finger at Matt, eyes flared with anger. 'She ran away. Poor Maggie was devastated.'

'And so was everyone else over what happened to Hope! For fuck's sake, Wal, show a bit of compassion.'

'She should have come home, where she belonged!'

Any sympathy Matt felt for his uncle evaporated. This was fucked. Wal would never understand what it was like to watch someone you cared about die while everything you did to stop it failed. He shoved back the chair and stood; the scrape of legs on lino was harsh in the sterile room. 'I'm going. I'll see you tomorrow.'

'Sit down. I haven't finished with you yet.'

He regarded Wal steadily. Matt had been ordered around by far more intimidating men than his uncle, and he wasn't in the army any more. He didn't have to take anyone's shit, least of all Wal's.

'I've work to do.'

'Too right you do. Starting with Glenmore.'

'What's Glenmore got to do with me?'

'Everything. Now sit!'

Across the room, Arthur produced a wheezy snuffle and rolled over. Both Matt and Wal watched him, but he seemed to have returned to sleep.

'Sit down, lad,' Wal said, tone conciliatory. 'There's something I need to talk to you about.'

Talk? That'd be a first. Matt scratched at his scar, thinking. Despite still wanting to thump the old man, curiosity tugged like an insistent child. What difference would a few minutes make? Decided, Matt lifted the chair back over and perched on the edge. 'All right. I'm listening.'

Wal sucked on his lips for a minute, observing his roommate before twisting his head toward Matt. 'Maggie knew she wasn't well. Heart problems like Tom. Happens in old people.' He made 'old people' sound like a species he didn't belong to. 'She was desperate to contact the missy but the address in Alice Springs that Michael forwarded led nowhere. The missy either didn't receive her letters or didn't want to reply. Bar jumping in the car and driving there or hiring one of those detectives, which she couldn't afford, Maggie had no other way of tracking her down.'

'Why did she need to contact Callie? Seems to me Callie made it pretty plain she never wanted to set foot on Glenmore again. She's only here now because someone has to clean the place out.'

'Maggie knew how to make her right.'

Matt shook his head. It was up to Callie to find peace in her own way. Everyone's demons were different. Going back had worked for him, but that didn't mean it'd work for her. 'Only Callie can do that.'

'Don't be a muppet. Stupid missy wouldn't know her arse from her elbow these days. Gone all citified like her mother.'

Matt leaned back with his arms crossed, breathing carefully in an effort to keep his temper in check. 'You have no idea what it's like to stand by helpless while someone dies, do you?'

'Maybe not, but I sure as hell know right from wrong. The missy has to stay. I made a promise to Maggie.'

Matt said nothing. From the hall came the clink of a wonky wheeled trolley.

'And I'm not the sort of man who breaks his promises.'

He wasn't either. Even as a boy, Wal assured Matt he would always have a room and a job at Amberton, and he'd never once reneged, even in the years when cattle and wool prices were dismal and the farm was doing it tough.

'All right, so what's this got to do with me?'

'I want you to keep her there. I can't bloody do it stuck in here, can I?'

'Right. And how do you propose I go about it? Chain her up?'

'I don't know. Use your bloody charms. Worked on her sister, didn't it?'

Matt jerked forward in shock. 'What do you know about that?'

'You think I didn't know?'

Matt could only stare at his uncle. Of course he assumed Wal didn't know. *No one* knew. It was his and Hope's secret. Their precious, private thing.

'Maggie knew too,' Wal added smugly. 'She noticed Hope wandering off just as I noticed you. I told her not to worry. That you were a good lad and wouldn't touch her.' The smugness disappeared. 'But you must have. That's why she went off the rails like she did.'

'What we did is none of your business, but Hope's drug taking had nothing to do with me. I hated it. It was because of that we broke up.' That and the fact she called him a boring country bumpkin who couldn't see past his great uncle's farm. Big call considering that by then, thanks to his mother, Matt had already travelled half the world and journeyed to cities a shitload bigger and busier than Melbourne. He might have preferred the country, but at least he'd developed that partiality from experience. Unlike her. Funny how even as a teenager he sensed what he wanted. Took him a while to see that though. Still, here he was, finding his way at last.

Now it was Wal's turn to be silent while he worked his mouth and mulled over that piece of information. 'Doesn't change the matter though. Still need to get the missy to stay.'

'I'm not doing it.'

What did Wal take him for? Some sort of gigolo? And the truth was he was afraid. He knew from experience Callie was just the sort of girl he'd fall for. Matt wanted to find new love, live new dreams, not get burned by someone hell-bent on leaving.

Wal's voice turned sly. 'I'll make it worth your while.'

Matt shook his head. This was stupid. He needed to get back to the farm. He glanced toward the door, catching the blue swish of a nurse's skirt as she passed. The wonky trolley began clinking again.

'I need to finish that fence.' He stood and squeezed Wal's shoulder. 'Let me know if you need anything.'

Releasing Wal, he headed toward the exit, tossing a 'And be nice to the nurses or they'll confiscate your bedpan,' over his shoulder as he went.

Two strides from the door, Wal called out. 'You haven't asked.'

Rolling his eyes heavenward, Matt debated whether to bite. Wal had an agenda Matt didn't like and playing games pissed him off. Setting his jaw, he kept walking.

'I don't have one.'

He stopped, one hand on the door jamb, and let out a tired breath. 'One what?'

'Will, you muppet.'

Matt briefly closed his eyes. He didn't want to know this. He didn't want to think about Wal dying. All he wanted was to get back to the farm and lose himself in work. 'In that case, maybe it's about time you thought about getting one.'

'I plan to. Soon. Man might even consider leaving all he owns to his nephew.'

Slowly, he turned around and stared at his uncle, heart thumping, unable to credit this was happening.

Casting a quick look down the corridor and then across to Arthur, who appeared to be dead to it, Matt strode back to Wal's bed and leaned in close. 'Let me read between the lines here. You want me to somehow convince Callie Reynolds to stay on at Glenmore, and in return you'll leave me Amberton?'

Wal nodded.

Matt shook his head in disbelief. 'Wal?'

'What?' replied Wal, expression innocent, as if he hadn't done anything even remotely questionable.

'Are you fucking crazy?'

Five

Scrubbing brush and plastic bucket in one hand, Callie stood on the back step inhaling clear, dew-scented air. She inspected Glenmore's rear yard, breathtakingly bucolic in the sun's early morning blaze.

A cracked concrete path led from the back step to a saggy-wired clothesline. Nanna's beloved liquidamber stood guard over the south-eastern edge of the yard, while the untidy remnants of her vegie garden and Honk's enclosure bordered the south-west. The home paddock's fenceline stretched behind those two markers, enclosing a narrow paddock that rolled away to the property's boundary in a patchwork quilt of pale yellow tussocks and verdant clover.

The memory of other summer mornings, days even more glorious and promise-filled than this, struck Callie like a punch: images of carefree sisters giggling girlishly as they bolted from bed and rushed outside in their pyjamas—Hope to collect eggs still warm from nesting hens, Callie straight to kiss her horse good morning—while Nanna and Poppy threw 'slow downs' and 'steady ons' in their granddaughters' overexcited wake.

She lowered the bucket and wrapped her arms around her waist, breathing hard. They were just memories. Selling Glenmore didn't mean she'd lose them. They'd still exist, locked in her mind—retrievable. Yet that didn't make Callie feel any better, or ease her feelings of betrayal.

She had to bear in mind the good the Hope Foundation could do with the sale money, how many girls they could educate about the dangers of drugs.

Perhaps the money would even save a life, prevent another family from enduring the terrible suffering hers had. What better gift for her parents than a funding boost for the thing they held dearest, their daughter-substitute obsession? After all, her own attempts at being the perfect Hope had proved disastrous. She'd tried, so very hard in the early days, but it was a legacy Callie couldn't live up to. But she could give them this, her most precious thing, and perhaps by doing so also assuage a little of her own guilt for not saving her sister that night.

She relaxed her arms and picked up the bucket. No matter how much it hurt, selling the farm was the right thing to do. The sooner she achieved that the better.

Her back straight and her shoulders squared, Callie strode past the liquidambar, following the much-trodden path to the house paddock. A hank of rotted-through rope dangled from one of the tree's sturdy branches, swaying lightly. Callie averted her gaze but she couldn't prevent herself catching its whispered creaks. Telling tales. Recapturing lost images. The way Poppy's fingers had moved with easy expertise as he knotted the tyre swing in place. The sharpness of his farmer's crow's feet as he grinned at his eager, dancing young granddaughters. Their squeals and calls of 'more, more' as he patiently pushed them in turn. The way they all laughed as if the world contained nothing but magic.

Jaw tight, Callie stalked on, leaving the shady whispers behind. She unlatched the home paddock gate, casting an eye over its new resident as she ducked round the edge and hooked the chain back in place. Phantom seemed happy enough, and so he should be on that pasture. Despite an infestation of wild oats, white clover colonised the clear spaces and clumps of cocksfoot shot coarse seedheads to the sky. Good pick for a horse, or so Callie recalled Poppy teaching her.

Alert for snakes, she made her way toward the water trough with her hand held out, palm down, enjoying the tickle of tall shoots and seeds against her skin. She halted in the compacted dirt at the trough's edge, dust rising around her ankles. Her nose wrinkled at the patches of algae floating on the trough surface. Brown and green slime clung to the concrete interior and draped superfine tendrils through the water. Lowering the bucket she caught a whiff of the trough's unhealthy scent, a sharp stagnant smell that made her nose crinkle even further.

Shame burrowed a hot tunnel down Callie's back. She sent Phantom a silent apology for not cleaning his water on her return from the hospital. At the time, all she'd cared about was locking the horse up as quickly as possible so she could crawl inside and nurse her distress. It wasn't until later that she registered surprise Phantom was still on the property. In her rush to follow the ambulance she'd left the main gate open, yet instead of bolting straight back to Amberton, the horse had stayed. Callie discovered Phantom by the machinery shed's rainwater tank, calmly picking at the tender shoots growing around its leaky tap.

Tugging the wonky brim of her fishing hat low over her brow, Callie set to work. Horses required a lot of water, especially in the heat, and while she might want to get rid of the animal, Callie would never deliberately let any creature suffer. Not even Honk, although after the painful snap he'd given her thigh when she'd locked him away last night, she wasn't convinced the rotten goose deserved any kindness.

She was scrubbing the last patch of slime when Phantom approached. Nostrils flaring, expressive brown eyes filled with curiosity, he nosed the empty trough, before nudging her arm, as though demanding an explanation for its emptiness.

'Well, hello,' she said, holding out her hand and letting him sniff.

The delicate hairs on his muzzle grazed her fingers, the tickle shooting an echo of another horse beneath Callie's skin, causing a fluttery delight. Greeting over, she stroked Phantom's nose, wincing at his poor warty face. Last night, as she sat at the kitchen table sipping a much-needed glass of wine, she'd used her laptop computer to Google warts on horses. Wal was right. They were harmless, non-contagious to humans, and would drop off in time, but that didn't stop her feeling acutely sorry for the animal.

He was a pretty thing otherwise. The type of bay whose coat was so light it appeared almost chestnut, but whose legs, mane and tail were a deep black, as though they'd been carefully dipped in gloss paint. She stroked his neck and shoulder, admiring the colour, the way the ends of his coat curled with sun damage and turned the red hairs rose gold.

'Nearly as bleached as my hair, hey, Phan.'

Phan. Four letters encapsulating so much loss, so much love, arranged into a word that didn't belong here. This horse wasn't Phan. There was only one Ghost Who Neighs and this warty thoroughbred wasn't him. Her darling horse was gone, likely dead, given the advanced age he'd be. He should be remembered properly, in her heart, not traded for a weak imposter.

Although she'd tried to dismiss them, Wal's harsh words still stuck and chafed like burrs. Sixteen years old or not, there was no denying she'd abandoned Phantom. If she'd really loved her darling horse, she wouldn't have let herself be kept from him. Or Nanna and Poppy, but when Hope began losing the plot all focus went on her, Callie's pleas for Glenmore ignored. Then when she died . . .

She wracked her brain for another name, something innocuous, without meaning or memory. 'I'll call you Morton,' she said, swallowing the spikes in her throat and giving the horse a light pat before returning to her task. No matter how enticing, how much his smell and soft nuzzles made her insides swell with longing, she couldn't afford to get attached.

Or worse, for him to become attached to her.

***

The real estate agent arrived mid-morning, twenty minutes late, which earned him a thick red cross against the desirable attributes list Callie had running in her head. As a young renter and therefore a species that ranked low on the affection count, she'd never been treated with much respect by agents, but this time round she had a valuable property to sell. Any agent who wanted her business would have to earn it.

He cruised up the drive in the sort of luxury SUV that made her immediately think 'tosser'. An opinion reinforced when he unfolded his long frame from the car and smiled at her from behind mirrored aviator glasses.

He wore a well-pressed white cotton shirt open at the neck with the sleeves folded neatly up, cream chinos and highly polished brown dress boots. An expensive-looking burnished stainless steel watch circled his left wrist, matching the broad silver ring on his wedding finger. His hair was too neat for it not to contain some sort of product, and as he approached, she caught the scent of an aftershave possessing too much subtlety and softness to be off the supermarket shelf.

Though the sunglasses obscured much of his face, something about his mouth and jaw sent a tingle of recognition through Callie. Then he whipped the glasses off, exposing dark-lashed brown eyes.

'Damn,' she said, waggling a finger at him. 'I know you.'

The agent's grin widened. He spread his arms and cocked his head in a jokey, look-at-me gesture. 'Well, I am pretty unforgettable.'

Callie rolled her eyes but his quip still had her smiling. 'Maybe it's just your ego I remember.' She studied him a moment while he regarded her with amusement, then she snapped her fingers as realisation dawned. How dumb of her not to make the connection, but she'd simply opened Nanna's out-of-date copy of the Yellow Pages and chosen the agency with the biggest ad without giving the name further thought. 'You're Wal's grandson. Tony, isn't it?'

'Anthony. And very much at your service.' He bowed slightly, before reaching out to shake her hand, his grip firm and dry despite the heat. 'How are you, Callie? Pretty good by the looks of things.' He nodded at her wrist. 'Nice tatt.' His grin quickly dissolved as he put the letters together. He dropped her hand, a tinge of colour rising up his neck. 'Sorry. I didn't mean to—'

'Don't worry about it,' Callie said quickly, before changing the subject. 'So how are things with you?'

'Can't complain. I've three gorgeous girls in my life plus a new baby boy, a growing business and—' recovered from his embarrassment he threw her a cheeky wink, '—it appears I'm retaining my unforgettable good looks.'

'Three girls, you say?' Callie shook her head. 'Now that's just being greedy.'

He laughed, bringing appealing lines to the corners of his eyes. Callie vaguely recalled acknowledging Tony Graney as extremely good-looking when she was younger, but that had been the extent of her interest. Back then boys were barely a blip on her radar. They didn't register much now either, especially married ones, but she was adult enough to appreciate an attractive man when she saw one.

'I'd have more if Deb would let me, but she reckons three's enough. You remember Deborah Harrison, don't you?'

'Yeah, I do. Couple of years older than me. Used to ride that mad chestnut. So you and Deb got married?'

'Six years ago now. We have twin girls, Maddy and Flora, and Jarrod's six months.' He reached into his back pocket and pulled out his wallet, flipping it open to expose a photo of his family and handing it to Callie. Deb sat on a picnic rug, head thrown back as she avoided the pudgy fingers her son was attempting to jam up her nose. Two doll-like girls, sharing identical cross-legged poses, bookended their mother, grinning so hard at the camera their gums showed.

'Cute. Although if those cheeky grins are any indication, I bet Deb has her hands full with those girls.' She passed the wallet back. 'I guess that means she doesn't have time to ride any more.'

He shook his head as he tucked his wallet away. 'She sold her horses when she went to uni and never got back into it. I think she misses it sometimes but it's too hard with the kids. And once the girls go to school she'll probably go back to part-time work. Doesn't have to but she insists it keeps her sane.' At Callie's enquiring look he clarified. 'She's a nurse. A very good one. Everyone keeps telling me how much they miss her at the hospital.'

Callie smiled at the pride in his voice, so nice to hear in a husband. 'You sound really happy.'

'I am. What about you? What have you been up to all this time?'

'Travelling, keeping busy. The usual things.' Having revealed all she was prepared to, Callie nodded toward the paddocks. 'So where do you want to start?'

Tony squinted up at the sky. 'Let's get the paddocks done first, before it gets too hot. We'll take my car if you like.'

'Sure. Just mind you don't run over Honk.'

'Honk?'

'Mad goose with a Napoleon complex.' At Tony's raised eyebrows she grinned. 'Short and very aggressive.'

'I'll keep watch.' He gestured toward her ute, a second-hand, late-model metallic bronze Proton Jumbuk that wasn't the most exciting of vehicles, but which had proved reliable and cheap to run. 'You'll be able to buy yourself something a bit better than that with the money you'll make off this place. Speaking of utes, I see Matt hasn't bothered to come and pick up Gramps's yet.'

'He's probably been too busy.' Although Callie wondered about that. She hadn't expected anyone to come on Monday, not after all the drama, and when she visited him on Tuesday, Wal had promised to send Matt around that same afternoon. But now it was Wednesday and the LandCruiser and float still hadn't moved. Given Matt lived only a few kilometres away, it seemed a bit slack. She'd have to remember to prod Wal about it when she called in to the hospital later.

Tony's BMW was pure luxury—leather seats, super efficient air-conditioning, and handing that made the Jumbuk feel like a go-kart—although Callie's ride in it turned out disappointingly short. Glenmore didn't have many improvements beyond the house, the machinery shed, aging timber cattle yards and a bore supplying water to the troughs. The country wasn't rich enough for dairying, nor did it have an irrigation licence, however it was still good quality grazing land.

Despite having had little done to them, the pastures remained in reasonable condition, but the empty paddocks, devoid of bovine stares and lows, left Callie feeling increasingly hollow. The solicitor had advised that, over the last year, as Nanna became increasingly frail and unable to manage, the property had been destocked. Good for Callie, as it was one less thing she had to worry about, but productive properties like Glenmore were meant to be used, not left to rot. Worse, the unchecked pasture growth posed an enormous fire hazard.

'You'll want to get onto this,' said Tony as he inspected a particularly overgrown paddock at the far eastern end of the farm.

'Don't worry, slashing's at the top of my to-do list.'

It was, although actually doing the job remained another matter. Poppy had let Callie sit on his lap while he drove the tractor, but had never shown her how it all worked. Still, she'd give it a go. The tractor was old but didn't appear too broken down, and she'd spied what looked like a mower in one of the machinery shed's bays. As Tony pointed out, even a small grass fire could wipe thousands off Glenmore's value. It was either learn or hire someone, and given Callie's anorexic bank account, the latter was out of the question. Besides, how hard could it be?

They returned to the yard. Honk trumpeted his displeasure but to Callie's relief remained out of harm's way. She'd had enough of his snappy mouth, and the tour with Tony had left her feeling tense and fractious.

'The house has been let go a bit,' said Tony, studying the front.

'I know. It would have been hard for Nanna to keep up maintenance on her own.'

'Your parents never came to help?'

'The Hope Foundation takes up a lot of their time.'

At her flat tone, he shot her a speculative glance but commented no further. He continued around the side of the house to the backyard and eyed Callie's makeshift repair to the water tank's pipe. 'Do you plan to do any work on it before listing?'

'Only the absolute minimum. I hadn't planned on hanging around.' She glanced across to where the newly renamed Morton stood, hanging over the fence, dozily watching them. 'But I might have to stay on a bit.'

'I know you're keen to sell but the better the property looks the more you'll get. It's a cliché but first impressions count. Although I don't suppose it matters in this case. Given the location, Glenmore will probably go to a developer who'll knock the place down anyway.'

Callie focused hard on Tony. 'What do you mean?'

'I mean you're potentially sitting on a gold mine. You haven't been here for a while but Dargate's had a massive injection of wealth, and people are looking to spend it. The demand for small acreages is huge, and Glenmore's in a prime location.' He indicated south. 'You're, what, a kilometre from MacLeans Bay?' His arm swept east. 'And if that wasn't enough, you have Becketts Landing and the river just over there, plus you're barely seven kilometres from town. The only place with more potential than yours is

Amberton, and Gramps refuses to sell even though it's the best thing for him.'

A sick feeling lodged in Callie's stomach. Glenmore broken up, the house flattened. The possibility had never occurred to her. 'But this is prime grazing country.'

'It is, but it's also prime hobby farmer territory.' Tony squinted across the paddocks, nodding. 'This'll sell fast, all right. I'd bet my reputation on it.'

A motorbike revved in the distance, causing both of them to swing toward the sound. Callie waited for it to come into view, but the bike remained hidden by forest.

'I hope you'll give the business to Graney's,' said Tony, turning back to her. 'We've a reputation for taking good care of our clients. I'll make sure you get the best price possible and seeing as you're an old friend of the family, I can even cut a deal on the commission.'

Callie swallowed. She stared at Honk, at Morton, at the paddocks and machinery shed, at the land her family had loved so much. 'I don't know.'

Instead of fading, the motorbike noise increased, carried toward them on the light sea breeze. Callie shaded her eyes, frowning as, to the south, a helmetless rider appeared at the edge of the forest and turned up the firebreak that ran along Glenmore's western boundary. Though the track was sandy and rough, the rider handled the terrain easily, standing in the saddle, legs and arms absorbing the bumps like springs, loose blue singlet billowing.

Tony glanced at the motorbike and when he spoke, an urgency tightened his tone. 'I know you're keen to get this moving. If you want I can have the sales authority drawn up today.'

Honk waddled under the clothesline and lowered his head to feed. What would happen to him if she sold? This was his territory, had been for over twenty years. She couldn't just leave him. Callie's gaze drifted back to Morton, still hanging his warty face over the fence, tail swishing at flies, eyes half closed as he snoozed in the heat. What if no one wanted to buy him? The only other place would be the knacker's and that fate was too sickening to contemplate.

Overwhelmed, she raised her eyes skyward, thinking of Hope, her parents, Nanna and Poppy, trying to stay strong against the terrible ache that gripped her heart and tightened her throat.

'Callie?'

But her attention didn't return to Tony. The motorcyclist had turned off the bush track and onto the road. She recognised Matt Hawkins just as he disappeared behind the house. A few seconds later he was cruising past Tony's car and pulling up behind the float. Rural quiet settled again as he kicked down the stand and switched off the ignition. With an easy throw of his leg, Matt dismounted, rubbing his hand over his head before approaching them.

He hadn't dressed to impress. His boots were dusty and scuffed. His singlet had a hole in one side and a grease stain on the other. One knee of his heavily faded jeans was rubbed so far through only strings remained but for Callie the look was far more appealing than Tony's pressed artifice.

Matt wasn't quite as tall as his cousin, who towered over Callie, but he was built far better. He had the naturally well-proportioned physique of a man who was born athletic, rather than made that way, with wide shoulders and muscled arms, but not heavily so. The sort of body that came from work, sport and good health instead of gym sessions and protein supplements.

He flicked green eyes at Tony before settling them back on Callie. 'Callie, how's things?'

'Good. You?'

'Not bad.' His gaze shifted. 'Tony.'

Tony let out an irritated breath. 'It's Anthony.'

'Sure. Sorry,' Matt replied, although from the way his eyes glittered he didn't seem sorry at all.

Callie couldn't blame him. She liked Tony well enough but the car, clothes and attitude signalled a man in possession of a monumental ego. Plus his insistence on being called Anthony, especially by a cousin who'd known him since childhood, smacked of pretension. It deserved a tease.

Stony-faced, Tony deliberately turned his shoulder on Matt and addressed Callie. 'About what we discussed, shall I go ahead?'

She glanced once more at Honk, now foraging in the shade of the liquidambar. As though sensing her attention, he raised his head and gave a trumpet. It was enough. The sale could wait until she had these animals sorted. Besides, if Tony was right and Glenmore would sell fast, a week or so delay wouldn't matter.

She shook her head. 'Not yet.'

Disappointment flickered on his face before it was covered with an understanding smile. 'Of course. It's a big decision.' Tony dug into his shirt pocket for a business card and handed it to her. 'Think of us though. Before you sign with anyone else. I meant it when I said Graney's look after their clients.'

She took the card and stared at the bright blue and gold design, fingers loose around the thick stock as she fought the urge to frisbee it across the yard. Instead she addressed him with a polite smile.

'You'll be at the top of my list, I promise.'

With nothing left to discuss, Tony nodded his farewell and, throwing a last unfriendly glance at his cousin, headed for his car.

As the BMW crunched back onto the road, Matt turned to her. 'Sorry to interrupt.'

Callie tucked the card into a pocket. 'Doesn't matter. We'd finished anyway.' Her gaze flicked to his scar. In unmerciful daylight it appeared more severe than at the hospital, giving the impression of bad-boy danger. Yet his kindness then and his tease of Tony today made her wonder. 'I thought you were supposed to come yesterday.'

'I would have but . . . you know.' He shrugged and looked away. 'How's Phantom?'

'Morton.'

He blinked. 'Morton?'

'Yeah, Morton. It's his new name. Like Tony with Anthony.'

Matt's mouth twitched. 'Not very glamorous.'

'Ah, but he's not a very glamorous horse.'

'No, he's not.' He thought for a moment. 'Warty-Morty. I guess that kind of works.' His expression turned serious as he watched Honk parade across the lawn. 'So you're going to list the place with Graney's?'

'Maybe. I haven't decided yet. I still need to talk to the other agents.'

'I suppose Tony told you it'd probably go to developers.'

'Yes.' She looked away and wrapped her arms around herself as stupid tears began to sting.

'Hey.' He moved closer but she held her hand up and stepped away.

Damn, she hated this feeling of wrongness. How could selling Glenmore be wrong? It was the right thing to do. For Hope and her parents. Besides, Callie was a barmaid, not a bloody farmer. And what the hell was she doing being such a sook in front of Matt Hawkins anyway? Callie didn't cry in front of people. Ever.

'So,' she said, dropping her arms and plastering a rigid smile on her face. 'Do you need help with the float?'

'No. I'm fine. I'll just load the bike into the back and tow the lot back to Amberton.'

She waited, expecting him to get the hint and leave, but he remained where he was, regarding her as though he wanted to say something but couldn't figure out what. Callie swatted at a fly, suddenly aware of her stinging skin. It was nearing lunch time and there they were standing in the blazing sun like a couple of foreign tourists. And she had chores to complete. Lots of chores.

'If there's nothing else . . .'

'Right. Sure. You've plenty on your plate and I need to get back.' He nodded, the strange, intense expression disappearing. 'I'll see you later.'

Only too aware how much work she had waiting but strangely compelled to watch him, Callie slid into the shade of the back eaves as Matt headed to the rear of the float.

In a few minutes the bike was loaded. Sighting her in the shade, he waved before walking to the LandCruiser's driver's door and tugging it open. He stared at the interior for a moment, then back at her. 'Come round for dinner. Tonight.'

Callie regarded him uncertainly. 'You mean like a date?'

Matt leaned his back against the cabin and puffed out his cheeks. 'How about calling it being a friendly neighbour?'

She thought on it for a moment then shook her head. 'Thanks, but I have a lot to do here.'

'You sure?'

'Positive.'

He blew out a long breath and gave a 'well, I tried' shrug. 'Your loss.'

'If you say so,' replied Callie, wondering if overinflated egos were a Graney family trait.

'I do. I cook a pretty mean steak, you know. I've even been known to serve it with salad.'

'I'm sure I'll survive.'

A lazy smile hooked Matt's mouth as he looked her up and down. 'Of that I have no doubt.'

With a last disconcerting wink, he ducked into the car, started the engine and headed out of the yard, leaving Callie blinking into the drifting stone dust, wondering what the hell had just happened.

Six

After Matt left, Callie retreated to Glenmore's cool kitchen for a cheese sandwich flavoured with some of Nanna's home-made tomato chutney and a cold drink. Confusion over the morning lingered in the still air, not only over Glenmore's fate, but also around Matt Hawkins.

She toyed with edges of her sandwich, pinching off tiny pieces of crust. On first meeting, she'd been too distressed over Wal to take Matt in. She noted his kindness, and wondered about that terrible scar, but little further. Then this morning he'd turned up looking at her in a way she couldn't fathom, asking her over for dinner while throwing lazy smiles and winks that stuck in her mind like mental hangnails.

Maybe it was as Matt said, and he was simply being a friendly neighbour, but Callie didn't think so. There'd been something too intense about his regard, an almost yearning quality to his gaze that even playfulness couldn't disguise, and it made her wary—wary, intrigued and annoyed that she hadn't pumped Wal for more information yesterday during her visit. She'd only brought Matt up because no one had come to fetch the car and float.

Matt proved to be the only subject during their conversation that Wal didn't grump over. Every other topic had left him lemon faced and rumbling like a volcano. She'd registered vaguely that Matt had come to Wal after leaving the army and wondered if he was one of those traumatised veterans who sometimes featured in newspapers and magazines. People so scarred from their experience of war—inside and out—that they struggled to return to society and sought refuge in isolation. Except nothing about Matt's behaviour during both their encounters indicated a damaged man. His face, perhaps, but not anything else.

Callie ceased picking at her sandwich. Speculation was pointless. She had jobs to attend to and a cantankerous old man to visit. Besides, what did Matt Hawkins matter? Even if she was intrigued—and if she was truthful with herself, a little attracted—Callie wasn't about to start anything with him. She had troubles enough.

Despite the air-conditioning running flat out, the sun-broiled ute interior seemed to take forever to cool down. Callie made a mental note to clear a space in the machinery shed so she could park the Jumbuk in the shade. The shed would need sorting anyway, and she should probably run a clearance sale before listing Glenmore. There were always people on the lookout for spare equipment and even out-dated machinery could be sold for scrap.

She let out a long sigh. Sorting Glenmore out was never going to be easy but Callie hadn't expected it to be this time consuming. Besides Morton and Honk, she had over three hundred hectares of overgrown pasture to slash and a house to finish cleaning out. Nor would her conscience allow her to leave until Wal was back on his feet, or at least at home.

Back in Airlie it had all seemed so simple. Get in, clean up and get out, but what she'd calculated would take a few days now had the potential to take a month, which would bring even more problems. The Jumbuk's purchase six months ago had wiped out most of her savings, and though she'd been careful, her bank account had remained unhealthily low. With her share of the rent still to pay on the Airlie apartment, and mobile phone, fuel and grocery bills, plus the potential of vet and farrier bills, Callie realised she would need to find a job. Fast.

Almost two kilometres of winding gravel road separated Glenmore from Amberton. Callie eased off the accelerator, noting the property's well-maintained drive, the old but tightly strung fences, the neat white sign proclaiming 'Amberton'. Details which made Glenmore's slow decay seem even starker and sadder. But where scrub encased Glenmore on three sides, giving it a sense of isolation, forest bordered Amberton only on the eastern boundary.

The property welcomed visitors with two burgundy-painted timber wings placed either side of a front double gate. Tracks carved by countless entrances and exits led away from the wings, leaving a natural strip of grass in the centre that was home to the white-painted steel drum that served as Wal's roadside mail drop. His house sat a hundred metres or so off Thiedeke Road, behind a thick cypress hedge that had been dense and old and full of shadowy secrets when Callie was a child. At some point the roof had been replaced, and now shiny burgundy Colorbond poked above the hedge instead of the dull grey of Callie's memory.

The farm entrance drifted behind, the scene expanding into open land dotted with thick-trunked gums and Wal's satin-coated Black Angus cattle. A needle of jealousy threaded through Callie's heart and was gone. Glenmore wasn't Amberton and even if it could be, she wasn't the one who could make it so.

She put her foot back down, leaving Amberton and her silly ideas behind.

It wasn't until she'd gone another kilometre that Callie became aware of the changed landscape. She frowned and leaned forward slightly, wondering how it had failed to register on previous journeys, if she'd become so urban and desensitised to country life that the sight of all those smallholdings failed to cause a tiny knot of concern. What was once open pasture populated with cattle and sheep now featured large, expensive-looking houses with immature but well-landscaped gardens and small paddocks containing the occasional pony, cow or sheep. One hobby farmer had two alpacas running in his high-fenced front paddock. As the ute passed, they looked up, brown eyes as huge and staring as Callie's felt.

Glenmore was far from idyllic but here, behind the neat fences, agrarian decay tentacled across the paddocks like a melanoma. The soil was weed infested and eroded, and the edible plant species that did remain were stunted, rank or made sour through lack of nutrients. The horse paddocks were the worst. She passed one which was almost all mustard weed, its resident pony standing forlornly in the shade of a small iron shelter, dust clouding around its legs each time it stamped a foot against flies.

The idea that this could be Glenmore's fate made Callie's insides drop and turn cold, as though she'd suddenly stepped close to the edge of an eroding glacier. She tried to swallow at the dryness in her mouth, brought on by the fear she was committing a terrible wrong—not to herself or even her grandparents, but to the land.

She shook the feeling away. She wasn't some sort of rural crusader. Towns grew. Progress happened. Glenmore was a few hundred hectares in a land of millions. Yet as she drove on, the bad taste remained.

Closer to Dargate a few cars began to appear, although fewer than yesterday, when she'd ventured into town to see Wal and grab a few groceries. Even the supermarket carpark seemed devoid of shoppers. Unsurprising, given the heat shimmer rising off the asphalt. Patterson Street, Dargate's main thoroughfare, was just as sleepy and Callie slipped into a park only a short walk from the newsagent's. Grabbing her purse and her computer memory stick she headed up the footpath, grateful for the shops' shady awnings and occasional blast of air-conditioning.

Fifteen minutes later she was out again, this time carrying a copy of that week's issue of *The Weekly Times*, half-a-dozen copies of her CV and two A4-sized 'For Sale' posters, each bearing a colour photo of a strangely wart-free Morton. It wasn't a bad image considering she'd snapped it on her phone, but the real magic was done on her laptop using its photo manipulation software. A half-hour's painstaking work and Warty-Morty had been airbrushed to handsome perfection, and his picture inserted into a jazzy poster. So what if she'd manipulated his looks a little? Morton was a sweet horse, the warts would drop off, and for the measly sum of $500 someone would score themselves a good animal, leaving Callie one less thing to worry about.

She hurried back to the car and placed the posters on the passenger seat before quickly starting the engine. The air-con blasted into life, drying the sweat on her arms and causing her to shiver. Reaching out to put the car into gear, Callie caught another sight of Morton and froze.

His innocent chocolate eyes seemed to bore into her. Her hand fell off the shift. She picked up the poster and held it in her lap, tracing a finger over Morton's long nose as something huge and prickly and sore lodged in her throat.

A man in board shorts cruised past, eyeing her. Several cars drove by. The Jumbuk's interior cooled and yet still Callie remained anchored by sadness and confusion, and an almost searing want. She tossed the poster aside and rubbed a hand over her face, squeezing at the outer corners of her eyes, unable to recall when she'd last felt so screwed up. Or so isolated.

Never letting anyone get close had been her way since leaving home, her protection against hurt, and she'd survived fine. Yet here, in Dargate, it felt worse somehow. She needed someone to talk to. Someone to reassure her that what she was doing was right, when her heart kept saying the opposite.

She dug her mobile out of the glove box and dialled Anna. If anyone could cheer Callie up it was her.

'Well, if it isn't our long-lost housemate.'

'Rowan?'

'The one and only. Saw your name flashing and thought I'd pick up. How's things? You freezing your bum off down there?'

'It's boiling, would you believe. Where's Anna?'

'Showering off Bruce. Oversexed buggers didn't get out of bed until lunch time. That's twice this week.'

Callie leaned back, pleased that Anna had come to her senses. He might not be the crocodile wrestler of Anna's fantasies, but Bruce was hugely likable, attractive in his own way, and most of all would love her like she deserved.

'Are we talking love here?'

'If the racket they make's anything to go by, I'd have to say yes. And I swear Anna called him "Bubby" last night.'

'Pet names. Always a sure sign.'

'Yeah, although surely she could come up with something better than "Bubby"? Makes Bruce sound like a complete wuss.' Rowan paused for a moment and when he spoke his voice was careful. 'You sound a bit down. Everything okay?'

Callie picked at a loose thread on the hem of her shorts. 'I'm all right. Things just aren't going as smoothly as I'd hoped.'

'It was always going to be hard, going back. You're braver than me. I still haven't visited where Des was killed. Mum and Dad and Ross go all the time, for his birthday and at Christmas. They put flowers by the tree and talk to him like he's still alive, but I've never been able to do it. I don't want to remember him there, all mangled up. You're probably the same with Hope and your gran's farm, not wanting to remember.'

'My sister didn't die at Glenmore, Rowan. She died in a nightclub.' On the filthy, drink-stained floor, with Callie beside her screaming for help, and no one able to hear over the whump-whump of dance music and their collective indifference.

'Oh.' Rowan's discomfort rattled through the phone's speaker. 'The shower's stopped. Do you want me to pass you on to Anna?'

'No, it's okay.' Calling Anna was a mistake. Her housemate was happy, in love. She didn't need Callie spoiling her mood as she had Rowan's. 'Just tell her I called and that I might catch her on Skype later.'

'Will do.' He waited a couple of heartbeats. 'I know you don't like to talk much about your life, but if you need us, either of us, we're here, okay?'

'Sure,' she replied quickly, desperate to escape the hot prickle that Rowan's kind words set behind her eyes. 'Thanks.'

'Sometimes even the strongest people need someone to lean on, Callie.'

Except Callie never had before, and she wasn't about to start. She'd get through this like she made it through everything else—by concreting on her stoic mask and pretending she was strong. With a last thanks to Rowan she hung up, fixed her seatbelt, and put the Jumbuk into gear.

As it had when she was a girl, a giant white plastic horse adorned the roof of Taylor's Saddlery. She smiled at its decoration—a hat with cork bobbles, the horse's white ears threaded through holes in the brim, and an Australian flag hanging limply from a thin plastic stick implanted in the hat's crown. Thanks to Peter Taylor's penchant for decorating the horse, no one in Dargate had any excuse for not knowing which national or local celebration approached. In this case, it was Australia Day, only a few days away.

A brass bell hanging from the door signalled Callie's arrival, earning her a yelled 'Be with you in a mo' from the rear workshop. The shop wasn't air-conditioned, only a solitary fan near the back of the display area circulated the fuggy, leather-scented air. Callie paused to take a deep breath and wallow in the smell, immediately thinking of Wal and his tack room, a place that had seemed like a treasure trove when she was young. Not that he'd allowed her to play in it much. She and Phantom were at Amberton to learn, not mess up Wal's belongings. Plus once Jacqueline Reynolds decided she rather enjoyed the pony club crowd, Callie had soon accumulated her own room full of tack to scrub with saddle soap and rub with oil.

A sewing machine started up, the whirr causing another flashback of Nanna wheeling out her ancient Singer and instructing Callie on how to mend Phantom's canvas rug. No matter how barbed-wire free they made his paddock, the horse always managed to find something to snag his rug on. Nanna refused to allow smelly horse gear near her beloved Pfaff, so rug repairs were relegated to the beautifully decorated black and gold Singer. Although a little temperamental, it was built so tough it could sew anything. In the days before Phantom took over her world, Callie and Hope were even taught to sew doll's clothes on the Singer. Another skill she'd long lost and, given her life, one unlikely ever to be regained.

As Callie had hoped, a large cork noticeboard still hung on the right-hand wall beside the saddlery's back counter. Trailing her fingers over a suede-seated western saddle as she passed, she made her way to the board and took a moment to study the advertisements already pinned to the surface. Her eyebrows shot up as she took in the prices: three thousand dollars for a second-hand dressage saddle. Six and a half thousand for a scratched and dented aluminium float. Fifteen thousand for an arrogant-looking black eventer, who, from the sales spiel, appeared not to have progressed beyond pre-novice status.

'Things have gone up since your day.'

Too distracted to have noticed the machine stopping, Callie spun around at the sudden words, hand on her thumping chest. Peter Taylor leaned against the workshop's door jamb, inspecting her up and down in much the same way Wal had on first meeting, albeit with a much more appreciative expression. Although older and more weathered, with his mop of curly hair now grey, Peter still possessed the same lean rider's body and hawkish good looks that had once made him very popular with Dargate's women. Callie could even recall her own mother giggling inanely on the rare occasion Peter directed his charm her way.

'Hey, Peter.'

'Callie.' His eyes twinkled. 'You've grown up.'

'Yes. I tried not to but . . .' She gave a 'what can you do' shrug, which earned her a very white, very straight-toothed grin.

'I bet I'm not the only bloke who's glad you did.' Peter left the door and walked behind the counter. 'You still riding?'

'No. But I do have a horse to sell.' She handed him Morton's poster, her stomach sinking as Peter's smiling expression turned serious.

He stuck a finger on Morton's nose. 'This is Lyndall Soriano's old horse.'

Callie said nothing. She wasn't sure she could. Wal had refused to tell her anything about Morton's history. According to him, it didn't matter. Whatever the horse's background, Morton was her responsibility now. That's all that counted.

Frowning, Peter looked at Callie. 'Thought his name was Phantom.'

'He's had an identity change.'

'So how did you end up with him?'

'Inheritance.'

'From Maggie, I take it. I was sorry to hear she'd passed away. Your gran was a lovely woman. Anyway, Glenmore's better for him than that pissy paddock he had at the Sorianos'. Horse kept getting colic from ingesting sand. Lyndall was mad about him though.' He threw Callie a puzzled look. 'Why get rid of him? He's a nice horse. Plenty of potential. Probably do all right with an experienced rider.'

She responded with a shrug. 'No room in my life for a horse.'

'No room? Rubbish. You've got plenty.' He stopped, expression turning grim. 'Oh, I see. You're getting rid of Glenmore too. We've all been wondering what would happen to it.'

'As a matter of fact, I am.' Callie kept her voice neutral, her mask of indifference fixed against his disapproval. What she did with Glenmore or Morton was no one's business but her own.

'I guess with property prices the way they are it's hard to say no to that sort of money,' said Peter, passing her the poster and tilting his head at the corkboard. 'Pin it up. I'm sure someone will take him off your hands. Might even be me.'

Digging out a thumbtack, Callie chose the bottom corner of the corkboard and attached her poster, then just as quickly untacked it. She flicked the corner of the paper, curling its edge, gaze not quite meeting Peter's.

'This girl, Lyndall, Morton's previous owner. Who is she?'

'Young girl. Twelve or thirteen maybe, something around that. You would have passed her place on the way into town. Big white double-storey house that looks like it belongs on a slave plantation. They're new to town. A couple of years, anyway. Father's a regional bank manager. The girl was horse mad so they bought Phantom from that shyster Maurie Cavendish, thinking the pair would grow up together.' He raised his eyes and shook his head.

'Common mistake for people who don't know any better.'

'Yeah. Poor girl was nervous enough, but one day she had a really bad fall at pony club and that was the end of her. Not the horse's fault, he just tripped. Lyndall came down hard, the horse on top. Hit her head and suffered a seizure.' His mouth turned tight. 'Frightened the bejesus out of all of us so it must have been even worse for her. Lost her nerve after that. Couldn't even enter his paddock. Parents decided the best thing was to sell the horse. Lyndall was devastated. Still comes in now and then just to look at stuff. Sad, really.'

Callie lowered her gaze as her own memories roused. She'd done the same thing in the days when her longing for Phan became too much. She'd sneak out to Ringwood on the train, to the big saddlery on Whitehorse Road, and spend an hour fingering saddles and bridles, running lead ropes through her hands, admiring jumping boots, sometimes trying on riding coats, imagining herself back in the ring with Phantom, overflowing with pride as a judge wrapped a blue ribbon around his thick grey neck. She glanced at Morton's photo and thought of another young girl losing the love of her life. The shame of abandonment that no reasoning could ease.

She folded the poster in half and then into quarters before regarding Peter once more. 'I might sit on this for a bit.'

'Good idea.' He smiled and winked. 'We could do with a few more pretty girls on the local show scene. And if you're worried about being rusty I can always give you lessons.'

***

Like the previous day, Wal was in a cranky mood when Callie called into the hospital with a fresh bag of grapes and *The Weekly Times*. Thanks came in the form of a grunt, but he kept sharp eyes on her when she dragged up a chair and sat down.

'Hope you're looking after Phantom properly.'

'I am.'

'And Honk.'

'Him too.'

Wal worked his mouth for a moment and Callie had to clench her teeth to stop from smiling. She'd known a lot of men like Wal from all the bars and clubs where she'd worked. Nine times out of ten the crankiness hid a kind soul. The saddest were the old men still coping with the loss of their wives. The pain was so acute they wanted to take their anger out on someone, especially the young who had so much in front of them, but scratch a little and they were simply lonely men, fearful for the future.

What Wal was scared of Callie couldn't fathom, but she planned to find out.

'What have you been up to?' he finally asked.

She picked up the paper and scanned the lead article—a furious condemnation of the big supermarket chains squeezing agricultural industries to death with price cuts. 'I had your grandson Tony out to look at Glenmore.'

Wal's mouth sank like a collapsed soufflé.

She flicked a page, feigning nonchalance. 'Apparently it's worth a fortune.'

'Should've known all you'd care about was money. Maggie was wrong. You're nothing like Tom. You've turned out exactly like your mother.'

Callie kept reading, using the newspaper's words to soothe herself, aware Wal only threw that line at her because he'd learned that it hurt. The noise of the hospital floated through the ward's open door. Callie glanced up as the elderly patient in the bed opposite let out a bugled fart in his sleep. Wal appeared too riled to notice.

'So Glenmore'll go to ruin like all the others.' He rolled his head to glare hard at her. 'You tell me, missy, what're we going to eat when all the land's gone? Dust? Weeds?'

'Australia's a big country.'

'With bugger all arable land.' He jutted a wrinkled finger at the paper, causing it to snap loudly. 'City people like you don't understand. You can't grow cattle and sheep and crops in the desert. Most of the dirt in this country's infertile rubbish. Meanwhile, every day another bloody housing estate gets built on prime farmland and lost forever. Land left to rot, full of weeds and vermin. It's a bloody disgrace. And people like you make it worse.'

'I'm entitled to sell the land, Wal. I can't be held responsible for what happens to it afterwards.'

'You could bloody-well do the right thing and farm it like it's meant to be.'

'Right.' Temper flaring, she slapped the paper into her lap. 'Like I know anything about farming.'

'Tom taught you some.'

'"Some" being the operative word.'

Wal's lips pumped back and forth while Callie tried to calm herself. She wasn't here to argue—there was nothing to argue about.

'I could teach you,' he said.

Callie smiled wryly and shook her head. 'Bit tricky when you're in here.'

'Then the lad could.'

Callie sighed. This conversation was pointless. She knew Wal was right and the thought of Glenmore going to waste like those hobby farms made her heart ache, but what was she to do?

She placed the newspaper back on Wal's cabinet. 'Do you want me to bring you the *Stock & Land* tomorrow?'

'You leaving?'

'Yes. I have people I need to see.'

'More bloody real estate agents I suppose.'

'Actually, no. I need to organise a job and once I've done that I'm going to call in to see Morton's previous owner.'

For a moment Wal looked completely flummoxed. 'Who's Morton?'

'Phantom. I renamed him.'

Wal's lip curled. 'Don't like the reminder, huh?'

A nurse padded into the ward, smiling hello as she made her way to the farting patient, and giving Callie an excuse to escape. It was probably Wal's wash time. Or his bedpan, and she wasn't about to stick around for that.

'No, I don't. I don't know what game Nanna thought she was playing with me but there'll only ever be one Phantom.' Even though he didn't deserve it, she leaned in to kiss Wal's cheek. 'You be good. I'll see you tomorrow.'

'She won't take him back you know.'

'Are you talking about Lyndall?'

Wal gave a smug nod, as if he already knew Callie's attempt to rid herself of Morton would prove futile. 'Too scared.'

'So Peter Taylor said. But that doesn't mean she doesn't still love the horse.'

'Maggie left him for you, you hear. You!'

'No, Nanna left him for a purpose. Maybe that purpose was to help Lyndall.' She patted his arm as she hid her distress at his words behind a rigid smile. 'I really have to go.'

Smile still determinedly fixed, she headed to the door.

'He was meant to make you happy again,' Wal called loudly, causing both the nurse and her patient to look up. 'Him and Glenmore. Maggie wanted you to see that here was where you belonged. The one place where you always felt at home. You really going to spit that back in her face? The woman who loved you, who left you—not her son, *you!*—the most precious thing she owned?'

Wal's words were like a horse kick to the heart. That wasn't fair. None of this was fair. Callie halted and wheeled around, holding her crumbling mask in place through sheer willpower. She would not cry in front of Wal, or the nurse, or anyone in this rotten place. Her plans were right.

'I'm sorry for Nanna, I really am. But I have to do this.'

For several long seconds Wal's brown eyes held hers, until he finally turned his head away in dismissal, his contempt so thick it coated her skin.

'Then God help poor Maggie.'

Seven

Callie kept her back straight all the way down the hospital corridor. Despite the soothing pastel decor and quiet vinyl flooring, tension twanged inside her like an overstretched rubber band. The urge to bolt was huge, and controlling it gave her normal athletic gait a jerky, almost robotic edge. She held every muscle clenched, like a boxer expecting a blow, but with no idea from where it would come. Close to the exit she passed a nurse and managed a closed-mouth smile, but the teeth behind it were locked together with almost painful intensity.

The automatic doors slid open, heat pummelling her body in a wave. Callie lengthened her stride, crossing the sticky asphalt carpark to the Jumbuk with eyes straight ahead. She didn't want to look back. She didn't want to think. She didn't want to give in to the awful fear and shame crawling inside her.

Only when she was safe in the confines of the ute with the air conditioner blasting did she claw her hands around the steering wheel, rest her forehead against its edge, and allow herself the choked sobs she'd been holding in so hard.

She'd known from the moment Wal handed her Morton that the horse was somehow a ploy to get her to stay, yet Callie had jammed that knowledge in the secret crevices of her mind where she hid all the other issues she never wanted to face, and ignored the message. If she didn't think too much, if she stayed focused on her goal, she wouldn't have to acknowledge her grandmother's wishes. But now there was no escape. Wal had made them real.

Callie pulled her head up and swiped at her eyes, breathing deeply, forcing calm through her veins. She stared through the windscreen at the manicured parkland surrounding Dargate Hospital and saw a landscape that mirrored her emotions. Heat had caused the grass to curl and turn dull, the vibrant green now tinged with grey. Even the decades-old oak trees appeared timorous under the weight of the impossibly huge sky.

She mulled over Wal's words, her brow furrowing deeper with every thought. Yes, Callie's time at Glenmore was the most joy filled of her life but that didn't mean she could be happy there again. Too much time had passed, too many familial ties unravelled. Her sister had *died*. Selling Glenmore would not only help ease her guilt over Hope, it would help Callie make peace with her parents. Yet how the hell was she meant to reconcile that with Nanna's wishes?

Callie chewed her lip, thinking about Hope, how she never quite felt the same about Glenmore as Callie did. She couldn't have, or Hope wouldn't have stopped wanting to come to the farm. It was boring, she complained. Nanna and Poppy were too strict.

There was a time when Hope was perfectly content to spend her time swimming or surfing at MacLeans Bay, or disappearing into the forest to wander the trails. Animal spotting, she called it. Being one with nature. A term that had made everyone roll their eyes and tease, and call her the household hippie. Then at seventeen that stopped, along with the swimming and surfing. Hope wanted to stay in Melbourne, seek urban adventure with her city friends. Suddenly her skirts became shorter, her tops tighter; the modern classic look she'd assimilated from Mum bastardised and cheapened. Make-up marred her clear skin. Secrecy became Hope's byword. Questions were answered in monosyllables, her mascaraed eyes never meeting anyone's. Men looked. A lot. And Callie noticed how much Hope liked it. How she played for it. Callie remembered the arguments that caused, between Hope and her parents, Hope and her sister. Regretful arguments; their legacy another layer to her guilt.

Even now, thoughts of that time still left Callie feeling confused. She loved

Hope, looked up to her. Her sister was beautiful, sporty, fun. People adored her. Sometimes Callie even wanted to be her, but she wanted to be at Glenmore too. And this new, rebellious, boundary-stretching Hope frightened her.

Then Callie learned about her drug experiments.

According to Hope, everyone did it; it made nightclubs fun. Callie wouldn't know because she was too young, too country and staid, like Nanna and Poppy. So Callie begged to be shown.

And oh, how she was shown.

One of the newspapers speculated that Hope was flaunting her coolness, taking more risks than normal because her sister was there. Though her parents tried to protect Callie from the media onslaught, she saw the article and took it as the truth. Not only did Hope die because Callie hadn't known what to do when she collapsed, her sister might not have swallowed those pills at all if Callie hadn't begged to tag along.

Nanna had it wrong. The farm had to be sold.

Maybe in the end Hope didn't care much about the farm but Callie did, which made this sacrifice right. Hope was dead, but the foundation created in her name lived. Callie couldn't give her parents their daughter back, but she could give them this cherished part of herself.

And with it would come forgiveness.

Equilibrium restored, Callie started the car only to yelp in fright as a tap sounded against the window. A chaotic-haired woman with a cherubic baby on her hip grinned at her. When Callie frowned and blinked the woman made a rapid 'wind down the window' motion. Finally recognising Deborah Graney, Callie forced a smile and obliged.

'Deb, good to see you.' She smiled dutifully at the dribbling baby and reached out to tickle his arm. 'Hello, you must be Jarrod. Aren't you cute?'

'Well, aren't you going to get out so I can give you a hug?'

Given her mood and the weather, a hug was the last thing Callie wanted but Deb had always been the tactile type. Callie received a warm, if rather squashed and baby-scented embrace, parting to find herself being eyed by two identical girls, each blessed with the same gorgeously curly hair as their mother.

'You two must be Maddy and Flora. Hello.'

The girls smiled shyly without speaking.

'The terrible twins. Literally.' Deb gave them an indulgent glance before boosting Jarrod back up her hip and regarding Callie once more. Her smile dropped and she leaned close. 'Oh, Callie, are you all right?'

'I'm fine. Honest.' At Deb's disbelieving expression she sighed inwardly. Even Callie's well-practised mask couldn't hide red eyes but at least a half-lie could hide the truth. 'Remembering Nanna, that's all.'

'It's always hard losing someone you love.'

Something Callie didn't need reminding of, but she nodded obligingly in response. Deb always was kind hearted, which was part of the reason her horses had got away with their naughtiness.

'Anyway, I feel like I owe you a big apology. Anthony told me you were back. I should have been in touch, organised to catch up for coffee, but between Wal and this lot it completely slipped my mind.'

'That's okay. I've been busy too. You look great by the way. Motherhood suits you.'

'Motherhood exhausts me, you mean.' Nose screwing up, Deb surveyed the carpark. 'God, it's baking out here. Are you free? We could chat in the cafe. Catch up.'

'I'd love to, but I have a whole heap of things to sort.' She grimaced. 'And I need to find a job.'

Deb cocked her head to one side. 'What sort?'

'Just bar work. Something casual.'

'Try the Royal. Ask for Doug Phelan. He might have something.'

'Thanks. I will.'

Deb smiled at her. 'I'll call you, okay?'

'Sure.'

Deb regarded her twins. 'Come on, you two. Time to see what sort of chaos your gramps has caused today.'

Callie retreated to the cool of the car, grateful for the break Deb had given her from her thoughts and glad to see her old pony club acquaintance so content. Deb was a nice girl. She deserved a good life.

She left the carpark, turning toward the centre of town instead of the shortcut around it. The Royal was on the Glenmore side of Dargate, at the far end of Patterson Street. Querying the pubs on this side of town first would save doubling back if Deb's tip proved unfruitful.

Fifty metres from the Commercial Hotel, Callie slid into a parking space, keeping the engine running as she checked her hair and face in the mirror. Her eyes remained slightly puffy and her tanned skin a shade paler than normal, but she'd pass. Publicans liked good-looking bar staff but experience was what really counted, and Callie possessed an overload of that.

Despite her credentials, she lucked out at the Commercial and again at the Imperial, although both kept her CV, promising to call if anything came up. At the Royal, her fortunes changed. Following Deb's suggestion, she asked for Doug and was led out the back to where a weathered-looking man with wide ears and a seen-it-all-before expression eyed her up and down before taking her CV and disappearing into his office. Ten minutes later he returned, this time with a smile on his face and a roster in his hand, and Callie had enough shifts to keep herself afloat. And little spare time to dwell on the costs of her decision.

Control, determination, activity—these were the things to help her hold it together.

With another chore ticked off, Callie headed out of town, driving slowly down Thiedeke Road as she hunted for the house Peter Taylor described. She didn't need to search hard. With its massive white rendered walls and two large columns propping up an ostentatious front portico, the Sorianos' property was impossible to miss. Even the gate consisted of two curved rendered brick wings. An engraved brass plate pinned to one wall declared the property 'Kelso'.

Callie indicated and turned, noting the empty timber-fenced paddocks either side of the drive. A green plastic feed tub sat near the gate of the right-hand paddock, the ground around it barren and compacted. A loop of baling twine remained knotted around the rail supporting the strainer post, ready for a leadrope to be threaded through—an old trick to prevent horses injuring themselves or breaking tack if they pulled back—but no grazing horse raised its head to eye her, and Callie's heart squeezed a little at the absence.

The drive widened into a neat gravel carriage circle, the centre decorated with a pretty fountain of a woman pouring water from a bucket into a lily-covered pond, her legs brushed by drooping fern fronds. Shade from the house made the area appear an oasis in the summer-burnt countryside.

As the Jumbuk crunched to a halt a very slim girl, around thirteen years of age, with razor cut black hair and a sulky expression, opened the front door. She leaned against the door edge, eyeing the Jumbuk with disdain as a Siamese cat wound round her legs and trotted purposefully to the end of the house before disappearing around the corner. Callie alighted and crossed to the portico, smiling through her sympathy for a girl she understood only too well.

'You must be Lyndall.' She held out her hand. 'My name's Callie Reynolds.'

Lyndall's gaze hesitated on Callie's tattoo, then politeness took over and she took Callie's hand in a brief limp grip. 'Hello.'

'I think I have an old friend of yours. A horse called Phantom.'

The sulk disappeared in an instant, replaced with eagerness and hope. 'You have Phan? How is he? Is he okay?'

'He's great. I've only had him a few days but he's in good health. Eating himself silly, in fact. He's a sweet horse. You must miss him.'

Lyndall nodded, lips flattened firmly together in a way Callie recognised, and she wished she could hug the teenager close and tell her that she could have her horse back, right now if she wanted. But things were never so simple.

The front door widened, revealing a worried-looking dark blonde woman with the same slender build as her daughter. Though her smile was polite, Callie noted the way she moved behind Lyndall and placed both hands protectively on her daughter's shoulders.

'Hello. Can I help you?'

Callie stuck out her hand. 'Callie Reynolds. I was in at Taylor's earlier. Peter told me about Lyndall, so I thought I'd drop by and say hello.'

'Callie bought Phantom,' said Lyndall.

'Ah.' Introducing herself as Kate, the woman reached across to shake Callie's hand, before returning to her proprietary stance behind her daughter, fingers nervously working the ends of Lyndall's dark hair. 'How is he?'

'He's fine. Stuffing himself with cocksfoot and clover.' Callie looked at Lyndall. 'I didn't buy him. My grandmother left him to me in her will.'

'Oh. So you don't ride?'

'I used to but I haven't been on a horse for years.' She flicked a glance at Kate before regarding Lyndall once more. 'Peter told me how much you loved him. I was wondering if you'd like to come and say hello.'

Lyndall raised pleading eyes to her mother, who regarded her pensively.

'He's out at Glenmore. It's a property only five or so kilometres from here, not far from Becketts Landing. I could take you out and drop you back.' Noticing Kate's hesitation, Callie suddenly realised how odd her proposal must seem—a stranger asking to take her daughter away. 'Or you could follow me out if that would work better.'

'Can we, Mum? Just for a while? I really want to see him.'

Kate stroked her daughter's hair and Callie saw the love there. And the worry. 'I don't know if that's a good idea.'

'Please, Mum.' Lyndall's eyes began to pool, hands twisting around each other. 'For five minutes. Just to say hello.'

Callie waited, hoping for the young girl's sake that her mother would give in.

'*Please.*'

After a few more moments' hesitation Kate relented. 'Sure.' She addressed Callie. 'When would be a good time?'

Relieved, Callie exhaled a slow breath and smiled. 'How about now?'

Kate followed in a teal-coloured Range Rover, which left Callie pondering their purchase of Morton. People of means usually bought press-button show ponies or been-there-done-that all-rounders that cost many thousands of dollars. Even when Callie was riding it wasn't unusual for an experienced pony club horse to sell for over five grand. If Peter Taylor's adverts were any indication, prices now were even higher. How the Sorianos ended up with one of Maurie Cavendish's saleyard specials was a mystery, but they wouldn't be the first to be suckered in by the smooth-talking horse trader's banter. The man was renowned for it.

'Watch out for Honk,' warned Callie, pointing to the madly complaining goose as Lyndall and Kate followed her across Glenmore's yard to the house paddock. 'He's getting seriously cranky in his old age.'

'They're meant to be wonderful guard dogs,' said Kate, smiling as Honk gave another outraged trumpet.

'They are. Although in Honk's case, only during the day. I can't leave him out at night because of the foxes.'

Lyndall cast Honk a dubious look. 'Does he bite?'

'He does.' Callie halted to point at the dark bruise on her thigh. 'And it hurts, but if you keep out of his way he's all right.'

Kate gave her daughter a quick shoulder hug. 'I'm sure you'll be fine.' She addressed Callie again. 'This was your grandmother's farm?'

'Yes. She died six weeks ago.'

'So you'll be living here now?'

'Only until it's sold.' Callie smiled tightly. 'Home for me is Airlie Beach.'

Lyndall threw her a worried look. 'Does that mean you'll be taking Phantom with you?'

'No. My plan is sell him. Although if I can find the right home I'd be happy to give him away.'

Morton was nose down toward the rear of the paddock, concentrating on developing his grass belly, when Callie arrived at the gate. Using the technique Poppy patiently taught her as a little girl, she curled her thumb and forefinger, placed them in her mouth and blew. A satisfyingly piercing whistle emerged, quickly echoed by yet another nasal grump from Honk and a softer, more welcoming noise from Morton.

Callie glanced at Lyndall. A delighted glow spread across the young girl's face, her brown eyes turning dewy as she watched her former mount hurry toward them, but instead of approaching, Lyndall remained a good metre away from the gate. Callie passed a querying look at Kate, who gave a subtle shake of her head.

As Morton neared, Callie opened the gate, making sure to latch it behind her so the young girl didn't panic. Showing off, Morton indulged in a happy pigroot and head toss before halting by Callie and, nostrils flared, used his long nose to bunt her in the upper arm and head.

Eyes enormous, Lyndall took a step backwards as horror turned her voice squeaky. 'What's happened to his face?'

Callie stroked Morton's nose, trying to keep her expression benign, while inside she cursed herself for not remembering the warts. 'He didn't have any grass warts when you had him?'

At the mention of warts, Lyndall looked even more appalled. 'No!'

'They're not uncommon, especially with young horses,' Callie explained matter-of-factly. 'And don't worry about catching them off him. They're not contagious for humans. He's perfectly safe.'

'What about Phantom?' Kate asked, concern in her tone. 'Are they painful for him?'

'No. Maybe a bit annoying but they don't hurt. Eventually his immune system will kick in and they'll just drop off. A few months and Morton'll be back to his normal handsome self.' Reaching between the horse's ears, she ruffled his black forelock. 'Won't you, Warty-Morty?'

Lyndall glanced from Callie to her mum and back again. 'Morty?'

'Sorry. I renamed him.'

As Callie spoke, Morton pushed past her to hang over the gate. He lifted his nose a few times, as if in greeting, then pawed the dirt before standing still and blinking at Lyndall. Stepping alongside, Kate reached out and caressed his jowl. Lyndall stayed where she was, eyes still huge. Callie's heart went out to her.

'He's such a lovely horse,' said Kate. 'Always on the hunt for pats. When Lyndall was at school I used to take my morning tea out and we'd chat.'

Callie smiled. 'You miss him?'

'I think I just miss having someone to talk to during the day. We had to put my old lab, Buffy, down a few years ago and the place feels empty without her.' Kate turned to her daughter. 'Do you want to come and say hello?'

Lyndall clenched her hands to her sternum, her fear palpable. She took a step forward, thin chest moving rapidly as she breathed in short harsh breaths. Though she now stood under a metre away from the gate it may as well have been a chasm. Desperate longing glistened in her eyes. Swallowing hard, her fingers trembling, Lyndall hesitantly reached out for her beloved horse.

Morton stretched forward to meet her only for Lyndall to snatch her hand away with a frightened cry. She skittered backward, her hands once more shoved hard against her ribs.

'Oh, sweetie,' said her mother, leaving the gate to wrap an arm around her shoulders. 'It'll be okay.'

'It won't!'

'Shh. It will.'

Callie felt as though someone had wrung her heart in their hands. She turned away and gazed at the lightly swaying forest canopy, wishing she knew how to make things better for Lyndall.

Bored with no one paying him attention, Morton wandered off to graze. With the horse at a safe distance, Lyndall broke from her mother's embrace to approach the gate and lean her chin on the backs of her hands.

Callie slipped through the fence and locked gazes with Kate, hoping she'd interpret her expression correctly. 'I'll fetch us all a cold drink.'

'I'll come with you.' Kate caressed her daughter's back. 'Will you be all right for a minute?'

Tight-mouthed, Lyndall nodded, her eyes locked on the animal she so desperately wanted to touch.

'I hate seeing her like this,' said Kate when they were out of earshot. 'It breaks my heart.'

'She loves him.'

'Desperately.' Kate spread her hands. 'But what else could we do? Lyndall wouldn't go near him and he was costing us a small fortune in feed and vet bills. We tried to help but nothing worked. The fall had just left her too traumatised. Finally Xav—that's my husband—made the decision he had to go.' Kate pressed her lips together. 'She cried for days.'

Of that, Callie had no doubt. Given the way Lyndall had acted on seeing her horse she probably still cried over his loss. What worried Callie now was where that grief was going, what emotions it was morphing into.

In the shade of Nanna's liquidambar, she halted and turned to Kate. 'Look, I know this is none of my business, but please don't let what happened to me happen to Lyndall.'

The other woman regarded her with a worried expression. 'What do you mean?'

Callie hauled in a breath. Time to be open for once. This wasn't about her. It was about a heartbroken and lost young girl, whose fate closely mirrored her own. 'I had a horse, a sweet grey galloway called Phantom.'

'Phantom?'

'Yes.'

Kate gave her a close look but to Callie's relief didn't comment further. She didn't want to explain her grandmother's game. Getting through her own story was trial enough.

'I loved that horse more than anything.' She touched the frayed rope end of the broken tyre swing, taking a moment to choose her words. 'We lived in Melbourne. Mum's a city girl but Dad was born and raised here, at Glenmore. So every school holidays and on weekends, when we weren't doing anything else, he used to bring us to visit Nanna and Poppy and let us loose on the farm. He wanted us to have some of what he had growing up, and I guess he missed it too.

'When I was eight, my grandparents finally got sick of my endless horse nagging and bought me Phantom. I couldn't come here enough after he arrived. I was so mad for that horse it was if nothing else existed in the world. He was like a best friend.' Callie shook her head. 'Actually that's a lie. He *was* my best friend.' She stopped talking as a choke formed in her throat.

'What happened to him?'

'He was sold, for similar reasons to Lyndall's Phantom. Things changed at home, which led to us not visiting as often. I tried to come but . . .' She shrugged as though it didn't matter anymore. 'I was young. Then my sister Hope died.' Callie let go of the rope and crossed her arms over herself as the familiar ache began to rise.

Kate's expression softened with sadness and sympathy. 'I'm so sorry.'

'Thanks. It was a long time ago.'

'I'm sure that doesn't make it any less devastating.'

'No. No, it doesn't.' Callie threw a look at Lyndall, still with her chin on her hands, watching Morton as he grazed, just as Callie used to do with Phan.

She turned back to Kate, willing her to understand, to see how important this was.

'After Hope's death, Mum and Dad set up a charity to remember her by. They worked really hard at it. I suppose it helped them cope, knowing they were doing something for her, but it also meant I never got to see Phan. Eventually my grandparents asked what they should do with him and Mum thought it best if he was sold. I wanted to object but with everything else it didn't seem right.' She blew out a breath. 'Things were really hard at home. I was trying to help, make sure my sister was remembered properly . . .'

She shook her head. 'I'm so ashamed I didn't fight harder for him. It still hurts. He was my best friend. I think maybe if I'd had him things mightn't have been so painful. I mightn't have run away like I did.' Callie gave a sad half-smile and spread her fingers. 'Who knows. But I do know what Lyndall's going through and you have to believe me when I tell you that she's hurting, really badly.'

Kate glanced at Callie's tattoo before turning away. For a long while she remained silent, her eyes riveted on her daughter, blazing with the sort of fierce lioness-like protectiveness and determination that only mothers possess.

Finally, she turned back to Callie. 'Lyndall's more precious to me than anything. More precious than my husband. More precious than my own life. And I will do anything, *anything*, to keep her safe and happy.' Her expression sank into helplessness. 'But I don't know how to deal with this.'

'Neither do I.' Callie smiled and touched Kate's arm in a sign of grateful solidarity. 'But that doesn't mean we can't try.'

Eight

Not bothering to open his eyes, Matt reached out and patted the bedside table as the raw opening guitar riff of AC/DC's 'Thunderstruck' broke him out of sleep. After a few seconds' scrabbling his hand finally closed around the vibrating shell of his phone. He brought it close to his face and half-opened one eye, unsurprised to find the cool, green-eyed gaze of his mother's professional profile staring back at him.

Awake now, Matt unglued his other eyelid and checked the time. Two twenty in the morning—mid-afternoon London time, although knowing Phoebe Hawkins, she could be anywhere in the world. His mother's private banking career meant his life had been punctuated with phone calls from all over the world, although for the last several years mainly China. Usually at inhospitable hours.

He slid his finger across the screen to unlock it and answer. 'Hey, Mum.'

'Did I get the time wrong again?' Phoebe said with her strange, Australian-mixed-with-the-rest-of-the-world-accent, a quirk developed from living abroad since her early twenties. Fluent Mandarin—and asset management expertise—had made her career, but she also spoke basic French and German.

He ground his palm into his left eye, rubbing the last of his sleepiness away. 'You always get the time wrong.'

'Sorry. You'd think I'd know by now.'

Matt thought so too. He doubted very much she ever stuffed up the time difference with her clients, but Matt was 'the mistake' and therefore rated low down on his mother's importance scale. He didn't hold it against her. Phoebe Hawkins simply had different priorities to other people.

'So where are you?'

'Home.' Which for Phoebe meant her barren, hyper-modern apartment in Islington. 'Although not for long. I'm leaving for Beijing tomorrow. Have you spoken with your father?'

Trust Phoebe to come straight to the point. He flattened his hand over his forehead and smoothed his palm back over his hair, well aware of what was coming and wishing he could just roll over and go back to sleep. 'Not yet.'

'You are going to though, aren't you? He owes you.'

'He doesn't owe me anything, Mum.'

Phoebe remained silent, her annoyance betrayed by the carrying sharp tap of a pen or pencil or fingernail against a desk. 'Then let me help.'

'I'm fine. Honestly. I've told you before I don't need anything from Kieran or from you.' Except perhaps a little bit of love, maybe a bit of pride in the son these two career-obsessed people accidentally created. Something other than this sense of being a cost on their lifetime balance sheets. But it seemed his parents could only ever relate to him in terms of money.

His father was the worst. The last time Matt caught up with Kieran Lynch-Moore was in Singapore's Changi Airport shortly before his second tour, when his scars were still raw and it had seemed so important to connect. His father was flying back to Luxemburg after a series of meetings in Asia and, determined to talk to the man he called Dad, but had never really known, Matt had flown in from Sydney. They were meant to spend the evening together at the Four Seasons Hotel. Instead they'd met in a crowded airport lounge, with his distracted father itching to catch his early flight out. The meeting lasted forty minutes, most of which was spent with Kieran on the phone, and ended with a pat on the shoulder and a promise to 'settle some funds on him'. Matt hadn't bothered to explain that he wasn't there for a handout. It wouldn't have registered anyway, but Matt had walked away vowing that if he ever had the chance to be a father then he'd be a far different man from Kieran Lynch-Moore.

'So how's work?' Matt asked, changing the subject.

'Challenging, in the climate.'

'You should slow down a bit. Maybe take a holiday.'

'I wish I could, but you know what this business is like. And stop prevaricating. I know you have this strange idea about not taking money from Kieran but you're forgetting that he never contributed a cent to your upbringing.'

'I'm not a bill that needs to be paid, you know.'

Phoebe must have caught the irritation in his voice for she softened her own tone. 'No. Of course you're not. But I'm concerned about your future. You can't stay at Uncle Wal's forever and I doubt you have much savings wise. The army doesn't pay that well.'

'Ah, now that depends which army you're in.'

His quip earned him a laugh. 'Isn't that the truth.'

Matt smiled into the phone. Growing up, laughter was a sound he'd rarely heard from his mother. Even now, he still savoured it. 'You don't need to worry about me. I'm all right. I'll work something out.'

Plus she was wrong about Kieran. Matt *had* taken money from his father: at eighteen, when he received a letter advising that a trust fund set up in his name had vested. It wasn't a huge amount and despite adding to it over the years, it still wasn't enough to buy him the farm he wanted, but it was a start.

'That's the issue, Matthew. You shouldn't need to. One word to Kieran and you could have the wherewithal to buy that farm you covet so much.'

'And where would be the fun in that? Come on, Mum, you of all people should understand that you have to work hard for what you want. I'm no different. And I don't know enough about managing a farm to take one on yet. I need this time at Wal's to learn.'

She sighed. They'd been through this before, after his stay with his old nanny, Antonella, when he'd realised what mattered most—family, contentment, love. Phoebe hadn't understood then either. It simply wasn't in her.

'I'm trying to help.'

'I know and I appreciate it, but I'll manage all right on my own.' After all, it was what he'd been doing most of his life anyway.

When she rang off he dumped the phone back on the side table and tried to fall back to sleep, but the conversation had triggered something in his mind. Despite what he told Phoebe, Matt's lack of experience hadn't prevented him looking at farms in the district. To his dismay, he'd found most were out of his reach. Those properties he could afford he doubted were big enough to make a living, and a smaller farm would mean he'd need to find other work. While he wasn't too proud to take on even the most menial of jobs, that scenario wasn't part of his dream. As fairy tale as it sounded, he wanted a life on the land with his family always close, where he could be a proper husband and father. A man made rich with happiness.

As he finally drifted back to sleep, he imagined Hope and wondered what his life would be like if they hadn't broken up. If he'd come to Dargate after school instead of joining the army. Would they be married, have kids? Cheeky little girls like Flora and Maddy. Perhaps a boy, too and a smiling blue-eyed wife, who made him feel special and wanted and protective.

His dream drifted, reshaping the face in his mind, until it settled once more. Only this time the smile he imagined wasn't Hope's.

It was her sister's.

***

Familiarity and time were slowly attuning Matt to Amberton's ebb and flow. Not to Wal's standard—the old bugger knew the place so intimately it was as though he could sense a flyblown sheep and the paddock it was in while sitting at the breakfast table—but each day Matt improved. It was the quiet that did it, the absolute peace of the place. A perfect balm for his soul after all the violence he'd witnessed.

He cocked his head and listened. The sound of a car decelerating on Thiedeke Road drifted over the farm. He waited, the hay he carried itching against his arms. Topanga cast him hopeful looks, his bottom lip quivering as he hung over the round yard fence, healthy chestnut coat a shimmer of gold in the sunshine. The car changed gear, the gravel crunch fading as the tyres swung onto a smoother surface.

'Sounds like we've a visitor,' he said to the colt.

With his free hand he unlatched the gate and carried the sheaves of hay to the old steel washtub that served as Topanga's feed trough. The horse followed behind, anxious for his feed and, Matt suspected, some attention. Since Wal's accident, he'd made sure the colt was well looked after, but Topanga was used to the old man's kind mutterings and fond mane scratches and rubs, whereas Matt struggled to justify the time. With so much else to do on the farm he couldn't help but view playtime as slacking off, plus he lacked his uncle's expertise. Wal's ministrations had a purpose—to condition the horse to human contact and develop trust—and Matt worried his ignorance could undo all his uncle's good work.

Ears still tuned to the car, he took a moment to stroke Topanga's silken neck as the colt snatched at the hay. The engine shut down, the quiet that followed broken by the dull whump of a car door closing.

'What do you reckon, Pang? Jehovah's Witnesses? Mormons?' But he'd heard only one door close and religious callers usually arrived in pairs. He sighed. It'd be just his luck to find an insurance agent banging on Amberton's front door, or someone selling vacuum cleaners or an electricity deal.

Giving Topanga a last mane scratch, Matt left the yard and took the worn path back toward the house. As he dodged around the trees shading Dolly's run, his step faltered.

'Look at you little cuties,' cooed a familiar female voice.

Supercallie.

A grin broke across his face. He took another step, careful to stay hidden in the shadows but angled closer so he could observe her without her knowing. She was crouched by Dolly's run, face animated with delight, as a mass of squirming, squeaking, soft puppies crowded against the fingers she'd poked through the mesh barrier keeping them safe and out of mischief.

A sudden memory struck him, one he'd long forgotten, of Hope meeting Wal's previous dog, Cooper, for the first time. Despite the threat of a cuff under the ear, he'd snuck the pup away from Amberton and met Hope in the firebreak behind the forest that separated Glenmore from Amberton. Her expression when she'd held the excited, licking puppy had made any risk worthwhile, flip-flopping his lovesick teenaged heart in a way that was almost painful. For days afterwards, he'd tried to figure out how he could buy her a pup of her own, but like so many of his ideas for them back then, he never managed to make it come true.

'You can have one if you like,' he said, moving out of the shadows and walking toward Callie. 'Wal's giving them away to good homes.'

She didn't start, making him wonder if she knew he'd been watching. Giving an ecstatic cock-eared puppy a last tickle, she rose and faced him, smiling.

'I doubt I'd make a good home.'

'You sure? They're pretty cute.'

'Ah, but cuteness isn't everything.'

He rubbed at his jaw, glad that he hadn't bothered to shave; the bristles helped make his scar less confronting. 'Probably just as well, otherwise I'd be stuffed.'

She studied him a moment, gaze lingering on his scar before sliding away. 'I'm sure you do all right.'

Matt's eyebrows rose at the half compliment but Callie was too busy staring through the trees to the yards with her hands on her hips to notice. Today she had her hair tied back low into two pigtails, giving her a girlish air. A sky blue singlet set off her eyes, her cuffed, faded red cotton shorts and worn out Dunlop Volleys showing off slender legs. Sweat or sunscreen cast a shine over her tanned shoulders and he was struck by how beach girl pretty she was. How she seemed to portray a kind of free-spiritedness, so incongruous to what he'd seen of her at the hospital and at Glenmore, when her reactions appeared those of someone who was anything but free.

She moved away from him, ducking under the branches to the edge of the shade, and nodded at Topanga, still chewing on his feed. 'That's a nice-looking horse. Is Wal planning to race him?'

'No. He's just breaking him in for someone.' Matt made a face. 'Although he's making noises about me taking over the job.'

'I didn't know you could ride.'

'That's the sticking point. I can't.'

A smile tugged her mouth. 'Yes. I could see how that would make things difficult.'

'You're the horsey one.' He cocked his head to the side. 'Maybe it's you he should be asking.'

'No thanks. I have enough on my plate.' She turned away again and swept her gaze around. If there was a purpose to her visit she didn't seem in any hurry to divulge it. 'This place used to seem like heaven when I was a kid. I was always so excited to come here.' She shook her head, expression slightly puzzled. 'I can't see it now. It just looks like a normal farm.'

'I imagine it was the horses.'

'Yeah. I always was a sucker for anything that neighed.'

'And now?'

Callie looked up at him from under lowered lashes. 'Now I'm a sucker for different things.'

He took a step closer and reached up to wrap both hands around an overhanging branch, gratified when her gaze skittered over his flexed biceps and chest. 'Callie Reynolds, are you flirting with me?'

'What makes you think that?'

'Oh, I don't know. Maybe the way you just looked at me.'

She shook her head. 'What is it about you Graneys? You all seem to have egos the size of elephants.'

'So what was that look for then?'

'That look, which you so badly misinterpreted, was merely that of a woman in need.'

'A woman in need?'

Humour lit her blue eyes but her voice feigned seriousness. 'A woman in *deep* need.'

Matt pursed his lips, nodding. 'This deep need of yours, would it happen to have something to do with Glenmore?'

'It would.'

He flipped through what help she could require and thought he knew. 'The tractor won't start.'

'Attractive and a mind-reader.'

'Attractive?'

'I'm a woman in need. Right now any capable man is attractive.'

He clutched his palms to his chest. 'You wound me.'

She laughed. 'I'm sure you're tough enough to take it.'

'Fortunately for you, I am. All right. I'll take a look, but I'd better warn you my assistance comes at a price.'

Callie crossed her arms and shifted her weight onto one hip, expression wry. The movement caused the strap of her singlet to fall to one side, exposing a very white bra strap. 'Oh, yes?'

Matt resisted the urge to lift the singlet strap back in place. The conversation might be borderline flirty but it hadn't progressed to the point of touching. And he wasn't sure that he was reading her correctly anyway.

Only one way to find out.

'Dinner, tonight. I'll cook you that steak I talked about.'

'Can't, sorry. I'm working.'

That threw him. What the hell would Callie need a job for? 'Working? Where?'

'Working, yes.' Noticing the strap, she adjusted it. 'Thanks in part to Wal lumping a horse on me, things are going to take a lot longer with Glenmore than I thought. Morton might be able to survive on clover but I can't, so I scored myself some bar shifts at the Royal to help tide me over.'

The idea she was staying on, even for a short while, appealed. A lot. 'What about Friday night then?'

'Working.'

He eyed her. 'Saturday?'

'The same. And thanks to it being the Australia Day long weekend, I have shifts on Sunday and Monday as well.'

He let out an exasperated breath. 'Okay, how about you just tell me what night you aren't working.'

'Smart play. Tuesday. I'm as free as a bird on Tuesday evening. You may impress me with your steak-cooking expertise then, but,' she held up a warning finger, 'only if you can get the tractor going.'

Matt pointed to his chest. 'Attractive, capable man, remember?'

***

Though Glenmore's Fiat tractor should have been retired from service years ago, Matt discovered nothing wrong with it—Callie simply couldn't fathom its gears.

Driving the ute and tractor, operating machinery and safely attaching and detaching linkages and PTOs was one of the first things Wal had taught Matt as a boy. At the time his mother had been unimpressed when she found out, but looking back, the old man had been correct to do so. Unfamiliarity and inexperience caused accidents, and the novelty made a marvellous respite from the monotony of boarding school. School was fun, but at Amberton lay adventure.

'You'll have to organise more diesel,' said Matt as he inspected Glenmore's small but fairly modern diesel-grade polyethylene fuel tank and pump system. Until Matt had pointed it out, Callie assumed Maggie had used the leggy, alien-looking drum that stood on rusted stilts on a concrete platform behind the machinery shed. Maggie probably would have had she'd been allowed, but as Wal so often liked to grumble, farm health and safety had so bogged them in rules and regulations it was a wonder they could farm at all. Matt supposed she'd been left no choice but to upgrade.

The tank registered around a third full. Not enough to keep a tractor as old as Glenmore's running for the work Callie had in mind. Given the Fiat's age and condition, an army Bushmaster probably had better fuel efficiency.

'More diesel.' Callie scratched at her arm, the tease-filled girl he'd seen at Amberton replaced by someone more pensive. 'All right. So how do I do that?'

'Just take the tank into Versace's. It's where Wal gets his diesel from. Maggie probably has an account too.' He rose from his crouch. 'There'll be paperwork around somewhere. Or you could just ring and ask.'

She looked away from him, studying her foot as she dragged it through some weed.

'How much will it cost, do you think?'

'I don't know. A reasonable amount I guess.' Matt looked at the tank and did a quick calculation. 'Three or four hundred. I don't really know. Wal would be the best one to ask. But you'll need more than one tank if you're planning to slash the entire property.'

She shook her head and walked away to stand at the edge of the concrete apron, arms crossed, as she surveyed the overgrown paddocks.

He watched for a moment before moving alongside her. Morton had retreated to the small stand of gums shading the far eastern end of his paddock. Bird chatter filtered from the forest, and on the rising breeze he could hear traces of the ocean. The forecast southerly change was at last approaching. If Callie wanted to make the most of the cooler weather she needed to get moving. But he kept his counsel, leaving her to think on whatever it was that caused that pinched, hounded look on her face.

'You ever had one of those days where you just wanted to run?' she asked quietly. 'And keep running until you've run so far you can never go back.'

'Plenty.'

Questioning blue eyes swivelled to meet his.

He shrugged. 'War's shit.'

She held his gaze for a moment, then her expression softened. 'Thanks.'

'What for?'

'For putting things into perspective.'

Genuinely puzzled, he frowned and tilted his head. 'How?'

'You reminded me how lucky I am.'

He thought of the terrified children he'd seen, and the women with eyes so haunted he wondered if they ever slept. The bodies. Stevie.

'Yeah, we're all lucky.' Feeling the need to lighten the mood, he pointed his chin toward the Fiat. 'Come on, I think it's about time you learned how to drive the beast.'

The tractor was cramped with the two of them inside. Matt stood in the cabin with his arms braced against the frame and a slouch in his back. Each time he tried to move, his leg brushed Callie's arm and he found himself constantly apologising.

'I can't get the seat to lower,' she said, fidgeting with the setting.

He stooped down for the lever, bumping her again. 'Sorry.'

'You don't have to keep apologising.'

'Yeah, I do. My old London nanny would smack me around if I didn't.'

'You had a nanny?'

'A nanny and a posh boarding school. I'm a well brung-up bloke.' He winked at her and pulled hard on the stiff adjustment. The seat suddenly dropped, bouncing Callie into his arm. 'Fuck, sorry. You okay?' She gave him a look that made him hold up his palms. 'All right, I'll stop apologising. You set now?'

Placing her hand on the wheel, she balanced her feet on the pedals and wriggled her bum a bit. 'Yep.'

'It's pretty straightforward,' he said, pointing in turn at the tractor's mechanics. 'Key, starter button, clutch, high and low ratio gears, handbrake.' And so the lesson continued, covering all the basics and safety issues he could think of until, finally, Callie was ready to take off. Tongue protruding slightly between her lips in concentration, she followed his instructions. The tractor lurched as she released the clutch too quickly before recovering to a sedate chug.

She grinned and leaned forward, bouncing in her seat. 'Easy!'

'Driving is. We still have to get you sorted with the slasher.' Matt straightened as much as the cabin allowed, wincing at the ache already forming in his back. He looked behind to give the mower a last check and pointed to an overgrown area past the main gate. 'Head over to that clearing. There's plenty of practice space, and around the house is where you should do first anyway.'

Though he suspected she knew most of it from watching her grandfather, Matt explained the mechanics of raising and lowering the mower, and the operation of the power take off. He wanted to make sure she understood the beauty and danger of machinery, and what to look out for when things went wrong, just as Wal had patiently taught him all those years ago. Within minutes Callie had it mastered, the slasher cutting a messy swathe through the long growth as pleasure in her achievement brightened her face.

Though his back ached and sweat soaked his T-shirt, Matt stayed on the tractor until she'd completed the entire area. She learned fast and, to his relief, took the task seriously, concentrating on getting the mower as close as possible to the fenceline while taking care to leave a safety margin, and monitoring the dials and machinery. Honk spent the entire time strutting around his patch with his head up and neck snaked, bugling his irritation at the noise. Not that Matt could hear him, the cacophony of the tractor kept the goose, and everything else, drowned out.

'Dinner. Tuesday,' Matt ordered when the tractor was safely returned to its bay in the machinery shed and he and Callie were making their way toward the house via the newly slashed front yard. 'And don't be late.'

'Late?' She thinned her lips and gave a rueful shake of her head. 'You never said anything about having to be on time. The tide might be right.'

'What's the tide got to do with anything?'

'Fishing.'

'Fishing?'

'Yes. Fishing.' She rolled her eyes. 'You know, rod, reel, bait, ocean.'

He stepped onto the spongy side lawn, another aspect of Glenmore that could do with some maintenance. 'As a matter of fact I do, but I'm not quite sure what that has to do with our dinner date.'

'Well, a day off means fishing.'

'It does?'

She nodded, expression serious. 'It does.'

'And you're prepared to be late for an evening with me—' he pointed to his chest, '—the attractive—your words—capable man who fulfilled his promise to get your tractor going, for the sake of dropping a line?'

'I am.'

Matt raised his eyes and made a tsk noise, as though he couldn't believe such an attitude could exist in a woman. 'Callie Reynolds, you are one strange bird.'

His display of mock disappointment proved a mistake. With his gaze averted, Matt failed to register Honk stalking around the edge of the house until it was too late. As soon as the word 'bird' was out of his mouth, the goose launched, great wings flapping, head streaking toward Matt's groin like a white and orange cobra.

He jumped backward, accidentally knocking into Callie, who'd ducked behind him. She grabbed his arm for balance, pulling him even further back just as he jerked his hips away from another lunge from Honk. The movement overbalanced them both and Matt only had enough time to grab Callie and spin her sideways before momentum sent him crashing to the lawn, Callie dropping painfully on his chest in an uncomfortable sprawl.

He blinked at the sky, unsure if it was his chest or the sprinkler head digging into his arse that hurt most. Callie rolled off him and they both lay staring, chests heaving, while Honk released a victory bugle.

'You all right?' Matt finally managed.

'Yep.'

'Interesting day.'

'It is.'

They stared some more, floored by a mad bird.

'Not quite what I had in mind.'

'No.'

Matt started to laugh. Callie joined in, giggling in a way that reminded him bittersweetly of Hope. For a yearning moment he wished he could talk to Callie about her, share the good times, the things they loved about Hope, keeping her alive through their united memories. But he and Hope had always been private. Secrecy was what helped make the relationship so intense.

Like so much else in his life, age had given him perspective. Hope might have broken his heart, but that didn't mean he didn't respect what they'd experienced. It'd been special the way only first loves can be. Sharing her now, even after Wal's revelation, would seem like a betrayal.

Honk sounded another smug trumpet, cutting their laughter.

'That steak,' said Callie, flopping her head to the side and regarding him with moist, mirth-filled eyes. 'Are you sure you don't want to swap it for roast goose?'

Nine

After the fun of Matt's tractor driving lesson, the thrill of operating heavy machinery and the satisfaction of seeing some progress on her Glenmore chore list, Callie thought slashing would be fun. If not fun, then at least not onerous, but the first full morning on her own had her reassessing that idea. By the end of her session on Saturday, she hated the job.

Driving monotonous laps of Glenmore's paddocks left her too much time to think, and Glenmore and thinking didn't co-exist well. The more she contemplated, the more confused she felt about her plans. Callie *knew* what she was doing was right, but since when did rightness feel so damn wrong?

Thanks to her poor financial situation, she'd had no choice but to dig into Nanna's cash account to pay for diesel, and while Versace's were sympathetic, business was business. If Callie wanted fuel, she had to pay upfront, which she did, heading straight for the newsagent's afterwards to invest in a ledger, driven by the irrational imperative to keep account of every dollar of Nanna's money she spent. Why, she wasn't sure. The land and cash were all hers anyway. The only person she was accountable to was herself, yet Callie couldn't shake the feeling she was stealing. From the Hope Foundation, from her parents. From Hope herself.

And while the weather remained cool, Callie had endless hours on the tractor to dwell on the thought.

Fortunately, when her mind finally tired of picking over the bones of her situation, she had Matt and her inconvenient attraction to him, along with

Lyndall Soriano's fear of Morton, to occupy her thoughts.

In the two days since his lesson on Thursday, Matt had been over each morning to check on her. He didn't stay long, just enough to give the machinery a quick once-over and ask how she was faring. They'd exchange a few minutes' banter and then he'd leave, Callie watching his ute as he drove away, flustered by the warmth he left behind.

Kate and Lyndall Soriano also became regular visitors, with Callie taking the lunchtime arrival of Kate's teal Range Rover as her cue to stop for the day. The paddocks might have needed slashing, but Lyndall's fear of Morton was pitiful. Callie didn't know what she could do to help, but she wanted to at least try.

While Lyndall hovered near the house with Kate, Callie would lead Morton out of his paddock to the shade of Nanna's liquidambar, chattering brightly as she brushed him down and cleaned out his hooves, doing her utmost to demonstrate that the gentle horse was harmless. Yesterday, Callie had vaulted onto his back and sat astride, savouring the long-forgotten joy of having a horse between her legs. She'd leaned forward, rubbing Morton's mane and tugging his ears until Lyndall's despairing expression sent her sliding back to the ground.

At a loss, Callie tried to ask Wal for advice when she visited before her shift at the pub, but the old man's mood turned filthy the moment she mentioned Lyndall's visits. After Wal's revelation about Nanna's plans, Callie understood his anger, although she was finding his temper increasingly difficult to tolerate. What worried her more was his appearance. The corrugations in his face seemed to have deepened, each furrow more shadowed. His disapproving mouth, always sunken, had submerged even further, forming a hollow in his face like a closed up sea anemone. Even his eyes appeared to have lost their healthy alertness, and there was a sheen to his skin, like a cold sweat, Callie didn't like. But if he was in pain, Wal refused to acknowledge it.

'Don't you worry about me, missy,' he told her when she voiced her worry. 'I'll be out of here before you know it.'

Callie hoped he was right, yet her unease remained.

That night the weather turned again. Callie woke to a Sunday morning made sweltering and dangerous thanks to a high pressure system over western Victoria and a gusting northerly wind. The Country Fire Authority's website had upgraded the fire danger to code red, leaving slashing and other machinery operations out of the question.

With a cup of tea in hand, Callie sat at Nanna's kitchen table and ran through the CFA's bushfire protection guide, wishing she'd had more time to prepare. Though the area in the immediate vicinity of the house was clear, weeds still grew rampant around the machinery shed. Wary of leaving herself short of feed, she hadn't slashed Morton's paddock—a mistake, given the horse's fussy eating habits. He hadn't touched any of the long growth, feasting instead on all the sweet clover patches and any tender young grass shoots he could find. The hayed-off older plants, with their ranker leaves and stalky stems, were left ungrazed. With each gust of wind, the seed heads bent and swayed, the paddock rippling like a silver-blonde ocean, as beautiful as it was hazardous.

Leaving the guide, Callie stared out the window and across the yard, rattled and worried. The groans of the house timbers as the wind tugged at its frame only reinforced her anxiety. Extreme bushfire danger days hardly affected her as a child. She knew they kept Nanna and Poppy busy, moving stock and checking water tanks and hoses, but they were always adult concerns. Other than the order that she and Hope remain close to the house, stinking weather merely meant playtime under the sprinkler or a quiet day inside sucking Nanna's home-made frozen cordial icy poles.

But Nanna and Poppy were both gone and though it was the last thing she wanted, Callie was now in charge. Childhood ignorance and irresponsibility applied no longer.

Drawing a notepad across the table, she returned to the guide and began making a list.

***

Callie spent the first part of the morning inspecting equipment, resisting the urge to give Honk a good hosing down when he ambushed her near the water tank. The goose was cranky enough without her adding to his temper, nor could she afford to waste water. Instead, she took her irritation out on the worst of the weeds growing around the machinery shed, pulling them by hand or, when that failed, using an old shovel to shear them off at the roots.

By ten am, Nanna's weather station read thirty-nine degrees Celsius. Patches of sweat left dark circles on Callie's shorts and singlet. Messy streaks covered her legs where rivulets had slipped through the clinging dust and sunscreen. Her blonde ponytail hung limp down her back, the hair under her fishing hat wet.

She retreated to the back step with an ice-filled glass, sucking on the cold cubes as she gazed across the paddocks to the wind-wracked forest, hazily wondering if Matt would call in. Callie glanced at her phone, lying on the concrete next to her hip. Perhaps she should call him at Amberton, ask his advice about what else she should do. The number would be easy enough to look up.

As though sensing her attention, the mobile released an electronic flourish. Wiping her damp hands on the leg of her shorts Callie picked it up, smiling as she read Anna's text asking if she was free to Skype.

Not shagging Bruce? she returned.

With Bruce. Not shagging. Skype? Anna shot back.

Callie texted back an *OK* and ducked inside for her laptop. Five minutes later she was grinning at a sleep and sex-ruffled Anna.

'Where's Bubby?' Callie asked.

Anna narrowed her eyes, speaker distortion turning her voice even harsher than normal. 'Let me guess, Rowan's been telling tales.'

'Pet names . . .' Callie sucked air between her teeth. 'You know what that means.'

A flush rose up Anna's neck but she didn't deny the allegation. 'Nothing wrong with pet names.'

'So where is he?' asked Callie, suspecting she already knew.

'He's around.'

Callie gave her a stern look. 'Wherever he is, he'd better be behaving himself. This isn't a sexcam.'

'I'm not that perverted.' Anna looked away from the screen, her expression slightly soppy. Rowan was right, after all her protesting Anna now had it bad. 'He's just rubbing my feet. I need it. The last few nights have been epically busy.'

'As long as that's all he rubs.' Callie took a sip of her melted ice. 'So how's things?'

'Pretty good. We miss you. Everyone does. Rowan said you called the other day.' Anna pulled her laptop closer and peered at her screen, frowning as she inspected Callie's image. 'He said you sounded a bit upset. Is everything okay?'

Though Anna's concern made Callie's throat thicken, she kept her face straight. 'Sure. Things are fine. A bit more work than I expected but . . .' She stopped. Why the hell was she lying to Anna? What difference would it make if she told the truth? 'It's not fine. It's hard, much harder than I expected.'

'You miss your nan.'

'There's that.' Callie swallowed and looked away, her eye catching on the tyre swing's broken rope. Yet another memory of Hope flitted through her mind: Callie urging her sister on as she swung dangerously high, Hope's back so arched her blonde hair dragged on the ground. Their shared whoops colouring the air. Even then her sister like to push the limits.

'There's more bothering you?'

Callie gave a half laugh and shook her head. 'You have no idea.'

'So share it with me.'

She stared at Anna's face, so pretty and open and warm. Callie wanted to talk, to tell Anna of her confusion, to ask for advice and reassurance, but the more she considered it, the more her skin began to prickle. Revealing confidences just wasn't her way.

'Thanks, but it's fine, really. I'm just being dumb.' She smiled brightly. 'You wouldn't believe what else Nanna left me.'

Her friend sighed. 'When are you going to learn that it won't kill you to get close to people?'

Shamed at the hurt in Anna's voice, Callie turned her face away. 'I don't do it on purpose.'

'That's the trouble. You do.' Anna let out another annoyed breath. 'All right, show me what I won't believe.'

Callie tried to ignore Anna's comment but it left a ragged wound, mainly because she knew it to be true. She *did* keep people at arm's length on purpose, but it was for their own good.

Tugging on her fishing hat, Callie rose and carried the laptop across the lawn toward the home paddock. Too hungry, dumb or simply oblivious to the heat, Morton was in the open, grazing. At her approach he looked up and slowly began to wander over, tail swishing at flies. Callie hoisted the laptop on a post, aligning the camera so Anna could see him.

'You have a horse?' Anna asked in disbelief.

'I do. A big warty one.'

'*Warty?*'

Callie eased the laptop out of reach as Morton stretched his neck out to sniff. She scratched his cheek, eyeing the screen to make sure Anna caught a good look at the horse's face. 'Very warty.'

'Oh, that's gross! Should you be touching him?'

'They're harmless grass warts. Not contagious for humans. They'll disappear in a few months.'

'For your sake I hope you're right. Although you want to be careful he doesn't scare potential buyers away.'

'All going to plan, he won't be here for much longer,' said Callie, treating Morton to a last ear tug before heading back to the house and shade. Already her shoulders were stinging with sunburn. 'I'm hoping his previous owner will take him back, but she had a bad fall and now she's frightened of him. I think she'll come good though. She's crazy about him.'

'What if she doesn't take him? You'll have to bring him here.'

Callie sank onto the step, balancing the laptop on her knees while she took a long slug of water. 'I don't think he'll fit in my room.'

Anna rolled her eyes. 'Don't be smart. You know what I mean.'

'I can't keep a horse.'

'Sure you can. You'd be able to paddock him somewhere. You love horses.'

'I do, but it's too much of a responsibility and they're damn expensive to run.'

'So find yourself a rich boyfriend.' Anna grinned. 'Just so happens I know of a good one.'

A surprised male voice sounded in the background. 'Who, me? I'm not rich.'

'I know,' said Anna, blowing a kiss to one side. 'But you, my darling Brucey-bubby, have other qualities.'

'Must you?' asked Callie, rolling her eyes.

Anna grinned at her. 'I meant Mark.'

'Not interested.'

'That was fast. Usually I get at least a bit of a spark.' Anna pursed her lips, eyes sharpening as she leaned in closer to examine Callie's face on the screen. 'Have you met someone down there?'

'No.'

Anna's eyes turned buggy at Callie's too-quick response. 'You have! Who? What's he like?'

'I haven't and he's not like anything. I have to go.'

'Don't you dare disconnect!' She pointed a finger at Callie, her voice rising to a squawk. 'Don't you dare!'

Her grin huge, Callie flapped her fingers in a series of tiny waves.

'Bye, Anna. Give Bubby my regards.'

By the time Callie's computer had completed its shutdown procedure, Anna's texts numbered five. Callie sent back only one message: *I have NOTHING 2 tell.* But when the sound of an approaching vehicle had her stomach doing a flip, only for it to sink in disappointment when the car kept on heading past, she wondered just who the hell she was trying to kid.

***

Compared with the previous night, the Royal proved a lot more subdued on Sunday. With plenty of daylight remaining and heat still in the day, the locals were either still squishing their toes in the sand and seaweed of MacLeans Bay or holed up in the shady cool of their homes. Doug warned Callie she'd be required in the main bar later, when the thirsty and overheated evening crowd started to arrive, but in the meantime she could look after the back bar, which catered for diners and poker machine players.

Happy to be on her own and away from the boisterous front of the pub, Callie set about unloading and reloading the glass washer and preparing for dinner patrons. She liked the back bar. Its flocked wallpaper and dark timber panelling gave the room an old-fashioned feel, reminiscent of what the pub must have been like in its glory days, when wool had made the district rich. The patrons tended to be an older, more polite group, whose interests lay in their stomachs or rattling another dollar through the ever-churning poker machines than in drinking themselves stupid.

'You do that well.'

Callie looked up to find Matt grinning at her. What a typical remark from him; innocent on the surface but somehow inferring more.

Unable to resist, she fired back a quip: 'You'd be surprised at what I'm good at.'

He rested his elbows on the bar and leaned toward her. Unlike his visits to Glenmore, when Matt turned up stubble-jawed and wearing stained work clothes, he was clean shaven. His green eyes danced, the colour deepened by his well-ironed green-and-white striped shirt.

'Callie Reynolds, is that a challenge? Do you have hidden talents you wish me to uncover?'

'No hidden talents, unless you count making cocktails. I'm pretty good at those.' Keeping her eyes slid sideways to watch him, she added another glass to the rack. 'So what are you doing here?'

'Oh, the usual for a newcomer to town. Feeling a bit lonely.' He winked at her, another habit of his. 'Thought I'd come down here and chat up a barmaid, see if she'd take pity on me.'

She raised an eyebrow.

He grinned. 'I'm meeting a couple of the guys from Dargate Rural Traders for dinner. Lucky for me they chose a pub with the best-looking staff.'

'If you mean Doug, you'll find him in the front bar.'

Matt shook his head. 'Not my type. Too jaded. Anyway, I prefer blondes.'

'If you think flattery will get you a free beer you're wrong.'

'Maybe it's not free beer I'm after.'

Shaking her head, Callie moved to the taps. The man had all the lines. 'So what can I get you?'

Wickedness flashed in his eyes. He took a few heartbeats to answer but when he did it was simply to order a glass of light beer. Callie poured it, glad for the reprieve from his banter. The game that had begun when she'd sought his help with the tractor seemed to grow a little more flirty with each encounter. It was fun, definitely, but the buzz it generated left her wondering if she shouldn't be more careful.

She placed his beer on the drainer and took his money. 'You didn't come over this morning.'

'No.' He took a sip, eyeing her over the glass. 'Did you miss me?'

'Not particularly.'

'Not even a little bit?'

Callie considered for a moment. 'Perhaps a fraction. Although it was more the capable man bit I missed.'

'*Attractive* capable man, let's not forget.' He took another mouthful, watching her closely. 'What's up?'

'Nothing really. It's just this weather. The fire danger.' She shrugged. 'I'm probably worrying about nothing.'

'That's not nothing. It's real.' He turned to scan the bar, waving toward the door as a couple entered. 'Looks like the boys are here. I'll come around tomorrow after I've seen Wal and picked his brains. We'll check things over.'

'Thanks. I appreciate it.' Then she grinned, relief making her reckless. '*Attractive* capable man.'

The look he shot back was so naughty schoolboy it sent the buzz into overdrive.

New patrons arrived, an elderly couple red-faced from heat. Callie tended to them, sympathising with their complaints about the broiling weather, her mood light. When she turned back, Matt had moved across the room to stand with two couples and a single woman. The men were around Matt's age, good-looking and well built. The sort of confident, ruggedly handsome country boys Callie had always admired. Standing close beside them were, she surmised, their partners. Both women were slim and dark haired, one wearing tight white Capri pants and a hot pink spaghetti-strapped singlet that matched her pink sandals, the other prettily feminine in a short, pale blue broderie Anglaise sundress. They looked young, healthy and carefree and, from the way the men had their arms slung around their shoulders, loved.

But it was the other girl who piqued Callie's interest. She hovered at the edge of the group, eyeing Matt from beneath long, made-up lashes. A snub-nosed redhead, whose hair fell in gorgeous ripples down her back, and whose pale, slender legs were shown off perfectly by a pair of cuffed shorts and leather wedges. However, her undeniable copper beauty was ruined by the sour tightness of her mouth. She reached out limp fingers toward Matt, barely managing a polite smile, before looking away with a bored expression.

Lifting his hand, Matt rubbed at his scar before letting his fingers drop and turning to the broader shouldered of the men. Callie's jaw tightened, her good mood evaporating at the obvious snub Matt had just received.

Irritated with herself for caring, Callie deliberately turned her back on the group. She crouched down at the rear, under-counter fridge and busied herself bringing stock forward, the bottles rattling as she clanked them together. Matt could look after himself. And she needed to mind her own business.

'A man could get used to a view like that.'

Callie looked around to find Matt once more at the bar, his head tilted as he eyed her bum.

'My shout,' he said in response to her surprised look. 'A Carlton Draught, a Cascade Light, two Diet Cokes, and a gin and tonic for my unimpressed blind date.'

'Blind date?'

'Yeah. Apparently the boys thought I needed one.'

She straightened and headed to the taps, sliding him a sideways glance. 'And do you?'

'I don't appear to be having much luck with the barmaid.'

Callie wasn't so sure about that. Not that she was about to admit it. Positioning glasses under the taps, Callie began pouring, regarding the redhead as she worked. Matt's blind date was leaning close to the Capri-panted woman, her hands twirling near her face, expression unhappy. As though sensing scrutiny, she suddenly looked up and caught Callie watching. Her gaze flicked to Matt, her hand quickly dropping as she muttered something to her friend, who jerked around to stab Callie with unfriendly eyes.

'She's very attractive,' said Callie, shovelling ice into a tall glass.

'Do you think? I've never been into redheads. Which is probably a good thing because she sure isn't into me.'

'Her loss.'

'That's what I reckon.' Although the words sounded confident, Matt's tone lacked its usual playfulness. He rubbed at his scar again in a way that made Callie speculate whether he even knew if he did it. It wasn't so much self-conscious as automatic. 'Anyway,' he said, smiling suddenly as though he'd just shaken off a bad thought, 'like I said, I prefer blondes.'

Callie placed the drinks onto a high-sided anodised tray, trying not to feel flattered by Matt's comment. It was simply his way, but knowing that didn't stop warmth spreading through her belly. He left with the drinks, returning a few moments later with the tray.

He didn't leave after he'd handed it over, fingers tapping on the bar, watching her as she fidgeted with wiping unnecessarily around the sink. 'What time do you finish?'

'Late.'

'How late?'

'Drive straight home and collapse into bed late.'

He nodded, and flattened his hand, fingers pointing toward her, leaving Callie with the sense he wanted to reach out. Instead, he patted the counter and pulled away. 'Watch out for 'roos.'

Matt didn't return to the bar again but that didn't stop Callie observing him. His group settled into one of the tables, the girls nattering at one end, the men at the other. Seemingly unperturbed by the redhead's snub, Matt appeared relaxed, gesturing animatedly as he talked, leaning back occasionally to laugh. He fitted in, like he'd been born in the town. He even carried himself the same as the other men, with confidence, as though he knew, despite his disfigurement, that he equalled their country-boy handsomeness and strength. It wasn't ego, as she'd first suspected, more a refined self-regard.

A man who knew who he was and where he belonged.

The thought made Callie strangely proud, and jealous. It was easy to admire Matt's fortitude but the natural, untroubled way he slotted in filled her with an unfamiliar yearning for a proper home. Unlike her, he had a place he belonged, whereas Callie belonged nowhere and to no one. Even the one place she held a deep connection with and adored, she wanted to cast off and run from.

Somehow sensing Callie's scrutiny, Matt looked up and winked, his smile so genuine and appreciative it seemed to illuminate the space between them. Something molten formed inside her, an exciting thing that bubbled and spread like sweet toffee. The sort of feeling that she hadn't experienced in years. That she'd tried very hard to never resurrect.

Disconcerted, heart thudding, Callie turned away, but not before giving voice to a heartfelt and despair-filled *Oh, damn.*

Ten

For the umpteenth time Matt berated himself for his stupidity. The longing that had walloped him hard in the chest in the pub the night before was pointless. Callie was selling up and leaving Glenmore and her painful memories behind forever. Time he came to his senses and ceased this stupid fantasising.

Yet as he drove through the gates of Dargate Hospital on Monday morning, Matt sensed it wasn't going to be that easy. Callie did something to him, aroused feelings he couldn't stop, made him act in ways he couldn't help. He wanted her, no question, but she wasn't the woman for him. His dreams were here. Hers weren't.

The hospital was noisier today but not with its usual medical industry. The air hummed with the chatter of Australia Day holiday visitors. Hospital sterility was softened by the drift of perfume and soaped bodies, of flowers and fruit, of outdoor life being brought inside. Each slide of the automatic doors dragged in scents of desiccated grass and thirsty trees, and the odd, slightly metallic aroma of super dry air. The heat blasts turned Matt's mind back to Callie and her worry over fire danger; her grin and the statement that had followed his offer for help.

Attractive, capable man.

Yeah. A bloke could get used to hearing those words.

Matt smiled to himself as he made his way to Wal's ward, only for his mood to plummet the moment he spied Wal.

'If you don't mind me saying,' he said, pulling up a chair close to the bed, sitting on the seat edge and leaning forward, 'you look like shit.'

Which wasn't a lie. Wal possessed the sort of pinched, greasy grey appearance of a person in deep discomfort.

His uncle threw back a sour look. 'You taking care of my farm properly?'

'As best I can.' Summoning patience, Matt picked Wal's *Stock & Land* off the bedside table and began to flick through it as he waited for the ritual to commence. Each day Matt would arrive, sit down, and attempt to respond to Wal's snapped-out questions about Amberton without losing his temper, until finally the old man turned to the subject he really wanted to discuss.

'Flystrike?'

'A couple.'

'You isolated them?'

Matt flicked over a page. 'Yep.'

'Cattle?'

'Fat, farty, burping machines, as per normal.'

'Troughs?'

Matt scanned an article warning of field crickets ruining pastures. 'No problems.' He turned the paper around and pointed. 'Is this something we should be worried about?'

'What?'

'Crickets. Black crickets eating pastures. Apparently it could be a problem.'

Wal's mouth flapped open and closed like a steam vent, sending his waxen jowls wobbling. 'Crickets?'

'Yes. It says here they're on the move. Do I need to watch out for them or spray or anything?'

'Don't be an idiot. Crickets like cracking soils.'

'Right, and I take it we don't have any of those.'

Apparently not, given the filthiness of the look Wal threw him. Matt bowed his head to hide his smile and feigned deep concentration in an editorial about the catastrophic decline in students wishing to study agriculture. Confined to bed, Wal could only simmer with frustration.

A gnarled hand reached out and snatched the top edge of the *Stock &* *Land*. 'Well?'

'Well what?'

'Don't you get smart with me, lad. You know exactly what. The missy.'

'She's a who, not a what.'

Newsprint scrunched in Wal's fist. Despite his unhealthy pallor, strength existed in his clawed grip. Any moment he'd snatch the paper up and start batting Matt around the head. Poor old bugger hated the hospital and detested being confined to bed even more than his painful physio sessions, a state Matt could relate to. He'd hated hospital too; the smell, the noises, and most of all the discomposing sense of helplessness. For an active, independent person, hospital could be hell.

Matt relented. Teasing Wal might be fun, but it wasn't really fair, no matter how much the cranky-arse deserved it. 'Yes, I've seen her. Last night at the Royal.'

Wal arched eagerly toward him. 'You took her out for tea?'

'No. She's working there. I thought she would have told you.'

'Missy doesn't tell me anything,' Wal muttered, slumping back. 'Just brings in bloody papers and grapes and talks about all the places she's been. Like I can't see what she's doing.'

'And what's that?'

'Pretending she doesn't give a tinker's damn about Glenmore.'

A few days ago Matt might have argued the point, but the haunted way she'd stared across the paddocks the day he'd helped her with the tractor had stuck with him. In the four nights since, during the drifting, contemplative moments of pre-sleep, Matt had rolled that expression around his mind, trying to decipher its meaning. Whether it was a product of Callie's sorrow for Hope and the loss her family had endured, or for herself and the heartbreak of abandoning a place that had comprised such a significant part of her childhood.

Perhaps more telling was her genuine worry for the property. Plus there was still no sign of Glenmore on Graney Realty's for sale list. Matt had been checking.

She'd wanted to run. The question was, from what? Her memories or her choice?

'Maybe she does care,' Matt said. 'But it's still her place. She can do what she likes with it.'

Wal let out a grunt that portrayed exactly what he thought of that statement. 'You're meant to be making her stay.'

'Not a proposal I recall agreeing to, but you'll be happy to know I've invited her around for dinner tomorrow night.'

'Good.' Wal nodded, mouth working in excitement at the news. 'Good.' His eyes narrowed and Matt could almost see the finely calibrated cogs of his wily mind ticking over. 'Show her Topanga. Ask if she wouldn't mind helping with him. Feed her some sob story about how he can't be left half broken like this. That it might give him problems later or something.' His lips puttered in and out like soft pistons. 'And while you're at it, see if you can't get her to take one of Dolly's whelps. Girls go funny over babies. Makes them susceptible.'

'Susceptible to what?'

Wal's left eyebrow sank with secretive man-to-man meaning as he tilted his head and bobbed his chin. 'You know.'

Cottoning on, Matt quickly slapped the paper down. This wasn't a discussion he wanted to continue and besides, Matt had his own agenda. He pointed to the small LCD television mounted on the ward's far wall.

'Have you been watching the weather forecast? Those hot northerlies are drying things off fast. Callie's worried about Glenmore. I said I'd ask you if there's anything she needed watch out for.'

'She can slash those bloody paddocks for starters.'

'Already onto it. She'd be finished if it weren't for the fire danger.'

'Good. Been bothering me, that.' Wal nodded his approval. 'Maggie had an old fire trailer. I checked it over for her back in November but you'd better give it another look just in case. Should've been replaced years ago but things got too tough after Tom died.'

'Anything else?'

Wal was silent for a while before rattling off a pile of chores that Matt wasn't convinced were entirely necessary, and sounded suspiciously designed to keep him at Glenmore rather than for fire preparation.

'I'll pass it on. Shit!' His voice choked as a foul odour suddenly engulfed the room. Matt jerked around to glare at Arthur's curled up, blanket-hidden body before turning back to Wal. 'Does he ever stop?'

Wal regarded his roommate with contempt. 'No. Always was a filthy bugger. Nurses won't move him either. Said I shouldn't be so uncharitable toward a dying man. Dying? I'm the one who's dying.' He jerked a finger at Arthur. 'Of that old bastard's stink!'

'You want me to ask for you?'

'No. No bloody point.' As though exhausted by his tirade, Wal sagged back onto his pillow, the pinched, afflicted expression returning to his face as he plucked the bed's pale blue waffle blanket up to his chest.

Matt leaned forward, elbows on his knees, and held his uncle's gaze. 'Okay, what's up?'

'What do you mean, what's up?'

'With you, Wal. I meant what I said when I arrived. You look like shit.'

His great uncle stared sulkily back across the room toward Arthur.

'Well?'

Wal's mouth scrunched up even further.

'Please yourself,' said Matt, planting his palms on the chair's arms and half rising. 'I'll just ask that young nurse I saw on the way in.'

'Problem with my waterworks,' Wal mumbled, still not meeting Matt's eye.

Matt sat back down. 'Serious?'

'Course not. Just a kink or something.'

'Is it because of your hip? A complication?'

'I told you, it's nothing. I'm fine.'

'Not from the way you're looking, you're not.' Matt stood and gripped Wal's shoulder as worry tangled his insides. 'Don't you go getting sick on me. We've still a lot to do together.'

'Stop your fussing, lad. I'm as strong as an ox.' But from the gruff texture of his uncle's voice and the glisten in his eyes, Matt could see Wal appreciated his concern.

He squeezed Wal's shoulder before letting go. 'You take it easy.'

'Can't do much else, can I?'

'You know what I mean.'

Matt left, thinking he'd stop at the nurses' station to double check there wasn't anything seriously wrong. With a bit of luck the nurse who remembered him from his early days in Dargate would be on duty. Aware Matt was looking out for his uncle, she'd been more forthcoming about Wal's health than the others, who had the irritating habit of referring him to Tony.

As Matt turned down the corridor toward the main exit he heard giggling, the sort of high-toned joyous bubble of noise little girls make. Seconds later, the space was filled with Tony and his family. Noticing Matt, the indulgent smile Tony was directing at his girls faltered. Sensing a stutter in the happy atmosphere, the remaining Graneys halted, looking from Tony to Matt. Even baby Jarrod turned in his mother's arms, eyes wide with assimilated anxiety.

Deb threw a worried look at her husband before directing a smile Matt's way. 'Matt, how are you?'

'Great,' said Matt, continuing toward them as though nothing was amiss. He glanced at Tony and nodded a greeting, before crouching to grin at Maddy and Flora, already gathered like blonde flowers around their mother's legs. 'How are the two prettiest girls in Dargate today?'

They looked at each other, communicating in that mysterious, silent way unique to twins, before grinning shyly back at him.

'You know that puppy of yours is still waiting for you to come and play.'

'Don't encourage them, please,' said Deb, exasperation in her voice. 'They haven't stopped nagging.'

'Really? Good work, girls.' He gave them a conspiratorial wink. 'Don't worry, we'll soon have her worn down.'

He rose and faced Tony, who regarded him with cool wariness.

'Wal's not looking too great.'

'No. Bladder infection.'

'Bad?'

'Just painful at this point. They're treating him with oral antibiotics but if it gets any worse they'll put him on intravenous.'

Matt nodded, satisfied and ready to leave them to it, but then he noticed the thick A4-sized yellow envelope in Tony's fingers, the paper held short end to short end so that it curled into a basket shape.

Wiry tension tightened Matt's neck. He looked meaningfully at the envelope before slowly lifting his gaze to his cousin's. 'Not planning to spring a trick on Wal, are you?'

Tony turned to Deb, speaking quietly as he ruffled baby Jarrod's hair. 'You go on. I'll see you in there.'

She pressed her lips together, jiggling Jarrod, whose mouth was already dissolving into howl-threatening trembles. 'Please don't argue. Not here.'

Tony stroked his fingers gently down her cheek, surprising Matt with the gesture's tender intimacy. 'It'll be okay. You go on.'

Matt watched Deb and the girls until they turned the corner, that same thick feeling of envy he'd experienced during their ill-fated family dinner once again lying around his heart.

'It's a will,' said Tony, as Matt turned to regard him once more. 'He needs one.'

'He does. I'm not disputing that. But it should be how he wants it, not you.'

Tony sighed and rubbed his hand over his forehead. 'I realise you have difficulty fathoming this, but I'm trying to do what's best for the family.'

'That property's Wal's.'

'A fact I'm very aware of, but you know what he's like. He could end up leaving it to some charity, just to spite us.' Tony held up the envelope, still curled like a protective container around his precious greed. 'At least this is fair.'

'Fair to you, I'm sure.'

Tony shook his head, his expression incredulous. 'Why do you think I'm out to scam him?'

'I don't know,' said Matt, cocking his head to one side. 'Why do you think? Could it be all those potential millions you were so keen to discuss the other night?'

Tony's expression turned to frigid hostility. He leaned in close, voice dropping to a deadly but clearly articulated whisper. 'It's a waste of time talking to you. You've never had a proper family so you've no idea what it's like. But *I* do.' He stabbed a finger toward his own chest. 'And I'll be fucked if I'll let some screwed-up cousin try to tell me what's best for it.' He straightened, jaw rigid, eyes glacial. 'Now if you'll excuse me, I'm going to visit my grandfather.'

Tony stalked away, leaving Matt concreted in place, a furnace scorching across his cheeks. *Screwed-up.* He'd never thought of himself that way before but maybe Tony was right. Maybe Matt didn't understand what family really was. And maybe it wasn't yearning he felt when he watched Tony with Deb, Jarrod and the girls, but the sludge of jealousy. The hankering for what Tony already had. The fear that he might never achieve it himself.

For a long, lonely minute Matt stayed unmoving, then he turned and walked on stiff legs through the hospital exit into the blasting heat of the day.

***

It wasn't until Matt spied the welcoming familiarity of Amberton's burgundy front gates that he regained some sense of composure. Throughout the journey from the hospital, he'd had to take his hands off the steering wheel to wipe them one after the other on his cargo shorts. Even then, and despite the Amarok's blasting air-conditioning, they'd remained slippery.

Anger, hurt and doubt kept swirling. How could he possibly know anything about family life? Apart from his time with Hope, the most loved Matt had ever felt was with his nanny Antonella and that hadn't lasted either: the year he turned nine, he'd been shunted off to boarding school, severing the only nurturing bond Matt had ever known. Perhaps something else was severed inside him at the same time.

Matt glanced toward the drive, tempted to crawl up its safe track and lick his wounds in the solitude of Amberton's quiet, but he'd promised Callie he'd come round and help. Besides, sulking alone never solved anything.

The forest separating Amberton and Glenmore ended, untangling into open country again. He grimaced at the state of the firebreak running between the scrub's edge and Callie's land. Someone should have been in to plough the break. Vegetation had been thick when he'd ridden the motorbike along it the previous week, but still with tinges of green thanks to residual soil moisture from the district's earlier bout of unseasonal rain. Now, after days of strong heat, the plants were sapped and wilted, forming a dangerous carpet of tinder across the break.

He slowed and turned in the gate, scanning the house and paddocks for Callie. Phantom—*Morton*, he reminded himself—was grazing near his water trough, black tail swishing lazily. As Matt braked in the yard, the horse looked up, nostrils flaring as he sniffed the air, before deciding the visitor held no interest and dropping his head again.

Matt scrubbed his hands down his shorts before reaching across to grab a Dargate Rural Traders baseball cap from the passenger seat. He tugged it on and threw open the car door. Heat swirled in waves over his skin, instantly drying his sweat. Although it made him feel about sixteen, he gave his armpits a quick surreptitious sniff. Satisfied his deodorant was holding out, he surveyed the paddocks again for Callie but the farm felt deserted, too overheated and wilted to do anything except let the incessant north wind ruffle its shorn pastures.

He trudged toward the house. Callie was probably inside, hiding from the weather, finishing the last of her packing. Making plans for the future, a new life far from here.

Suddenly her voice cracked the quiet. 'Will. You. Just. Stop!'

Matt halted, frowning as he tried to assess what the fuck was going on.

'Owww!'

Blood rising, he broke into a run, only to skid to a halt a few seconds' later in the space between the water tank and house, gawping at the sight before him.

Callie stood bailed up in the corner between the vegie patch and the back fence, her face red with fury as an equally furious Honk took pot shots at her legs. A raggedy cotton hat covered her head, two blonde plaits sprouting from underneath; her knees and hands were dark with dirt. A neat stack of tomato stakes now edged the derelict vegie patch, a growing pile of pulled-out dead tomato plants nearby.

Suppressing a laugh, he crossed his arms and leaned against the side of the house. 'I take it you were ambushed? You should be more careful. A girl could get hurt.'

She narrowed her eyes at him. 'A little bit of assistance wouldn't go astray, you know.'

'Why would I assist? Looks bloody dangerous. Anyway I'm having far too much fun watching.'

Callie refocused on Honk and took a careful step to the side. The goose lowered his head, hissing.

'Quite a temper for a goose,' Matt remarked mildly.

'My sister's fault. She sexed him.'

'Hope sexed him?'

'Yep. Never been the same since.'

He nodded as though unsurprised. 'Of course she did. Perfectly natural thing to do.'

'Stop it!' she ordered Honk as he shot another snap her way. 'Hope thought so.'

'Okay, I'll ask the dumb question. Why?'

'She wanted to know if Honk was a goose or a gander,' Callie replied, her eyes never leaving Honk as she edged another step. 'Poppy suggested she discover for herself. So she did.'

'How?'

Callie rolled her eyes. 'How do you think? We held him down and she shoved her fingers up his vent.'

'She—' He shook his head. That was such a Hope thing to do.

'I think he might have post-traumatic stress disorder.'

'Understandable. No one likes their vent invaded.'

'She said she stroked his penis.'

Matt's mouth began to twitch. 'Kinky.'

'Maybe for some,' Callie replied with mock seriousness, 'but Honk isn't a loose goose. Except in the bowels.' At Matt's raised eyebrows she broke into a grin. 'He pooed all over her.'

'A bum-bardment.' He nodded in approval. 'Well done, Honk.'

They locked gazes, and suddenly laughter burst from Matt like water from a fountain. He clutched his stomach and slid down the wall, landing with a hard thump on the hot concrete. Eyes moist with mirth, he tried to speak but couldn't get any words out.

Affronted at being outdone, Honk joined in the racket.

'Oh, shut up, you. This fight's over.' And with a whoop, Callie ducked, feinted again and bolted, Honk charging behind, wings wide and flapping, squat legs pumping hard. He scored a hit on the back of her calf, causing her to stumble, but she regained her balance and shot across the lawn like an Olympic sprinter, blonde plaits flying out behind her. Unable to keep up, Honk halted, tail waggling over and over as he trumpeted furiously at the sky.

Callie collapsed on her hands and knees in the grass in front of Matt, plaits swinging either side of her face. For a moment she kept her head bowed, back heaving as she sucked in air, then she looked up at him, grinning broadly.

'Well, that was an adventure.'

'It was.'

'Nice of you to assist.'

Matt shrugged. 'Just helping you adjust to life in the country.'

'Why thank you. You're all heart.'

Nose crinkling cutely, Callie inspected her dirty hands, before clambering to her feet and heading to the water tank. Matt rose and followed, backside stinging from the burning concrete. He crossed his arms and went to lean against the tank wall but thought better of it when he felt the heat radiating off its metal exterior. Instead he waited nearby, watching her as she soaped her hands and scrubbed her knees, using a cracked yellow bar set inside a stocking tied to the tank's tap.

He couldn't remember the last time he'd laughed so hard. He couldn't remember feeling this damn good about someone either. Not agonisingly lovesick, like when he was teenager, more happy. Simple, clean, natural happiness. If Callie could do that after the fucked-up morning he'd had, imagine what she could do if they really got it on.

He reached out and brushed the back of his fingers over the angry red blotches on her upper arm. 'Honk got in some good shots.'

She stilled, and for an uncertain moment Matt thought he felt a slight tremble in her skin. The sensation passed as Callie returned to scrubbing her hands, leaving him to wonder if it was just his wishful thinking.

After brushing down her wet knees and flicking the last of the water off her fingers, she straightened and turned to him. 'He did, the little shit.' She stared across the lawn, shaking her head before catching his gaze again. 'I need a cold drink. You probably do too. And while we're doing that you can fill me in on what Wal said about fireproofing Glenmore.'

Pulling off his cap, Matt followed her inside, expecting to find a room filled with bags and boxes. Instead he found a neat kitchen, its floor swept and the sink and benches tidy. The china cabinet sported knick-knacks on doilies. A roster printed on Royal Hotel letterhead was pinned to the fridge front with faded plastic alphabet magnets. An old cake rack with some kind of slice cooling on top rested on the stove, while the kitchen table sported an open laptop, a notebook filled with Callie's loopy writing at its side.

He glanced at her but she seemed oblivious to his scrutiny, too busy fetching glasses and a jug of water from the fridge.

'Take a seat,' she said, handing him a moisture-beaded glass. 'Hungry? I made a slice. Nanna's recipe.'

'Sure, thanks.' He pulled out a chair, noticing a cardboard box that had been hidden from view by the laptop's screen. A blue ribbon lay bundled in the top. He reached out but before he could touch it Callie plucked up the box and moved it to the top of the china cabinet. Nothing about her expression suggested anything other than a person tidying for her guest, but he sensed the rebuke anyway. Whatever the box held, it wasn't for him to see.

He drank his water, watching her closely as she cut two fat pieces from the slice and placed each on a plate.

'Date slice,' she said, sliding the plate in front of him. 'It used to be our favourite.'

'Our?'

'Mine and Hope's.' She avoided his eye, staring out the window as she rubbed at her tattooed wrist. 'I'd forgotten about it until I saw the recipe in Nanna's book.'

The way she looked made Matt wanted to touch her again. Instead he took a bite, mouth filling with moist crumbs, the flavour sweet, spicy and moreish. 'It's good.'

Callie smiled and took a sip of water before picking up and biting into her own piece. Her eyebrows lifted. 'It's not bad, is it? Not as good as Nanna's, but nothing to be ashamed of.'

'Definitely nothing to be ashamed of.' Matt finished his slice to prove it.

'Thanks.' Slice done, Callie dragged the notebook toward her. 'I made a bit of a list from the CFA website but Wal probably knows better than anyone what needs to be done here.'

'He does. If you have the time, it's probably easier to walk around and show you.'

'Only if you can spare it.'

'You just made my morning,' he said, picking up his plate then Callie's and taking them to the sink. 'I can spare it.' He turned on the tap and rinsed the plates off, before placing them in the drainer.

'You're well trained.'

'Comes from having to fend for yourself from a young age.' He leaned against the edge of the sink and surveyed the room. 'I expected boxes everywhere.'

She ran her finger down the side of her glass, not looking at him. 'It's a slow process.'

'Painful too, I imagine.'

'It has its moments.'

Callie finished the last of her water and rose to place the glass in the sink. He shifted aside but still she was close. A soft scent rose from her skin, sweat mingled with something nicer. The angry red blotches on her arm now held a tinge of blue, bruises in development. Once more, he found himself grazing fingers over skin and once more she stilled, her face strangely expressionless as she stared out the window.

'You shouldn't do that,' she said, though there was nothing in her voice that told him she wanted him to stop.

'You don't like it?'

'I didn't say that.'

'Then why should I stop?'

She brushed away from him. 'We should get to work. I'm sure Wal has a list as long as my arm.'

'Callie.'

She halted at the door and looked back over her shoulder at him. 'You don't want this, Matt.'

'Why don't you let me decide for myself?'

She opened her mouth to say something then closed it again and looked away. 'Come on.' With a yank on the door and a gush of heat, she disappeared outside.

After puzzling for a few moments, a smile began to play around the edge of Matt's mouth. Callie's words were that *he* didn't want this. No mention of her feelings, and that meant something. What, he wasn't sure, but it was something he intended to explore. With care and patience, if his intuition had it right. Fortunately for him, it appeared time was on his side.

Because if the lack of progress with the house was any indication, Callie Reynolds wasn't going anywhere in a hurry.

Eleven

Years of practice should have allowed Callie to keep her expression neutral. She was expert at donning her mask. The one that gave nothing away, cloaking the turmoil inside her like a dropped theatre curtain. But Matt Hawkins had a way of making the heavy drapes draw apart, tugging on the ropes with his smile and those knowing green eyes.

Callie studied him as he crouched in the long grass at the back of the machinery shed inspecting the fire trailer's hoses. In the unforgiving outdoor light his scar seemed harsher, furiously slashing across his cheek and jawline in an arrowhead gouge to his chin. On another man it might have turned his features ugly, but for Callie the scar gave Matt a sexy, almost mysterious appeal. It posed questions, ones she wanted to dig into. She wanted to ask how it happened, how badly it hurt, how he felt about it. That he'd been injured in Afghanistan she knew from Wal, but there had to be a bigger story. A story that fitted the man she was beginning to think he might be.

The man she wanted to know everything about.

Angry with herself and the futile direction in which her thoughts were heading, Callie crossed her arms and looked away, toward the east and the river. She watched a bird float on the fevered wind before it ducked back into the swaying treetops. The forest edges held a deceptive, thirsty grey hue, as if the scrub wouldn't last another day without rain. It would, though. This country was tough, its spiky plants evolved to survive summer's aridity until the autumn break, still a good few months away, brought relief. Callie would be long gone by then, lodged in the distant safety of Airlie Beach and her uncomplicated life with Anna and Rowan.

'Everything looks fine,' Matt said, straightening and patting the rusted tank. 'Although Wal's probably right that it's due for replacement. She's a pretty old rig.'

'A problem for the next owners,' said Callie, the words coming out harsher than she intended, but after the incident in the kitchen, Matt needed to understand. She had nothing to give and he deserved better.

If he registered her tone he didn't let on. Instead he tugged off his cap and used the back of his forearm to scrub sweat from his brow before looping the hat back over his head. 'You've listed Glenmore for sale then?'

'Not yet.'

Matt squinted across the paddocks. 'I wish I had the money to buy a place like this.' He looked back at Callie and shrugged, irresistible smile dancing. 'Can't have everything though. Right, let's check this shed.'

She followed him as walked the perimeter of the machinery shed, thinking on what he'd said. 'Is that what you want to be? A farmer?'

'Yep.'

'Funny, I thought you were a soldier.' Callie frowned. 'That you were just recovering here or something.'

'Nope. Here for good.' He scratched at the light stubble growth around his scar. 'I miss it a bit though.'

'I thought you said war was shit.'

'It is.'

She tossed him a curious look.

Matt shrugged. 'It's hard to explain.'

Callie paused by a pile of ancient fenceposts, stacked only a few metres away from the shed. Perhaps Matt was like those other soldiers she'd read about and didn't want to elaborate. 'Too painful?'

'No.' He grimaced. 'Some I'd rather forget, but I'm not fucked up about it if that's what you're thinking. If anything, Afghanistan taught me the best lesson of my life.'

'And that was?'

'Life's short. You need to get on with it.'

'So you've come to Dargate for that?'

'No better place.'

Callie wasn't so sure about that. She slid her eyes sideways, letting them travel over his scar. The scar that made that girl in the pub judge him so severely.

'Your blind date?'

'You mean Jasmine? What about her?'

'Jasmine.' Callie pursed her lips. 'Pretty name.'

'Pretty girl. Just not my type. If she was blonde I might have been interested.'

'Really?'

'No.' He regarded her seriously. 'Women who think they can judge a man simply from his looks definitely aren't my type. No matter how attractive.'

Callie reached down to test the weight of one of the posts. Heavy. She'd need help to move the pile a safe distance away. Although a convenient place to store firewood, even she could see its position was dangerous. 'Did it bother you?'

Matt reached for the same post, muscles flexing as he hauled it up. 'Did what bother me?' He let it drop again. 'We need to shift this pile. It's too close to the shed.'

'I think Nanna must have been raiding it for firewood.' Callie indicated an axe-chewed block, weathered slivers of timber forming grey litter at its base, before inspecting the pile once more. The posts hadn't even been stacked, simply dumped as though tipped from the back of a trailer. Perhaps Nanna had meant to shift them away but couldn't manage the task single-handedly. The thought spiked Callie with guilt.

'Probably full of snakes,' she said, prodding her toe at a bottom post, trying to cast away the thought of Nanna out here in the bitter winter, old bones aching in the southerly wind chill, trying to cope on her own. No one caring.

'Probably. We'll need long trousers, good boots and gloves for this lot.'

'We?'

'You won't shift it on your own.'

Callie had to concede Matt was right. The old hardwood posts were too heavy for her and this wasn't something she wanted to do alone. Not in snake season and not with Nanna's ghost hovering. 'You have enough to look after with Amberton.'

'I can do both.' He moved away from the woodpile to continue his inspection. Pausing at the shed's rainwater tank, he crouched to test the tap but it appeared rusted in place. 'I'll bring a shifter back for that. You haven't answered my question, by the way.'

Callie blinked. What question? She was still caught on his shifter comment, how he seemed to take for granted that she would accept his help. That she would want him hanging around fixing her problems. Callie didn't want her problems fixed. She just wanted to get this over with and escape. Trouble was, the world seemed determined to keep her netted, every struggle only worsening the tangle in which she found herself. Wal, Morton, Honk, Lyndall, Nanna's ghost, and now Matt. All conspiring.

'You mentioned Jasmine,' he prompted. 'Then wanted to know if it bothered me, and I asked if what bothered me.'

She shook her head. 'It doesn't matter now.'

He wandered on, clicking his tongue at the overgrown grass. Callie crossed her arms again, sulky with the feeling she was being judged. This wasn't her mess. She'd been here exactly one week.

A girl couldn't do everything.

Besides, she was damn well meant to be gone.

'If you meant how she immediately judged me by my scar,' he said, answering her question anyway, 'then the answer is no.'

'Not even a little bit?'

'No.' He caught her expression and made a face. 'All right. So it stung a bit. But I'm not going to get myself down just because someone thinks I'm ugly.'

'You're not though.' Silently cursing her errant mouth, Callie turned her face deliberately to the roof, crushing her arms tighter across her chest as she pretended to inspect the shed's guttering.

'No?' He grinned, and shifted closer, expression jubilant.

Ignoring him, Callie stalked on, halting at the old fuel tank on stilts and gesturing toward it. 'Any ideas on what I'm meant to do with this?'

'Pray we don't get a fire.' He cupped his hands around the points of her bare shoulders and regarded her square on. 'Look, you're never going to get everything perfect.'

'I know. I just don't like this weather.' Moving backward so he was forced to release his grip, she threw a hand westward and swept it to the south. 'And there's so much dry growth.'

'So stop fretting. It might never happen.' He smiled. 'Anyway, I'm here.'

'Superman, huh?'

'A Superman for a Supercallie.'

Callie stilled, her sweat-sheened skin suddenly frosting. *Supercallie*. Hope's pet name for her. The name they used to giggle over, that had once meant sorority, an 'us' versus 'them' coalition of siblings. How could such a silly name trigger so much pain?

Easily—because when it really counted, Callie had proved far from super.

'You must have work back at Amberton,' she said, deliberately keeping her voice neutral. 'And Lyndall and Kate will be here shortly to see Morton.'

'Callie.'

'I think I have an idea of what I need to do here.' She gave a brittle smile, the sort of short, insincere twitch she loathed receiving from other people but the only expression she could manage at that moment. 'I probably need to do bucketloads more but as you said, I can't do everything.'

Matt studied her, his mouth thin, gaze penetrating. She held it, determined to pretend nothing was amiss when it was patently obvious she'd calcified the amiable atmosphere with her regrets.

'Are we still on for dinner tomorrow night?' he asked finally.

'Depends on the tide.'

'Fishing. Of course. How could I forget?'

She cocked a finger at him. 'Not just any fishing. Day-off fishing. The best kind.'

'You'll let me know?'

Callie nodded, although she wasn't entirely sure she would. She needed to mull, rearrange her thoughts back where they belonged. Focus on the task she'd arrived so determined to complete seven days ago. Think of Hope.

Hauling in a breath, she headed pointedly for Matt's car, leaving him to follow.

He'd parked near the house, on the weed-savaged crushed limestone apron separating the backyard from the shed. Though dusty, the car's newness emphasised Glenmore's disrepair. Callie stood a short distance from it, reflected heat from the duco and limestone radiating around her body as she waited for Matt to catch up. He hadn't immediately followed, no doubt vexed by her sudden change of attitude. Good. If he thought her fickle and difficult, it might give him cause to back off.

But no annoyance registered in his tone when he arrived, hands in pockets and wearing a thoughtful countenance, merely inquiry.

'Lyndall's Morton's old owner, isn't she?'

'Yes. Although I'm hoping she'll take him back once she regains her confidence.'

'Wal mentioned she was pretty scared of the horse.'

'She'll come good,' said Callie with more conviction than she felt. 'Kate's determined to help her overcome her fear.'

'Do you mind if I stay for a bit?' He shrugged when Callie eyed him. 'Maybe having a man around might help.'

Callie's jaw tightened. She wanted to refuse but she also suspected Matt might be onto something. Lyndall might feel safer knowing he was close. And Matt possessed an easy-going kindness that might help the frightened teenager to relax. The way things were progressing, Callie and Kate needed all the help they could get. No matter what they tried, Lyndall's fear remained.

Any answer was saved by the drone of a car. Seconds later, the Sorianos' Range Rover eased into the drive and pulled up alongside Matt's ute.

***

With Honk safely locked in his run, Callie and Kate sat in the shade near the house water tank watching Lyndall as she chatted easily with Matt. On first introduction, when Lyndall's gaze had widened at the sight of Matt's scar, he'd simply apologised for looking a bit freakish before explaining that he'd been injured by a roadside bomb in Afghanistan. The teenager's mouth had dropped in astonishment, curiosity burning across her face, but Lyndall was too well mannered to give into her urges and probe—a fact Callie couldn't help feeling mildly annoyed about.

From then on the pair settled into a surprising rapport, Lyndall helping to corral Honk while Callie fetched Morton, the teenager breaking into giggles when the extremely put-out goose managed to land a good peck on Matt's backside. When he'd asked to take Morton from her, Callie had passed the horse over without argument. Now Matt stood in the liquidambar's shade, Morton tethered to his hand at the end of a long rope and happily cropping the lawn, while Lyndall hovered deeper in the shadows, still nervous but looking far less anxious than she had during any of her previous visits.

'Matt seems nice,' said Kate, reaching down to pour some more iced water from the jug Callie had made up.

'He is.'

'Pity about that scar.'

Callie frowned, pondering the statement. Half the time she didn't notice Matt's scar. It was simply a part of him, another facial feature like his straight nose and pleasantly formed mouth.

Girlish conspiracy pinking her cheeks, Kate leaned closer. 'Nice body, though.'

'And there I was thinking you were a happily married woman.'

'I am, but that doesn't mean I can't look.'

Using Kate's observation as an excuse, Callie indulged in a long perv at Matt. Kate was right, he did have a nice body. Fit, masculine without being brawny, and definitely a candidate for Anna's crocodile-wrestling fantasy. She'd noticed before, of course. Callie was as appreciative of a well-developed male as the next woman, but with him her admiration seemed deeper, more complex. And that, more than anything, made it dangerous.

His words filtered toward them. 'Hurt like crazy but there were others worse off than me.'

Realising the subject, Callie tuned in.

'What did you do?' asked Lyndall, voice breathy with wonder.

'Went to help. Which wasn't easy because we were being shot at.'

'Weren't you scared?'

'Terrified, but you can't let that control you.' He shrugged. 'My mates needed help. So I kept going.'

Lyndall didn't say anything for a moment. Callie held her breath, caught by Matt's words, a strange feeling in her belly.

'You never went back after though, did you? I mean, after you were better. That's why you're here.'

'As a matter of fact, I did.'

Lyndall's eyes bugged out.

'Once I was patched up and better I went back for another tour.'

'But why?'

He reached up and wrapped his palm around a branch. 'I didn't want my time there to be defined by that one incident. It wasn't all shooting and bombs. There was mateship, loyalty, the feeling we were doing something right. It's beautiful there, too. Not like here but in a weird way. Sort of ancient.' His mouth twisted. 'Hard to explain.' He let go of the branch. 'The main thing was that I sorted it all out in my head properly so that when I discharged I knew I had my life right. That I had something to aim for and didn't have to worry about the shit stuff dragging me down because I'd settled it for good.'

Lyndall focused back on Morton. 'I wish I was brave like you.'

'I wasn't brave, Lyndall. Just determined. You are too. I can see it in the way you look at Phantom.' He tilted his head. 'You love him, don't you?'

She nodded, front teeth dug into her bottom lip, on the verge of tears.

'Then you can be determined too. For him.'

'How?' The crack in her voice was heartbreaking.

'By taking a step.' He smiled and held out his hand. 'Come on. You can do it. You've a soldier protecting you.'

Mouth thin and tight, Lyndall glanced from Matt to Morton and back again. Kate leaned forward, silently urging her daughter on. Finally, with a last glance at her mother, who nodded in encouragement, Lyndall reached out for Matt's hand. Grasping it tightly, she took the step she needed.

'Good girl,' said Matt. 'I knew you could do it.'

A wobbly smile eased Lyndall's lips.

A proud choke rose in Callie's throat. She glanced at Kate. The other woman had her fingertips pressed to her mouth, eyes glistening.

Turning back to Matt, Callie caught his triumphant wink and grinned, but victory proved short lived. Sensing his mistress, Morton jerked his head up, a happy whicker rumbling in his chest as he headed purposefully toward the shade and Lyndall. With a whine of distress, Lyndall wrenched free from Matt, scampering back into the shadows with her hands clutched against her chest and eyes bright with frightened, hopeless tears.

Kate's head dropped in disappointment. Callie leaned across to touch her shoulder but she too could feel the weight of their failure.

To Matt's credit, he kept at it, far longer than Callie would have had the patience for, but other than a few tentative steps toward Morton, Lyndall never returned to Matt's side. After an hour he led Morton back to the paddock, Lyndall trailing at a distance, before once more taking up her vigil behind the safety of the gate.

'It's no good,' said Kate, slumping back in her seat as Matt freed Honk from his run.

Callie secretly agreed but didn't want to say so. Her own hopes needed to be kept up. 'She made it closer than she has before.'

'And then shot off like a mouse the moment Phan lifted his head.'

Casting wary looks over his shoulder at Honk, Matt returned to the water tank.

'Sorry, the ice has all melted,' said Callie, passing him a drink.

'Doesn't matter. It's wet.' He finished the glass and refilled it from the last in the jug, taking a smaller sip before addressing Kate. 'I'm sorry I couldn't do more.'

'That's okay. You tried.' She sighed and stared toward her daughter. 'I wish I knew what to do.'

'It's only been a few days,' said Callie. 'It'll take time to build her confidence again.'

Kate rubbed a hand over her hair, the blonde even darker today because of the heat and her sweat. 'I know. But school holidays will be over soon and then what will we do? And you can't stick around forever.'

Callie shifted her gaze to the old swing rope before looking away. 'Don't worry about me.'

'I think it's his size.' Matt looked from Callie to Kate. 'As much as she loves him, he's too intimidating. If we had something smaller, like a pony, she might find it less frightening. It'd get her used to being around horses again but without the same association with danger that Morton seems to have. One of those really quiet ponies you can stick a baby on might do the trick.'

Callie smiled wryly. 'The original Phantom would have been perfect. He wasn't much bigger than a pony and completely bombproof. Never mind.' She reached for the empty water jug and stood.

'Don't worry,' Matt said to Kate as the pair took the hint and followed Callie's lead. 'We'll sort her out. I'll track us down a pony. Wal's bound to know of one.'

'That's really kind, but you don't have to.'

'I don't mind.' Matt smiled at her before settling his green gaze on Callie. 'Besides, I never was one to walk away from a challenge.'

Twelve

Matt picked up his phone, checked the screen and when it didn't provide the assurance he sought, tossed it back onto Amberton's pine kitchen table. He opened the fridge then closed it again before wandering to the oven and opening its door. A tray of neatly cut chat potatoes sat inside, wafting a delicious herby scent from the fresh rosemary he'd tossed them in, their skins crisp and brown. Letting the oven door close, Matt leaned his bum against the bench and glanced at his watch. Ten past seven. She should have been here by now.

He crossed his arms and legs and scowled at his phone, then scratched at his scar and tapped his foot on the lino as more seconds ran by. His gaze flitted to the door, hearing tuned to the unbroken country quiet. Finally he dropped his arms and straightened.

'Fuck it.'

Ten minutes later the potatoes were in a foil-covered bowl. The green salad he'd prepared was in a plastic container on ice in a cooler along with two properly aged rib-eye steaks, half-a-dozen beers and the carefully chosen bottle of rosé Matt had picked up that morning from the bottle shop. Packed in a crate in the back of the ute next to the cooler was Wal's butane-fired camping stove, a cast-iron skillet, plates, cutlery, plastic tumblers and a pair of Dargate Rural Traders stubby holders.

Despite his gut telling him it was a waste of time, Matt journeyed the short distance to Glenmore. The metallic bronze tailgate of Callie's ute glittered from the shed but a quick yell through the back door of the house remained unanswered. He checked the home paddock, Honk strutting and tooting in frustration from behind the wire wall of his run as Matt passed. Morton stood at the far fence, staring southward toward MacLeans Bay.

Matt's shoulders slumped a little. He had to face it, Callie really had stood him up to go fishing.

He eyed Honk, tossing up whether to cut his losses and head back to Amberton for a night of beer drinking in front of the day–night limited over cricket broadcast. Like any bloke with brains would do.

'Fuck it,' he said for the second time. He'd cooked for her. She could bloody well eat it.

Though plenty of daylight remained, the sun was beginning to lower as Matt drove down the firebreak, its rays shooting white, orange and gold flickers through the trees like a kaleidoscopic fireball. The track rose as it crossed into coastal dunes and the forest began to thin. Stringybark and tea-tree gave way to coastal wattle, grasses and succulent, purple-flowering pigface. Matt wound down the window and breathed in the smell of ocean and seaweed as the tide churned in counterpoint to the Amarok's diesel chug.

He manoeuvred the ute over the final boggy dune and nosed onto the beach proper, leaning forward, hunting the coastline for Callie as he bumped toward firmer sand. Matt spotted her a few hundred metres to the east, tide lapping her ankles, fishing rod tucked against her belly, one hand gripped around its handle. A light breeze billowed her unbuttoned white shirt, whipping the tails like a flag end and exposing the blue and white stripes of her singlet.

At the sound of the car she turned. The tatty fishing hat she favoured shadowed her face, the two blonde plaits sprouting from beneath the hat bouncing against the ballooned back of her shirt.

Matt decided against driving to where Callie had left her tackle box, choosing to park further away on the steadier sand. Besides, it wouldn't hurt her to walk to him—she was the one who'd stood him up.

Within minutes he was settled on the picnic rug, beer in hand, the hiss and spit of grilling steaks joining with the foamy roll of the incoming tide.

After the swelter of Amberton, the beach, with its scented breeze and dazzling light, was glorious. As much as it hurt his ego, he couldn't blame Callie for coming here.

He stared up the beach. Another woman and he probably would have taken the hint and backed off but for some reason with Callie he couldn't. Maybe he just wanted sex. It'd been a while and she was an attractive girl, except it was more than that and he knew it. She had a narcotic effect on him, buzzing him with feel-good sensation, and his body demanded more.

He took a suck of beer and swivelled away to flip the steaks. When he turned back, Callie was wandering toward him, rod in one hand, tackle box in the other, and the sun throwing tawny rays over her body.

'Hi,' she said, stopping in front of him.

'Hey.'

She indicated the steaks. 'They smell good.'

'They do, but I'm not sure you deserve any.'

'What can I say? The tide was right.' Her mouth curved a little. 'You were warned.'

'True.'

'So you're angry?'

He studied her a moment. Maybe she wanted him to be. 'Nah. The beach is a better place for dinner anyway.' He tilted his head at the cooler. 'Beer in there if you want.'

Matt poked at the steaks while she dumped her gear and rummaged for the beer. At the hiss of the opening bottle he shuffled over, making room for her on the rug. Taking the hint, she sat beside him, crossing her legs and accepting his proffered stubby cooler with a smile of thanks.

'Catch anything?'

'No. But I didn't really expect to.' She squinted up the beach. 'It's quiet.'

'Everyone's back at work.' Matt waved his tongs at the sea. 'No surf either.'

'I like it like this. It's peaceful.' She angled her face toward him. 'Good day?'

'Not bad.'

'How's Wal? He didn't look well when I called in.'

'No. Poor bugger's managed to score himself a bladder infection.'

Alarm widened her eyes. 'Will he be all right?'

'He'll be fine. It's not serious and they're good at the hospital.'

Although that didn't stop Matt worrying. The antibiotics were fighting the infection but Wal remained in pain, despite his steadfast refusal to admit it. Plus Matt didn't know what was happening about the will Tony had foisted on his uncle, which bothered him almost as much as Wal's bladder infection. When he probed during his morning visit, the old man refused to discuss it. Matt didn't like thinking about him upset and hospital wasn't a great environment for contemplating a subject as sensitive as mortality.

He pressed his tongs into the steaks, assessing their springiness.

'Can I help?' she asked as he began to arrange the salad and potato bowls.

'Nope. Got it all under control.' He loaded her plate with a steak, its caramelised surface sleek with juice, and passed it over. 'I hope you like it medium.'

'Medium's perfect, thanks.'

'Help yourself to spuds and salad. Spuds are probably a bit cold though.'

'My fault.'

'Doesn't matter. You're here now.' Matt reached into the cooler. 'I have wine if you want. Some rosé.'

'Sounds good.'

Other than Callie praising his cooking, they didn't talk much over dinner. Seagulls and tide noise filled the space, familiar sounds that made the quiet more comfortable than awkward. When they finished, Callie took the plates and cutlery to the water to rinse them off while Matt packed up the burner and bowls. He half expected her to grab her things and head for home but she settled back down on the rug with her arms wrapped around her shins and her chin on her knees.

'It's beautiful, isn't it?' she said, mesmerised by a sea that glittered as though sprinkled with gold and copper confetti.

'Very.'

'Sunset comes too fast in the tropics. One minute it's bright sunshine and the next it's all moon but here . . .' Callie smiled and shook her head. 'It's like some great god has spread a billion diamonds across the sea.'

'You make it sound romantic.'

'Not romantic, just . . .'

'Like here is where you'd rather be?'

Her mouth pressed closed and she nodded as though the answer dried her throat too much to speak. Taken aback by the sadness of her expression, Matt reached out to trace a finger down her sleeve only for his hand to fall away when she took a swig from her tumbler.

'I need to get this over with.'

'This?'

'Selling Glenmore.'

'And then what?'

She shrugged. 'I'll go back to Airlie I suppose.'

'Leaving the attractive, capable man who cooked you the perfect steak behind?'

Her mouth twitched. 'There'll be other girls for you to cook steak for.'

He rubbed at his scar. 'Do you think?'

'I should hope so. I didn't call you an attractive, capable man for nothing, you know.'

'I thought that was just a woman in need thing.'

'It was, but the best lies come with an element of truth.'

Matt regarded her steadily. 'You know what? Life's too short to fuck around. Right now I don't want other girls. I just want you.'

For a long while she said nothing. Matt couldn't blame her. Trouble was, what he'd said was the truth: he *did* want her. Badly. Happiness and caring and protectiveness and a hundred different other emotions battled inside him whenever she was around.

'I don't do relationships, Matt.'

'Not sure I was thinking that far ahead.' He grinned, aware he was fibbing but not caring. 'Well?'

'Well what?'

'You know.'

Time snagged on the way she met his gaze: hopeful and hesitant, like she wanted to grasp the moment but didn't know how. His hand crept along the rug, dragged by the desire he thought he recognised in her eyes. As his fingers touched the edge of her shirt she turned back to the sea.

He waited, holding onto his optimism, only for her to suddenly down the remainder of her wine and rise.

'Time for home.'

So he'd gambled and lost. This time. Matt wasn't the most sensitive of men but he knew hesitation when he saw it.

'I'll drive you.'

'I can walk.'

'You don't have to worry. I won't try anything.'

'Ah, but that's the thing,' she said with a shallow smile. 'It's not you I'm worried about.'

***

Matt paced the return journey, taking more care than was necessary. After Callie's comment, he wanted to draw out their time together. Her words gave him hope she might at least acknowledge the attraction between them. Open up that discussion and he might even get to kiss her. And who knew where kissing might lead? The thought left his stomach clenching in anticipation.

The Amarok's headlights lit up the forest, the encroaching darkness making the thick interior appear impenetrable. A red-necked wallaby eyed the vehicle before dashing away into the undergrowth, while through the lowered windows came the raucous chatter of birds settling in for the night.

'Look,' said Callie, a thrill in her voice.

Matt followed the line of her finger to see a wombat shuffling across the track. He smiled, as delighted as Callie. Wombats were rare, especially this side of the river.

Leaving the wombat to its nocturnal fossicking, Matt turned down the firebreak that led to the Glenmore, scanning the paddocks as he steered.

'Looks like Warty-Morty's given up.'

Callie leaned forward, peering through the windscreen. 'He's up by the gate.'

'Waiting for you.'

'Not me. Apples. I bought a bag the other day. He gets one a night.'

'The way to a horse's heart.'

She sat back. 'They're so funny. One bite and he gets this look on his face that's almost orgasmic. Phan used to do that.'

'You still miss him.'

Callie crossed her arms and rubbed her shoulder, twisting to stare out the side window. 'Yeah.'

Matt's left hand lifted off the wheel, then dropped back down. Though the gesture would be purely compassionate she might interpret any touch otherwise and he'd promised not to try anything.

'I'm fine. Really,' she said when Matt insisted on carrying her fishing gear to the house.

'Aren't I allowed to be a gentleman?'

'A gentleman who cooks steaks. Ever heard of too much of a good thing?'

Matt released a theatrical sigh. 'You women. No wonder us blokes get confused. We're either not doing enough or doing too much. Can't win.'

'We just like to keep you on your toes.'

'Trust me,' he said, falling into step beside her. 'I'm so far up on mine I'm a ballerina.'

'Nice image.'

He grinned and winked. 'You wait till you see me in a tutu.'

Her laughter broke as she passed the water tank, the noise reverberating, buzzing his body with warmth.

Suddenly it ceased.

'Lyndall?' Callie dashed to the back step and knelt in front of the teenager, collecting the quietly sobbing girl's limp hands in hers. 'What's happened? Are you all right?'

Lyndall raised her head. Tears streaked her cheeks. Her mouth trembled, and a drip ran from her nostril. Sniffing it heftily back, she regarded Callie with pooled eyes, voice coming in a choked, hiccupy wail.

'It's D-Dad. He doesn't w-want me coming here anymore. H-he doesn't want me seeing Phan.'

'Oh, Lyndall, I'm so sorry.'

The young girl broke into heaving sobs. Callie wrapped her tightly in her arms, rocking and shushing her gently. When the spasm was over, Callie settled back on her heels, Lyndall's hands once more in her own.

'Tell me what happened.'

After a few shuddery breaths Lyndall related how she'd come downstairs to find her parents arguing in her father's office.

'Then he said he wished Phan had broken his leg, that way he would have had to be shot and none of this would be happening.' Her face crumpled, threatening more tears, but a burst of anger held them at bay. 'That's when I barged in and said that Phan was sweet and good and it was him that deserved to be dead.' She sank her teeth into her bottom lip. 'Then I ran out.'

'And came here.'

Lyndall nodded.

Callie glanced at Matt before turning back to Lyndall. 'They'll be so worried about you.'

'No they won't. They don't care about me.'

Callie reached up to stroke her hair. 'You know that's not true. Your mum adores you and your dad does too. They're just worried, that's all. They're probably going frantic looking for you right now.'

With a teenager's typical self-absorbed impracticality, Lyndall jutted her chin and folded her arms across her chest. 'I'm not going back there.'

Keeping his movements slow and quiet, Matt rested Callie's rod against the rainwater tank and placed her tackle box alongside it. This was way out of his realm but he couldn't stay silent.

'Parents don't like to see their children hurting,' he said. 'It makes them weird. That's why they're acting the way they are.'

Lyndall gave a derisive snort.

Matt glanced at Callie, whose despairing look told him she was as lost as he was. Brilliant. Neither of them had any idea what to do. He studied Lyndall's mutinous expression; this required a delicacy he wasn't sure he possessed. Resigned to a long night, Matt made his way to the back step and sat alongside her with his knees up and wrists draped casually over their tops. A friend there for a chat.

'You're lucky, you know,' he said. 'I never had the kind of family you do. In fact, I'm pretty sure the only reason I even exist is because Mum couldn't find the time to fit an abortion into her schedule.' Lyndall threw him startled look. Matt shrugged. It was a harsh thing to say about his mother but not, he suspected, very far from the truth. 'She's not a monster. Just someone who values her career over family and children. She had me, hired a first-class nanny to do all the mothering stuff, and carried on as usual. Then when I turned nine, Mum decided I was big enough for boarding school and packed me off to Australia.'

'You must hate her.'

'No. I wish she was different but I don't hate her. She's just a woman with flaws.' He smiled. 'We all have them.'

The sulky expression returned to Lyndall's face. 'My parents especially.'

'Parents aren't perfect, Lyndall, they're just human. They make mistakes, but most of the time they're only trying to do what's best. My mum realised her limitations. She did what she could, which in her case was to pay for the best care she could find. I was looked after, received a good education, but I missed out on what you have. That really special thing called family. You might think it's dumb but I'd trade a lot for that.'

Lyndall dropped her head. 'I can't not see Phan.'

'So tell your dad that.'

'He won't listen.'

'Have you tried?'

Callie's eyes met Matt's. Even in the poor light he could see her approval radiating. The warmth he'd felt earlier grew, strengthening him.

'Do you want me to talk to him for you?'

Lyndall's jaw dropped. 'You'd do that?'

Matt pretended to think for a few beats before sliding her a sideways look. 'Does he own a shotgun?'

'No!'

'Then, yes, I'd talk to him for you.'

'I thought you were meant to be a brave soldier.'

He pressed his shoulder against hers in a gentle nudge. 'There's a difference between stupidity and bravery, you know.'

'I can talk to him too,' said Callie. 'I lost my Phan. I'm not going to stand by and see you lose yours.' She gripped Lyndall's wrist. 'You're not alone in this.'

To Matt's relief, Lyndall began to come round, though it took another twenty minutes for Callie to gain Lyndall's permission to call her mother. As soon as she had the go-ahead, Callie strode with her mobile to the end of the yard, setting Honk into a brief flurry of wing flaps and trumpets. The goose's outrage faded as Kate's panicked tones fractured the night air.

'Are they angry?' asked Lyndall on Callie's return.

'No. Just very worried and relieved that you're safe. They've been searching everywhere. Neither of them imagined you'd run all the way out here.'

'It's not that far.'

'Far enough for a young girl on her own,' said Matt, standing and holding out his hand. 'Come on. I'll drive you home.'

Callie threw him a look he couldn't interpret before addressing Lyndall. 'Do you want to say a quick goodbye to Morton?' Callie waited until Lyndall was past the liquidambar before addressing him with quiet urgency. 'I'll take her.'

'I can do it. My car's just there.'

'I know you can, but you need to remember she's a thirteen-year-old girl.'

Matt stared at her, confused. 'And?'

'And you're a man. Think about it.'

Realisation dawned. 'Right. Of course.' He shuffled. The idea he might be thought of as some sort of child molester had never occurred to him. 'You'll be all right though?'

'I'm a big girl. I'll be fine.'

'I can wait here until you get back.'

'You've done enough.' She smiled. 'Beach dinner, wine, convincing a distraught young girl about the importance of family. That's a big day for anyone.'

Matt repaid her with a saucy look. 'I'm up for more.'

Callie laughed. 'I'm sure you are. Unfortunately I'm not.' She glanced at

Lyndall, still standing a metre from the gate, Morton hanging over the fence in hope of a scratch. 'I'm sorry I didn't call.'

'Doesn't matter now.'

'I suppose I should also say that you told the truth about your steak cooking prowess. It was good. I mean that.'

'See? I'm not just a pretty face after all.'

'No, you're definitely more than that.' She looked Lyndall's way again, expression clouding when she saw the teenager turning back to the house. In the smooth, moonlit line of her neck Callie's pulse ticked faintly as though calling for the touch of his lips. An uncertain tension seemed to fill her, as if she'd ratcheted up her strength and held it in check with a hair trigger. Then she turned back, collar once more hiding her throat, and shoved her hands into her pockets. False brightness turned her voice high. 'Anyway, thanks. It was great.'

Matt touched her upper arm and was rewarded with a lift of her chin, followed by a hesitant, hopeful part of her lips. He could kiss her right now, he knew it as sure as he knew the moon existed, but they weren't alone. A teenager was picking her way toward them, and panicked parents anxiously awaited their daughter.

Plus kissing Callie merited privacy and time. Lots of privacy and time, because once he started, Matt didn't intend stopping.

Smile teasing, he lowered his head to place his mouth near her ear. 'You can thank me properly tomorrow.'

Matt straightened, tossed a wave toward Lyndall, and sauntered off to his car. He didn't look at Callie. He didn't need to.

The shallow fast breaths caressing his neck had said it all.

Thirteen

'Damn,' Callie muttered as she shuffled down the hall toward the kitchen in her shortie pyjamas. The curse had nothing to do with the lumpy mattress on which she'd twitched and flipped all night, or the ache in her back and hips. It came from somewhere far deeper than her bones and muscles. Somewhere visceral. It was a feeling as powerfully undertowed as the tide she'd fished yesterday.

She straggled her way to the kitchen entrance and slumped against the wall, eyes closing in dismay as memories of last night bubbled to the surface. 'Damn, damn, damn, damn, damn!'

A groan followed, then a rub of her tired, sleep-filled eyes. She was absolutely knackered. And it was all one person's fault.

Matthew Hawkins.

Dropping her arm, she focused on the kitchen. Dull morning light spilled through the window over the sink, giving the room a greyish hue that matched her mood perfectly. The weather must have turned overcast, although Callie couldn't recall that being the prediction. Endless heat was the bureau's forecast last time she checked, but it wouldn't be the first time they'd misjudged western Victoria's fickle elements.

What did she care about the weather anyway? She had bigger worries. The biggest owned laughing green eyes and a manner that made her insides pop and jingle. Not always in a good way either. For some unfathomable reason, in Matt Hawkins's presence her emotions became unruly, frothing beneath her mask, raising it up and exposing the frailty beneath. And he'd be over again today. Claiming his 'proper' thanks. Thanks she'd desperately wanted to give last night.

Must have been the wine.

'Damn,' she muttered again, knowing it had nothing to do with the wine. Callie simply wanted him in that primitive, gut-driven way she'd hoped she'd inured herself to over the years. Keep busy, that was the only remedy. Concentrate on what needed to be done. Fight this lunacy. Because that's exactly what it was—lunacy. Callie couldn't afford to have feelings for Matt— or anyone else—here. She was leaving.

Once she had Lyndall and Morton sorted.

And Wal was out of hospital.

And Honk taken care of.

And Nanna's house properly cleared.

None of which would be achieved by flopping about, moaning. Straightening, she stepped onto the lino, trying to decide where to start. Her gaze settled on the china cabinet, where Nanna's beloved porcelain toreador and bull faced each other in an eternal standoff.

Treasures existed behind the cabinet's glass doors. Memories. Each time Callie thought about clearing the cabinet, she'd found something more important to do, but the time had come, just as it had for sorting the other rooms: the lounge, with its photo frames and knick-knacks and bag of knitting, still open as if Nanna would settle into her recliner at any moment and create something warm and wonderful; the spare room, with its wardrobe of children's clothing that Callie had taken one look at and slammed the door on, breathing hard. Hope's favourite navy cable-knit jumper, neatly folded. The riding coat Callie had once taken so much pride in wearing, traces of grey horse hair still clinging to the sleeves.

As painful as it was, she had to stop being a coward and face the memories and relics of her childhood. The sooner she did, the sooner she could leave Glenmore and Matt Hawkins and everything else behind.

She rubbed her eyes again. First, breakfast and coffee, then at least the world might look less dreary. Pausing momentarily to fire up her laptop,

Callie padded to the sink, grabbed the kettle and began to fill it, staring blankly out the window while the tap ran. When the kettle was full, she plugged it in, but didn't flick it on. Instead she frowned, hand hovering over the switch as a horrible prickle of wrongness crept up her spine.

That wasn't cloud.

She jerked back to the sink, palms gripped against its steel edge, straining forward as she took in the view. A nightmare sky festered across the horizon. Where bright sun and cobalt blue should have blazed, the atmosphere instead churned with charcoal menace. Further in the distance, past the river and into the national park beyond, hovered a terrifying orange glow.

Bushfire.

'Please, no.'

Callie darted to her laptop, clicking madly on the news sites, opening webpage after webpage in the hunt for information, breath shallow and rapid and choked with dread. The blaze had started during the night just south of Dartmoor. At first it'd been a grass fire, but as the wind rose, the flames began to race, tearing across desiccated summer pasture until it hit the tinder brush of the park. There, it exploded, gobbling up the forest undergrowth, whipping skywards through the stringybark, strafing the country with hungry sparks and cinders that caught and fed and grew.

Now a ravenous maw of flame pushed southwest toward the river and Becketts Landing.

Fear sluiced cold shivers down Callie's back and arms. She wanted to whimper, to hug her knees to her chest and rock, but she didn't have time for weakness—she needed to act. She bolted to her room and dragged on jeans and her long-sleeved fishing shirt. Thick socks and leather boots followed. With clumsy fingers she tied her hair into a tight knot at the base of her neck then jammed on her fishing hat. Stopping only to check the CFA's website for a warning upgrade, she tore outside.

As she sprinted across to the shed, Matt turned into the yard. He pulled up alongside her and alighted quickly.

'It's all right.'

'No, it's not!'

He grabbed her shoulders. 'Stop. Look at me. Units have been called from all over the district. Fire bombers are being organised. The front is still a good four kilometres away and there's a thumping great river between it and us. We have time.'

Screwing out of his grip, Callie faced the horizon, her eyes beginning to fill. 'I shouldn't have taken that stupid job. I should have been here, making Glenmore safe.' Her voice rose. 'Not serving drunks or going fishing or wasting time on a stupid teenager who can't even touch her own horse!'

'Hey!'

Callie pressed her palms hard against her forehead. 'I can't let anything happen to Glenmore. I just can't.'

'And nothing will.'

'You don't know that!'

'Look,' he said, and she could see from the tightness of his jaw that Matt was trying to hold his temper. 'I know you're scared, but you need to think rationally. The odds of that fire crossing the river are low.' He let out a breath. 'And even if it does, panicking won't help matters.'

'I'm not panicking.'

He raised his eyebrows.

She turned away. The wind tugged at her shirt and hat bringing with it the smell of danger. Matt was right. Here she was running around like a headless chook with no plan other than to hook the farm's fire tanker to the ute. After that she had no idea.

'I don't even know what I'm meant to be doing,' she admitted.

'If it's any consolation, neither do I.'

'That's not helpful.'

'Maybe not, but I'm pretty good at following orders and figuring shit out. We'll be all right.' He bumped her shoulder, confident and weirdly sexy in faded black jeans and a flannelette shirt. Any other man would have looked like a bogan.

'So what do we do then?'

'Prepare, monitor and wait.' Matt shrugged. 'It's all we can do.'

***

With Matt busy at Amberton, Callie spent the day clearing what she could, which, to her fear-filled mind, still wasn't enough. The fire tank was full and ready, attached to her ute, with the small plastic knapsack unit she'd discovered in the garden shed in the tray. She laid sprinklers around the house but didn't start them. Even though the outside taps were fed by bore, Callie saw no point wasting precious water—it'd only evaporate in the wind and heat anyway. She phoned in and cancelled her shift at the Royal, relieved when Doug expressed his understanding. He was a farm boy himself, and his brother still ran the family's grape-growing and grazing property over the border at Wrattonbully. Besides, with everyone knuckling down for the fire effort, the pub would be dead.

She kept the Jumbuk's doors open and the radio turned up, listening for updates and emergency warnings. Following Matt's advice, Callie downloaded the CFA's FireReady app to her phone and checked it regularly, while in the house, the laptop remained on, its browser windows open on the CFA, Bureau of Meteorology and news websites.

Though her anxiety refused to wane, Matt's reality check kept the panic at bay. She worked and worried and constantly reviewed warnings, but there was only so much she could achieve. Glenmore's fate lay mostly with the weather gods.

Kate and Lyndall arrived at lunchtime, Lyndall in a panic over Morton's safety, but when Callie carefully suggested they move the horse to Kelso, Kate said no. Morning had brought further drama to the Soriano household; the relief of finding Lyndall safe had worn off, and now her father had grounded her. Glenmore was out of bounds, but for her daughter's sake, Kate was secretly defying the directive. Even with the threat of fire, their domestic situation was far too delicate to take Morton home and, like Matt, Kate had every confidence the fire wouldn't breach the river.

At five, having done all he could at Amberton, Matt returned towing Wal's horse float, an agitated Topanga stamping in the back.

'His owner wants him home. Best place for him anyway. Horse is restless without Wal.' He indicated Morton, who had remained near the gate since Lyndall's visit, as if sensing it was the smartest place to be. 'I asked if she had room for another and she said she did.'

'Thanks,' said Callie. 'I asked Kate to take him but she couldn't.'

'Things not good with Lyndall?'

She shook her head. 'Diabolical by the sounds of it. But Kate's working on it.'

'They'll sort it out.'

'I hope so.' But Callie wasn't so sure. If anyone understood how fraught the relationship between a teenager and her parents could get, it was her. Some fights everyone lost.

With Morton loaded, Matt took off again, promising to be back in an hour. Callie stood in the yard, watching the sky. It seemed to heave like a living thing, every fiery breath shooting dense smoke across the firmament, swelling her anxiety with it. For a moment she wished she hadn't sent Morton away, that he was still here, hanging his sturdy neck over the fence, giving her something to cling to. A mane in which she could bury her stinging eyes; comforting solidity she could breathe her fear-filled sobs into. But the only animal remaining on Glenmore was Honk, and the goose was far too cantankerous to be a comfort to anyone.

Matt returned, this time with Amberton's modern water tanker in tow and a cooler filled with cold corned beef, salad and bread, the sight of which made Callie's stomach rumble.

'Have you eaten?' he asked as he carried the supplies inside.

'I forgot.'

'I suspected that might have been the case.' He dumped the cooler, plucked a wooden chopping board from the drainer and settled it on the bench before opening the kitchen's top drawer and rummaging around in the cutlery.

'Make yourself at home,' said Callie, leaning down to inspect the laptop screen.

'Don't gripe. Someone has to look after you.'

'I'm perfectly capable of looking after myself, thanks very much.'

'Yeah, that's why you haven't eaten.'

Ignoring the jibe, Callie sat down to pore over the latest updates. Nothing had changed. The fire remained uncontrolled. She switched through to the news websites, eyes widening at the devastating scenes captured on the ground and in the air. The fridge door opened, providing a welcome blast of cold to Callie's sweat-soaked back. She flicked through more photos. Images of weary, soot-streaked firefighters. Of scorched paddocks and singed wildlife. Of a farmhouse in ruins. A world turned hellish.

'Don't you have any butter?'

She swung around to find Matt still peering into the fridge, a jar of Nanna's chutney in one hand and a perplexed expression on his face.

'Try the butter keeper.'

'Ah.' With a sheepish grin he extracted a tub of margarine from its flip-top storage.

Callie rolled her eyes. 'Boy looker. Rowan does exactly the same thing.'

He glanced over his shoulder. 'Okay, I'll bite. Who's Rowan?'

'Flatmate.'

'That's all right then.' He kicked the door shut, throwing her a wink at the same time. 'Wouldn't want to think I had competition in the attractive, capable man department.'

Sandwiches made, he carried them outside and settled on the lowered tailgate of his ute, waiting for Callie to sit alongside before handing her half a sandwich.

'So what do we do now?' she asked between mouthfuls.

'Wait. Pray.' He released a long breath. 'I don't know.' He glanced at the horizon. 'I hope they're all right.'

Callie swallowed, interest in her sandwich waning as she imagined the terrifying conditions the fire fighters were facing. 'I hope they are too.'

She finished her dinner in silence, eating only because she knew she had to. Matt seemed equally unenthused, chewing slowly, eyes searching the land and sky, ears tuned to the radio.

'I hope Wal's all right,' said Callie. 'I missed seeing him today.'

'You still might yet. The old bugger's threatening to discharge himself from hospital.'

'Now why doesn't that surprise me?'

Matt looked down at his boots. 'I thought he might have had more faith in me.'

Alerted by the disappointment in Matt's voice, Callie studied him. One hand rubbed his jaw, fingers scraping the base line of his scar in that distracted way he sometimes had. Except this seemed more than distraction.

'He's just worried,' she said with a touch of his shoulder. 'Like all of us.'

His hand dropped and he smiled slightly. 'Yeah, you're right.'

'You must care for him a lot.'

'I do. He's a pain in the arse but he's the closest thing to a father I ever had. It kind of matters what he thinks.' He regarded his boots again. 'Funny, it never used to. I guess I've changed.'

'Growing up does that.'

'No, thinking you're going to die does it.'

'Did you? Did you really think that was it?'

'For a while.' He smiled at her. 'Fortunately it wasn't.'

She smiled back. 'I'm glad.'

His eyes locked on hers. Fluttery things launched in her stomach only to be grounded by the sombre tones of another radio update, reminding Callie that a world existed outside the flights of her foolish wants.

Night fell early, the day obliterated by smoke. For a while both the western and eastern horizons hung with orange-red incandescence—one side Heaven, the other side Hades—then the sun went down, leaving only fire glow. Callie locked up an unusually subdued Honk, who waddled to his run with barely a protest. She made tea, checking websites while she waited for the kettle to boil, hoping for a miracle, finding none.

Weary, she traipsed outside again. Matt had found himself a higher perch, atop Glenmore's rusted tanker.

'It's solid,' he said, taking the mugs from her.

'It better be or we're in strife.' She hoisted herself up next to him and sipped her tea. Wind caught loose tendrils of her hair and fluttered them around her face. She watched the silhouetted treeline, wishing more than anything for the tops to still, for the wind to lull to a safe whisper.

'Can I ask you something?' said Matt.

'You can ask. What answer you'll get is a different matter.'

He smiled slightly then sobered, seriousness in his eyes. 'This morning, you said you couldn't let anything happen to Glenmore.'

Aware of where this was going, Callie looked away.

'Why sell if you love it so much?'

'I have to,' she said past the spiky lump in her throat. 'Mostly for Hope. For her memory, the foundation, but for Mum and Dad, too.'

One piece of her heart for a family filled with broken ones.

'Even if it makes you miserable?'

'Some things are more important. Anyway, I'll be all right. In the end.'

The wind kept up its rough rustle, bringing with it the scent of smoke. Callie finished her tea, swallowing her emotions back where they belonged. Notices and warnings came over the radio; the instructions for this side of the river remained unchanged. Time trudged, clinging weariness to her bones.

'You should go home,' she said. 'There's nothing to do here.'

'There's plenty.' Matt leaned closer, eyes twinkling. 'I told you, someone has to look after you.'

'If you think it'll make me want to have sex with you, it won't.'

He shrugged and straightened. 'Fine by me.'

'Fine?' She blinked. 'You've changed your tune. Last night that's all you wanted.'

'Last night I was lying.'

Callie stared at him.

He spoke matter-of-factly, as if revealing his heart was something perfectly normal. 'I learned something the day we were hit, something life changing. I had half my face torn off. My mate Stevie looked like he'd been pushed through a mincer, the rest of our patrol didn't look great either, and some arsewipe was firing at us. There I was, crapping myself, trying to maintain cover and help Stevie when I could hardly see past my own blood, and not once did I think I hadn't fucked enough. Not once.

'There are some things that matter, Callie. *Really* matter. And love's one of them. Not sex, *love*. And when there's a chance of it, you just have to go for it because tomorrow it could all turn to shit. Don't believe me? Take a look at the horizon.'

She swallowed, overwhelmed by the power of his speech. 'I've been here less than a fortnight. You can't feel like that. Not about me.'

'Can't I? People fall in love every day, some fast, some it takes a while.' He shrugged. 'There are no rules.'

'You're nuts.'

'Yep.' He grinned. 'About you.'

'Okay,' she said, sliding off the tank and pacing. 'This is dumb and stupid and just plain wrong.'

'Why is it wrong?'

'Because I'm *leaving*!'

'What, tonight? Tomorrow?'

'No,' she said, drawing the word out in exasperation. 'When everything's done, of course.'

'And how long do you reckon that will take? A week?' He slid off the tank to join her. 'A month?'

'I don't know, do I?'

'So why not try us on while you're waiting? What have you got to lose?'

'We're not a frigging coat!'

He grinned at her. 'You know, not once have you said you're not interested.'

'Oh, shut up!' Callie glared at him but the infuriating grin remained. 'You know your problem?' she said, thrusting a finger in his direction. 'You're too cocky.'

'Not cocky. I just know what I want. And right now I want to try for something with you.'

She halted. No one had ever spoken to her like this. Callie had never allowed it. She shook her head. 'I'm sorry. I just can't.'

'Can't or won't?'

'What difference does it make?'

He thought on that. 'None. I'll still keep trying anyway.'

As Callie's mouth opened to tell him to bugger off, the radio broke into an emergency warning signal, their mobiles immediately sounding in tandem.

The fire had reached the river.

Fourteen

Callie watched, listened and worked in a state of increasing despair deep into the night. The smoke-obscured darkness made preparations challenging and, in some cases, dangerous, a situation not helped by Glenmore's structural decay or Callie's anxiety-induced clumsiness. Blocking the house gutters so she could fill them with water proved near calamitous when the cracked concrete on which she'd placed one foot of the ladder collapsed, tilting the ladder with it. Only a quick grasp of an eave prevented Callie's fall. She'd stopped momentarily, breathing hard, before setting her shoulders and continuing.

As soon as they'd heard the warning, Matt had driven Wal's water tanker to Glenmore's eastern boundary to patrol for embers, leaving her with the promise that it would be all right. Perhaps it would, perhaps it wouldn't, either way, Callie was thankful for his presence and the calm with which he faced this potential disaster; the belief he had in his choices, even the impossible, lunatic ones.

When the gutters were filled with as much water as she dared, the house well hosed and the sprinklers running, Callie left to join him with Glenmore's tanker. A last look at her laptop had provided some hope for a wind change, but as she climbed out of her ute, her confidence waned. Gusts tugged at the knot of her hair, her untucked shirt flapping around her sweat-soaked skin, while the trembled rush of a million wind-beaten leaves carried across the paddocks from the forest.

She joined Matt. He stood close to the Amarok's open door and droning radio, hands on hips, scanning the dark. 'Anything?'

He shook his head. 'Not a spark.'

Callie released a relieved breath. 'Should we start wetting things down or something?'

'No. Save the water for when it's needed.' His tone changed, strong with determination. 'It won't get across.'

'It's a big river,' said Callie, feigning hope she didn't feel.

'Bloody deep gorge there.'

The depth of the gorge wouldn't save them, though. It was the width that counted, the distance the embers had to travel before they caught dry grass or flammable, oil-laden leaves. Structures existed along the gorge—timber moorings, dilapidated boathouses, holiday shanties—and, clinging to the western slope, the tiny riverside village of Becketts Landing. The river was a haven for fishing and waterskiing, a getaway for Dargate locals, with even a few brightly painted houseboats available for hire. There were bush trails and camping grounds, but most of all there were trees. A lot of trees. And that made the entire area vulnerable.

'Looks like they're moving in,' said Matt, pointing to the road, less than half a kilometre distant, and the blue flash of a police vehicle.

Though their number had dwindled as time slunk into the early hours, all through the evening, Thiedeke Road carried a steady stream of cars. Too engrossed in her own work and worries, Callie had paid little attention. If anything, the traffic annoyed her. While she noticed at least one fire truck, most vehicles appeared to be sedans. Dargate townies out for a rubberneck, thinking they were safe, when all they were doing was clogging up the road, putting themselves—and others—in danger.

'About time.'

Matt's mouth formed a grim line. 'People never learn.'

'They think they're safe, that's the problem. But we're not.' Tears threatened. Embarrassed, she braced against the Amarok's tray and ducked her head to stare at her boots and the stubbled dry grass that surrounded them. 'We're not safe at all.'

'Hey.' Matt ran a hand over her back. 'We'll be all right. They're still predicting a wind change. All we have to do is hold out.'

Ten minutes later, the radio announcer solemnly relayed the death of a volunteer firefighter. Others were missing, feared deceased. Callie walked away, unable to bear any more news. A truck stormed down the road, another following quickly behind. She clutched herself and rubbed, seeking comfort, only for a siren wail to strike splinters down her spine.

Matt brought over a bottle of water. She took it gratefully. The stinking air coated the inside of her mouth and throat and lingered no matter how many swigs of water she swallowed or how many times she washed her mouth out. The caustic flavour of smoke and fear.

With nothing else to do but monitor and wait, Callie paced. Matt regained his perch on Glenmore's water tanker, watching for cinders and any hint of flame. In the darkness, all they could see was the fire's hot glow. Occasionally, a freakish orange moon appeared before smoke obscured it once more. On the road, headlight glares that once pointed to the river moved toward town as emergency services ordered people from the area.

Matt tried to get her to rest several times but Callie wasn't interested. Vigilance mattered. The thought of being asleep, even briefly, and missing a single cinder sent jitters through her legs. So she continued her nervous pacing.

Morning began to bleed into night. With it came a still dawn.

Callie halted, tuning her fatigue-dulled senses in to the day. A flutter launched in her chest. She turned to Matt. 'Do you feel it?'

'Feel what?' Matt frowned, then his eyes widened. He held up his palm and twisted it around like a radar. 'It's gone.' A grin broke. He slid off the tanker to join her on the grass, regarding her with bright eyes. 'The wind's dropped.'

She nodded, barely able to contain her relief, not wanting to celebrate too much in case she upset the wind gods. Matt took her hand and squeezed. With a smile she squeezed back, before turning to watch the sun leech strange streaks into the polluted sky.

The wind stayed low for nearly half an hour before rising again, this time from the south. The flames turned back on themselves, into the ruined, charcoaled land, and smouldered. Firebombers worked to extinguish hotspots to the north, where the river curled back on itself, but by midmorning, Callie began to breathe properly again. The worst was over. Glenmore was safe.

After a much-needed breakfast of more corned beef sandwiches and too-sweet tea, Matt returned to Amberton, leaving Callie with instructions to call if anything, *anything*, looked even remotely wrong.

'You held it together,' he said, kissing her forehead, lips lingering, palm cupped around her upper arm. 'Be proud.'

'I think I'm too tired to feel anything,' she replied, but his words curled and warmed and left her wishing for more than one chaste kiss.

When he'd gone, she let Honk loose onto the soaked lawn before regarding the house's roof. The gutters sagged with the weight of water trapped inside. Though fatigue sapped her muscles of strength, Callie fetched the ladder and climbed up to unblock the makeshift plugs. By the time she'd finished, she could barely hold her legs straight enough to stand in the shower. Bed beckoned. She slid onto its surface in just her knickers and called to sleep.

Only for it to answer with dreams of Matt, Glenmore and impossible futures.

***

Showered and dressed in her work clothes, Callie stood in the kitchen toying with her phone, scrolling backward and forward through her contacts, hovering between her father's mobile and her parents' home number. Names and digits she'd kept loaded but never dialled. The fire had stirred something within her, a need to reconnect. It had been eight years. She was different. They would be too. Yet that didn't guarantee any change in their relationship.

She stepped outside, putting off her decision for a few minutes longer. Not that she had many to spare. Her shift began in just over forty minutes and though it was tempting to call in sick, rent was due on the Airlie apartment this week and she didn't want to let Anna and Rowan down.

Early evening smeared the sky with gold and blue. The smoke had been pushed away thanks to a blissful southerly. Occasionally, on a fickle gust of wind, the taint of destruction puffed then faded. The drone of planes had gone, along with the sirens and strange low roar of fire that Callie hadn't noticed through the night but was now conspicuous because of its loss, like cicadas in a tropical summer, suddenly stilled. Traffic on Thiedeke Road had picked up again: sightseers wanting a view of the blackened landscape; holiday shack and boat owners returning to summer normality.

After a lap of the house she stopped near the clothesline and regarded her phone once more. Dad. It had to be him. Calling was hard enough and Callie still wasn't sure how she felt about her mother. Lyndall's passion for her Phantom had resurrected too many old grievances.

With a deep breath she pressed the dial button.

'Michael Reynolds.'

She closed her eyes. Soothed by the sound of his voice and yet still anxious. What to say after all this time?

'Hello?'

'Hey, Dad.'

'Callie?'

'Yeah. It's me.'

Her father didn't respond immediately and Callie's eyes began to smart with the thought that maybe he didn't want to talk, that the damage she'd done was irreparable. Finally he shook a long breath out. 'It's really good to hear your voice, honey.'

Callie closed her eyes in relief. 'And yours, Dad.'

'You got my letter then?'

'I did. It was delayed though. I moved to Airlie Beach a while back and it took a while to get to me.' She paused. 'I'm really sorry about Nanna.'

'We all are. Me especially.'

'Was the funeral nice?' Callie winced at the term. How could a funeral be nice? Why couldn't she talk to him properly? Say what she wanted.

'I think so. A good turn out. Lots of praise for Mum. She was well liked around Dargate.'

'She was.'

'So you're living at Airlie Beach now? That's a nice place. Maybe your mother and I could come visit you one day?' The hope in his voice made Callie's heart stumble.

'Actually, that's what I was calling about. Right now I'm at Glenmore.'

'You're at the farm? Is everything all right? I saw about the fire. It didn't occur to me that you'd be there. We assumed you were still in Alice Springs.'

'Everything's fine, Dad.' She glanced across the paddocks. Not fine, but Glenmore was what it was and soon it'd be something else. Something very different. Callie shook the thought away. 'Look, I'm only here for a short while, just to clear things out. I thought maybe there'd be a few items from the house you might like. Photos, knick-knacks. There's some of Hope's things here too. Old clothes mainly . . .' She bit her lip. Old or not, of course they'd want Hope's things. They coveted everything of hers.

'That's really good of you, honey. Thanks. But what I'd like most—what we'd both like—is to come and see you. It's been too long.'

'Has it?'

'You're our daughter. Of course it's been too long.' His voice softened. 'Please. Tomorrow? Around lunch time?'

Callie swallowed. 'Sure. Okay. That'd be good.'

'We'll see you then. And Callie?'

'What?

'We never blamed you. Remember that.'

She pondered his assurance all the way into Dargate. They hadn't blamed her, not in words, but the house she'd grown up in had become unbearable all the same. At the start, lost in her grief and guilt, Callie had tiptoed around her needy parents, barely making eye contact, avoiding the desperate way they looked at her, as if at any moment she might morph into Hope and give them all back their lives.

Callie remembered the loneliness: Dad in the lounge, television turned up to smother the noise of his sobs; Mum in Hope's room, sitting on the edge of the bed, staring vacantly, a piece of Hope's clothing clutched tight to her body. Nights when Callie would retreat to her room with earphones jammed in her ears and music turned up painfully loud to block out the silence of her sister's absence.

And then came the Hope Foundation, sucking everything they had left. Suddenly Hope began to dominate their lives even more in death than she had in life. The more Callie tried to keep her sister alive, the more she shrank inside, until the only option remaining was escape.

No, they hadn't blamed her. But every second of Callie's life overflowed with the memory of a sister she didn't save, and could never replace.

***

The following morning, after three cups of coffee, breakfast, some serious perusal of news websites, a text conversation with Anna, a fielded courtesy call from Tony Graney to check all was okay, another from his wife asking the same, two loads of washing, a bout of Honk dodging, and no success at all in settling the thrumming nerves that had arisen over her parents' impending visit, Callie finally braced herself enough to tackle the china cabinet.

She sat cross-legged in front of the first door and scratched her arm. Beside her, retrieved from the newsagency before her shift yesterday, lay a wad of butchers paper. Several flattened wine boxes, which she'd snaffled from the Royal's bottle shop, leaned against the wall along with a roll of packing tape and a pair of Nanna's sewing scissors.

Callie gave up scratching her unitchy skin and sighed. She had to do this. It was part of the process and at least the china cabinet was better than the spare room cupboard. That, her mum and dad could deal with.

She opened the frosted glass door. A black china horse stood frozen in a prance, mane flying, nostrils flared, but where it should have had a curling near foreleg, only a snapped-off eggshell edge of china showed. The damaged leg rested on a wad of folded tissue beneath the horse's belly. Pressing her lips hard together, Callie reached out a shaky hand, picked up the horse and brought it to her lap.

'Beauty,' she whispered.

The statuette had stood on the dresser in the spare room, picked up by Nanna at a bric-a-brac sale years before. Not specifically for Callie, but because she liked it. Callie, though, had taken one look and fallen in love, naming the horse Beauty and playing horsey games around the lounge room floor when the weather was too inclement for outdoor play.

She'd forgotten about Beauty, too distracted by emotions and everything else to register his absence, but she felt it now. Nanna must have knocked him while dusting and placed him in the cabinet for safekeeping until she got around to having the break repaired.

It wasn't the first time Beauty had been injured. A fine, blistered line split his left hock where Poppy's glue had oozed from the repair, paint shiny where it didn't quite match the original glaze. Hope had accidentally kicked the horse when Callie left him on the floor to answer Nanna's summons to the kitchen. The ensuing fight was furious. Callie screaming at Hope, her sister blaming Callie for her carelessness. They barely spoke for days afterwards. Like most of their fights, the crisis eventually passed, although it took a stern talking to from Nanna and Poppy to thaw the ice.

Callie gathered up the broken leg and fitted it into the break. The local hardware store would have the right glue. Perhaps even specialist paint she could apply to cover the spot where a scab of glaze had broken away and been lost. She placed the horse and broken leg on the butchers paper and stared at it. It was a china horse, damn it. Just ash and clay and glaze. And yet . . .

Stupid sentiment. She couldn't keep everything. Where would she put it anyway? Her room in Airlie was tiny and what if she moved again? More boxes of stuff to drag her down. Callie picked at the paper edge, preparing to wrap, then stopped as Honk released one of his trademark guard dog trumpets.

Matt, no doubt. She glanced at Beauty and bent to retrieve him from the floor. Maybe she'd have a shot at repairing him before donating him to the Salvation Army. Some little horse-mad girl might get as much pleasure from the horse as she once had. With an indulgent smile, she placed him next to Nanna's haughty china toreador and wiped her sweaty hands on the back of her shorts. She breathed in and headed to the kitchen door.

The man standing at the door with his fist raised, ready to knock, wasn't Matt.

'Dad!'

He smiled. 'We're a bit early. Blame your mother.'

Jacqueline Reynolds stepped to his side, tentative smile fixed on her face. 'Hello, darling.'

Callie's heartbeat hammered as a tornado of emotions swept through her. The urge to burst through the door and fall into her parents' arms fought with uncertainty and years of distance. She glanced at the microwave clock. It wasn't even ten o'clock—they must have left Melbourne around five am, perhaps earlier. Callie hadn't showered or done her hair or changed into decent clothes. She wasn't ready for this. How could she be? They'd barely communicated since she was eighteen.

'Can we come in?' her dad asked when Callie made no move to open the door.

She took another quick glance around the kitchen, strewn with her possessions: the coffee things left out, laptop on the table; her box of precious memories, first blue ribbon laced through, half spilled from her nostalgic rummages.

'Sorry. Of course.'

The screen door released a testy squawk as Callie pushed it open. She stepped back, letting them pass, her mother wafting expensive perfume, that strange brittle smile still cemented on her face.

Her parents stood awkwardly together in a space that now seemed too small. Her father's gaze swept over Callie, before lingering on her right wrist and its vibrant tattoo. His blue eyes lifted, overloaded with sorrow. Callie breathed in hard, wishing the horrible creepy feeling puckering her skin would stop, but the more she stared, the worse it became.

Her dad had aged, badly. His hair, once dark blond, now held streaks of grey. He was fifty-two years old, yet his eyes had the sunken, landslide appearance of a man much older, as though the muscles were too weak to hold his skin in place. Lines had developed deep ruts around his mouth, dragging his flesh down into the start of a double chin.

In contrast, her mother appeared as perfectly coiffed as she always had, diamond-ringed fingers clawed around a leather handbag held at her waist. Though the day was hot, she wore tailored fawn slacks and a silky white long-sleeved shirt, and loafers the same tan as her bag. Heavy gold jewellery circled her wrists and neck. Yet, like her husband, age and loss hadn't left her unscathed. Tiredness raked lines around that fixed, fragile smile and even expertly applied make-up couldn't veil the blue-grey tinge under her eyes.

Even now her parents' grief still defined them.

'You look so grown up,' Michael said finally.

'Just like your sister.'

Callie threw her mum a sharp look before looking down, ashamed at the tremble she'd caused in her mother's lips.

'Honey,' said her dad, moving close. 'I'm so glad to see you.' He placed a moist hand on her upper arm before brushing a loose strand of hair behind her ear like he used to when she was little.

The longing for her father's love was too much. Callie raised her eyes and looked at him, so old now. So missed. His eyes pooled with tears, setting off a flood in her own. With a sob she collapsed into his fold.

When they parted her mother took over, stroking Callie's messy, unwashed hair, pressing her daughter against her pristine shirt. Callie breathed in her mum smell, the combination of perfume and body lotion and make-up instantly familiar.

Clearing her throat, Callie brushed at her eyes and indicated the fridge. 'Would you like a drink? I've cold water. Or I could make some tea.'

'Tea would be good.'

'Sure. Just give me a minute and I'll clear some space for you. I've been packing. Things are a bit untidy.'

Jacqueline reached for the box containing the blue ribbon, but Callie beat her to it. Her mum stepped back, and Callie's stomach clenched again. She hadn't meant it as a rebuke, but Phan remained a raw subject between them.

She retreated into the comfort of ritual. A pot of tea left to brew on a trivet. A plate of date slice Callie doubted any of them would eat. Mismatched china teacups and saucers fetched from the cabinet, rinsed and dried before being reunited on the table. Sugar bowl, spoons and a jug of milk prepared and set on a placemat. Activities to cover her nerves until there was nothing else to do but sit and talk.

Despite their best efforts, awkwardness lingered. Wariness coloured

Callie's conversation. The sting from her mother's remark about her resemblance to Hope lingered. It was as though, even now, Jacqueline Reynolds could see no further than the daughter she'd lost. Nor did Callie want to talk more than superficially about the foundation or her years of wandering. Both would lead to a confrontation she wasn't ready for. They had made a connection, albeit fragile. Only time would see if it would strengthen.

Each time conversation faltered, Callie filled the lapse with unnecessary industry, rising to fetch more water or tea. Finally, when they'd all run out of things to say, Callie suggested her parents check Hope's things.

Her mum's eagerness hurt, but Callie was used to hiding her feelings. Expression detached, she left them to the spare room, Jacqueline tenderly touching her daughter's clothes, while a ball of thorns scraped Callie's throat and caused her feet to thud on the hall floor.

Heat seared her skin as she stepped outside. A part of her wished she'd had the courage to sort Hope's things herself. Handing them over, ready wrapped in a garbage bag, would have been so much easier than this.

The screen door screeched. She turned around to find her father walking toward her.

He placed a hand on her shoulder. 'Are you all right?'

Mouth tight, Callie nodded.

For a while he said nothing, surveying the paddocks with that hangdog expression he'd developed. 'So do you know what you're going to do? With Glenmore, I mean.'

'Yes.' She winced at the word. 'No.' Callie let out a breath. 'No, I don't. I thought I knew. I was so certain and then . . .'

'Mum must have had something in mind when she left you the farm. Maybe she wanted you to keep it.'

She smiled a little. 'You sound like Wal.'

'Wal? How is the old sod?'

'In hospital with a broken hip. Not very happy about it either.'

He threw her an enquiring look.

'Horse accident.'

'He gave me an earful about Mum at the funeral.'

'Don't worry, he's been giving me one too.'

They shared a smile and Callie wondered why it was always so much easier with her dad—not perfect but less tense than with her mum. Perhaps it came down to something as simple as him being country bred. Her mum was always uncomfortable at Glenmore, whereas Callie and her dad adored it.

Gently, Michael lifted her arm and inspected her tattoo. Callie fought the urge to tug her wrist away, forcing herself to relax as he traced a finger over the letters.

'Must have taken a while.'

'It did.'

He caught her gaze. 'This is your tribute?'

'Sort of.'

Michael's hold slipped until he held Callie's hand between his. 'It took me a long time to realise how hard it must have been for you, living with us. We were so fixated on what happened to Hope that we didn't stop to consider how it affected you.'

Callie's jaw clenched. 'I don't want to talk about this, Dad.'

'We have to sometime.'

'Yes, but not today.' She glanced toward the house. Not while her mother was in there sobbing over Hope's things. Not while Callie felt so weighed down by all her old insecurities. 'This sun's got some sting. Best we get into the shade before we get burnt.'

'Callie?'

She halted on the concrete path.

'Don't shut us out again.' He stepped toward her. 'Losing one daughter was bad enough. Don't let us lose two.'

Callie regarded the screen door, somewhere behind which her mother still lingered.

'I'll try.'

Right then, it was all she could offer.

Fifteen

The moment he clattered down the float ramp onto Glenmore's crushed limestone yard, Morton propped, stuck his head in the air and released an ear-splitting 'welcome me home' whinny.

'You right?' Matt asked before succumbing to Morton's nudge and rubbing his nose. He may have sounded annoyed but Matt appreciated the horse's sentiment—every time he set foot on Glenmore he felt like whooping too.

Except perhaps not today.

Callie had a visitor, and if her strained appearance at the window when he pulled up was anything to go by, it wasn't an easy one.

He eyed the white Camry again, glancing from it to the house as he registered the Hope Foundation sticker adhered low on the rear window. The Reynolds. No wonder she was tense. Though he had some appreciation of their loss, Matt couldn't help taking on some of Wal's umbrage over the way they'd abandoned Maggie. Or the way they might have treated Callie. Eighteen-year-old daughters from well-to-do families didn't leave home to go wandering the country alone without reason.

Michael Reynolds emerged around the corner of the house. Matt's heart gave a slow judder as he took in the ruin that Callie and Hope's father had become. It had been years, ten at least, but where Matt would have expected the tell-tale signs of middle age, Michael had the startling, shrunken demeanour of a man atrophied by loss.

As Michael looked up, Matt changed his assessment slightly. Atrophied was probably too strong. Callie's father didn't look that worn; it was more that he exuded the air of a man who'd simply given up on life. Where a man of vigour would have strode to his vehicle, Michael slugged: his shoulders didn't stay quite level; his back wasn't quite straight. And he looked tired. Really tired.

Her expression inscrutable, Callie trailed a step behind, alongside Jacqueline Reynolds. From her reddened eyes, Callie's mother had been crying yet her mouth was fixed in a stiff curve that was more contortion than smile. Otherwise, she appeared the same as he remembered: expensively dressed and made up; stylish in spite of the half-stuffed garbage bag she carried. Given she was Hope's mother, Matt had tried to like Jacqueline on the few occasions they'd met, but he'd always found her standoffish. To be fair, he supposed that could simply be a result of her feeling out of place. Wal, in his black-and-white way, preferred the label 'snob'.

Michael smiled at Matt. 'Is that a gift horse?'

'As a matter of fact it is. Not from me though.' Matt led Morton over, and held out his free hand. 'Mr Reynolds, good to see you again. It's been a long time.' He nodded at Jacqueline. 'Mrs Reynolds.'

Michael turned to Callie. 'So he's yours?'

'He is. Apparently Nanna wanted me to have a horse as well.' She flicked a rapid, unreadable glance at her mother before regarding her father once more. 'She named him Phantom.'

'Ah,' said Michael before also casting a look toward his wife, whose set smile faltered a fraction before relocking.

'But he's called Morton now, aren't you, boy?' said Matt, scruffing his fingers into the centre of Morton's black mane the way Wal taught him and that he'd learned horses adored. 'Warty-Morty.'

'I renamed him,' Callie explained. 'It suits him better.'

As he stroked the horse's nose, Michael scanned Matt's scar. 'Looks like you've been in the wars.'

'I have. Literally.' He pulled Morton back as the horse zoned in on Callie's dad for a full-on forehead rub, before answering Michael's unspoken question. Funny how people didn't want to ask, as if the war he referred to might be related to gangs or drugs or something else other than a fight Australia, and he, had signed up for. 'Afghanistan.'

Michael nodded. 'Glad to see you in one piece. Others haven't been so lucky.'

'No,' said Matt, thinking of Stevie. 'Others haven't.'

'Callie mentioned you've been helping out on the farm,' said Jacqueline. 'That's very kind of you.'

'Only a bit. She's been doing pretty well on her own.'

Michael gave his daughter an indulgent look. 'She always was a capable girl.' He turned back to Matt and nodded. 'Good to see you again.'

Matt knew a dismissal when he heard one. Probably not a bad thing. There was a whole lot of shit going on between Callie and her parents that he didn't understand. His first instinct was to protect her, but that wouldn't help them sort out their problems and from the way they were acting, they still had plenty. Plus maybe Callie's dad was the one who could convince her to keep Glenmore. After all, it'd been his home too.

He returned Michael's nod and led Morton to his paddock, the horse tugging the lead as he kept looking back at Callie as though hurt she hadn't greeted him.

'Stop being a sook. You'll get your turn.'

He stayed at the gate, watching Morton, flicking surreptitious glances at Callie, until he heard the car leave and her approaching footsteps crunching over the grass. She leaned on the fence strainer rail and rested her chin on her folded hands. Though the sun burned with typical summer brilliance, the southerly that had brought an end to their dramas continued to blow, keeping conditions mild.

Matt leaned his elbows on the gate, sucking in grass and forest scented air and the pleasure of a perfect day. Any other time he'd feel dozy but Callie's presence kept his senses on alert.

She tilted her head to regard him. 'First time I've seen my parents in eight years.'

Matt said nothing, leaving the space for her to fill if she wanted.

'Dad's aged.' She squeezed her eyes shut as though against some internal pain, her voice thick with sorrow. 'Really badly. It's horrible. Makes me so sad to see him like that.'

'They've been tough years. For everyone.'

'I know.' She rubbed her face. Matt let Callie be, giving her time to recover. Huffing out a breath, she reversed position, leaning her back against the rail with her arms and ankles crossed. 'Mum's still the same. A few more lines but not much else different.' She contemplated her feet. 'She spent most of her time in the spare room crying over Hope's things.'

That must have hurt. Eight years and Callie's dead sister still took precedence. He flicked the leadrope's spring clip, trying to think of something soothing to say but Callie spoke first.

'I think she still blames me.'

'For Hope?'

Gaze heartbreakingly sad, Callie nodded.

Matt wanted to belt something for seeing her like this. 'How could it be your fault? You didn't force those drugs down her throat. She wanted to take them.'

'But she might not have if I wasn't there.'

'What do you mean?'

'I begged her, Matt. I wanted to come along. I should have known she'd have wanted to show off, put on the sophisticated big sister act.'

'That's bullshit.'

'Is it? The papers said that's what happened.'

'Fuck the papers. Hope did what she did because she thought it was cool and she liked it.' She'd said as much to Matt when things started to go bad between them. He hated drugs, whereas she seemed to regard taking them as a rite of passage. 'Listen to me. What happened wasn't your fault.'

'I know, I know,' she said, grimacing. 'The rational part of me understands that but seeing Mum . . .' She rubbed her face, digging the tips of her fingers into the corners of her eyes and pressing hard before letting her hands fall and sighing. 'This isn't doing any good.'

Matt couldn't agree more. 'At least you've made a start with them.'

'Yeah. That's something.' And to his relief she smiled, blue eyes regaining their spark. 'More than I had before.'

'Much more,' he said, winking at her to lighten the mood further. 'Your parents, me. This place is providing all sorts of new starts. Maybe you should stick around, see where they lead.'

But Callie merely rolled her eyes and pushed off the fence, leaving him twirling the leadrope like a lasso and grinning at the glorious sky.

No straight out refusal.

Progress. Definitely progress.

***

Matt glanced at the puppy in the passenger side footwell of his ute as it attempted once again to bounce up onto the seat.

'You're not going there.'

The pup turned his head and panted, eyes bright.

'What did I say?' he said, leaning across to gently dump the pup back to the floor, cursing himself yet again for not thinking of a way to restrain the pup in the ute tray. Already the pup had piddled on his mat. Any moment the little brat would start chewing something.

Poor Deb, as if a toddler and twins weren't enough, she was about to be terrorised by a black-and-white ball of fluff. A very cute, very naughty ball of fluff.

He flicked the indicator and turned up the road leading to Snob Hill and his cousin's oversized house, wishing instead he was heading back to Glenmore and Callie. She was busy though, packing up her nanna's china cabinet and then off for a hectic Friday shift at the Royal.

The morning's events swept back into his mind. Callie seemed sick with worry for her parents, and with good reason, given how crap Michael looked. As for Jacqueline, Matt didn't know what to make of her. He hoped like hell what Callie suspected wasn't true. Blaming Callie for Hope was beyond unfair but a blind man could see the gulf between them.

At least she hadn't said no to his suggestion that she think about staying. Maybe she was even considering the idea.

He grinned. Imagine how happy *that* would make his uncle.

Interpreting the grin as approval, the pup made another leap up to the seat, this time succeeding. Mouth open as though in laughter, he placed his paws on the centre console to look at Matt, one ear perked up, the other flopped over, tail waggling in glee. Matt threw him a dirty look, and for a moment the tail stopped its wagging, but the pup was nothing if not plucky and was soon ducking and wriggling again, desperate for attention.

Matt reached out his hand and scratched the pup's ears. 'Know how you feel, little buddy. Know exactly how you feel.'

As he'd hoped, Deb was home, baby Jarrod motoring over the floor like a plump miniature tank, releasing joyous *ahhs* as he attempted to escape his mother's clutches. The twins were playing at a lurid green child's table set, dolls, dresses, baubles and cosmetics strewn around. They greeted him like a pair of gaudy clowns, mouths covered in startling pink lipstick and eyelids smothered in bright blue eye shadow. Their eyes widened when they spied the puppy.

Deb took one look at the pup and groaned, before stooping to scoop up Jarrod as he attempted to scurry out the front door. 'I can barely cope with this lot. How do you expect me to handle that as well?'

'The girls will keep him occupied.' He peered past Deb and winked at Maddy and Flora. 'Won't you, girls?'

They nodded vigorously in response.

'Can't refuse now,' he said to Deb.

'You're a terrible man.' She pushed the door open wider. 'Come in.'

Maddy and Flora stood side by side, jittery with excitement. Matt placed the puppy on the floor and pushed him toward them. The two girls were on the pup in seconds, cooing and stroking, the pup almost turning himself inside out in squirmy delight.

'Would you like a cuppa?' asked Deb, leading him to the kitchen.

'That'd be great, thanks.'

Like the rest of Tony's house, the kitchen was a slave to architect indulged minimalism and as impractical for children as a modernist art gallery. Finger smudges pasted the stainless steel appliances. The glossy white cupboards showed the tell-tale signs of spills and adventures with crayons. But Deb had made it feel homely, with the girls' artworks pinned up, photos of the family on the walls and handmade craftworks lining the windowsill.

She handed him Jarrod to nurse while she set to work. The baby regarded him solemnly, torn between wanting to howl for his mother and curiosity about the man holding him. Matt made faces, delighting in Jarrod's hysterical reaction. Every contortion made the baby giggle as though it was the most hilarious thing he'd ever seen, his chubby little body quivering like warm jelly. Matt handed Jarrod back with reluctance when Deb opened her hands for the baby so she could strap him into his high chair.

Coffee turned out to be lattes brewed from an alien-looking automatic espresso machine. Deb slid a trendy handle-less glass toward him and caught his amused look.

'I know,' she said, 'but Anthony likes them.' As she picked her own glass up for a sip, the puppy raced into the kitchen, skidding on the white tiles, little claws clattering, only to be followed by two giggling girls. The pup propped and yipped before succumbing to a fit of over-excitement and piddling on the floor.

'You'll pay for this,' said Deb, setting down her glass. With calm efficiency she plucked the plastic spoon he was noisily drumming against the table from Jarrod's hand before crouching down to wipe the floor with paper towels. Towels dumped in the bin, she washed her hands, passed Jarrod a less cacophonous squidgy toy, ordered the girls to take the dog outside and sat down again.

'So how are things at Amberton?' she asked.

'Good. Keeping me busy. Wal's list of instructions is, anyway.'

'Terrible about the fires.'

'Yeah. Didn't look good for a while.'

Deb rotated her glass with her fingertips. 'This will business—'

'Wal's not telling me anything, Deb.'

'Anthony's worried sick about what he'll do.'

Matt wanted to make a disparaging remark but restrained himself. Deb deserved better, and she had the pinched look of someone who wanted to talk but was unsure if she should. Bitching about Tony would only cause her to clam up and Matt was curious to know what they'd discussed.

'I know what you're thinking,' she said, holding his gaze. 'You think he only cares about the money he could make off the place, but that's not true. He's genuinely concerned about Wal. And the family. Things were so tough before this boom came along, when his mum and dad had the business. It's a well-kept secret, but there were a few times when they nearly lost it. Anthony can't stand the idea of going back to that worry.' She reached out and touched the back of Matt's hand. 'He's a very loving man who wants only the best for his family. You can see that by the way he looks at us.' She withdrew her fingers and looked down at her glass. 'He thinks you don't understand. But I think you do. I think you want exactly what he does.'

Matt stared through the kitchen window at the girls being chased by their new puppy, the family's dopey chocolate labradoodle, Canute, joining in the fun.

'I'm sorry. That was a bit rude of me.' She smiled. 'I just wanted you to not judge him so harshly.'

'It's hard not to when he wants Wal to sell. Losing that place would kill him.'

'I know. I think Anthony sees that now. But that still doesn't solve what will happen after he dies. Will you talk to him?'

'Who? Wal or Tony?'

'Wal, but it'd be nice if you and Anthony could get along again.'

One of the girls released a high-pitched squeal. Matt swivelled in time to see her rolling on the ground with the puppy trying to lick her silly, Canute bouncing around like a curly jack-in-the-box, his tongue hanging out.

'Although if that dog starts digging holes in Anthony's precious lawn like Canute did, you might be pushing it. He paid a fortune for that turf.'

'I'll try, but only because you're too nice to refuse and Jarrod laughed at my funny faces. No promises though.'

Matt left the Graneys' feeling lighter, as if he'd dumped more than a puppy at the house. The kitchen deep and meaningful had helped a little but he still wasn't convinced about his cousin. Tony's pushing of Wal, both at the pub and in the hospital with the will, seemed too calculated to be all familial concern. Matt had no doubt that he cared deeply for his family, he only had to look at Tony with his girls and baby to see how precious they were to him. His anger in the hospital toward Matt spoke volumes too. Although whether that was more from thwarted plans, Matt couldn't be sure.

It didn't matter. What mattered was that Matt had made the first move. The next was up to Tony.

***

Matt's weekend dragged. Callie had taken on double shifts at the pub and when she wasn't sleeping away her exhaustion, she was packing up the house, or attempting to. By his estimation there seemed to be more toying around than packing, with only a few boxes making it to the taped up and labelled stage. It wasn't that he didn't have plenty to keep him occupied—each visit to Wal had him leaving with another list of jobs—it was that he simply couldn't wait for Monday to come around so he could deliver his surprise to Callie.

A passing remark to Wal about Lyndall and her need for a bombproof pony had unearthed the astonishing fact that Phantom—Callie's Phantom—was not only alive, but thriving. The news launched Matt into immediate action. Disappointingly, and despite much cajoling, Phantom's owners refused to sell. A situation Matt soon accepted when he heard how precious the pony was to them. But the gods were clearly on his side. Perfect timing meant he could borrow Phantom for a period of two weeks, enough, he hoped, to give Callie back some of the childhood joy she'd lost. And perhaps restore Lyndall's confidence.

At six on Monday morning, after doing his rounds of the farm, he hooked the horse float to the Amarok and drove two hundred kilometres eastward down the Princes Highway to Warrnambool, still unable to believe his luck.

By the time he drove through Glenmore's gate nearly five hours later, Matt was chafing like a racehorse waiting for the starter. Keeping half an eye on the house, he parked the car near the shed, circling so the float's tailgate pointed toward the river.

Callie was hanging clothes on the line when he walked into the yard. Even with a peg in her mouth she looked sexy—athletic, tanned and with her body shown off gloriously in a pair of denim shorts and fine-strapped white singlet. She wore her hair in milkmaid plaits again, a look he found curiously arousing.

'You're looking smug today,' she said, pulling the peg from her mouth and hanging up a pair of skimpy knickers.

'There'd be a reason for that.' He held out his hand. 'Come here.'

'Why?'

'Don't argue, just come. Please. It's important.'

Her eyes narrowed. 'What are you up to?'

'You'll see.' He stretched out and snatched her hand, holding it firmly so she couldn't escape. Though her suspicious expression remained, she followed him to the end of the house. 'Now close your eyes.'

'No!'

'Please, Callie. It's important.'

She held up a finger. 'Don't even think of playing a trick on me.'

'It's not a trick, I promise.'

Callie fixed him with a long stare before sighing and closing her eyes.

Matt led her across the yard, stopping her at his ute's right front fender. Grabbing her shoulders, he spun her gently to face the house. 'Now don't move, and whatever you do, don't open your eyes.'

'This had better be good.'

'Trust me,' he said, kissing her lightly on the forehead. 'It's so good it's a bloody miracle. Now stay, and no cheating.'

As quietly as he could, he lowered the float's tailgate. Phantom stood patiently with one hind hoof cocked. Matt ducked inside, whispering nonsense as he untied the horse's lead. A slight nudge and Phantom backed out.

Matt caressed his ears. 'Now, no messing about. This is important.' He poked his head around the side of the float to check on Callie. She stood with her arms crossed, weight on one hip but still facing the correct way. Making a clicking, come-on noise, he led Phan forward. Two metres from Callie, Matt halted, heart drumming.

'You can open your eyes and turn around now.'

Callie turned. Her eyes rolled. 'Oh, if you've bought me another hor—' Her fingers went to her mouth. She glanced at Matt, eyes flooding. 'If this is some sort of joke then it's not funny.'

'It's not a joke, Callie.' He stroked the pony's forelock. 'It's Phantom, your pony. He's alive.'

Sixteen

Callie's fingers trembled against her lips. Her eyes began to sting with hurt. Presenting her with a fake Phantom was a cruel thing to do to someone, and from Matt, of all people.

'Phan's dead. He has to be. It's been too long.'

'He's not.' He led the horse closer. 'I promise you this is Phantom. *Your* Phantom, alive and looking pretty bloody good for his age.'

Callie shook her head but she couldn't deny the creature in front of her. The stumpy horse had Phan's lovely dapple-grey colouring. His off-side front hoof was white, as Phan's had been, and he had the same sweet long lashes as her beloved horse. Her heart took several skips, tripping over her rising excitement. She glanced at Matt, who smiled encouragingly, and let hope flow through her veins.

She took a step to the side, hungrily scanning the gelding's flank, and there it was—the triangular scar where he'd caught himself on a piece of scrap iron after yet another Houdini escape from his paddock. Proof.

'It's really him.' A tear slid down her cheek, her voice gravelly with emotion. Callie looked at Matt; his green eyes glittered as though he, too, found the moment affecting. 'It's really him!'

'Yep.' He cocked his head toward Phan. 'Well, go on. Don't just stand there. Say hello.'

Stepping back to Phan's head, she held out her fingers to let him smell her, then stroked the lovely curve of his nose. Callie had always loved the little dish in it, imagining he was really a romantic Arabian. In the summer, she'd ride him down to MacLeans Bay and race him bareback across the sand, pretending they were galloping across the desert to a secret oasis. They'd had so much fun, so many adventures. The best friend she'd ever had. Losing him had intensified the agony of Hope's death and cut something from her soul, leaving her bereft of comfort. Two friends—two loves—gone.

And now, after all that yearning and regret, she had one of them back.

Overwhelmed, Callie wrapped her arms around Phan's neck and buried her face into his deliciously horsey-smelling mane. She breathed him in hard, loving the warmth of his body against hers, the lovely bristle of his mane against her cheek, the short sleekness of his summer coat; the touch of a strong, healthy and perfectly, wonderfully alive Phan.

'I can't thank you enough,' she said, looking up at Matt. 'How did you find him?'

'It wasn't that hard. Wal knew where he was all along.'

'He never said!'

'Probably because you didn't ask.' Matt gave a wry shrug. 'You know what he's like.'

Letting go of Phantom, Callie stroked her hand down his neck, then across his back and hindquarters, checking him over. Though obviously aged, with his dapples faded, his back dipped, and his muscles not quite as hard as she remembered, her horse appeared in excellent health. His coat gleamed like burnished stainless steel, his hooves were well-trimmed and without cracks, and his mane and tail were clean and knot free. Callie couldn't stop touching him, as if at any moment he'd disappear from her life again. She returned to his head and cupped it, telling him how handsome he was between kisses.

Phantom accepted her attentions with equanimity. A sturdy little bombproof horse who'd seen it all before.

'Listen, Callie, I'd better warn you. He's only on loan.'

She looked sharply at Matt. On loan? Phantom was *her* horse. She didn't want him on loan.

'I'm sorry, but he has to go back. The owners need him.'

'What do you mean "need" him? What for?'

'For their son, Ethan.' Matt pointed toward the house. 'Come on, let's get everyone watered first and I'll explain.'

To avoid a Honk ambush, Callie led Phan to the backyard via the front of the house where it was easier to watch for the mad goose's approach. She'd had one horse accident already and wasn't about to risk another. Callie walked on Phan's near side, Matt his off, the little horse plodding obediently between them. One sniff of the back lawn, with its spurt of tender growth thanks to the heavy watering Callie had given during the night of the fire, had Phantom perking up considerably. Though he still followed, every step involved a snatch at grass. Prepared to indulge her old friend anything, Callie let him have his head.

Honk was grazing in the far corner but on spying the trio, he raised his beak, bugled loudly, and raced toward them, wings beating like great clappers. Callie tensed, Matt's step faltered, but Phan simply lunged at the goose with long snapping teeth and sent him scuttling off back to his corner in a series of frightened squawks.

'I'd forgotten you did that,' Callie said, ruffling Phan's forelock. She grinned at Matt. 'Phan was the only person Honk ever showed respect for.'

'Person?'

'You know what I mean.'

Callie handed Phan's lead to Matt while she ducked inside to fetch a bucket of water. Returning, she sat cross-legged on the lawn and watched Phan suck greedily at the contents, admiring his gorgeous dark eyes and sweet flicking ears. Having taken his fill, the horse returned to grazing, biting into the sward with sloped yellow teeth. Each chomp left a scoop of exposed pale thatch, as if a golfer had run wild and left divots over the lawn.

Morton paced the home paddock, halting occasionally to neigh loudly across the fence, but Phan seemed just as disinterested in him as he was with Honk. The horse's one-track mind hadn't changed. There was food to be had and he wasn't about to let it go to waste.

Returning from his own trip to the house, Matt handed Callie a glass of water and sat down next to her. The smug expression he'd worn since his arrival hadn't faded. Callie couldn't blame him. If she'd tracked down something as precious for him she'd be feeling pretty smug too.

'You okay?' he asked.

'Very.'

'You're not, I dunno, upset?'

Callie eyed him. 'Why would I be upset?'

'Because you can't keep him.'

'A little, but I guess I'd better hear about this Ethan before I start judging.'

Matt took a sip from his glass and leaned back on his hands, legs stretched out and crossed at the ankles. 'Just so you know, your nan and pop kept Phan here for as long as they could. Well after your parents suggested they sell him.'

'Mum. It was Mum who said he should be sold.'

'She was probably only doing what she thought was right.'

'I know.' Callie picked at some grass, plucking the blades in sharp jerks. 'Still hurts though. Anyway, go on. Tell me what happened.'

Matt regarded her for a moment before continuing. 'Wal heard about a family—the Jennings—who were looking for a pony for their son Ethan. Riding for the Disabled had changed his life apparently.'

Callie breathed in hard as she realised where this was heading. 'It takes a very special horse to be a Riding for the Disabled horse.'

'It does. Wal says your nan agonised over whether to let him go, but the moment she saw Ethan with Phan she knew it was the right thing to do. He's been with the Jennings ever since, spoilt rotten.'

She gazed at Phan, sad that she'd lose him again, proud that he'd been so cherished. 'So how long do I have him for?'

'He has to be back by the fifteenth. Ethan's in respite care for a couple of weeks while Belinda and Darren take a well-earned holiday.'

Today was the fourth of February. Callie had ten full days. She had to make the most of it. For herself and, she realised, for Lyndall.

She turned to Matt. 'Thank you for this. It's . . .' She hunted for the right phrase to express her gratitude.

'Just what you'd expect from an attractive, capable man like myself?'

'Not quite what I was going to say,' said Callie dryly.

'You know,' he said, edging on to his hip and leaning on his elbow, fingers in the grass close to her leg. 'I should probably add self-serving to that list.'

She raised her eyebrows, aware of his hand, so close to her bare skin.

He grinned. 'You owe me two kisses now.'

'Two?'

'One for the other night with Lyndall, one for Phan.' He affected an innocent air. 'Not that I'm counting.'

'Much.'

He slipped a finger down her bare leg, leaving a shiver of goosebumps in its wake.

'Well?'

Callie clenched her teeth against the pulse in her groin, against the urge to slide alongside him, drape her leg over his and drag him to her like an over-hormoned adolescent.

'Well what?'

'You know.'

'Don't you have work to do?'

'I do. But some things are more important.'

She looked at him sideways. Damn, he was tempting with his sparkling eyes and confidence. He made her stomach lollop and flutter. He made her want to reach for a future she didn't believe she deserved. He made her want to love.

Callie breathed in hard. She stared at the house, at the paddocks and forest. At all she had promised her sister and family. At the peace she had hoped for herself. He was right. Some things were more important.

Anchored again, she stood, dusted off her backside and reached down for Phan's bucket before regarding Matt once more. 'Come on. We'd better get these horses introduced.'

'Callie—'

But she was already leading Phan away.

***

Kate was almost as excited as Callie to learn of Phantom's homecoming, but with school returning Tuesday morning, the timing of Lyndall's rehabilitation sessions proved problematic. Callie's shift at the Royal began at four. School didn't end until three. Allowing time for Kate to bring Lyndall to Glenmore and for Callie to belt into town for work, they had half an hour at the most for Phantom to work his magic.

At least—thanks to Kate's persuasive powers—Lyndall was no longer grounded and they didn't have to conduct the activity in secret. Having experienced enough drama from Hope's deceits, Callie had never felt comfortable with the lie. Kate was only trying to help but Lyndall was at an impressionable age. Deception was the last thing she needed to be shown as acceptable, and as far as Callie could determine Xav Soriano was a loving parent who merited more respect.

'God, I hope this works,' whispered Kate as Lyndall observed Phan from beside the safety of the liquidambar's sturdy trunk.

'Me, too,' Callie replied before walking forward to untie the horse from the clothesline. She scruffed Phan's mane and bent toward his tufted ear. 'Not to put too much pressure on, but there's a whole lot riding on this, Phan my man. But you can do it. You're the Ghost Who Neighs.' She straightened and smiled at Lyndall. 'This is my Phantom. Isn't he gorgeous?'

Lyndall eyed him dubiously. 'Isn't he a bit small for you?'

'A little but he's very strong and, most of all, completely bombproof. You could stick a baby on him and he wouldn't move. Look.' After looping his lead over his neck, Callie kissed Phan's nose and then crawled on hands and knees beneath his belly. Once underneath, she stopped and shoved her head between his front legs, looking up to grin at Lyndall. Phan curled his neck to sniff at her hair before returning to his half doze. Demonstration finished, Callie slipped out the other side. 'See?'

'He looks quiet,' Lyndall replied, sounding only half convinced.

'Very. That's why he was chosen to help teach a disabled boy to ride. It takes a pretty special horse to do that.' After clipping Phan back to the clothesline, Callie walked over to the teenager, brushing white hairs off her black work skirt as she walked. 'Why don't you come and meet him?'

An anguished look crossed Lyndall's face. She wrung her hands, staring at Phantom.

'You can do this, sweetie,' said her mother. 'I know you can.'

'A few steps?' asked Callie.

Lyndall inhaled long and hard, holding her breath as she jerked a few nervous nods.

'Good girl.' Callie held out her hand. 'You can hold my hand if you want.'

She blew out her breath but shook her head. 'I'm okay.'

'So a couple of steps?' Callie took one, smiling when Lyndall followed, hesitant but moving forward all the same. Feeling hopeful, Callie took another. They were still a good three metres from the horse but for Lyndall that was close. A few seconds' reluctance and the young girl followed again.

Callie let them stand there for a few moments, chatting about some of the adventures she and Phan used to get up to. How they'd disappear for hours, riding the paddocks and forest trails, dreaming her big horse dreams.

'How are you feeling?'

'Okay.'

Callie observed her for a moment. The fall and subsequent seizure must have been terrifying for the teen to be so affected but if Lyndall wanted this she had to forge past her fear.

'Do you think you could manage another few steps?'

When Lyndall nodded, Callie went through the slow process again. Lyndall's eyes rarely left Phantom. One move and Callie was sure she'd bolt, but Phantom remained his dependable, stoic self and stayed exactly where he was, making no move bar the occasional swish of his tail and mane to fend off flies.

Fifteen minutes of step-by-stepping and Callie managed to coax Lyndall within a metre of the horse, far closer than she'd even dared hope on their first try. A foot stamp finally sent the teen throttling backward, a mewl of fear escaping her mouth. Kate sighed but Callie remained optimistic. They'd made excellent progress and for the first time, instead of misery, hope flowered in Lyndall's expression. A few more sessions and Callie envisioned her having enough courage to touch Phan's nose.

The week quickly fell into routine. Mornings Callie spent making half-hearted attempts to finish sorting the house but mostly delighting in

Phantom's presence. She let the pony wander where he liked, leading him out of the paddock each morning and letting him loose on the back lawn while Honk watched sulkily from a distance, and Morton neighed his jealousy. Callie stopped work often to come and chat or just observe, soaking up the precious time she had.

Phan may have been spoiled silly at the Jennings', but Callie made his time at Glenmore horse nirvana. She bought bags of carrots and apples, bales of lucerne hay, a special pellet mix for aged horses. She oiled his hooves with an expensive proprietary hoof grease that Peter Taylor swore was the best on the market, and shampooed and conditioned him with showhorse products. Combed out his mane and tail until it flowed with silvery silkiness, only to find the next day that he'd rolled dust and manure through his coat and swished his tail back into tangles.

Despite Phantom's age and outwardly placid nature, the mischievous horse Callie remembered from childhood still existed. On Wednesday morning, she wandered outside with a cup of tea and an apple to discover Phantom had pulled half her washing off the line and was wandering the backyard with a pair of her underpants caught over one ear. He proceeded to skitter about, tossing his head and prancing away from her, refusing to come near even when she pleadingly rattled a bucket of pellets. Frustrated, she left him, hoping the knickers would fall off, only for Matt to turn up at lunchtime and discover Phantom still wearing them. To make matters worse, the pony trotted happily to Matt's side and let him laughingly pluck the knickers off and wave them about like a lacy pink flag.

Thursday proved almost as bad. Intent on finally clearing the house of some of the boxes she'd packed, Callie left the screen door propped open as she carted them to the Jumbuk to take to the thrift shop. Returning from her second trip she walked inside to discover Phan standing as happy as Larry in the kitchen, the date slice she'd made that morning and left to cool on a rack now on the floor in pieces and Phan chewing blissfully. It took several minutes' coaxing, the entire cake and two apples to get him outside again.

When she wasn't doting on Phantom, providing an increasingly sooky Morton with some love, helping Lyndall, working, or exchanging banter with

Matt, Callie wandered the house and farm deep in thought. Hope remained always at the forefront, along with her father's words about blame.

When the letter had arrived at her flat in Airlie, it had all seemed so simple: get in, clear up, get out. Put the past behind forever. Now, she didn't know what to do. She didn't know what Hope would want. But most of all, Callie couldn't decide what she wanted for herself. Surely, like her finite days with Phan, these weeks were her time for farewell, to find solace in the past before leaving it behind for good? Staying would risk her turning into her mother, forever trapped in memory and loss. And that she couldn't face.

Yet nor could Callie deny the pull of Glenmore. Or Matt.

Stay or go. Stay or go. The question nagged relentless, kept unanswered only by the objectives she'd yet to fulfil. But once they were all reached, there'd be no more putting it off.

Callie would have to decide.

***

'You're looking pleased with yourself,' Callie said to Wal as she walked into his ward on Saturday afternoon. He did, too. The antibiotics had done their work. Wal's skin had lost its greasy-grey pallor and instead of lying collapsed and weary, he had the bed pushed up so he could watch television and the ward goings on in between shooting daggers at poor, dying farty Arthur. A walker stood near the bed where the physical therapist had left it, a rubber-topped aluminium cane nearby.

'Going home tomorrow,' Wal replied, glee twinkling his eyes. ''Bout bloody time too. Quack said I could've been out already if it wasn't for that little setback.'

'That's great news.' Callie dumped the tatty photo album she carried on the guest's chair and a copy of the *Saturday Age* on the end of his bed, and leaned in to kiss his bristled cheek—the first she'd given him since their argument about Nanna and her wishes for Glenmore. Wal's crankiness and Callie's wariness, combined with the deliberate brevity of her visits, hadn't permitted much showing of affection. It was more a case of Callie marching in a few minutes before she was due at the Royal, uttering a polite 'How are you?' as she presented a newspaper, some fruit or whatever thing she decided might keep Wal entertained, followed by a bolt out the door. Today though, Callie clutched a secret. 'Matt'll be glad to have you back at Amberton. He doesn't say, but I think he misses you.'

'I hear you been spending a lot of time with the lad.'

'Not really.' Callie gathered up the album, pulled the chair close to the bed and sat down, album resting on her knees. 'He just comes around at lunch mainly. Although yesterday he said he was going to help me fix the guttering.' She frowned. 'He probably won't have time now with you coming home. You'll need him close to look after you.' Her face turned bright. 'Doesn't matter. I'm sure I'll manage on my own. Can't be that hard.'

'Never you mind about me, missy, I can take care of myself just fine. I'll make sure the lad helps out.' Wal's gaze settled on the photo album, wrinkled mouth working in and out as he contemplated its meaning. 'What's that you got there?'

Callie smoothed a palm over the faded cover. 'Just something of Nanna's I found.'

'Oh, yeah?'

'It's a photo album. I thought you might like to see some of the pictures.' She met his gaze. 'I found a really interesting one toward the end.'

Wal's mouth puttering ceased. Caution crept across his face. 'That so?'

'Yep.' Callie rolled in her lips to stop from smiling. 'It's one of you and Nanna together.'

'Plenty of them about,' mumbled Wal, eyes darting away.

She reached over and covered his hand with her own. 'You loved her, didn't you?'

'She was a good woman, Maggie.'

'And you loved her.'

Wal's chin jutted. 'Friends, we were. Good friends.'

'Yes, and you loved her and that's why you care so much about what happens to Glenmore. And me. Because *she* cared.'

Her statement hung. Wal's gaze remained averted, his body tense, hand curled tight beneath hers. Callie didn't mind. She hadn't expected him to tell her the truth. She didn't need it anyway. The photo radiated all she needed know.

Releasing his hand, she opened the album and turned to the page in question, smiling as she grazed her palm over the protective plastic film.

It wasn't an intimate photograph. The size and quality suggested it'd most likely been snapped for the *Dargate and District Times* or one of the rural newspapers. There was no sign of touching, no hand-holding or pressing together of shoulders. Simply a snap of two people smiling at one another as they leaned on a saleyard fence, sharing a look they thought was private but which in a shutter-click had been stilled and condensed into a single powerful portrait.

Another time and Callie would have missed it, but she'd been seized by the familiar look on Wal's face. Pulse rising, she'd studied the picture closer, recognising the softness around his eyes, the longing they held. A mirror of the expression that his great-nephew had worn only yesterday, and other days previously. An expression she still wasn't sure she could accept.

'Look,' she said, dragging the chair closer so she could balance the album on the bed edge. 'See the way you're looking at her.'

Wal stared, the wrinkles around his mouth puckering as his lips fell inward. His eyes drooped as sadness and love fought for ascension. He traced his finger over Maggie's happy face before snatching it away and setting his features, as though the show of intimacy had never occurred.

'Like I said, good woman.'

'She was,' said Callie. Then she smiled and leaned forward to hug him tightly. 'Thank you.'

'For what?'

'For caring for her.'

Wal laid two awkward pats on Callie's back. 'Good woman.'

Although whether he meant Callie or her nanna, she didn't know.

***

As Callie predicted, with Wal home, Matt's free time became limited. Matt grumbled that the old man was ruining his love life until Callie pointed out that he didn't actually have one—not one she was aware of. Matt merely regarded her steadily and said he did, it just didn't involve any sex. Yet.

Despite the cravings of her body, Callie wasn't convinced it ever would. Time was sliding by. Of the goals she'd set herself, one had already been achieved and the others progressing. Wal was home and on the mend. With Phantom's trusty help, Lyndall was making excellent headway. On the house front, Callie had managed to strip the kitchen of everything except the essentials and those items she couldn't bear to part with. Some boxes had already been deposited at the Salvation Army collection depot in Dargate, others remained stacked in the machinery shed on a makeshift pallet while Callie decided their fate. Of the rooms remaining, only the two hardest to tackle were left, a chore she was determined to labour through during the coming week.

Plus she'd made a discovery, one with the potential to solve her Honk issue. Closer inspection of Glenmore's paperwork had revealed that the house and home paddock were on separate titles to the rest of the farm. She could sell the farm, while retaining the house and home paddock as a rental, guard goose included, with the income funnelled directly to the Hope Foundation.

All goals achieved, just as she'd planned, and with their fulfilment, the freedom to leave.

Except early Wednesday morning, as she led Phan down to MacLeans Bay to soothe his old legs in the lapping salt water, lightweight rod and tackle box in one hand, Callie fretted whether it would be that easy. Whether she could drive away without looking back, without fear that she'd done something terribly wrong. That she'd forsaken happiness and the chance of love for a dead person and a debt that didn't need repaying.

Fishing didn't have the placatory effect that she'd hoped, although Phan delighted in his paddle, bashing his hooves at the waves and flicking Callie with water. Beyond the tide mark, she'd let him off his lead to roll, the horse squirming his back over the squeaky sand, legs kicking as he rubbed one side and flipped over to the other. They'd sauntered back to Glenmore, Callie chattering all the way to cover the ache in her chest, too aware that her time with him was finite. As it was with Glenmore.

The ache dissipated when she reached the back of the home paddock and spotted Matt's ute in the drive. Wingbeats of excitement lifted her stomach and her pulse skipped in anticipation. Unnecessary urgency lengthened her stride.

She finally spied him at the front of the house. Matt stood on a convertible ladder of the type that could be adjusted into a scaffold, head tilted back as he peered at the gutters, rattled brackets and tapped timber.

'Have you developed some handyman fetish or something?' Callie asked as she led Phan toward him. 'Or are you on the run from Wal?'

'Not on the run. Wal ordered me over. Anyway, I've heard some women find handymen sexy. Thought I'd give it a try.'

Callie halted as Matt climbed down, thinking there might be some truth in the sexy tradie statement. He'd dressed in work clothes: a pair of fawn, multi-pocketed cotton drill pants and a long-sleeved blue shirt with the cuffs rolled up. The trousers wrapped his thighs and hips perfectly, the shirt style accentuating his shoulders. A few darkish hairs sprouted between the V of his collar. The sight of them made her fingers twitch.

She dug them into Phantom's mane instead. 'How is he today?'

'The same. Frustrated. Dreading the physio. Doing more than he's meant to.'

'Can't keep an old farmer down.'

'No.' Matt eyed her rod and tackle box. 'Catch anything?'

'Not really. Some slimy rock cod that I threw back. I missed the tide so was just fishing for the hell of it. Phan enjoyed himself though.'

'He's going to miss you.'

Callie dropped her arm until it circled the pony's neck and hugged him close. 'Not as much as I'm going to miss him.' Hug over, she indicated the roof. 'So, Mister Handyman, what's your verdict?'

'Put it this way, you'd better hope we don't have a downpour any time soon. I don't think they'd cope.'

Callie agreed. The guttering had held the water when she'd filled it during the fire, but only just, and the weight of it had taken its toll. Sections that had previously run straight now sagged heavily where the brackets had pulled away from the eaves.

'It's not the timber though, is it? I had a poke around yesterday but it all seemed pretty solid. Not that I have any idea what I'm looking at.'

'I'm not sure I do either but I can take a good guess at things,' said Matt, picking up the scaffold and moving it to the other side of the front door. 'So far I'd say it's just the bracketing that needs replacing. Maybe the odd bit of gutter. Nothing too serious.'

'So I should have it sorted in a few days then?'

He hesitated before answering, 'Probably.'

Callie knew what he was thinking. She'd been contemplating it herself all morning. But now she'd had an idea.

'Good,' she said, grinning at him. 'Because once that's done I can start on painting it.'

'It?'

'The house. If I'm going to rent it out I can't leave it like it is, can I?'

The worry fled his expression. He stepped close, palmed one of her plaits and slid his hand down its length, hand coming to rest lightly on her collarbone. 'Painting the house. That could take a while.'

Never had such an innocuous statement sounded so sensual, so filled with promise. Her skin goosebumped, little dimples of exhilaration extending across her arms and shoulders, creeping to her chest.

'It could.'

'Not a job you should tackle alone.'

Her breath turned shallow. 'I can manage.'

'It'll be easier with two.'

'You have Amberton, Wal.'

'Neither of which are as sexy as you.' He let his fingers spread, thumb brushing the sensitive skin of her throat. Aware of the thin fabric of her singlet, she moved her arm to cover her breasts, feigning a scratch of her arm. It didn't conceal enough. He followed the movement, lips parting slightly.

Matt's gaze hovered on her mouth before meeting her eyes. 'Have you any idea how much I want to kiss you?'

If his desire was anywhere near hers, then Callie had every idea. She didn't want to just kiss him either. She wanted sex. Giggly, roll-about, passionate, fun sex. With him. Right there, right now. And the consequences could go jump.

'I have Phan,' she said, wincing at the lameness of her excuse.

'So?'

'He needs a drink and a hose down.'

His thumb continued its sensuous stroke. 'Afraid you won't be able to stop?'

She nodded.

Matt leaned in close to her ear, the touch of his breath on her skin like a caress. 'Me too.'

Callie swallowed, hard. She had to break this up. Now, before she caved in and subjected poor Phan to a human sex education lesson.

Stepping back, she pointed dumbly toward the yard. 'In that case I should go and . . . you know.'

'Yeah. And I should get on with this. Though I'm not sure I'll be much good. Bit hard to concentrate.' He peered down at himself, Callie following suit. The front of his trousers bulged with an impressive erection.

Her mouth parted, brain scrambling with it. This wasn't in her plans. Not this invasion of lust. If leaving seemed difficult before, it was even worse now.

'Matt, this is—' She frowned, too muddled to work out what she wanted to say. 'You're making it worse.'

'Maybe that's the point.'

She shook her head. Nudging Phan, who'd dozed off, she began to lead him away. At the end of the house she stopped and regarded Matt over her shoulder. 'I'm still planning to leave, you know that.'

'I know.'

'So why keep pushing?'

'Because you're sexy and funny and strong and fragile and frustrating.' He shrugged. 'I'm nuts about you. Can't help it. And if I get hurt, I get hurt.'

'And what about me?'

Matt's gaze intensified. 'What do you mean?'

'What if I get hurt?'

'That won't happen. Not while I'm around.'

But as Callie led Phantom away, she wasn't so sure. Every choice she faced promised pain. The question was which one would damage her heart the most—losing Glenmore or the man she was beginning to love? And what would letting down Hope and her parents cost her? Whichever way she looked, a price had to be paid.

She took a few more steps and halted, thinking. If whatever path she took ended in pain, maybe she should stop stressing about the endpoint and consider having some fun on the journey instead.

Callie looked over her shoulder again. Matt stood with his legs apart scratching his scarred jaw, watching. A great hunk of fun just waiting for the go-ahead.

All she had to do was say yes.

Seventeen

On his return to Amberton, Matt found Wal on the back verandah, Dolly panting and obedient by his side, the two remaining pups at his feet, heads angled up like attentive fluffy schoolchildren. Though Matt had tried his hardest, and so had Wal by all accounts, homes for the last pups remained elusive.

'Well?' he asked, the moment Matt appeared on the path.

'Looks like only minor repairs. Brackets mainly. Should be done in a few days.'

Wal grunted and leaned on his cane. The walker stood nearby, probably left over from the physio's visit, but Wal hated the contraption. A cane had some dignity, the walker gave him none.

'Have to try something else with the missy then.'

Matt considered telling him about Callie's plan to paint the house and dismissed it, curious to see what scheme his uncle devised. The old man was still obsessed with Callie staying on at Glenmore, even more so now he'd returned home. She had to, he said. Maggie wanted it and he'd promised, and a man's word mattered.

Matt wanted Callie to stay too, as badly as Wal, but it was her choice, and he was stuffed if he was going to manipulate her. Especially not after her parting words today. Callie had experienced enough hurt for one lifetime.

Wal used his cane to point at the pup with the crooked markings. Instead of the typical collie mark of a neat white stripe along the nose that widened over the top of the head, leaving the dog's ears and eyes black, only the fur over the pup's left eye and ear was dark. The right side of his face was pure white, his eye a disconcerting pale blue. 'That one.'

'What about that one.'

'We'll give it to the missy.'

Matt suppressed a sigh. Wal was going about this the wrong way. If a horse couldn't make Callie stay, a dog stood no chance. 'I don't think she'll take it.'

'Course she will. Look at it!'

The pup cocked its head as though it knew it was under discussion, bright and button cute despite its mismatched eyes.

Matt's negative response turned Wal's expression vinegary. 'Wouldn't have to resort to this if you were doing your job right.'

'She's not some fucking chore, Wal. She's a person. And who says I'm not doing things right by her? We could be shagging each other stupid for all you know.'

Eagerness illuminated Wal's face. 'Are you?'

'None of your business.'

The hopefulness dimmed. Wal eyed him before jutting his cane in Matt's direction. 'You know your problem? You can't see past *her*.'

'Who?' asked Matt, flummoxed. 'Callie?'

'Her sister, you muppet!'

Matt regarded his uncle with a granite gaze. 'In case you've forgotten, Hope's dead and what we shared died well before that. So you can get that stupid idea out of your head right now. You need anything? I'm going to sort this chook shed.'

He marched off, fists clenched, jaw rigid. But it wasn't anger toward Wal coiling his muscles like compressed springs, it was fury at himself. Over the past few weeks, as his desire for Callie deepened, he'd forgotten all about his relationship with Hope. At the start he'd thought his feelings for Callie were some resurrected by-product of a long-forgotten teenage love, but he'd soon discovered they were better than that. Bigger, and far, far more complicated. He'd fallen in love with her and he thought—hoped—that even though it scared the crap out of her, Callie might feel the same.

Which meant that at some point he had to make a decision whether to tell her about Hope.

At the chook shed, Matt halted and stared at the wire enclosure with his hands on his hips. The roost was empty, the hens all out poking about the yard. The pungent smell of chook manure and soiled bedding hung in the air. Some time down the track he'd clean the entire run out and give it a good wash with disinfectant, but that could wait for a cooler day. He glanced around, not in the mood for this. Right now he needed to sweat, dispel his brewing anger and, most of all, think.

In a cleared area at the side of the house, past the clothesline, Matt spotted Wal's wood pile. Grimacing, he strode to the shed where the axe was kept.

He grunted with the weight of the first strike, smiling at the satisfying sound of metal splitting wood. It took several swings and feet adjustments to get his position steady, but once settled, he sank into a monotonous rhythm, muscles stretching, hands chafing, mind set loose.

Was it a lie, not to tell? Perhaps the answer would depend on whether Callie ever asked, and he doubted she would. Matt didn't want to know about any of her past lovers, so why should she want to know about his? Trouble was, it felt wrong. Really wrong, like a betrayal. So many times he could have mentioned it, yet he never did. He'd kept his relationship with Hope secret, and secrecy gave things power they didn't merit.

The axe thwacked again and again, wood splinters darting like missiles, the air redolent with the spicy aroma of cleaved timber. Sweat soaked his shirt and trickled down the line of his spine into his trousers. His shoulder muscles ached, his hands began to burn, and still Matt couldn't rid the worry that he'd played this wrong.

But that wasn't the worst of it. The worst thing about this entire fuck-up was that he hadn't the faintest idea how Callie would react when she did find out. His head told him that if he explained it properly she'd understand.

The rest of him, though, wasn't so sure.

***

The following afternoon shone too glorious for argument but that didn't stop Matt trying. To save Wal a laborious hobble across the yard, he'd driven the

Amarok to the house and now stood holding the passenger door open for his uncle.

'You're wasting your time,' he said. 'She won't take it.'

Wal tossed back a dirty look before snapping his fingers at the pup and ordering it inside the ute. The pup skittered over to the driver's seat, overexcited body quivering from head to tail. Matt observed it suspiciously. If it piddled, it was out, regardless of his uncle's demands.

'Will. Girls like pups.'

'I'm telling you, she won't.'

'What would you know about women? Nothing, that's what.'

Matt gave up. No, he wasn't an expert on women, but he knew enough about Callie to know Wal's present would be dumped straight back into his arms. Besides, it really was too nice a day for this, although his appreciation might have had more to do with spending time with Callie than the weather's magnificence.

For the short drive to Glenmore, Wal kept the puppy perched on his lap, the pair of them as quivery and adventure hungry as each other; if Wal had owned a tail, it would have wagged. Instead, he peered through the windscreen, inspecting the passing landscape, keen-eyed and confident, convinced he'd come up with another way to keep Callie at Glenmore, and completely oblivious to the real reason she'd invited him over.

Given the old man's moods, Matt wasn't sure Callie's plan was such a great idea, but Phantom was due back in Warrnambool the following day and Callie and Kate were willing to try anything. He glanced at his watch. They had fifteen minutes or so before Kate and Lyndall were due—an hour earlier than their usual time, but Kate had decided this was more important than an hour's schooling.

He pulled up near the house and, spotting Callie by the water tank, signalled an okay. Her return grin tripped his heart. That and the way she looked, all country fresh and sunshiny. He liked how she never dressed up, always casually pretty in shorts and singlets that showed off her athletic body but in an unselfconscious, almost wholesome way. The naturalness of her made her far sexier than other women he'd known. Not that he'd had that many. The scars left by Hope's dumping made him cautious. At least they had until war and a roadside bomb changed everything.

'I'm not a bloody invalid,' muttered Wal as Callie attempted to assist him from the car.

'Suit yourself,' she said, stepping back with her arms crossed. She remained close enough for Wal to lean on her if needed, her attention sharp.

The pup sat thumpy-tailed on the driver's seat while Wal eased himself out. When she caught sight of the dog, Callie's warm welcome smile had iced over. Lips pursed, she'd thrown Matt a 'don't even think of it' glance. Matt had shrugged and responded with a wry 'blame the old man' expression that left her raising her eyes heavenward.

Feet square, cane propped between his legs and one hand on the ute, Wal called to the pup. It scampered obediently to the edge of the passenger seat, looking up at him. 'Down,' he ordered, and in a few leaps the pup was out and by his feet. 'Good dog. Now go meet your mistress.'

'Oh, no you don't,' said Callie, palms held up.

'Too late,' said Wal, shutting the ute door. He gripped his cane and, with nothing else to say, set off on his shuffling journey to the house.

Callie followed alongside. 'I'm not taking him, Wal.'

'Dog needs a home. You're it.'

Releasing a frustrated growl, she stopped, hands on hips, to examine the pup which, with a hand signal from Wal, had propped to regard her.

'Don't look at me like that. I'm not your mistress.' The dog whined softly and raised its paw. She closed her eyes for a moment, shaking her head. Finally, after tossing another filthy glance Wal's way, she scooped the pup up, carried him back to the ute and deposited him gently in the tray. After ruffling his head she cupped his jaw and addressed the pup eye to eye. 'Now you be a good dog and sit there, okay?'

Though the pup whined plaintively and tried to lick her hand, as Matt predicted, Callie remained strong. She strode back to Wal.

'Don't try that trick again. I have enough animals to deal with. Now,' she said, perking up, 'come and say hello to your old friend Phan.'

The horse was on the back lawn in his usual grass-snuffling position, silver-coated in the sunshine. From the buckets of horse care products lined up against the house wall, Callie had spent another morning lovingly pampering her old mount. Phantom's tail even sported trendy show-pony kinks where she'd plaited the length and let it dry. Water puddled the path where the coiled-up garden hose had leaked the last of its contents. Honk waddled nearby, poking his beak around and releasing disgruntled toots.

It was all comfortingly rural but Matt barely noticed any of it. The horse could have been dyed purple with fluorescent green zebra stripes and Honk roaring like a lion for all he cared. Dampness had turned the thin fabric of Callie's white singlet translucent and clingy, adhering to her skin and exposing the pink lace edge of her bra. He couldn't stop ogling her. Soon he'd have to make an excuse and hide to save embarrassment.

Leaving Wal chatting to Phan, Callie slid to his side. 'Are you all right?'

'No.'

'What's the matter?'

He bent close to her. 'White singlets and water don't mix.'

She glanced down then darted a look toward his groin, gaze lingering in a way that only made his suffering worse.

'Sorry.'

'Liar.'

'I am. Really.' She smiled sympathetically. 'Not great timing. I'll go change. Keep an eye out for Kate and Lyndall for me?'

'In this state?'

'Good point. I'll be quick.'

She dashed inside. After pausing to check Wal was fine, Matt wandered over to pat sooky Morton—anything to keep his mind from thinking of Callie's small, perfectly formed breasts bouncing as she dragged the damp singlet from her silky skin and over her head.

She returned wearing a disappointingly loose navy T-shirt and slid him a look from under lowered lashes. 'Better?'

He dug his hands into his jeans pockets, trying to ease his discomfort, then leaned close, keeping his voice low so Wal wouldn't hear. 'Not when you look at me like that.'

'No control.'

'I have plenty.'

Her mouth twitched, blue eyes gleaming. 'Do you?'

'Play your cards right and you might find out.' He glanced over his shoulder at Wal and straightened, too well versed in his uncle's ways to be fooled by his feigned nonchalance. Wal might appear to be massaging Phantom but his head was tilted in a manner that suggested far too much interest in the goings-on of others. Matt made a show of checking his watch. 'Kate and Lyndall will be here any minute. You'd better prime him.'

'I suppose I'd better.' She sighed and turned to scrutinise Wal. 'Wish me luck. I have the feeling I'm going to need it.'

Thanks to Wal's ministrations, Phan was in a state of equine ecstasy, the expression on his long face that of a dosed-up junkie. With each dig of Wal's magic fingers, the horse's back curled deeper, like a dog arching away from a delicious scratch. Relaxation had caused his penis to flop out and swing pendulously below his belly. Callie grinned and threw Matt a wink that had him digging his hands even further into his pockets.

'Pony been walking stiff?' Wal asked when Callie approached.

'No, why?'

'Bit of arthritis in his back. You can feel it.' Wal indicated for Callie to put her hand near his and rub. 'See?'

She frowned. 'I'm not sure what I'm meant to be feeling.'

'Rough bits, on the bone.'

Callie shook her head. 'It feels normal to me but I'm not a great horseman like you.' She dug some more before giving up. 'You were always the best with horses. And riders. You taught me pretty well.'

The compliment merely earned her a grunt. 'You used to listen back then.'

Ignoring the dig, Callie went on. 'Which is why I'd like to ask you a favour.'

Wal withdrew his fingers and leaned both hands on his cane, eyes narrowing. 'A favour, huh? Well, spit it out.'

'Help me help Lyndall overcome her fear of horses.'

'Think I'm stupid, don't you, missy?'

'No, I don't. I think you're very smart and I also know that beneath all that bluster there's a kind man who cares about people, which is why I'm asking you for help.'

Wal poked a finger toward her chest. 'Maggie bought that horse for you. Not for some spoiled brat.'

'She's not a spoiled brat. She's a sweet girl who's lost her confidence and I want to help her get it back.'

'Help her then. Disregard your poor grandmother's dying wish and give her the horse. Do what you bloody well like. You will anyway.' He made a dismissive gesture before clutching back at his cane and hobbling toward the path. 'Just don't expect me to get involved.'

'Come on, Wal,' said Matt, forsaking his better judgement and joining in. 'Lyndall loves that horse.'

'Please, Wal.' Callie clutched at his arm. 'I'm not doing this to hurt Nanna. I'm doing this because I don't want Lyndall to hurt like I did.'

'And whose fault was that?'

Callie said nothing, but the sag of her shoulders made Matt want to hug her close and not let go.

Wal appraised her for a moment, mouth slumped in a subsidence of wrinkles. 'All right,' he said suddenly. 'But on one condition.'

'What?'

'You take the pup.'

'Oh, Wal, you know I can't. I live in a shared flat. The others would never allow it, nor is it fair on the dog.'

Wal resumed his uneven lumber out of the yard. 'Take it or leave it.'

Callie stared despairingly at Matt. He walked to her side, rested a hand on her back and rubbed gently.

'I'm sorry. He won't budge now the idea's in his head.'

Her head dropped. 'Damn.'

As soon as she said the word, car noise filtered from the road followed by a crunch of tyres on gravel as a vehicle turned into the property.

Callie jerked up. 'Damn.' She stomped a foot. 'Damn, damn, damn!'

'It's okay. Lyndall will come good eventually.'

'She won't, I know she won't. Kate will give up or Xav will put a stop to her visits again. Today's our last chance.' Pressing the edge of her curled fist to her mouth she considered for a few seconds. Then she dropped her arm, uttered another heartfelt 'damn' and marched after Wal, leaving Matt shaking his head in wonder.

Despite everything, the old man had won.

***

'So what are you going to call him?' asked Kate, fondling the puppy's ears and trying to avoid his friendly but needle-like bites.

Matt, Callie and Kate had parked themselves near the house to give Lyndall space. Not that she'd required a lot. Fifteen minutes after meeting Wal, in what had seemed like an act of magic to all of them, Wal had her stroking Phantom's nose. Ten minutes later she'd walked a circle all the way around the horse, hand not leaving Phantom's shiny coat. Now, half an hour on, she sat bareback on Phantom, expression rapt as she listened to Wal's instructions.

'No idea,' said Callie, turning to Matt. 'I don't suppose you have one?'

Matt considered for a moment. 'You could name him after Wal.'

'Call him Wally, you mean?' She smiled. 'That has possibilities.'

'What about Patch?' asked Kate. 'For his markings.'

'Patch.' Callie held up the pup and inspected him nose to snout, savouring the name. 'Patch,' she said again, and the pup responded with a squirm and a deftly placed lick on her nose.

'I think he likes it,' Matt said, feeling dumbly soppy at the charm of it all and more than a bit disconcerted. Callie had the ability to either completely unman him or leave him pumped with testosterone.

She held the pup against her chest, stroking it fondly. 'Patch it is then.'

Name decided, they turned back to Wal and Lyndall.

'He's amazing,' said Kate.

Callie smiled. 'He is, isn't he? I should have introduced them earlier, when Wal was captive in hospital. Might have saved me being lumped with a dog.' She looked down at Patch and kissed the top of his head. 'Not that you're not a little sweetie. He was a brilliant teacher when I was kid. Everything he said made sense. And it was so simple too. Like how horses don't judge, they just act in response to fear. So when they kick or bite or misbehave, it's not because they're being naughty or stubborn or mean, they're just frightened, and that fear can only exist because we did something to make it. Change our behaviour, teach them to trust us, and everything will fall into place.'

'Obvious when you think about it. They're prey animals after all.'

'Exactly. Their behaviour is simple and instinctive. It's the modification of our behaviour that's hard.' Lowering Patch to the ground, Callie squinted at the sky and then down at Matt's wrist. Realising what she wanted, he held his watch up for her. Her nose screwed up when she read the time. 'I suppose I should get ready for work.'

'You could call in sick,' said Matt, only half kidding. He still couldn't shake the image of her lacy bra.

'And leave the poor beer-drinking public to Doug alone. I'm not that mean.'

Kate squatted to play handshakes with Patch. 'What are you going to do with Patch while you're gone?'

Callie looked at Matt for guidance.

He shrugged. 'Lock him inside?'

She regarded the dog dubiously. 'He'd chew the place to pieces.'

'Laundry?' suggested Kate.

'Honk's enclosure?'

'Then where would Honk go?' Callie crouched down to inspect Patch. 'I suppose I could tie him to the tank.' She let out a sigh. 'I can't do that. It's mean.' She cupped the pup's jaw. 'Laundry for you, but if you even think about chewing anything you'll be back with your mum before you can yelp.'

When she was ready, Matt walked with her across the yard to her ute, sneaking looks at her legs and bum, pert in her short black skirt.

'How much longer will they be, do you think?' asked Callie, glancing back for the third time, as though she couldn't bear to leave her animals.

She'd knotted her hair into a loose bun, blonde tendrils drifting in the light breeze. The style exposed the smooth skin of her neck and Matt felt the urge to place a tender kiss on its satiny surface like a magnet pull.

'No idea.'

'Are you sure you don't mind looking after Patch and Honk?'

'Not a bit.' He grinned. 'But it'll cost you.'

She rolled her eyes. 'According to you, everything has a price. I'm beginning to think you're a soldier of fortune.'

'That's me. Complete mercenary.'

'Now that implies someone mean and selfish.'

Matt struck a haughty pose as they halted by her ute. 'I can be mean and selfish.'

Her eyebrows shot up.

'I can be anything you want.' He glanced down at her black leather-clad feet. The thick soles and elastic inserts reminiscent of nurses' shoes. 'It's those sexy shoes. They have me at your mercy.'

She laughed and playfully slapped his chest, then opened the door and slid into the driver's seat. 'You really are crazy.'

Balancing his hands on the chassis, he leaned in close. 'Yeah, about you. I wish you could come tomorrow.'

'I wish I could too, but Doug's insistent.' Her face turned gloomy. 'I hate work parties. Especially on a Friday. They always get messy.'

'I'll drop by when I get back. Make sure you're okay.'

'Thanks, but I think I'll be safe. Dargate's bound to be tame compared to the Alice.' She grabbed his arm and twisted his wrist, wincing at the time. 'I'd better get going.' She bent forward and turned the key, the movement gaping her shirt and providing him with an unobstructed view of her lace-covered left breast.

'Callie?'

She reached back to tug on her seatbelt. 'What?'

Ducking his head, he leaned in and curled his hand around the line of her chin. Her mouth parted, eyes widening in surprise, then he registered nothing more except the exquisite, heart-walloping sensation of her soft mouth on his.

The kiss was intense, brief and meaning laden. Exactly the way he wanted.

'Happy Valentine's Day,' he said, pulling away but leaving his palm in place. Her eyes were huge, her breath shallow, and all he wanted to do was kiss her again. And more. So much more.

Instead, he pressed his lips against her forehead, holding them there a moment with his eyes closed, before finally releasing her. 'See you first thing tomorrow.'

As Matt stood in the shade of the shed, watching as she reversed out, noting the way her uncertain gaze repeatedly flew back to his as though seeking reassurance this was real and safe and right, he knew he couldn't lose her.

His secret about Hope would just have to stay hidden.

Eighteen

Callie pressed her wet cheek against Phan's and wrapped her arms around his neck. The horse didn't move, accepting her teary farewell with his usual stoicism, content with a belly full of apples.

She pulled away and gave him one last kiss on the nose. 'You be a good boy, now. Be nice to Ethan and don't go escaping your paddock.' Phan blinked his silvery lashes and bunted her in the belly. More tears slid down Callie's cheeks, her throat thick with sorrow.

Matt placed a steady hand on her back. 'The Jennings said you can visit him any time you like.'

She caressed Phan's silken muzzle. 'Long drive from Airlie.'

His fingers tensed; a fractional change of pressure that threaded a needle of guilt through her conscience. Their kiss yesterday had changed a lot. She wanted so much to grab what he offered, to give in to her longing and embrace the joyous honesty of love, yet her resolve continued to waver.

Last night, although weary and a little bit heartsore from a Valentine's Day shift laden with starry-eyed couples, she'd sat on the back step, Patch snoozing at her side, and pondered her situation. She'd thought of Hope; her heartbroken parents; Nanna and Poppy. Emotional forces orbiting like electrons, each in competition. She was wrenched by the desire to do right by all of them, trapped by indecision and the call of her own heart. Then she'd thought of Matt, his sexy confidence and certainty, how he made her feel wanted and admired and special. The way he'd made her insides float with just one short kiss. The future he made her yearn to embrace.

Midnight had passed, cool and cascaded with stars. Goosebumps ranged her arms and legs. Phantom drifted across the paddock, almost pearly in the moonlight, Morton, his body dark and shadowy, following. Insects darted and whirred. A rabbit crept to the edge of the lawn and skittered off. Callie should have been in bed, but she was too lost in introspection.

Another hour of mulling brought no change. All Callie decided was that she still didn't know what to do. She wasn't sure she ever would.

Matt broke into her thoughts. 'We have to go, Callie.'

'I know.' She tossed him a watery smile. 'I'm going to miss him, that's all.'

'At least you'll know he's safe and looked after.'

She nodded and turned back to give Phan another hug. Pressing her mouth close to his fuzzy ear she whispered a last 'I love you' then hauled in a long, tight breath and walked him to the float, Patch scampering alongside.

Instructing Patch to sit, she led Phan into the float and tied his lead to a loop of baling twine while Matt secured the tailgate. She smiled as Phan nibbled at her loose hair, rubbery lips caressing her arm. Love for this tough little horse made her heart swell. This time, if it was truly goodbye, she wanted to say it properly.

She held his head between her hands once more. 'Phan my man, The Ghost Who Neighs, Phanny Mae, Pharty Phan, you are the best horse in the world. The sweetest, kindest, loveliest animal ever born. Thank you for being my friend.'

With a last kiss on his grey nose, she left the float.

'Done?' asked Matt when she stepped down.

Too choked up to speak, she nodded and followed him to the ute.

He settled into the driver's seat and wound down the window before dangling his hand out. Stepping close, she took it, liking the tenderness of his fingers as they gently squeezed hers. 'You take care at work today, okay?'

'I'll be all right. Doug will be there.'

'Be careful anyway. Dargate mightn't be Alice Springs but that doesn't mean it doesn't have its share of dickheads.' He sighed. 'I have to go. It's already seven and they're collecting Ethan at ten.' Callie made to step back but Matt tugged on her hand, head tilted toward the window. 'Come here.' He smiled, the affection in his green eyes magnetic, promising happiness. 'Please.'

Insides fluttering, she moved closer.

'Now bend down.'

Her stomach flutters turned into wingbeats. Drawn by longing, she leaned toward him, mouth close to his. 'How far?'

'A bit further.'

Her lips hovered at the edge of his, her voice soft and husky as though she feared being overheard. 'Enough?'

'Never enough. Now hurry up and kiss me.'

She obeyed; a brief, hard and potent connection that left her soaring. Callie drew away, heat flushing her skin. 'Drive carefully.'

His hand gripped hers. 'I don't want to leave now.'

Callie didn't want him to either. 'You have to.'

'See you tomorrow?'

She shook her head. 'Double shift.' The hold on her fingers didn't loosen. He stared grim-faced through the windscreen. 'Are you going?' she said when he still didn't let go.

'Do I have to?'

'*Yes.*'

His pleading, puppy-dog expression could have given Patch a run for his money. 'Kiss for the road?'

'Go!' Callie ordered, laughing as she tugged her hand from his to scoop Patch into the safety of her arms, using his fluffy paw to wave goodbye. 'Now, or I'll sic my savage dog onto you.'

With a grin and a horn honk, he finally departed.

***

Callie was up a ladder dressed in a daggy pair of cut-off denim shorts, an ancient singlet and her fishing Dunlop Volleys when Matt turned up early Sunday morning. Callie followed his progress from her perch, laughing as Honk ambushed him near the water tank. Excited by the drama, Patch erupted into a frenzy of high-pitched yipping, racing around the goose and getting under Matt's feet.

'Fuck,' he said, tripping hard against the water tank, the bouquet of vibrant sunflowers he carried in his right hand swinging as tried to regain his balance. Steady again, Matt threw Honk a furious look. 'Do that one more time and you're a roast.' He switched focus to Patch, still yapping and bouncing like a black-and-white tennis ball. 'As for you, you little shit, sit!'

Patch sat and held up his paw. Grim-mouthed, Matt shook his head at the dog.

Callie pointed her paint scraper at him. 'Aren't you Mr Happy.'

He looked up, expression immediately softening. 'Sorry. Wasn't expecting to be attacked.' He held up the flowers. 'Wal ordered me to bring these around.'

'Wal?'

'Yeah. Sly old bugger saw more than he was meant to on Thursday, so now he's turned Cupid. I told him not to bother. The arrows have already struck.'

'Have they?'

He held her gaze, eyes brilliant in the morning sun. 'You know they have. Are you coming down?'

Callie descended, kissing his cheek as she took the sunflowers. 'As lovely as these are, a convertible ladder and a wire brush might have turned me on more.' She smiled at the bright, happy blooms. 'They're gorgeous.'

'Like you.'

She regarded him, thinking the same. He'd teamed a pair of faded but neat jeans with his green-and-white striped shirt, the sleeves rolled up to expose his tanned forearms. A clean soapy smell drifted from his body, the damp ends of his hair curling around his collar. 'You're not looking so bad yourself today.'

'I was hoping I could drag you away from here. Maybe duck across the border for lunch at one of the wineries.' He nudged her. 'Should have known my date plans would go awry.'

'Sorry.'

'I forgive you.' He scanned the house walls. 'Big job, scraping all that back.'

'Actually it's kind of therapeutic. Although not as therapeutic as yesterday morning.' At Matt's raised eyebrows she explained. 'I hired a pressure washer. Gave it all a good blast to clean the grime away. There's something a bit sexy about shooting that water gun.'

'Disappointed I missed that.' He eyed her again. 'I'll go home and get changed, bring a ladder back.'

'I'll put these in water.'

He touched her cheek. 'Back shortly.'

Calling Patch to heel, Callie took the flowers into the house, only to head out again when she realised the perfect vase was packed away in a box in the machinery shed. She found it in the fourth box—a tall, cut-crystal vase in need of a good clean—and a piece whose fate she'd dithered over.

The vase had the heavy weight of high quality lead crystal and though she wasn't certain, Callie thought it had once belonged to her great-grandmother. She'd packed and unpacked it twice before repacking it again. A vase wouldn't bring Nanna back and its disposal wouldn't mean Callie didn't love her. But now, as she dug it out of its papery cocoon, Callie experienced a surge of satisfaction, as if she'd corrected some karmic wrong.

The sunflowers looked glorious in the washed vase, their colour refracted in the sparkling crystal. Callie took her time arranging the stems just so, smiling to herself as she worked, thinking of Matt and his kindness while anticipation of his return buzzed like an electric charge across her skin.

Unable to resist, she picked up her phone and snapped a photo of the flowers, then forwarded it to Anna with a message.

Present from local farmer type. Suspect crocodile wrestling capabilities. What 2 do?

Anna's message came back less than a minute later. *KNEW IT! Drives ute?*

Laughing, Callie texted straight back. *Yes.*

Sexy?

Very. With war scar.

RU SERIOUS? Hot in bed?

Unknown.

Make known then if pass test marry.

A few seconds later another text came through. *Can u send pic?*

No. Don't want 2 make u jealous.

Cow.

A car sounded in the drive. Callie pumped out a final text. *Is here. Later!*

Knowing Anna and her capacity for never-ending text conversations, Callie turned the phone off. Except for work, no one else was likely to ring, and the last thing she wanted was her day off ruined with a call from the Royal.

Matt had changed into a pair of daggy cargo shorts, an old blue polo shirt, long football socks pushed down to the ankles and a pair of work boots.

Callie eyed him up and down. 'You look like a plumber.'

'As long as I don't smell like one.' He didn't. Despite the work clothes he still smelled of soapy cleanliness. 'Wal's sulking.'

'Why this time?'

'He expected the flowers to work miracles but I told him you only wanted me for my tools.'

'He's right. The question is which tools.'

Matt angled his head and appraised her. 'You know you've just given me a hard-on.'

Callie glanced down but his shorts were too baggy to tell. 'No control.'

'Want to test the theory?'

'It's a kind offer but right now I have other dirty things on my mind.' Tool tray in hand, she marched off to the back of the house, halting at her ladder and squinting up at the wall. The paint guy at the hardware store had warned her that scraping the paint was the worst part of the job. Given her minimal progress she could believe him.

'Maybe I should just pay someone,' she said when Matt caught up.

'Why when you can do it yourself?'

'I don't know. It's just such a big job.'

'Made easier with two.' He dropped his ladder and slung an arm around her shoulder, earning a jealous yip from Patch. 'Bugger off, Patch. I saw her first.' He kissed Callie on the temple. 'We'll get it done.'

She smiled up at him, her heart flip-flopping as she took in his indulgent expression. Even now, the rational part of her brain registered that he wasn't a traditionally handsome man, but that didn't stop him being sexy as hell. 'Thanks.'

He smiled back before releasing her to pick up his ladder. 'You can kiss me proper thanks later.'

***

The morning drifted in a haze of scraping, sweat, old timber smells, the odd curse and a lot of perving. By eleven thirty, they'd completed the entire rear wall and the concrete path was strewn with paint flakes, as if the house had shuddered itself free of dandruff. Despite multiple orders to cut it out, Patch had run himself silly with his attempts to herd Honk. Each time Callie turned her back, the pup resumed his sneaky stalking, only to be caught out with a hissy counterattack from Honk that set Patch running in yappy circles.

She wished he'd stop. The cuteness was making her love him.

After a brief discussion, they decided it was best to tackle the worst parts first, even if it did mean working in the sun. After taking it in turns to regrease themselves with sunscreen, they carted their equipment to the badly weathered western side of the house. Declaring that the tool-bringer gets to decide who uses it, he banished Callie to Wal's low-set scaffold and took over the under eaves work on the ladder.

'What are you looking so pleased about?' she asked when she caught him grinning down at her.

'Nothing.'

She narrowed her eyes and pointed her scraper at him. 'You're up to something.'

He feigned innocence. 'Me? Never.'

Callie watched him for a moment before resuming her work. A minute later a flake of paint dropped between her breasts. She frowned and picked it out only for another to hit her shoulder.

'Great view from up here,' he said, one eye closed as he aimed another paint scrap at her chest.

214

The scrap stuck on the swell of her right breast. She picked it off, rolling her eyes.

'Very schoolboy.'

'I can be very adult if you want.'

Callie did want. Scraping this side of the house was a mistake. She was hot, sweaty, bored and, after a week of non-stop work, in need of some fun. She gave him one of her sideways looks, mouth quirking in an 'I dare you' smile.

He sobered fast. 'Keep that up and there'll be consequences.'

'Oh, yeah. What sort of consequences?'

'Like I said, keep that up and you'll find out.'

'A girl could be tempted.' Callie dug the scraper into the paint edge and removed a solid run. More scraps landed on her shoulder. She brushed them off without looking up, feigning interest in a timber knot she'd uncovered. When she thought he wasn't watching, she glanced slyly upward only to meet Matt's gaze. She smiled again.

'Last warning.'

'And you'll do what?'

'Put it this way, you won't get any more of the house done today.'

'Promises, promises.'

'Right,' he said, climbing down. 'That's it.'

Callie's heart beat an excited tattoo. Dumping her scraper, she jumped down from the scaffold, using it as a fence between them.

'That won't save you.'

She feinted right and rushed left but Matt had already guessed the manoeuvre. In one sweep he had her pressed hard against the wall, one hand holding her wrists above her head. He cast a lazy look over her stretched, quivery body, stripping her.

'You look hot.'

'Literally or figuratively?'

'Both,' he said, tucking a finger under the fine strap of her singlet and running it down to the top of her breast and back up again.

She licked her lips. 'I'm sweaty.'

'So am I. And right now looking to get sweatier.'

'Here?' She winced at the squeak in her voice.

'Yeah. Why not?'

'What about Honk and Patch?'

The hold on her wrists slackened. He pressed a delicate kiss on the inside of her collarbone, voice vibrating against her skin as he spoke. 'They're animals. They'll understand.'

More delicate kisses followed; a slow fluttery trail over the curve of her chin that paused just below her ear. He released her wrists, scraping his palm down her arm and side to rest lightly against her waist as the finger under her singlet strap began another slow journey downward.

An exquisite spasm shot up Callie's spine, making her arch against him, breasts brushing his chest. He was hard all over, tense and aroused. Her arms curled around his neck, signalling her want. He understood, nipping delicately along her jawline and upward before finally capturing her lips with his.

This was nothing like their previous kisses. This was pure passion, hungry and desperate. He pressed her harder against the wall, breath coming as rapid as hers, hands roaming until they cradled each breast, thumbs brushing her nipples in an electric jolt.

Callie made a noise that had him kissing her harder, bodies compressing against the wall. She slipped her hands inside his shirt, delighting in his muscular frame and lean stomach, and used her index finger to trace the furry line between his belly button and waistband.

His mouth left hers to trail across her cheek, ear and arched neck. Kisses winged down her throat, making her shudder. As though joining in the celebration, Honk released a series of trumpets, Patch following with sharp yips.

'I think we've excited them,' said Matt, looking up to grin at her, only for his smile to drop as a car door slammed. 'Fuck.'

Callie blinked, still afloat on her desire. Another door banged shut. Voices drifted. Lyndall calling out to Morton.

Matt backed away and ran a hand over his hair. 'You'll have to sort them out. I can't face anyone in the state I'm in.'

'I'm not sure I can either.'

'Callie?' Kate called at the back door. Any moment she'd appear around the corner.

'Damn.' She knocked her head back against the wall. 'Sorry.' With a squeeze of his hand and a check that her top and bra were arranged properly, Callie let out a shuddery breath and walked briskly to the corner of the house, glancing back in time to see Matt slip around the front to safety.

'How's things?' asked Kate when Callie appeared. 'Hot by the look of you. Not the best time of day to be working on the house. I hope you don't mind. Xav's gone into the office and Lyndall wanted to see Phan. I didn't want to say no. I can't help worrying that all the good work Wal did with her will come undone now your Phan is gone.' She peered at Callie's face. 'Are you all right? You look a bit feverish.'

'Fine,' said Callie ultra brightly. 'Just hot.'

Kate frowned and hunted behind Callie. 'Where's Matt?'

'Oh, he's just . . . busy. You know, doing stuff.'

Realisation turned Kate's eyes wide. 'Oh, god. We've intruded.'

'No, no. You're fine.'

'And you're a terrible liar, Callie Reynolds.' Kate touched her arm. 'I should have called. I'm sorry.'

'Wouldn't have made any difference. I turned my phone off.'

The older woman nudged her, delight sparkling her eyes. 'Can't help feeling pleased though. He's a good catch.'

That Matt was a good catch Callie couldn't dispute. It was whether he deserved to be caught in the impossible snarl of her life that was the issue. She thought of him languishing at the front of the house in discomfort, waiting for her return, and all she wanted to do was go to him and pretend life was normal. That she could be happy with him. Here, in the place she loved.

Instead she crossed her arms and began to stroll down the path to the liquidambar. 'How's Lyndall?'

'Better. She and Xav are talking at least. He's trying to be understanding but he's so worried for her.' Kate's mouth thinned. 'He's scared that if she starts riding again she'll have another fall.'

'You must be too.'

'I am, but I'm more worried about what will happen if she doesn't ride.'

'Ask Wal for help. I'm sure he won't mind. And it'll give him something to concentrate on while his hip heals properly.'

They reached the fence. Lyndall stood in the paddock stroking Morton's coppery bay coat. After Callie left for work on Thursday, Wal had continued his lesson, coaxing Lyndall into the paddock with Morton. Though nervous, she could now approach and pat the horse. Riding would take time yet.

'Callie's busy,' Kate warned her daughter. 'Say your hello and we'll be off.'

'It's all right,' said Callie. 'You take your time.'

'No,' said Kate firmly. 'It was bad manners of us to turn up unannounced.'

'I don't mind, really.'

Kate dropped her voice and indicated the house. 'You mightn't but someone else does.' Callie turned. Matt sat on the back step watching her, Patch panting at his feet. 'I might be an old married woman, but I still remember what it was like. At it like rabbits.'

'We haven't got that far yet.'

'All the more reason for us to leave.' Kate raised her voice again. 'Time's up.'

The teenager's 'Aww, Mum' was silenced with a glare. Leaving Morton with a last pat, Lyndall approached the fence, casting a hopeful look at Callie. 'Perhaps I can come back later?'

'Not today.' Kate regarded Callie. 'Maybe Monday after school?'

'Any day after school is fine. I'll be at work every day except Wednesday, but the house will be open if you need a drink or the loo.'

Kate hugged her. 'I'm so pleased. You belong here. I've thought that from the start.'

'Thanks.'

Kate released her and waved Lyndall toward the car. 'You have fun.' She threw a look at Matt before grinning back at Callie and delivering a not very whispered, 'Half your luck!'

Callie smiled, waving them both farewell before walking slowly back to the house, eyes locked with Matt's. At the step, as the Range Rover's engine faded into the midday quiet, she edged her way between his legs and placed her hands on his shoulders. Matt's palms slid up her thighs to her hips. He tilted his head back to regard her; scarred and sexy and hot and bothered, and overloaded with everything she'd forsaken for the last eight years.

'Now,' she said, bending toward him. 'Where were we?'

Nineteen

It was a struggle to get past the kitchen. Given the way they'd attacked one another, Callie supposed they were lucky to even make it into the house. If it weren't for the close call with Kate and Lyndall, they probably wouldn't have.

Matt pressed her up against the hallway wall, continuing the ravenous kisses that hadn't stopped since she'd first lowered her mouth to his. Callie was naked from the waist up, arms around his neck, legs wrapped around his hips and crossed at the ankles to anchor her in place. Her singlet was draped over the china cabinet, her bra, god knew where. The top button of her shorts was undone, the zip open, her groin pressed against Matt's.

She'd removed Matt's shirt on the step and tossed it into the yard where it was probably being destroyed by Patch's sharp teeth. His cargo pants were halfway down his thighs, causing him to shuffle awkwardly. He cradled her bum, fingers following the centre seam of her shorts as he stroked between her thighs.

Callie broke away from his mouth to point in the general direction of the spare room.

'In here.'

Matt stumbled his way to the single bed until they fell in a tangle of sweaty arms and legs amid creaking springs and laughter. Callie's shorts winged across the room, following his cargo pants, the last of her underwear sling-shotting after them. Callie laughed as Matt's jocks caught on his springy cock, enjoying his hungry, almost pained expression as she levered him out and tugged them over his hips and down his legs. Grinning, she twirled the jocks around her finger before flinging them toward the wardrobe.

Nudity brought a pause, the atmosphere sultry with anticipation. In the quiet, their breaths sounded raspy and rapid, the squeaking complaints of the old bed loud.

Matt sat back on his heels to look at her, scanning her breasts and continuing downward, a lazy smile on his face. 'Better than my dreams.' He shifted his gaze back to hers. 'And I've been having a few lately.'

'So have I.'

He grinned and leaned forward, mischievousness and desire widening the pupils of his eyes, turning the green darkly compelling. His hand slid up her inner thigh as he lowered his mouth to her belly and laid a delicate kiss on her hypersensitive skin. 'Did it involve this?'

Catching her lower lip between her teeth, she nodded. 'And more.'

His hand slid higher, causing her breath to halt. 'More?'

'Much more.'

'I think I'd like to hear about these dirty dreams in detail one day.' A finger caressed. 'But right now, I think we should live them.'

'Couldn't agree more,' Callie replied, arching as the finger slid inside, her mouth curving into an O.

His lips returned to her belly, his breath as hoarse and accelerated as hers. Gasps mingled with moans and soft whispers, the sounds overlaid with creaks from the bed. Matt's mouth ventured everywhere, his hands further. Callie clutched at his hair, arms, anywhere, wanting all of him all at once, but he was, as he'd promised, a man of control. Only when she'd been reduced to shuddering ecstasy did he lick his way back up her belly and kiss her hard.

'Had enough?'

'You're kidding?'

'Good.' He kissed the tip of her nose. 'Because I haven't even started. Don't move.'

She smiled as he eased out of bed and rummaged through his shorts. Matt had the tautest arse in history, not to mention other impressively firm bits. 'You've a scar on your shoulder.'

'Yeah,' he said, finally pulling out a pack of condoms. He waggled the pack, winking at her. 'A soldier's always prepared.'

On the few occasions Callie had allowed herself a fun romp she'd made sure at least one of them was well supplied with protection, and if they weren't, it simply didn't happen. With Matt, for some unfathomable reason, safe sex hadn't even registered. Probably because she'd spent too long convincing herself it was never going to occur.

He returned to the bed and sat down, tearing at the packet with his teeth. She traced her finger over his shoulder scar, red and ridged like the one on his face. 'It looks bad.'

'It wasn't. Not really.'

'Tough guy, huh?'

'You bet.'

Callie smiled and plucked the condom from his fingers. Kneeling behind him, she kissed his scarred shoulder before resting her chin on top and reaching over to make a game of sheathing his cock.

He looked at her sideways, returning her smile. 'Tease.'

'This isn't teasing. Real teasing I'll show you later.'

'Later,' he said, rolling her back onto the bed, firm and ready against her leg. 'I like the sound of that. But then I like the sound of everything you do.' He slipped his hand under her knee and slid it along her calf, stretching her leg up and out, before sucking hard on the tight bud of her left nipple.

'And I like everything you do,' Callie replied. His cock teased. 'Oh, damn.'

'Even that?'

'Especially that.' She arched against him. 'Oh, god.'

'No, just Matt.'

Callie's giggles turned to gasps. The bed resumed its creaking, this time in earnest. Her arms tightened around his neck, her legs around his hips. The bedhead began a rhythmic thump against the wall. They shared a smile and then Callie was too lost to care how much noise they made.

***

'There's a dolphin on your arse,' said Matt later, kissing it.

Callie lay face down on the bed, sated and sleepy. Annoyingly, Matt seemed wide awake, intent on a languid exploration of her body, despite having fondled and kissed most of it already.

'I know. I hate it.'

'It's not the best tatt.' He traced a figure eight around the globes of her bum. 'So why'd you get it then?'

'Thought it was a good idea at the time.' She rolled over to prop herself on her elbow, head resting on her palm, mimicking his pose.

'You only have scars, not tatts.'

'I don't really like them.'

She raised her eyebrows.

'Except on you.' He kissed her forehead. 'You have great breasts. I especially like these.' He tweaked each nipple in turn, causing goose bumps to rush across Callie's shoulders and thoughts of more sex to tumble into her head. He smiled as if reading her mind and let his fingers trace lower. 'I like this bit too.'

'Aren't you tired?'

'Are you?'

She gave him her special underlashed smile.

'Consequences.'

'I like consequences.'

'I guess that settles it then,' he said, reaching for her.

***

It was after four by the time they crawled out of bed and then only because Matt was hungry and wanted to fix the loose bedhead before the entire frame collapsed. Callie wanted a shower but the rumble of her stomach drove her first to the kitchen. She sat on the bench swinging her legs and watching Matt as he made scrambled eggs wearing nothing more than a pair of jocks.

He poured the lot into a bowl and used a spoon to feed it to her, sucking up any spilled scraps straight from her skin. The bowl took a long time to finish.

As did the shower.

Finally, they made it outside into the sunset glow and Patch's relieved welcome. Honk was waddling near his run, ruffling his feathers in readiness for bed.

'I liked that shirt,' Matt said, holding up the wrecked polo shirt and poking his finger through a large rip in the side seam.

Callie ran her fingers through the dark line of hairs running from his groin and up across his chest. Now that she'd started, she couldn't hold back from touching him. 'I prefer you without it anyway.'

He grabbed her hand and kissed her fingers. 'Don't start what you can't finish.'

'Who says I can't finish?'

'Your animals.'

'You're an animal.' She blew him a kiss. 'Kinky boy.'

'Who's calling who kinky? Thanks to you, my days of normal showering are over.'

'So are mine with scrambled eggs.'

They grinned at one another and Callie couldn't remember the last time she was this happy. Stupid, floaty, can't-stop-grinning happy.

Matt seemed to feel it too. He wrapped his arms around her and pulled her close.

'A moment like this deserves champagne.'

'There'll be other times.'

'Good. Because I have ideas.'

She smiled. 'So do I.'

He kissed her, cradling her face, catching and holding her gaze when he'd finished, the look lingering as if he wanted to say something. She kissed him again to stop the words. The day had been enough.

Sick of being ignored, Patch wormed his way between their legs and whined. They looked down at him like indulgent parents.

'Probably hungry.'

Callie sighed. 'I suppose I'd better feed him. Do you want to look after Honk?'

'No, but for you I will. Then I need to go.'

The thought of sleeping without his lean, muscled body against hers left a hollow in Callie's belly but she tried not to let it show. Wal needed Matt too. So did Amberton. He understood his responsibilities, while she, with her indecision, could only continue to tread water. But it was the sort of warm, joyous water a girl could swim in for decades.

'What time's your shift tomorrow?' Matt asked as they meandered around the outside of the house hand in hand ten minutes later, taking the long way to his car.

'I'm on days until Thursday. Lunch until six.'

'I'll come round and cook you dinner again.'

'Scrambled eggs?'

He smiled. 'If you want. I was thinking more along the lines of steak and salad.' He bumped his shoulder against hers. 'You need to keep your strength up.' At the car he leaned against the fender and drew her between his legs, arms braced around her waist. 'Pretty perfect day.'

'Except for the interruption. That wasn't so much fun for you.' Tilting her head, she thought for a moment. 'And fishing would have been more exciting than paint scraping.'

'We could have made love on the beach.'

The way he said 'made love' sent her heart thudding. 'It's probably not as good as it sounds. All that gritty sand.'

'You've never done it?'

'Have you?'

'No. But I'm planning to. Soon.' He smiled. 'There's this sexy blonde I know.'

'What happened to nurses' shoes and milkmaid plaits?'

'Tomorrow?'

She returned his hopeful expression with her special smile.

Matt pressed his forehead against hers. 'I don't want to go.'

'You have to.'

'Callie—'

She pressed her finger against his mouth. 'Don't.'

Hurt flickered across his eyes and disappeared. 'Okay, but that coat's still there. Waiting for you.'

'I know. I just . . .' She dropped her gaze, ashamed of her prickling tears. She hated herself for doing this to him, but she needed more time to reconcile her feelings. Hope was dead, her family fused to its loss, and yet here Callie was, happy. In love. 'I'm still deciding.'

'Hey,' he said, using the curl of his index finger to lift her chin. 'Take all the time you want. I'm not going anywhere. Okay?'

She nodded then kissed him hard in an attempt to recapture the mood. 'Attractive, capable man.'

'Angel,' he replied, kissing her even harder back.

Impossible though it seemed, as she watched his taillights merge with the sunset, her heart soaring high on love, Callie actually felt like one.

***

At eight thirty the following morning, in need of a cold drink and a break after two solid hours of paint scraping and without Matt to make it fun, Callie sat in Glenmore's kitchen, fired up her laptop, and called Anna on Skype.

Anna regarded her owlishly through the computer screen from the dishevelment of her bed. Her hair was sleep mussed, her blue eyes bloodshot. It had, by the look of her, been a big night.

'Where's Bubby?' Callie asked before Anna could start complaining about the ungodly hour.

'Work. Do you have any idea what the time is?'

'Yep. I've been up since six.'

Anna flopped her head back on the pillow and groaned. 'I hate Sunday seshes. I had an eighteen-year-old Scottish backpacker vomit on me last night. Ash just told me to hose off and get on with it.'

'Poor you. Good thing you have Brucey-bubby to make things better.'

Anna poked her tongue out. 'Your phone's been off.'

'I've been busy.'

'I left twelve texts.'

'Thirteen,' Callie said. 'I counted them last night when I was trying to sleep.'

Pulling the laptop across, Anna shifted onto her belly, pillow tucked under her chest, settling in for a girly chat. 'Well?'

Callie smiled. 'Well what?'

'Don't play cute. Your farmer. Spill.'

'His name's Matt.'

'And?'

Callie deliberately took a drink of water. 'And he's nice.'

'Nice? I thought you said he was a ute-driving crocodile wrestler.'

'He's that too.' She put the glass down and smiled across the table at the sunflowers, still gloriously golden in their crystal glass. 'And more.'

'You had sex,' said Anna, grinning.

'I did.' Amazing, heart-whumping sex that made her feel more alive than she had in years. Fingers around the heavy base, Callie twirled her glass and studied the water as it sloshed the sides. 'Anna?'

'Yeah?'

'You and Bruce, what changed?'

Anna frowned. 'What do you mean?'

'You were just playing around, never serious, and now . . .'

Anna's frown dissolved into a smile. 'I did what you said. Took a chance. I opened my eyes and really looked. And you know what I saw?'

'What?' asked Callie, leaning toward the screen.

Dreaminess softened Anna's expression. 'I saw how much he loved me. How good he was. Not just in bed, but inside—' she pressed a hand to her upper chest, '—where it matters.'

Good, inside, where it mattered. Callie looked away. That was Matt.

'I don't know how to do this, Anna.' She turned back, her throat tight. 'I'm so scared I'll hurt him.'

'You love him?'

She nodded.

'Does he love you?'

'I think he might.'

Anna smiled. 'Then it'll be okay.'

That evening after her shift, Callie returned to Glenmore to find Matt in the kitchen chopping a cucumber, the table cleared and laid with a tablecloth, plates and cutlery neatly arranged at right angles, sunflowers decorating the centre and a bottle of red wine open beside two crystal wine glasses that Callie distinctly remembered packing up. The room was warm with the scent of grilling steaks and the contentment of home.

He smiled at her. 'You want a glass of champagne or should we save that for another time?'

'Another time. Do I have time for a shower?'

He glanced at the stove. 'If you're quick.'

She placed a hand on his shoulder and stood on tip-toe to kiss his cheek. 'I'll be back.'

Five minutes later, skin still glittering with drops of water that she'd missed with her hasty towel swipes, smelling of vanilla body wash and expectation, Callie walked quietly to the end of the hall, stretched up her arms and placed them on the jamb, angling her hip to pose with one knee bent like a fifties pin-up. Ready, she called out to him.

'Matt, I'm hungry.'

'Good,' he replied, turning around. 'So am— Fuck.'

Kicking her leg to show off her foot, she lowered her lashes and curled one corner of her mouth, well aware she didn't need to give him 'the look'. The milkmaid plaits, lacy bra, matching knickers and nurses' shoes had already done their trick.

He didn't say anything further. He simply put down his knife, flicked off the stove and came at her, kissing the breath from her lungs and turning her inside out with his passion as he manoeuvred her onto the table. The cutlery ended on the floor. Only quick thinking from Matt saved the wine, glasses and plates. The sunflower vase fell over, splashing the table and lino with water. Callie didn't care. She didn't care about anything but being with Matt.

'Still hungry?' he asked when he'd finished reducing Callie to a panting, quivering lump of jellified joy.

'For you?' She ran her finger along his bottom lip. 'Always.'

'Always? A bloke could get used to that.'

'I could get used to you.'

He kissed her nose. 'That's the whole idea. Come on, as much as I could stay here all night, I've spent the day shovelling chook shit and I'm starving.'

'Romantic.'

'That's me. Attractive, capable and romantic. And you—' he planted another kiss on her nose, '—are my sexy milkmaid angel.'

A detour via the shower meant it was another hour before Callie sat down to dinner, this time buzzing with pleasant exhaustion. With the tablecloth relegated to the laundry, they ate without it, sneaking hand holds like a pair of teenagers.

'Wal wants you to come round for dinner tomorrow night for an Amberton lamb roast.'

'We'll have to behave.'

'He probably wouldn't mind if we didn't. He's over the moon about us. Silly old bugger can't stop grinning. Reckons Maggie can rest easy now.'

Callie smiled, thinking of the photo of Wal and Nanna at the saleyards, the adoration in their gazes. 'They were lovers, did you know?'

'I suspected as much, the way he talked about her.' He squeezed Callie's hand. 'Bet they weren't as energetic as us.'

'Or as kinky. That thing you did against the dresser . . .' Her gaze drifted with the memory.

'Shit,' he said, putting down his fork. 'I need to take you to bed again.'

'Okay.'

To Callie's delight Matt stayed. She woke sometime in the deep night and lay watching him breathe, mesmerised by the gentle rise and fall of his body. Moonlight threaded a silvery beam through a gap in the curtains, the pure light blessing his skin. He might call her his angel but in the glow of night she knew that it was Matt that deserved the name.

She reached out to hover her hand over the place where the moonlight touched, and the beam caught her Hope tattoo. The colours lit up, the blue like lapis lazuli, the leaves, flowers and birds coming alive, swirling around the letters, embracing her sister's name. Gravel formed in Callie's throat, painful roughness she could never swallow away.

Movement shifted her attention. Her gaze met Matt's.

'Don't leave,' he whispered, taking her hand, his eyes glistening. 'That coat doesn't fit without you.'

Callie closed her eyes and tried not to cry.

Twenty

Callie checked the clock for what felt like the fiftieth time. She'd only been at work an hour and another five dragged ahead. Five long hours plus a few minutes' driving time and a shower to wash the pub smell from her skin, and she'd see Matt again.

'I'll do a run through the back,' she said to Doug, who nodded and continued his glass polishing.

Tuesdays were typically quiet. The Royal's usual collection of diehard punters lined the sports bar, turf guides snapping as they turned pages and reread forms and compared odds, gear changes and track ratings. Out the back, where Callie was heading, the bistro hosted only a table of five—young mothers, including Deb Graney, with babies in pushers, sipping the cappuccinos and lattes Callie had made them earlier.

'Any more coffees, ladies?' she asked the table, earning head shakes all round. Deb pushed her cup and saucer toward Callie, other arm holding a contentedly breastfeeding Jarrod. The twins were at Debbie's parents being spoiled silly.

'How are things out at Glenmore?' asked Deb with a sly smile.

'Good. Great.'

'Yes, I imagine they are with Matt hanging around all the time.'

'He's been a help.'

'I bet.'

Callie tried to remain cool in the face of Deb's teasing grin but it was hard when the other four women started discussing Matt and what a great catch he'd make. That Deb knew about Callie and Matt was hardly surprising given the family connection, but it still left her a little dismayed. She wasn't used to sharing her private life, and hearing her lover being dissected by a bunch of women she hardly knew was even more disconcerting.

'We'll have to have you both over for a barbecue soon.' Deb touched Jarrod's head as he shifted in her arm. 'And Wal now that he's back on his feet.' She smiled. 'Be nice to have a family get-together.'

A family get-together. That was a step Callie definitely wasn't ready for. How could she be when she was still working out her place in the world? Anna might believe love solved everything, but Callie's decisions encompassed more complex issues than whether to turn a fun shag into something permanent.

Keeping her doubts hidden, Callie gave a non-committal nod before gathering the dishes and carrying them behind the bar. Half an hour later, the women left, Deb pausing by the bar to tell Callie she'd be in touch about the barbecue, which did nothing to ease Callie's distraction.

Knock-off time ticked around. She barely registered the drive to Glenmore, her mind running over the past few weeks. Wal was home, Lyndall well on the way to recovery and regaining Morton, the house was almost cleaned out, and Callie had discovered a solution to her Honk issue. Painting the house's exterior was now just an excuse; with the sale of the second title, she could pay someone to do that. So why hadn't she made a decision?

After freeing Patch from the makeshift dog run she and Matt had constructed in the shade of the liquidambar, Callie trudged to the house, the pup's squirmy body soft in her arms. Holding the screen door open with one hand, she set him down. The pup exploded from her arm like a fluffy cannonball. Before she could order him to heel he was off, little claws scrabbling across the floor. Yipping with glee, he pinballed off the fridge and tore around the lino, racing toward the china cabinet.

'Patch!'

But the pup wasn't listening. He barged straight into the coiled laptop cord. Wire began to unravel, caught by his little legs. Powered by momentum and excitement, he kept coming. Callie leaped for the computer but it was already falling, dragging the crocheted doilies and Nanna's precious figurines and Beauty with it.

The laptop crashed to the floor but Callie barely registered the sound. All she could hear was the sharp clink of china breaking as first the toreador and then Beauty hit the lino.

Patch halted, panting, his mismatched eyes intent on Callie. She crouched by the ruins, a low, extended 'no' reverberating in her throat. Whining in alarm, Patch sank to his belly and edged to her side. She placed a hand on his head, knowing it wasn't the dog's fault. She shouldn't have stored the laptop on the china cabinet, but with Matt and her making love on every other kitchen surface, it had seemed safest.

A rough tongue tickled her palm. 'It's okay, Patchy-baby, it's okay.' But the words were more for herself than the pup.

The toreador's head had snapped off at the shoulders in what looked like a clean break. She shifted her gaze to Beauty. His broken near foreleg had been joined by a fractured hind hock. A little moan escaped as Callie suddenly realised which leg it was. Her chin dropped to her chest. She closed her eyes, wishing the sight away but it was locked as hard and fast as the memory of the first time she'd seen Beauty's in pieces.

Callie's phone buzzed. Patch licked her fingers and sat back on his haunches. She surveyed the mess again and tugged her mobile from her pocket with a leaden hand and glanced at the screen.

A message from Matt. *On your way?*

Callie was. But to where, she had no idea.

***

Wal's cane thudded across Amberton's kitchen floor as he headed toward Matt. Callie kept her gaze on the television. The screen flicked from a shocking railway level-crossing accident back to the newsreader as Wal's hoarse whisper filtered from the kitchen.

'What's wrong with the missy?'

Matt's reply was too low to work out, but she sensed his worried glance.

After a quick tidy and shower, she'd arrived at Amberton to an ardent welcome from Matt and a warm fug of delicious smells and homeliness. But instead of feeling content, Callie couldn't shake the crawly sense of foreboding that had affected her from the first moment she saw Beauty's broken leg. Emotions in turmoil, she'd retreated into the polite blankness that had held her in good stead all these years. To Matt and Wal's enquiries, tiredness came as an easy and valid excuse for lack of spark. Exhaustion caused by too much sex, work and paint scraping. Almost the truth but not quite.

And Matt hadn't believed her for a second.

Neither, it appeared, had Wal. He wasn't much of a talker but the man had spent a lifetime assessing the body language of animals. Callie's demeanour was barely a challenge.

A timer sounded, signalling Matt's roast was ready for carving. With a long breath, Callie left the safety of the lounge for the kitchen and Wal's shrewd gaze.

She touched him on the back as the old man fetched spuds from the oven. 'Anything I can do to help?'

'No, you just sit down, let us men sort it.'

'Matt?'

'You heard the boss,' he said, giving a long carving knife a last expert stroke down a sharpening steel.

Callie's smile was genuine when Matt placed an overloaded dinner plate in front of her. He'd gone to a lot of effort and the result looked and smelled delicious.

'Thanks. I haven't had a proper home-cooked roast in ages and this looks perfect.'

He squeezed her shoulder before serving Wal and then himself, finally settling down and pouring everyone a glass of cabernet merlot from the open bottle on the table.

To Callie's relief, conversation stayed on safe topics. Amberton, Dargate, the upcoming relocation of the pony club and the design of the town's proposed new library, which had divided the community. Though unable to summon much animation, Callie joined in the conversation as best she could, smiling at Matt as he occasionally reached across to touch her hand or back.

Meals finished, Callie ordered Wal out of the kitchen. 'You go sit down, we'll clean up.'

Wal winked. 'You two just want time alone, I know.'

'No, we just want to make sure you take it easy.'

'Nothing wrong with me, missy. Fit as a fiddle.'

'So that's why you walk with a cane, huh?'

Beaten, Wal hobbled from the room, leaving Matt and Callie grinning at one another.

'You shouldn't tease,' Matt said, squirting detergent into the sink.

'I know.' She leaned her hip against the bench, watching Wal's progress. 'He's all right though, isn't he? His hip's healing okay?'

'Yeah. Physio said he's making amazing progress, given his age.'

'That's good.' She nodded, eyes still on Wal. 'That's really good.'

Matt's hands stilled in the sudsy water. 'What's wrong, angel? You're not just tired. It's something else.'

She held his gaze, lips pressed tightly together, eyes wide to halt the onset of tears. The urge to tell him welled huge. Except she couldn't. There was nothing to tell. Not yet. Only a heavy weight in her chest that wouldn't shift. Callie shook her head and angled away.

He pulled a saucepan from the suds and rinsed it. 'My mum rang this morning. She's going to be in Perth this weekend. She wanted me to fly over.' He regarded her. 'I said I had important things going on here.'

'When was the last time you saw her?'

'Start of last year.' He shrugged. 'She's hard to catch up with.'

'You should go over.'

'I don't want to leave you.'

'I'm a big girl. I can cope on my own.'

He placed another pot in the sink. For a moment she thought he was going to say something then he resumed scrubbing.

She touched his arm. 'You should see her, Matt. She's your mum.'

'I know. I just get pissed off with her summoning me when it suits her. She knows how much I care about family and I hate the way she exploits that. But mostly I'm worried about you.'

'I'm fine, Matt.'

'So you keep saying.' He stared at the pot. 'I don't know what's worse. Knowing there's something wrong or that you don't trust me enough to tell me.'

They finished the dishes to the sound of the television and crackling unease.

'You'd make someone a good wife one day,' she said, when the last dish was stacked away, relieved when Matt played along with her clumsy attempt at reconciliation.

'I'm available for marriage, if you're interested.'

'I'm not the marrying kind.'

Matt grabbed her from behind, spinning her around and planting a noisy kiss on her neck. 'Live in lust then?' He pressed his mouth to her ear and dropped his voice to a whisper. 'You, me, sexy nurses' shoes. What a life.'

She rested her head against his chest. 'You make it sound so easy.'

Matt stroked her loose hair. 'It is easy, angel. If you let it.'

Callie said nothing for a long while, content in his hold. Finally she looked up. 'Will you come home with me?'

He kissed her forehead. 'I'll always come home with you.'

At Glenmore they made love in the creaking single bed. As though sensing her need for comfort, Matt indulged Callie everything. Hand in his, he led her to the centre of the room, where the setting sun glowed through the window and cast blazing streaks through his hair.

He undressed her with slow seduction, placing fluttery kisses on every scrap of skin, tracing lines over the dips and hollows of her body, until she stood naked and quivery, breath coming fast. Lifting her, mouths joined, her legs around his waist, Matt carried her to the bed and used his lips and tongue to pleasure her into exquisite ecstasy. Only when he'd reduced her to molten contentment did he undress himself and join her, skin to skin, teasing her with a love she couldn't find a way to accept.

She curled against him, dozing, her head to his chest, arms and hands wrapped against her body. Matt kept his arms protectively around her, his lips on her hair.

Sometime in the night, when the sun had fallen and moonlight streaked the room, she told him about Patch's accident—the laptop, the toreador and, in faltering words, Beauty. 'His leg, the hind one, it was the same one Hope broke when we were kids.' She plucked at the sheet. 'It's stupid, I know it is, but I can't help thinking it means something.'

'Angel, it was just an accident. You can't read anything into it. It was just one of those chance things. You want something with true meaning?' He took her palm and pressed it against his chest. 'I'll show you. This is where truth lies.' He covered her hand tightly with his own. 'I've told you before, I've learned what really matters in life. And it's not statues. It's what lives here.'

She smiled slightly. 'You know, for a man you're an incredible romantic.'

'Only when it comes to you.' Gaze riveted on hers, he lifted her hand and kissed her fingers. 'Now come here and let me show you my big, strong, masculine side.'

'I've seen it.'

'Not enough,' he said, nibbling his way up her arm. 'Definitely not enough.'

***

Callie woke feeling dispirited and, despite Matt's best efforts, still disturbed by the previous day's events. She wasn't one for superstition, nor was she religious, even horoscopes barely held her interest but, irrational as she knew it was, there was something unsettling about the the breakage—accidental or not—of both statuettes.

Matt took his time leaving, lingering over his cereal, toast and tea, touching her constantly, alert green eyes following every move. They'd made love in the shower, draining Glenmore of hot water again and forcing Callie to boil the kettle to wash the dishes. Matt stood behind as she washed, kissing her neck and whispering sexy nonsense in her ear.

'I'll come back at lunch,' he said, as she walked him to his ute.

A southerly had blown in overnight, bringing with it cool conditions and a sense of fading summer. Patch scampered and skidded over the crushed limestone yard, chasing tumbling leaves and yapping at the wind. Morton stood near the trough with his rump pointed south and his tail blown backward onto his hocks. The trees rustled as though whispering. Callie shivered and wished she'd donned a jumper.

Noticing, Matt draped an arm around her shoulders tugged her close to his side. 'Wal's got a few things he needs done but I'll see if I can sneak a few hours to help you with the house.'

'I don't know if I'll work on it. I was thinking of going fishing.'

'Bit cold.'

'I have jumpers.'

He wrapped his other arm across her front, enclosing her. 'Not as warm as my arms.'

'Nothing's as warm as your arms.'

They shared a smile as they walked the last few steps to the car.

'Angel, about last night—'

'I'm fine, Matt.' She held his gaze. 'It's all right.'

'I worry about you, that's all.'

'I know. You're an attractive capable man and a hopeless romantic who worries too much.'

'You forgot to mention my big, strong, masculine side.'

Callie pressed her nose against his. 'Okay, so you're an attractive capable man and hopeless romantic whose big strong masculine side is very, very—' she grinned at his raised eyebrows, '—masculine. Now go before you get into strife with Wal.'

Despite her order, Matt dallied and played around another ten minutes before departing. He kept dragging her close for kisses, sneaking his hands up her top, making her laugh with ridiculous promises of what he was going to do to her later. Finally he left, window down, arm out and fingers stretched as though wanting to hold her hand one last time. Callie cuddled Patch, using his paw to wave back.

The ute disappeared past the forest, its dust trail vaporising in the wind. She set Patch down and the pup took off once more across the yard, chasing shadows cast by clouds. Cold without Matt's warm touch, Callie crossed her arms around herself and inspected the sky. The clouds were low, most white but with a spattering of bruised types. The southerly's strength kept them scudding across the sky and it was unlikely she'd see more than a light shower. Nothing to prevent her going fishing. Not that the tide was right—that wouldn't be optimal until lunch time—but with her feet in the soggy sand, the tide's mesmeric lap and the loop and pull of the line to watch, Callie could clear her mind and let it drift.

She whistled for Patch, the smile she'd worn for Matt loosening as she walked back to the house. Why couldn't she shake this off feeling? It was an accident, nothing more and yet the symbolism of Beauty's broken leg continued to nag.

***

Three solid hours of being battered by wind and salt water brought Callie no closer to a decision about Glenmore. She hadn't really expected it to. The reality was, she didn't want to decide because the moment she did, she'd pay. Callie could do the right thing by Hope, her parents—even, in part, by herself—but doing so would dishonour Nanna and leave her own heart cleaved from the loss of Glenmore. As for Matt, leaving him didn't bear contemplating.

To her surprise, she'd bagged half-a-dozen good-sized King George whiting, making her choice to walk further along the bay to where a deep gutter formed between two reefs worthwhile. She'd cleaned the fish on the beach, wading out into the cool water to wash the blood and dangling entrails away while seagulls screeched and squabbled over the scraps, the birds rising and falling like breakers in the wake of Patch's galloping raids. The walk and catch had rekindled memories of her grandfather and summer days spent fishing in his company while Hope wandered off on one of her rambles along the forest trails and firebreaks.

Matt arrived at lunchtime as promised and as sexy mouthed and touchy as ever. Making up for future lost time, he called it. His mother had sent e-tickets through and he'd decided to make the trip to Perth after all. Life was too short to hold grudges, and for all her faults, Phoebe was still his mother.

Thanks to Matt's endless games, filleting the fish took far longer than usual. To keep him occupied, she set him to salad preparation while she dusted half the fillets lightly in flour and grilled them for lunch, the other half kept aside for Wal. With the wind still cool, she and Matt ate in the kitchen, Patch whining and scratching at the back door, the radio tuned to the Country Hour.

A stage set with all the ingredients of home, yet unlike their other days together, there was an air of falseness, as if her happiness was all an act, and now the play had to end.

Matt ducked off again mid-afternoon, leaving her to continue with the house, although Callie had no enthusiasm for the chore. In his absence her efforts were desultory, progress slow and more than once she wondered why she was bothering. Restless, she called for Patch and spent an hour and a half trailing around Glenmore, trudging to its farthest reaches, where the forest encroached and the land began its downward drift toward the river. She rested, watching Patch snuffle and duck cutely through the grass chasing mice and butterflies, his lithe puppy body twisting with excitement, tripping and tumbling with joy.

She arrived back at the house in time for Kate and Lyndall's visit, smiling as she watched Lyndall stride to the gate. Since Wal applied his magic, the teenager had blossomed, her confidence soaring as she reconnected with her horse. The way she walked, the brace of her shoulders and back, how easily she smiled—all pointed to a girl who had reclaimed a passion she'd thought lost. Whatever happened with Callie and Glenmore, Lyndall's transformation proved at least that her time here had some purpose.

'I've a present for you,' said Kate when Callie wandered over to the car. 'A little thank you gift for helping Lyndall and allowing us to visit Phantom.'

'You don't need to thank me, Kate. I wanted to help. And the truth is I need to find a home for the horse.'

'I don't care what your motives were, my daughter's a different girl because of you.' She opened the Range Rover's back door and reached inside, hauling out a poster-sized dark timber frame. Smiling, Kate balanced the frame on the toes of her trainers, its back facing Callie. 'And I've found a friend. So I'm going to say thanks whether you like it or not. Now,' she said, turning the frame around. 'This is for you. So you remember.'

Her fingers to her mouth, overwhelmed, Callie stared and stared.

The frame contained a collage of photos, each containing the heart-tugging image of a stumpy grey horse in various poses. Phan with his head held nobly, nostrils flared. Phan munching grass on Glenmore's back lawn, Honk watching warily in the background. Morton and Phan sharing a scratch, Phan too short to reach the taller horse's neck properly but trying anyway. Phan with his coat buffed to polished silver, his tail clean and silky. Phan with his eyes half closed in bliss as apple juice dribbled from his greedy lips.

There were also photos of Callie with Phan. Pictures she wasn't aware had been taken, bar one. In the centre of the frame was the one Callie knew of. It was her favourite, a photo that Matt had snapped on his phone of Callie, crouched, with her arms around her beloved horse's neck and her cheek pressed against his jowl. A broad grin split her face, her blue eyes vibrant from the sun and love, while Phan's sleepy eyes and half-curled muzzle suggested an almost comically smug expression.

'Oh, Kate,' said Callie, her eyes filling. 'It's beautiful.' Mindful of the frame, she embraced the other woman. 'Thank you. It's the most perfect gift.'

Kate returned her hug. 'I'm so glad. Lyndall was worried you'd be upset because you had to let him go again.'

'Not at all.' She released Kate to admire the pictures once more, stooping to trace her finger over Phan's face. 'It's wonderful. Really, really wonderful.'

Thanking Kate once more and admiring the photos as she walked, Callie carried the frame to the house, leaving it propped carefully against the water tank before joining Kate as she headed to the home paddock's gate.

'Do you like it?' asked Lyndall when they arrived within earshot.

'Love it,' replied Callie, ducking through the fence to give her a hug. 'It means a lot.'

She released Lyndall to give Morton a scratch. Callie hadn't spent much time with the horse since Lyndall had begun caring for him. Though his nose still appeared as if covered in some alien creature's droppings, Morton's sweet, gentle manner remained unchanged. Summer had curled the ends of his bay coat even further, giving it the colour of gold-shot taffeta. His combed mane and tail shone glossy black, his hooves slick with oil. Callie inspected his black-dipped legs, noting a sprinkling of tiny yellow bot fly eggs.

She knelt down to pick at them with her fingernail. The larvae that hatched from the eggs were revolting creatures, lodging and developing in the horse's mouth before being swallowed down where they attached to the stomach. 'Do you have a bot-knife?' she asked Lyndall.

'At home. I'll bring it tomorrow.' Lyndall knelt down to help.

'Callie?'

'Yes?'

'Will you give me a leg up?'

Callie ceased her picking. 'Sure. Do you want me to fetch a halter so I can hang onto him while you sit?'

Lyndall shook her head, her hand on Morton's upper foreleg. 'Mr Graney says trust goes both ways. Phan trusts me, I think. So I should trust him back.' She stroked his leg. 'I won't need a halter.'

The teenager took her time, smoothing her palm over Morton's coat, chattering to cover her nerves. Callie glanced at Kate, who remained behind the gate, watching, and debated whether to call her over. She decided against it. Lyndall needed to do this on her own.

Callie made a stirrup with her interlocked hands. 'Are you ready?'

Lyndall nodded, fists knotted in a hank of mane. As though sensing the importance of the moment, Morton kept his head up and didn't stir.

'Okay, one, two, three.'

On the third count, Lyndall vaulted onto Morton. She sat with both hands seized in his mane, legs clenched, teeth locked over her bottom lip.

'You're doing great,' said Callie, patting her thigh. 'Relax your leg. He's not going anywhere but if you keep too tight a hold he might take that as an aide to walk on.'

Giving Lyndall's loosened leg another pat, Callie walked to Morton's head, distracting the horse with ear tugs and forehead rubs to give Lyndall time to settle herself. Every now and then she threw a reassuring glance at Kate but the other woman didn't seem to need it. Her face fairly glowed with pride at Lyndall's achievement.

She stroked Morton's cheek. 'I can't believe how far you've come. Not so long ago you couldn't step within a metre of the gate, now look at you.'

'I know. I can't believe I was like that. It seems stupid now.' Lyndall ran her palm up Morton's mane. 'What you said, that first day I came here, about how you'd give him away to the right home. Do you still mean it?'

'I do.' Callie softened her gaze. 'He's your horse, Lyndall. He always was. In fact, I'd love for you to take him back home today, but it's not my choice. That's something you need to talk over with your mum and dad.'

Lyndall's head dropped. 'Dad's still not sure.'

'Then you'll just have to convince him otherwise.' Callie smiled. 'I wouldn't worry. You have your mum on your side and from what I know of her, when it comes to looking after you, she's a pretty tough nut.'

They stayed in the paddock half an hour longer, Callie traipsing winding paths through the long grass, encouraging Morton to follow with Lyndall on his back. The horse, as they'd both expected, behaved impeccably. By the time Lyndall slid off her cheeks were flushed and her confident walk had almost become a swagger.

In a better mood than she'd been all day, and deciding she should make up for her lax afternoon with some paint scraping, Callie gave Kate and Lyndall a last thank you hug and left them at the gate, stuffing Morton with carrots. She sauntered to where she'd left the frame, raising it up and balancing it on her knee so she could feast again on her beloved horse. She was still picking through the photos, smiling at Phan's expressions, when the Range Rover's engine started. The horse could pull the goofiest faces and there was always a hint of mischief in his gorgeous brown eyes. He and Patch, with their naughty playfulness, would have made great friends.

As she looked up for her puppy, she heard two quick thumps, like sacks being dropped. The engine noise ceased. Car doors opened, then a sharp cry.

Frigid horror washed through Callie. Her eyes darted around, hunting for Patch, but the only animal they located was Honk. She wanted to call for her puppy, watch him streak across the grass and bounce into her arms, pink tongue flopping and mismatched eyes alive with delight, but the call stayed inside, blocked by a whimper.

With exaggerated care, she placed the frame against the house wall and, letting icy numbness settle in her chest, turned on stilted legs down the concrete path toward the yard.

Kate appeared at the end, her face stricken. 'I didn't see him, I swear. I didn't know he was there.'

'It's okay,' Callie replied, her voice sounding strange, as though it was a dream person speaking instead of her. 'It's not your fault. I forgot to call for him.'

She crossed the yard to where Patch's motionless body lay. Lyndall crouched nearby with her hand on his rump, tears staining her cheeks. The breeze ruffled his fluffy black-and-white coat. If not for the blood leaking from his nostrils and staining the grey limestone, Patch could be asleep in the sun.

Callie knelt by his head and stroked his silky fur, holding her hand over his chest in the hope of a breath or heartbeat, but she felt nothing. His glazed eyes had already revealed the truth. The Range Rover was a heavy vehicle; his body soft and fragile. From the first crush there'd been no hope.

Though she wanted to bawl and howl, Callie's eyes refused to moisten. The dull lump around her heart sucked all emotion except resignation. This was the price for not heeding the first sign. Fate had tried to steer her toward the right path but she'd lacked the courage to take it.

'He's dead,' she said, unnecessarily confirming what they all knew. 'I'll have to bury him.'

'We'll help.'

She shook her head and, noticing Kate wringing her hands, straightened to rub the distraught woman's upper arm. 'It's okay. It wasn't your fault.'

'I didn't think to look!'

'Please don't blame yourself. It was an accident. One of those things.' She turned to Lyndall. 'Are you all right?' The teenager nodded, although her face was as pale as her mother's. Callie focused again on Kate. 'Will you be okay to drive home? You've both had a bit of a shock.'

'I shouldn't leave you.'

'I'm fine, Kate, really. And Matt will be here any minute.'

'Are you sure?'

'I'm sure.' Callie squeezed her arm. 'Go on. Look after Lyndall.'

Though reluctant, and continually casting Callie puzzled looks as if confused by her calm, the Sorianos finally departed, Kate hunched over the wheel like an old woman.

As soon as the car was out of sight, Callie set to work with the burial. She wasn't going to wait for Matt and his sympathy. She didn't want him to see the fear she could barely contain—or her resignation. He'd only start trying to reassure her again.

But she knew. Oh, how she knew.

The time for prevarication was over.

Twenty-one

Callie buried Patch out of sight in the tough dirt behind the machinery shed with nothing to mark his grave. Though she'd raised a hefty sweat digging, the bone chill remained. Her back teeth ached from the tight clench of her jaw, and her cheeks stung with windburn from the morning's fishing expedition. Even her muscles, which should have been loose from exertion, felt stiff. She couldn't stop looking over her shoulder—at the yard, paddocks and forest—as if she feared fate had turned human and stalked the landscape. Each time she saw nothing, but her ears didn't miss the sad whistle of tree whispers and wind.

On her return to the house she discovered two texts: the first was from Anna, asking when she was next free to Skype; the second, her voicemail, which led to a message from her father, asking how she was, wanting her to call. Callie dumped the phone back on the table, messages unanswered. She wasn't in the mood to talk to anyone, not even Matt, but any moment he'd land on her doorstep with his sexy smile and wandering hands and she had to be prepared. Lack of courage meant she'd stretched this too far, and made a difficult situation so confused every solution seemed wrong. No longer. Tomorrow she would decide once and for all and act, and as selfish as it was, she wanted one last night of happiness with him. One last night imagining what her life could be like if the world turned differently.

And deep down, where her heart beat strongest with longing, Callie wanted him to sway her. To wrap her in that coat and fill her so full of his warmth that it cancelled all the cold and doubt. She wanted to wake tomorrow loaded with the strength to say that the right path was the one where she walked with peace and love instead of guilt.

She halted by the china cabinet where the broken statuettes lay cushioned in tissue. Poor Beauty with his broken legs and chipped coat. The once proudly strutting toreador with his snapped off head. Picking up Beauty, Callie fiddled with fitting the pieces back, somehow hopeful that, like her and Matt, he could be saved. But the damage was too great and her heart was too sore. She didn't want either statuette now anyway. Their message hurt too much.

She gathered the pieces with shaky hands, folded the tissue around the statuettes' ruined bodies, and took them to the bin, kicking the lid up with her foot. For a heartbeat she hesitated, then she clenched her teeth and opened her palms. The clunk as they hit the bottom sent a shiver along her back. Jaw still tight, Callie closed the lid and headed for the shower.

Two minutes later, naked and frantic, Callie raced back into the kitchen and exhumed the bodies, releasing a long, relieved breath when unwrapping the tissue revealed no further damage.

Things might be looking bleak but she wasn't ready to lose hope yet.

***

'Where's Patch?' asked Matt, frowning at the door.

Callie stopped stirring the pasta sauce she had simmering and wiped her hands on a tea towel. Of course he'd noticed Patch's absence, she was stupid to think he wouldn't. The puppy was always scratching at the back door, whining to come in and play. Tonight there was only wind.

She leaned her back against the sink, fingers curled hard around the steel edge. 'There was an accident. My fault. I forgot to call for him when Kate and Lyndall were leaving. He must have been chasing a butterfly or something and didn't see the car. By the time I reached him, he was already gone.'

'Oh, angel.' He crossed the room to hold her. 'Are you all right?'

She nodded into his chest. 'Bit upset.'

'I can imagine.' He cupped her face and studied her expression, and his honest worry made tears prick. 'You know it doesn't mean anything.'

'I know.'

'You sure?'

'It was an accident, Matt.' Callie struggled to hold his gaze but she had to. A lie was less hurtful than her real feelings and her future wasn't set in stone yet. She could still decide to stay. 'I'm more worried about Kate. Poor thing was beside herself and for it to happen after she'd given me the Phan collage was really unfair. She and Lyndall were so happy I liked it.' She twisted her head to kiss his palm. 'I need to put the water on for the pasta.'

'Where is he? I'll go bury him while you finish.'

'I've already done it.'

'Fucking hell, Callie, you should have waited.'

She lit the gas for the water and concentrated on stirring the sauce, her back to him.

'What for? I'm not that squeamish.'

'It's not about being squeamish.' He wrapped arms around her belly and pressed his lips to her neck. 'In case you hadn't noticed I want to look after you. Makes me feel manly.'

'You've already proven your manliness.' Relieved to be on safer ground she curled in his arms until she faced him. 'Multiple times.'

She played with the bottom button of his polo shirt, her favourite green one that matched his eyes. During their first few meetings he hadn't cared how he appeared—torn clothes, unshaven, grease, sweat and dirt crusted—now he always took care. Matt Hawkins was a man who didn't need to tell her how he felt. He showed it in everything he did.

Tugging on the button, Callie presented him with one of her seductive looks. 'You could prove it again if you liked.'

'What about dinner?'

'I can put the pasta on to cook or you can take me to bed. I guess it all depends on what you're hungrier for.'

He answered as she'd hoped—by reaching behind her, turning off the gas and, clasping her hand firmly, marching her straight to the bedroom.

An hour later Callie led Matt back out, fingers loosely joined with his.

He'd been gentle and loving, letting her escape, just for a while, the sadness and worry that had settled like a leaden raincloud on her life.

A dawdling summer sunset cast the kitchen in a glorious orange glow. Elvis glittered above the sink. Even the lino sparkled, and for a few beats, Callie had the fanciful notion Glenmore was calling her. That this moment, this spangled beauty, was its way of asking her to think again, to look hard at what she would be giving up. A glance at the china cabinet and Beauty's broken body culled the idea from her mind.

Except, as she caught Matt's loving gaze and the way the light framed his hair like a golden halo, a glimmer of optimism remained.

'Why don't we crack that champagne?' she said and then frowned. 'Or is that too weird after what happened today?'

Matt was already opening the fridge. 'Not weird. Call it celebrating his life.' He extracted the bottle and returned to her side, kissing her temple before opening an overhead cupboard and retrieving some wine glasses which he regarded dubiously. He shrugged and placed them on the bench. 'They'll do.'

Callie glanced out the window. Toward the east, the forest blazed with rays from the setting sun. Long shadows from the house, water tank, shed and liquidambar stretched toward the paddocks as though reaching to snatch the last warmth from the day. Yearning gripped and tugged. How could she leave this place, with all its memories?

Except memory was the very thing demanding she leave.

She plucked the glasses from the bench. 'Let's drink it outside.'

'You'll be cold.'

'I have you to keep me warm.'

Matt moved the chairs from the liquidambar's shade to the western wall of the house so they could make the most of the dying sun, placing the arms so close they touched. A small thing but an act that made her yearning tug even harder. It was the little things Matt did that made him the man he was. The way he cared and acted selflessly, even in bed when she teased him to straining point.

'I'm the barmaid,' she said, attempting to take the bottle from him.

He swung it out of her reach. 'All the more reason for me to do it.

Everyone's entitled to a break, even barmaids who wear hot nurses' shoes.'

The cork released with a satisfying pop. Callie held the glasses as Matt poured, loving the way the sun turned the hairs on his arms coppery.

'What are you smiling about?' he asked, setting the bottle on the concrete path and sitting down.

Callie passed him a glass. 'You.'

'That's all right then. For a moment I thought you were laughing at my technique.' He pressed his glass against hers. 'To Patch. He was a good dog.'

Callie swallowed, and forced herself to act unconcerned when the mention of Patch's name brought the afternoon's despair back. 'Patch.' Toast and champagne sip over, Callie sat back to stare across the lawn, trying not to think of Patch's wriggly soft body and happy gaze. 'I suppose I should call in on Wal tomorrow and tell him.'

'I will if you like.' Matt reached for her hand and squeezed. 'Don't stress. He's been around a long time. He knows stuff like this happens.'

She remained quiet, content to watch the changing colours of the land and absorb its sounds and smells. The air was loud with bird clamour as they settled for the night and the whirs of insects on the hunt for a mate. Pasture and forest scents mingled, occasionally spiced with the smell of horse dung and Honk's enclosure.

As if on cue, the goose sauntered around the corner of the house and across the lawn, releasing a churlish trumpet as he passed in unsubtle reminder that this was his territory. Callie followed his progress with a small smile. In one way, the goose was the cause of all this. Without Honk she would have been long gone but the goose and his cranky ambushes had started something. Love, thanks to a mad goose. Hope would have laughed herself stupid over that. Instead of sadness, the idea felt somehow warming.

She turned to Matt. 'Let's go inside. I want to eat and then I want to do things to you.'

'Things?'

'Yes. Lots of things.'

He rose and tucked the champagne bottle carefully under his arm so he could keep hold of her his glass as well as her hand. 'I love it when you talk dirty.'

***

Despite exhaustion, Callie couldn't sleep. She laid awake listening to Matt's breathing, his occasional mutters, the sound of his closeness. No matter which way he slept, he always seemed to be holding her. A palm on her hip or below her breast, his fingers tangled in hers. She loved it most when he curled over her, stubbled chin digging pleasantly into her collarbone, his arm across her chest and his heart beating strongly against her back.

With the curtains closed, only a sliver of light entered the room and she had to stare closely to make out the handsome profile of his face, marred by a scar that she'd grown so used to that she barely noticed it.

He woke early, stretching noisily before rolling over to kiss her.

'Good morning, angel.'

'Good morning, attractive, capable man.'

He studied her for a moment. 'Bad night's sleep?'

'Not as good as yours. You were like a snuffly baby.'

Smiling lazily, he curved a hand around her breast. 'That's because I had something warm and soft to cuddle up to.'

'I had something hard.'

The lazy smile widened to a provocative grin. 'And getting harder.'

Callie broke into giggles as he tickled and teased her into liquid excitement until passion took over. She closed her eyes as their bodies joined, holding him with a ferocity that bordered on desperation.

'Fuck,' he panted, as Callie arched beneath him, fingers digging deep into his flexed bum. She stayed that way until the last of her trembles subsided, lids hooded as she sank back into the mattress. Matt rested a moment before kissing his way to her mouth and pressed his forehead against hers, eyes gleaming. 'And you wonder why I can't get enough of you.'

She traced a finger over the muscles of his back. 'I thought you cared more about love than sex.'

'That wasn't just sex.' He kissed her nose and rolled aside to cradle her close. 'What are you up to today?'

She snuggled against him. 'I need to go into town. Sort a few things. Then work, I suppose.'

'I'm going to miss you.'

'You're only away one night.'

'Ah, but that's one night with you I'll never make up.'

As they embraced and snuggled, a new day bloomed across the room, threading through the curtains and illuminating the weave of their bodies around the sheets and each other. Callie fixed on the creeping light, willing it to stop, but its path remained inexorable. Dawn touched his arm, his shoulder, his neck and face before sliding across to burnish her own skin. Callie closed her eyes against its bright hurt and rested her head on Matt's chest. She had to accept it now. The night was over.

Decision day was here.

'Matt?'

'Yes, angel?'

But she couldn't find the words. She wasn't sure which ones were the truth.

When she remained silent, Matt tucked his finger under her chin and tilted her head so he could see her face. For a long moment he studied her, then a smile began to tug. His gaze softened as though he could hear the silent words in her head, the 'I love you' she wanted to say but couldn't. Slowly, he bent to kiss her.

Something powerful and elemental swamped Callie. An inner strength that had been there all along, hidden below her need for penance and the irrational idea that her life wasn't her own to enjoy. An inner strength now fortified by that most special of human emotions.

And for the first time since her arrival at Glenmore, Callie knew that the choice she made today would be the right one.

Twenty-two

Dargate was bustling with pay-day shoppers by the time Callie arrived in town. Thursday was sale day at the livestock exchange, and utes and four-wheel drives hogged the parking spaces along Patterson Street. Farmers sauntered the footpaths, peering in shop windows with their fingers tucked into their pockets, creating knots in the pedestrian flow as they caught up with friends and acquaintances. Callie smiled at them as she strode up Patterson Street toward her bank. Every one of them reminded her of Matt, their wives a future she could reach for.

'Callie!'

Callie looked up to find Deb Graney pushing a stroller rapidly toward her, one hand on the handle, the other linked to her skipping, mop-haired girls. She smiled as Deb halted in front of her, pinked-cheeked and puffing, palms on the heads of the twins as they settled in by her sides.

'Hey, Deb. How's things?' Callie crouched down to the twins. 'How's that puppy of yours?'

'In big trouble,' said Deb as Callie straightened. 'He keeps digging holes in the lawn. Anthony's going mad.'

'He'll grow out of it.'

'Who? Anthony or the pup?' They shared a grin until suddenly Deb's good humour faltered. She glanced around with a pensive expression, a hand returning to the stroller's rubber handle and twisting it. 'Listen, do you have a minute? I really need to talk to you.'

'Bit tricky right now. I have to get to the bank and then work.'

Deb touched her arm lightly. 'It's about Matt Hawkins.'

The way Deb said his name, the way she regarded her, had Callie's stomach knotting, and she experienced an infantile urge to slap her hands over her ears. Instead she settled her expression into polite enquiry.

'What about Matt?'

Deb glanced around and frowned. Patterson Street's footpath wasn't wide and they'd halted in front of a souvenir shop with display racks of postcards out the front. Pedestrian traffic snarled around them. 'Look, I really don't want to do this here. Come around the corner.'

Callie didn't want to do this either, whatever this was. Her good mood was already evaporating. She pointed past the newsagent's. 'I really need to get to the bank.'

'Please. This is important.'

An unpleasant sense of prescience told Callie to refuse and walk away, but Deb remained insistent. She trailed Deb and the girls as they pushed through to the back street carpark, halting in the sparse shade of a red flowering bottlebrush on a concrete bay at the perimeter. Heat from the surrounding asphalt and cars wove around their bodies.

'What is it, Deb? I really don't have long.' Callie pulled her phone from her pocket and deliberately checked the time.

Deb's fists tightened around the handles of the pusher as though priming herself. 'I know this is none of my business and Anthony said not to say anything, but what he's doing isn't fair.'

'What are you talking about?'

'Matt.'

Alarm rattled Callie's insides. 'What about Matt?'

'He made a deal with Wal. For Amberton. Anthony and I only learned of it yesterday. I know a lot of the staff and patients at the hospital.' She spoke in staccato bursts. 'I bumped into Sally McPherson. We got talking about Wal and she told me what she heard. I didn't believe her but she said Arthur Metcalf heard it too. I rang Anthony and he said to check. So I did. Arthur confirmed it and he has no reason to lie. He's too close to death for games.'

Callie shook her head in confusion. 'Arthur confirmed what?'

Deep sympathy darkened Deb's eyes. 'The deal Wal made with Matt. That if he kept you at Glenmore like Maggie wanted, Wal would leave him Amberton.'

Callie swayed and Deb grabbed her arm.

'I'm so sorry. I didn't think he was like that either, I really didn't, but owning a farm here is his dream. He's made no secret of that.'

'No,' said Callie faintly. 'He hasn't.'

'I'm really sorry. Anthony told me to keep out of it but the moment I saw you in the street I knew I couldn't. It's too unfair.' Deb peered at her. 'Are you okay? Do you need to sit down?'

'No.' Callie cleared her thick throat. 'No, I'm fine. Look, I really have to go.'

Deb appeared on the verge of tears. 'I'm so sorry. I really thought he wasn't like that.'

Although her skin felt so icy any movement might crack it, Callie forced a stoic smile. 'Neither did I. But you did the right thing, telling me.' She glanced at the twins. 'You'd better get the girls into some shade and I'd better get to the bank.'

'Callie?'

'It's okay, Deb. You did the right thing. I'll see you.'

She strode away, determined to show nothing was wrong. Callie was good at this. She'd done it for years, holding her mouth just so, her shoulders and back straight, striding confidently and carefree when inside she was near collapse.

Confusion churned. This wasn't the Matt she knew. Nor was this the kind of mean scheme she'd expect from Wal. He might be gruff and liked to get his own way, but he wasn't cruel. But both of them also possessed strong desires. Matt to own his own farm, have a family, capture what he believed really mattered in life; Wal to fulfil his promise to Nanna.

Powerful desires, no question, but enough to do this?

Forgoing the bank, Callie walked back up Patterson Street to her car, legs like concrete blocks. She climbed stiffly behind the wheel and stared blankly at the tail-lights of the car parked in front.

She'd been searching for signs since her arrival. How ironic that on the morning she'd decided to believe in herself, another had appeared. The fire, Beauty and the toreador, poor darling Patch and now this. All signs in a sequence of many; omens that she would never find happiness at Glenmore. Except the last sign couldn't be true. It just couldn't.

How convenient that Matt was on his way to Perth. Callie couldn't even confront him. But she could talk to Wal. And if what Deb revealed was true, then the world really had signalled its imperative. And this time, no prevarication, no doubts, Callie would obey its call.

***

Callie pulled up near the house and quickly alighted. A high-pitched yap revealed Wal's location. Dolly's pup—now christened Dash—guarded the front verandah step, yapping madly, its fuzzy, soft body rocking with ecstatic welcome. Her step faltered as memories of Patch and his happy bark crowded her mind. She thrust them away, determined to get this done.

Dash bunted her legs as she knocked on the screen door and yanked it open. She let him inside and followed his trail to the kitchen. Wal looked up from his papers and steaming cup of tea to regard her before frowning at the dog.

Callie planted her feet and set her hands to her hips. 'Did you make a deal with Matt over Amberton?'

'What?'

'You. Matt. Amberton. He convinces me to stay and you leave it to him. Well? Did you?'

'Yes, but . . .' Wal's brow lowered, mouth disappearing in a maze of wrinkles. 'Who's been telling stories?'

Callie didn't reply. She had her answer. Now there was work to do. Throwing him a last, filth-laden look, she stalked out of the kitchen, leaving behind the sound of Wal's chair scraping across the lino.

'Don't you turn your back on me, missy! Don't you dare!'

Callie slammed the screen door shut and kept walking.

'He's a good lad!' Wal's cane thumped across the timber. He yanked open the door. 'You dump him and you'll be no better than your sister!'

She spun around. 'What?'

'She didn't know a good bloke when she had one either. The lad loved her and all she did was spit in his face.'

Matt and Hope? Impossible. Except it wasn't, and she knew it. He'd called her Supercallie.

The pain in her chest worsened. Her sister. Always her sister. The person who everyone Callie loved wanted her to be. And now even Glenmore had joined the chorus.

Well, it and everything else could go to hell. At least in Airlie people accepted her for who she was.

Wal stretched an arm out. 'Come inside. Have a cuppa and we'll get this sorted properly.'

Callie shook her head. 'I have work to do.'

Back like iron, she walked to the car, leaving Wal leaning on his cane, frowning and sucking in his mouth.

At the end of Amberton's lane she braked, leaving the car to idle as she fumbled for her phone and scrolled through her contacts. Finding Tony's number, she hit connect. The receptionist put her straight through.

Tony's voice was polite but wary. 'Callie, how are you?'

'Fine, thanks. Look, Tony, I want you to list Glenmore.'

'Maybe you should wait a few days. Deb just called me and—'

'On the market today, Tony. I want it sold.'

'Callie, please, I know this business with Matt is upsetting—'

'This has nothing to do with Matt. This is about me. Understand? Me. I want that property sold. Today if possible. You must have contacts?'

'I do,' he said, tone now business-like, much to Callie's relief. She wanted his real estate expertise, not his personal advice. 'I've already sounded a few people out about Glenmore, suggesting it might come on the market. They certainly made all the right noises, and only last Monday we had an enquiry from a person interested in purchasing a property just like it.'

'Call them all. Get an offer. I'll be around in half an hour to sign the sales authority.'

She hung up then placed another rapid call to Doug, citing a family emergency as the reason for cancelling her shifts until further notice. Throwing the phone on the passenger seat, she put the car into drive and skidded off in a hail of stones toward Glenmore. A few clothes and toiletries, the animals cared for, and she'd be away.

Thirty-five minutes later she was in Tony's office, ignoring his worried looks as she double-checked the sales authority. Several times he'd tried to talk to her and each time she cut him short with a cold stare or curt response. She was like a robot. No feelings, no expression. Existing only to get this done.

'This affects us too, you know,' he said. 'What Wal does with Amberton.'

'Then I'm sure you'll have a great deal to discuss with him.'

'I do. Look,' he said, clasping his hands and leaning forward, 'I'm aware of Sally's and Arthur's claims, and I know Deb believes that neither has a reason to lie, but you know what this place is like. Maybe they misunderstood. Wal has his faults but this?' Tony shook his head. 'He mightn't care much about me but I know he cares about the kids, and it'd be them he'd be cheating if this went ahead.'

'I checked with Wal. The deal's real. He admitted it.' She shoved the paperwork his way and stood. 'Call me when you have an offer.'

Business complete, she strode back out to her car. A hastily packed overnight bag sat in the ute's tray. She'd wanted to clear up properly but that would have taken too much time. The compulsion to face her parents over-rode her desire to pack and bolt, so she'd left the rest of her things at Glenmore, the back door locked for the first time since her arrival. After an infuriating chase, she'd hunted a loudly protesting Honk into his run, leaving him well stocked with water and enough prepared feed to last a couple of days. Morton scored a quick once-over, his trough the same. Satisfied the animals would survive her absence, she'd left, not once looking back.

Just as she wouldn't look back now.

Forty kilometres from Dargate, where the winding forest road reconnected with the Princes Highway, Callie called her father.

'Callie, honey. Thank god. I've been so worried. You didn't return my call. Is everything okay?'

'It's fine, Dad. In fact, I'm on my way to see you.'

'You're coming home?'

'Just for tonight.'

'That's great. Really great. Your mum will be thrilled.'

The comment left Callie feeling even more hollow. Her mum's visit to Glenmore had revealed all too poignantly how much Jacqueline Reynolds still agonised for Hope.

'So when can we expect you?'

'Later this afternoon. I'm not even at Heywood yet, so I'll be at least four hours, probably more by the time I get across town.'

'We'll be here. I'll fire up the barbie and burn some sausages. Get Jacq to make a couple of salads. Sit outside on the verandah like we used to.'

'Sounds good.'

And perhaps it would be for a while, but after dinner they were going to have that talk her father wanted. Clear all the muck out before it clogged their lives any further.

'Drive safe, honey.'

'I will.'

Callie hung up and turned on the radio, tuning into a local commercial station and its mind-sapping programming of adverts, banter and easy-listening music. Determinedly flushing Matt from her mind each time he crept into her thoughts, she zoned out to the rumble of the road and radio noise until, on the outskirts of Port Fairy, her phone buzzed. After checking the screen, she pulled over.

'Tony.'

'We have an offer. A reasonable one, but if that's their starting point I imagine we can push for more, especially once the others I've spoken to come back.'

'Take it.'

'Don't you want to know what it is first?'

'Fine. What is it?'

He relayed a figure that made her breath catch. 'But given their interest I think we can get more.'

'Didn't you hear me? I said take it.'

Tony didn't like it and said so, but the commission on a property of Glenmore's value was a powerful persuader. He argued then capitulated, as she knew he would. Twenty minutes later it was over.

Only when Callie passed through the new housing developments of Melbourne's far western suburbs did her stomach begin to roil. Where once cattle and sheep grazed, houses and bitumen ate into the land, stealing it block by block in a massive sprawl of endless roofs, tiny backyards and clothes lines. They weren't Dargate's hobby farms but the result was the same. A fate soon to be shared by Glenmore.

'What have I done?' Callie whispered, her nausea rising as the housing sea sprawled and rolled to the left and right. Exactly what she should have done from the start, that's what she'd done. The right thing. For Hope, for her parents, for her.

She had to believe that.

Because to countenance anything else would destroy every remaining scrap of self-regard she had left.

Twenty-three

Phoebe Hawkins didn't stuff around when it came to accommodation. Although this was Perth, where a man wearing work clothes and coated in rust-coloured dirt could be a billionaire, Matt couldn't help feeling self-conscious when he approached the Sanctum's front desk. The boutique hotel's receptionist didn't blink at his casual attire and ragged backpack. She simply checked him in before politely indicating the way to the business centre where his mother waited.

He checked his watch and mobile for the umpteenth time and compared them. Quarter past six Perth time, which meant nine fifteen Victorian time. Callie should have been home.

He dialled again, and again the call went straight through to voicemail. 'Me again. Can you call? I'm worried.' He hesitated then went on. 'I love you.'

He hung up, feeling dumb. Doug had probably offered her an extra shift. He was stressing over nothing, but that didn't stop the churning apprehension that had settled in his stomach since landing, when he'd turned his phone back on and found not a single missed call or message from Callie.

The lift's lurch did nothing to ease his anxiety. He thought again of the weird phone conversation he'd had with Wal during his Adelaide stopover. If nothing was wrong, why had Wal called to ask if Matt had spoken to Callie? It wasn't like him to chase up like that. As if Matt didn't have enough uncertainty prickling his back, Wal's mutter about having to go into Dargate to talk to Tony only made the prickles spread further. By the time he'd hung up, Matt was so full of worry he'd thought about cancelling the entire trip, but with one flight a day between Dargate and Adelaide he'd had no choice but to stick to schedule.

The lift doors slid quietly open. Matt followed the plush, immaculately carpeted hallway to the Hancock Room, where he'd been told Phoebe was working, and knocked. When no one came to the door he pushed it open anyway and found his mother at the back of the room, a laptop open in front of her and a mobile phone pressed to her ear. She glanced up, waved him inside, and went straight back to what she was doing—talking in Mandarin while tapping a pen against a notepad.

After dumping his backpack on one of the black leather chairs, Matt made his way around the jarrah meeting table and planted a dutiful kiss on his mother's cheek. She looked up and quirked her mouth before nodding at whoever was on the phone. It was a look he recognised all too well from childhood, when he'd walk in, heart leaping with hope that today would be the day she dropped everything and smiled just for him. Except that day never happened and never would. He'd learned not to mind but today her distraction irritated.

'Mum?'

Green eyes flashing, she frowned and sliced her hand through the air, continuing the conversation.

Matt checked his watch again. Six twenty-three and still no call, no text, no nothing from Callie. He strode to the window and stared out. Past Perth's verdant parkland, the city sprawled like a Lego set. Heat shimmer rose from a landscape made entirely of angles, making him long for the soft, calm edges of home. What the fuck was he doing here? He hated it. This concrete, heartless mess that pulsed money. He wanted Callie and Glenmore. He wanted what mattered. Lost in worry, Matt didn't notice his mother had stopped talking until she said his name.

'Matthew,' she said, rising from her chair and approaching. 'You're looking very rural.' She hugged him in that uncomfortable way she had, as if she didn't know where her arms and body belonged.

Now she'd returned to her version of a normal person, he studied her. Despite cool green eyes and symmetrical features, she was more nice-looking than beautiful, but it was her elegance that made passers-by look twice. Phoebe was tall, almost Matt's height, and slim with it, her figure accentuated by expertly tailored clothes. Her blunt cut, shoulder-length hair hung silky and straight. Thin, shaped eyebrows widened her eyes, her long, pointed nose lengthening her face. A severe mouth was disguised with lip liner and lipstick. The only frivolity appeared to be a platinum and diamond drop necklace, but even that, nestled against her pale skin in the V of her jade-coloured silk blouse, appeared as classy as the rest of her.

Wal's sisters once described Phoebe Hawkins as being like an old movie star except they hadn't meant it as a flattering comparison. She was, they agreed, lovely to look at but her ambition destroyed all warmth. They were right, but that didn't stop Matt loving her. For all Phoebe's frailties, she was still his mother.

'And you're looking very bankery.' He held her at arm's length. 'But I mean that in the best way.'

'You always were excellent at stating the obvious.' She glanced over her shoulder at the computer as it made a pinging noise. 'Ah, that's probably your father. We've been having quite a conversation.'

His mum and Kieran in conversation? Now that was something new.

'How is he?'

Her mouth tipped a little. 'Rather furious with me at the moment.'

'Don't tell me you've beaten him to some major deal?'

'Not quite.' She held out her arm, indicating a seat, as if he was a client instead of her son. 'Best get settled.'

Matt waited for his mother to reveal more but she merely took her seat and turned the computer toward her, mouth quirk heightening as she clicked and read. Matt studied her, his confusion growing. It wasn't like Phoebe to play games, she was always business like. The only moment of foolery she'd ever had—that Matt believed—occurred the night she and Kieran had sex.

The enigmatic expression stayed as she clicked the mouse, making her appear young and very pretty, like the girl she must have once been before ambition steeled her edges. Finally she closed the laptop lid and folded her hands in her lap.

'All right, Mum. What's going on? The last time I saw you look this smug was the night you signed Mr Zhao as a client.'

'Do I really look that pleased?'

'You do.'

She smiled again. 'Well, I have organised something special. And, I must say, with perfect timing. It's rather pleasing to be able to tell you this in person.'

'Tell me what in person?' said Matt, unable to stop impatience from entering his tone. He loved his mother but right now he wanted to be back at Glenmore, with Callie, not watching her gloat over some business deal in a posh hotel.

'Your father and I have bought you a property.'

Matt blinked, unsure if he'd heard correctly. A property? Did she mean a farm?

Phoebe smiled. 'You were never going to get one on your own and your father owed you. And I owed you too.'

'You don't. Neither of you do. I'm doing okay on my own.'

'Living with Uncle Wal?' She shook her head before sitting up very straight and regarding him steadily. 'Look, we—Kieran and I—both appreciate we haven't been the ideal parents—'

Matt pushed his chair back, cutting her off. He stood, running his hand over his face. He was here, away from Callie, because his parents, after twenty-six-plus years, had decided to go on some bizarre guilt trip? 'This is nuts.'

'Not quite the reaction I expected.'

'I'm sorry but . . .' Matt breathed out hard. If only Callie would call, he might be able to think clearly. He forced himself to sit back down. 'Okay, let me get this straight. You and Kieran bought me a property—a farm, I take it—to make up for—' he raised his hands and eyes to the ceiling, '—fuck knows what. And I'm grateful, I am, but you didn't have to. I can make my own way.'

Phoebe tapped a manicured nail against the laptop lid, assessing him steadily, cool businesswoman once more. 'It's a commercial decision as well. If you fail, the land has excellent development potential. You'll be secure either way, as will our investment. As it stands, you own fifty-one per cent of MPK Holdings. Kieran and I own the remaining forty-nine per cent, split twenty-five per cent my way, twenty-four to your father. That way, should he change his mind—which he'd better not—he can't pull it out from under your feet.'

Matt let his hands flop between his legs, wondering why he felt so upset when his parents had effectively handed him his dream. 'Okay, so where is this property?'

'The perfect place. Right next door to Uncle Wal's.'

The tamped-down fear that had been haunting Matt since his arrival rose in a flood. Horror spread across his skin like swarming ants.

'You mean . . .' He couldn't say it, but the property name screamed in his head anyway.

'Yes,' announced Phoebe triumphantly. 'We bought you Glenmore.'

Twenty-four

Callie pulled up at the front of her parents' suburban Malvern house and took a moment to gather herself. She'd hit peak-hour traffic and the journey across town, with its endless horn honking, squashed-in traffic and rude driving, had sapped the last of her energy.

She dug her fingers into the corners of her eyes. Tired. So damn tired. And heartsore. The day's events weighed on her chest as though tied to a thousand lead sinkers. She'd been so certain of her path this morning, only for a single conversation to sour the sweet happiness she'd tasted.

She didn't want to think about Matt. She couldn't. What was done was done. All Callie wanted now was to complete the plan she'd devised at the start, make proper peace with her parents and move on.

With weary movements, she gathered up her turned-off phone and bag and trudged up the path toward the house. Little had changed. The Queen Anne-style house retained its brick and timber elegance. Roses still bloomed along the fenceline, a Japanese maple taking pride of place in the centre of the manicured fescue lawn, but as she opened the timber gate, hints that all wasn't well became apparent. Moss grew between the path's brickwork. Paspalum spread coarse leaves across the lawn's margins. One of the decorative timber roofline frets near the entrance had broken away. Unswept leaves and grass colonised the corners of the porch.

The front door opened before Callie could knock. Her smiling, watery-eyed father unlatched the screen door. 'Honey,' he said, opening his arms.

Callie slumped into them, the urge to howl against his chest enormous.

'It's so good to have you home,' he whispered, rubbing his cheek against her hair. 'We've missed you so much.' He pulled away and gathered himself. 'Now, let's get you inside before Jacq starts fussing. She's in a big enough state as it is.'

Callie sniffed and swiped at her cheeks. She'd forgotten how comforting a Dad cuddle could be. She might be grown up, but his embrace still possessed the power to soothe.

Photos of Hope, from birth to pretty, unsmiling seventeen-year-old, adorned the walls. A life locked in glossy paper, chemicals and silver frames, partially lived, never to be completed. There were photos of Callie, too. All years old, as if, like Hope, she'd been swallowed into a void as a teenager and never let out. Feeling guilty, Callie made a mental note to send her parents some new snaps to hang—joy-filled ones.

As she entered the kitchen, her mother rushed at her, stopping Callie in her tracks. The hug was strangely standoffish, Jacqueline's body not quite connecting like her arms, as though she didn't know how far to go with it. After several seconds she stood back, hands still on Callie's shoulders, and the same brittle, hopeful smile that she'd worn at Glenmore on her face.

'I'm so pleased to see you. And here too.'

'Thanks, Mum. It's good to be home.'

'Can I get you something? Glass of wine?' Her brow furrowed with sudden distress. 'Maybe you prefer beer? Or perhaps Coke?' She blinked rapidly, hand fluttering to her mouth. 'I don't know what to offer. Isn't that awful?'

'A glass of white wine would be lovely, thanks.'

'Sauv blanc?'

'Whatever you're having is fine.'

Jacqueline buzzed off in a nervous flurry leaving Callie staring wide-eyed at her dad.

He sidled alongside her. 'She's just excited you're here.'

Callie frowned and watched as her mother poured them all a glass of wine. The kitchen bench was laden with salad bowls, condiments and a plastic-covered plate of chops, sausages and steaks. Enough food to cater for twice their number at least.

'Well,' said Michael, taking a glass from his wife, 'I think this requires a toast.' He held up his drink. Dutifully, Callie followed suit. 'To family.'

'To family,' Callie murmured and took a sip.

Silence lingered as they flicked glances and awkward, solicitous smiles, waiting for the other to talk. Callie's mind crowded with things she needed to say but she could sense now wasn't right. They needed time to relax, to get used to being together again, before she bombed them with her desperation to get the hell away.

She looked around, expression polite when inside she rattled as badly as her mother.

'It's still the same.'

'Yes,' replied Jacqueline. 'It never felt right to change it.'

Callie dropped her gaze to the floor. Of course her mum didn't want to change the kitchen; she never wanted to change anything. Even Hope's room had remained the same as the night she left it. Callie might not have been home for eight years but she would bet her ute that if she walked upstairs and entered her sister's bedroom right now it would be like walking backward in life.

'I should light the barbie.' Her dad closed a firm hand around her shoulder. 'Want to come give me a hand?'

'Sure.' She tamped down her pointless brooding and glanced at her mum. 'Can I help? Set the table or anything?'

'No, no. You go out with your father. I'm fine.' As if to prove it, Jacqueline returned to the bench to arrange bowls that didn't need moving, apprehensive false smile fixed in place.

Callie looked away. Damn this was hard. For all of them.

She followed her dad out onto the back patio. A high hedge still separated the Reynolds from their neighbours and half shaded the garden, its shadow long in the fading evening light. Past the patio's paved edge, the underwater lights of the family pool turned the surface an unnatural ocean turquoise in the encroaching night. The colour made Callie think of Airlie and the home she'd soon return to.

She walked to the edge, wondering when someone last splashed in the cool water. When laughter last rang from the Reynolds' yard.

'Your mum's not handling this well.' Her dad stepped alongside, barbecue scraper in one hand. The hiss of gas flame mixed with insect whirs. The oily scent of the heating barbecue plate filled the air. He held her gaze. 'She thinks you blame her.'

'For what?'

He shrugged. 'For forcing you away.'

Callie thought of how hard she'd tried to gain her parents' attention, to be good for them, to make up for the daughter they'd lost, that she'd failed to save. How they'd thrown all their energies into the Hope Foundation. How, even silenced by a coffin and layers of dirt, the house had vibrated with her sister's presence.

Her mum was the worst, always bringing up foundation news. The girls they could save. A never-ending reminder of what Callie couldn't do. Yeah, Callie blamed her mum back then. But it was nothing compared to how severely she blamed herself.

'I left for a whole bunch of reasons, Dad. Not just because of Mum.' Callie regarded the shimmery pool surface. 'Phantom hurt though. I know to everyone else he was just a horse, but he was more than that to me. I really needed him.'

'I know. And we never understood how much until it was too late.' He stroked her hair, smiling. 'But we're going to make up for that, I promise. Anyway, enough. There'll be plenty of time for this later. Let's get this dinner going before your mother decides to make another salad.'

***

Thanks to her dad, dinner was eaten with more talk than quiet. Callie could see him doing his best to relax both the women in his life, teasing her mum over how much food she'd prepared, asking Callie about Airlie and the other places she'd lived.

Callie tried to play along but her heart was so leaden with sorrow it was a slog. Her mind kept drifting to Glenmore and Matt. Two more things she'd loved and lost.

She insisted her mother remained seated while she and Michael did the dishes. The fridge was crammed with leftovers, and Callie tried not to think how much Patch would have loved a spare sausage or chop bone to gnaw on. But he was gone too.

With the last dish put away and every surface wiped clean, Callie apologised and ducked off to the loo. She sat on the toilet with her eyes closed and her palms held together in front of her face, their edges pressed to her mouth as though praying. The urge to bolt back to her ute clawed at her, but the time for running from her family was over. She was an adult, not a confused eighteen-year-old, and they needed to talk. For all their sakes.

If only she weren't so tired and hurt.

Cold water splashed on her face helped shock her system back to alertness. Though a large mirror hung over the bathroom sink, Callie avoided inspecting her image too closely. She knew how she looked—ragged and sorrowful—and she didn't want to contrast who she was now to the girl who'd so fleetingly danced with happiness at Glenmore.

Stiff-backed and determined, Callie returned to the kitchen. Her mother regarded her with a tentative smile over the steam of a boiling kettle. A prepared coffee plunger stood beside it. Three small coffee cups were grouped on the polished timber dining table, along with a sugar bowl, milk jug and plate of Tim Tams.

'Want a port?' asked her father from his position near the sideboard. Eyebrows raised, he held up a small glass. 'There's scotch if you prefer. Or I think there might be some of your mother's Cointreau hanging around in the cupboard.'

'I'm fine, thanks.' Callie had already had too much wine and she needed a clear head for what was to come.

She took her seat and waited for their return, crossing her arms then uncrossing them, trying to stay calm. To occupy herself, she studied the room again only for her gaze to become locked on the wall behind her mother's chair, where a series of photographs formed a rectangular pattern. Callie stared as she recognised images from early Hope Foundation events. Her parents looked nothing like they did now. Jacqueline Reynolds mingling at a fundraiser. Confident, perfectly groomed, her drive evident from the spark in her eyes and the way she pointed at a brochure as she spoke to a pair of smartly suited men. Her father addressing a group of attentive teenagers, arms held out from his side, leaning toward them, impassioned.

Callie sank back, disturbed at the change, and glanced toward her dad. He nodded slightly, as if to say, 'I know', then quickly turned to shove his wife's chair out of the way as she carried the filled plunger to the table.

Jacqueline placed it down before dragging her chair back and pushing the plate of biscuits toward her daughter. 'Tim Tams. They used to be your favourite.'

Callie shook her head.

'Oh. I have others.' Jacqueline made to rise but Callie stayed her with a hand on her forearm.

'It's fine, Mum. I've eaten far too much as it is.'

'Are you sure? I think there are some mint chocolates somewhere if you'd prefer.'

'Positive.' She smiled. 'Now sit down and let me sort your coffee.'

'No, no. I'll do it.'

Callie didn't see the point of arguing, activity seemed to help her mother cope. She waited until they were all seated with steaming cups before looking from her dad to her mum and back again.

'I need to tell you both something.' She fingered her cup handle as a thick burr blocked her throat.

Her mother's hand crept toward her but didn't touch. 'What, darling?'

'Callie?'

The prickly burr grew thorns. She lifted her gaze up to meet her father's. 'I sold Glenmore today.'

'Oh, honey.'

'I'm sorry,' she said, distressed by the devastation in his voice. 'I should have talked to you first but I thought it would help make things right between us. If I gave the money to the foundation. To make up for letting Hope down, for not being like her.' At her father's expression she began to crumble. 'It was your home. I should have asked. And Nanna—' Tears began to seep again. She covered her face. 'I'm so sorry!'

A chair clattered to the floor. Arms lifted Callie, snatching her into a fierce hug.

'You stop. You stop this right now.'

Callie could only shake her head. She'd let them down again. One look at his face and she'd seen the horror contained there.

A soft hand gripped hers, pulling it away from her face. 'Callie, darling, please.'

She opened her eyes. Her mum's face was close to hers, overflowing with concern and tears.

'You have nothing to be sorry for. Nothing.' Jacqueline gave a watery smile. 'It's us who need to be apologising.'

Her dad eased his hold. 'Your mum's right, honey. We're the ones who had it wrong.'

'Me especially.' Her mum touched her cheek. 'I'm so sorry about Phantom.'

Overwhelmed, Callie shook her head.

'Don't you dare say it doesn't matter because it does.'

'It doesn't, not any more. I'm letting it go.' Taking a step back, she hauled in a long breath and swiped at her wet cheeks. 'I'm sorry. I know you loved her and I did too, but I'm so tired of Hope's death ruling my life. The money from the sale of Glenmore can go to the foundation but after that . . .' She held her hands up and dropped them. 'I can't keep doing this, trying to make up for what happened.' She looked at them, knowing the next words would hurt. 'I'm going back to Airlie.'

Her mother's mouth trembled. 'But you've just come back.' She wrung her hands. 'I haven't—' Anguished, she looked at her husband. 'Do something!'

But Michael shook his head. 'Callie needs to do what she thinks is right.' He held Callie's gaze. 'But one thing's for certain, we're not taking the money. That's yours. It's what Mum wanted.'

'It's not. What Nanna wanted was for me to stay. That's why she left me the horse. To make up for Phantom, but it turned out Glenmore didn't want me the way I wanted it.'

He frowned, not understanding.

Callie smiled crookedly. 'Long story. Maybe another time.' She placed a gentle hand on her mum's back. 'Come on. Our coffees are getting cold. And I think I need a Tim Tam after all.'

***

They talked into the night. About Callie, about Hope, about Michael and Jacqueline and the weariness of extended grief that had worn them down too. Although her dad glimpsed the truth, her mother hadn't realised how much it affected their lives. They'd lost a daughter, but that didn't mean they had to wallow in her loss.

To Callie's shock, when she climbed the stairs for her old room, she found it exactly the way it had been when she left.

'You kept it the same,' she said to her hovering mum.

'Well, yes. Of course.'

With a laugh, Callie hugged her tight, her mum responding in kind, although with a bewildered expression.

After Glenmore's gravity-fed rainwater trickle, her parents' shower was an indulgent pleasure. Callie stood under the cascade for longer than she should, letting the water thump her scalp and back, stripping away the day's difficulty.

Even the shower couldn't halt the drag of her fatigue but when she snapped off the light, slipped into bed, and pulled the sweet-smelling sheets up to her chin, wakefulness persisted. Her thoughts tumbled between her mother and father, Matt and Glenmore. She let them roll, hoping tiredness would see them fade, but her heartache was too acute. Giving up, Callie reached for her phone and turned it on. Texts, missed calls and voicemail alerts crowded the screen, every one of them from Matt. She deleted the lot without reading or listening to them, even though part of her longed to hear his voice, to feel that special cocoon of love again.

When the screen was clear and Matt erased, she dialled Anna.

It was nearing midnight on a Thursday. Anna should be awake, either at work or winding down after it. Callie hoped for the latter.

'About time you called me,' Anna accused in her nasal quack when she answered.

'Sorry. Been a lot going on. So what's happening?'

'Heaps!'

Callie's nerves began to jingle at her flatmate's overexcitement. Something major had happened; it rang through Anna's voice like a klaxon. 'Oh yeah?'

'Bruce asked me to move in with him and I said yes!'

'That's really great, Anna,' said Callie, trying to keep her dismay at bay. 'I'm pleased for you. Next we'll be hearing wedding bells.'

'Maybe. He's been hinting but I want to see how it goes first.'

'So it'll be just me and Rowan then.'

'Ah, well,' replied Anna hesitantly, 'that's the thing. With me moving out and the lease coming up, Rowan decided that now was a good time to get out too. He's moving to Mackay so he can go to uni full time.'

Callie sank back into the bed and stared into the darkness. 'Right.'

'I'm sorry. After we spoke I thought, you know, that you and that bloke you met—'

'It didn't work out.'

'Oh.' Anna sounded on the edge of tears. 'I'm so sorry, but you seemed so happy.'

'Yeah, I was.'

'Don't worry. You will be again.'

They talked for a little longer, making arrangements that only made Callie feel worse. Finally, she rang off and rolled onto her side. As sleep at last lapped, Callie whispered a final prayer, wishing for the future Anna was so certain could be hers. Fearing that, without Matt and Glenmore, it might never come.

Twenty-five

Callie woke at five in a tangle of sheets and a greasy layer of sweat. She rubbed her face and lay back for a few seconds, recalling the events of the previous day. The leaden ache that had weighted her heart yesterday returned at the thought of Glenmore. A memory and love-filled home now relegated to nothing more than another profitable parcel of land in some developer's business plan.

And then there was Matt.

She cupped her hand over her eyes as if it would shield her from more pain but there was no keeping him at bay. Callie didn't know which hurt most: his deal with Wal or his relationship with Hope.

Why hadn't he mentioned it? He'd known Hope, loved her, and yet he'd said nothing. They could have talked about her, remembered all that she was, learned new things, good things, and savoured old ones. How comforting it would have been to hear from him that Hope had known love too before she died. The heart-filling, wondrous type Callie thought she'd found herself before it all went wrong.

Maybe Matt had answers to some of Callie's questions about Hope. Perhaps he knew why her sister changed the way she did.

Perhaps he was even the cause.

Wouldn't that just be the icing on the whole rotten mess.

Callie released a bark of irony-heavy laughter and tossed off the sheets. The day was creeping awake. She needed to get to Glenmore, pack the last of her things, lead Morton to Kelso and leave. Get in, clean up and get out, just as she planned from the start.

Showered and packed, she padded downstairs to a kitchen already aromatic with brewing coffee.

'We heard you moving around,' her dad said as he kissed her good morning.

Callie crossed to her mother at the bench and kissed her too, the gesture strange but also liberating. As if, out of all the mistakes, she'd also achieved something good.

Over breakfast, Callie filled her parents in on her plans. She would leave for Glenmore after breakfast, finish the last of her chores and head north to Airlie. The flat needed to be sorted, the furniture she'd left behind either sold or put into storage until she made other arrangements. Of her plans after that she made no mention. Not out of residual wariness, but because she simply didn't know what they were. It wasn't important. Where to settle she could decide on the way, let the vast Australian landscape call her to a new home.

The one thing she knew for certain was that wherever she landed this time, it'd be for good. Callie's days of running were over.

She left at seven, promising to be in touch. The embraces she shared with her mum and dad felt more real than she'd ever remembered; love made more poignant by the lingering memory of another farewell eight years earlier, and regret for the wasted years that followed.

Pausing only to top up with fuel at Geelong, Callie drove to Glenmore's gate, her eyes filling as she spied the house and its half-scraped walls. The idea of renting it out had always been an excuse. She understood now that had she not learned of Matt's betrayal she would have stayed, keeping the house and home paddock, satisfying at least part of Nanna's wishes. The rest she would have sold. As much as she loved the land, Callie wasn't a farmer, and regardless of how her parents felt, Callie needed to give a piece of her heart for Hope. If not for penance, then for at least her own peace. The foundation provided a wonderful drug-education service, the money would ensure its future.

Callie reversed so the ute's tail faced the back path. Glenmore's buyers had accepted her condition to take it fully furnished, and though she'd managed to clear the house of most things bar the essentials, there was still a ute-load awaiting collection and disposal.

Leaving her belongings in the passenger well, she got out, taking a moment to gaze across the hayed-off countryside. A rising northerly tugged at the summer blonde grass of Glenmore's ungrazed paddocks. Over the next few months, provided nature was kind, the land would see summer yield to an autumn break and a carpet of green. In a perfect world, the rains would restart the farming cycle. Autumn drop calves would gaze cutely from under their mother's legs. Lambs would cavort and the land would be vibrant with industry as local farmers prepared new pastures and hay crops.

Except the world wasn't perfect. A few months would probably see the paddocks dotted with surveyors' flags. Perhaps a sign would face Thiedeke Road, advertising the coming development, urging buyers to secure their smallholdings in the face of brisk demand. Within a year the first houses would begin to grow. Hobby animals, driveways and thick, decorative fences would appear. In two years the area would be unrecognisable.

Thank god she wouldn't be around to witness the change.

Two steps past the water tank, taking full advantage of her distraction, Honk unleashed his ambush. Huge, furious and hissing, he attacked in a flurry of wing beats and beak darts. Callie squawked, only to have Honk respond louder and longer with an outraged squawk of his own. Yelping as a wing bashed her thigh, she scooted to the other side of the tank before ducking sideways to take refuge behind the liquidambar's trunk.

'Who let you out?'

But Honk was already strutting off, beak lifted triumphantly heavenward, tootling his victory to the sky. Callie waited until he was well past the clothesline before coming out of hiding.

She frowned toward his run, positive she'd left Honk's enclosure securely latched. No wonder the goose was cranky. He'd probably had no sleep for fear of foxes.

Unless Matt was back and had been over.

Matt. She didn't want to think about him, or all the text and phone messages she'd deleted. Or the soreness in her heart that refused to ease.

Throwing a last wary look Honk's way, she set her jaw and marched toward the house, only to be halted this time by a ute appearing in the lane stretching from the eastern boundary of the property.

Her stomach lurched as she recognised Wal's old LandCruiser. Wal she could handle, but Matt would be too much. No point hiding. Whoever it was would have already spied her ute.

She waited at the edge of the yard, relieved when the car came close enough for her to recognise Wal's gnarled face peering through the windscreen. Instead of stopping, he continued to the front gate and, in an impressive parallel park, jammed the LandCruiser sideways between the entrance's two strainer posts.

After climbing carefully out of the cabin, Wal dumped a broad-brimmed hat on his speckled head, walked stiffly to the ute's tray, tugged a director's chair from the back, and snapped it open. Next came a plastic storage box from which poked what looked like the lid of an old thermos, which he placed alongside the chair. Finally, he lifted down a wriggling Dash and placed him on the ground with a head pat, Dolly leaping after them. With a last inspection of his amenities, followed by a satisfied nod, he settled his backside into the chair.

Callie pursed her lips. So the stubborn old fool wanted to block her leaving. Fine. Other exits off Glenmore existed and with only one Wal, he couldn't cover them all. Let him sit there and stew in his obstinate juices. Her plans were set. She would be leaving whether Wal liked it or not.

***

Callie carried the last box to the back of her ute and jammed it into place. The tray sat low over the wheels from the weight of its cargo. The journey back to Airlie would be slow, but time wasn't an issue. A fortnight remained on the Airlie flat's lease. She could wander around if she wanted, indulge in some blue sky thinking time.

Throwing Wal a speculative look, she ducked back into the laundry for Morton's halter and lead, experiencing a pang of guilt for what she was about to do. No matter what her grandmother hoped, Morton was never Callie's horse, he was Lyndall's. He belonged at Kelso with the girl who adored him.

A polite person would have called to relay her plans but Callie couldn't risk Kate saying no. Besides, phoning would entail turning on her phone and Callie had no intention of doing that until she was long gone.

Aware of Wal's scrutiny, she spent some time rubbing Morton's face and ears, ordering the horse to be good to Lyndall, before leading him out of his paddock toward the gate. Wal remained in his chair, a mug in his hand, Dolly and Dash standing guard nearby.

Callie halted a metre away and held his gaze. 'Can you please move your ute? I need to walk Morton to Kelso.'

'No.'

She drew in a long breath, ordering herself to remain calm. 'Please, Wal. I've a long journey ahead. I can't afford to wait around for you to get sick of this game and leave.'

'Not my fault,' he said. 'Lad ordered me to keep you here until he gets back.'

'What for? So he can have one last crack at fulfilling your stupid bargain? No thanks.' She swallowed down her rising upset. Mentioning Matt *hurt*. 'All I want is to get the hell out of here.'

Wal took a sip of tea, his hand stroking the pup's head, carrying on as if what she said or did were of no consequence. He set the mug between his knees and glanced at the sky with narrowed eyes, his nose screwed up. 'You may as well head back inside. He'll be a few hours yet.'

'Go to hell, Wal,' she said, tugging on Morton's lead and marching off toward the lane, only to arrive at the loading yards ten minutes later and discover every exit padlocked. A trek to the rarely used far eastern gate found it similarly barred.

With her jaw flexed so hard her back teeth throbbed, Callie tromped Morton back to his paddock, setting him loose with his halter still buckled. Pulling the gate closed, she knotted the lead over the top bar and stalked over to the machinery shed. Somewhere in the junk a bolt cutter existed. And if she couldn't find a bolt cutter, there were bound to be wire cutters. One way or another, she was getting out.

Concerted digging unearthed wire cutters. Her temper growing fouler by the second, dust and sweat-smothered, Callie stomped back to Glenmore's gateway.

'You,' she said, waggling the cutters at Wal, 'are a horrible old man.'

Wal merely tilted his head. 'Make sure you do it properly. Don't want wire springing back onto the dogs. Bloody dangerous.'

'The d—' She shook her head. What was the point? Departing with an irritated growl, she stormed off along the fenceline.

The trouble was Callie had no idea how to go about the task of breaching a barbed wire fence safely. Common sense told her danger existed in snapping wires willy-nilly and she wanted to escape, not kill herself. Or anything else.

Halfway between the gate and the boundary paddock, almost opposite the house, she halted and tugged on the wires of a bay that appeared less taut than the others. The road fence was the oldest on the property, existing in this section only to keep a border in place and stock from wandering in rather than out. Callie could only remember Honk and Phan grazing around the house, occasionally a small mob of sheep and, once, in the far distant past, a scarily horned goat. Never cattle.

Callie released the wire and let a smug smile slide across her mouth. Time and a lack of need for straining had seen the fence tension slacken. With a few hefty pulls, some well-hammered cleats and a bit of snipping, she would have her escape route.

After a quick trip to the shed and another dusty rummage for a hammer, cleats and a thick pair of leather gloves, Callie was back. Mindful of Wal's warning she took care to secure each wire well, tugging it as hard as she could, then fixing it into the post with three deeply hammered cleats. She continued through the strands, nailing them secure before moving to the bay's opposite post and repeating the process. Satisfied, she returned to the first post and, leaving enough of an end to twist back on itself, snipped the top wire. Her relieved exhalation when the wire curled safely away sounded harsh in the dozy afternoon.

More snips and wire twists followed until, at last, the fence was down.

As she pulled the wires aside out of danger, Wal hobbled up, Dolly following at his heels, her offspring frollicking behind. Chin jutting, he inspected her work before pausing in the centre of the open bay and pointing. Immediately Dolly parked on her haunches at the spot. He patted her head and with a hand gesture, signalled her to drop. Dog in place, Wal whistled to Dash and made his laborious way back to his seat with his hands in his pockets.

Callie eyed the collie before regarding Wal. Her mouth tightened as the old man raised his mug in a self-satisfied toast.

She looked back at Dolly and tapped the cutters nervously against her leg. Surely the dog wouldn't hurt her or Morton? Dolly was a sweet thing and Wal would never hurt a horse. Then again, she'd never thought he'd make stupid deals with Matt. Or turn Glenmore into a prison.

Still, there was only one way to test his mettle. Throwing Wal a 'stuff you' look, she stomped off to fetch Morton.

Callie was still over ten metres away when Dolly began to growl a warning. Morton baulked and jerked his head, feet paddling backward, the lead rubbing Callie's hand as the rope slipped through her grip.

'Hey, shh,' she said, trying to soothe the horse. 'It's just Dolly. She won't hurt you. She's a good dog.'

But as Callie coaxed Morton forward, it became clear that Dolly wasn't about to disobey her master. The growls became more menacing. The dog's hackles spiked. Callie shifted her grip higher up the lead as Morton danced in agitation.

'Stop it, Dolly. Sit.'

Dolly ignored her, instead casting a glance Wal's way. Teeth bared, she lunged forward, barking nastily. Pain streaked Callie's palm as friction from the slithering lead caused her skin to burn. Biting against the agony, she tried to keep her grip but Morton was in a panic. With a last wrench he was free, tearing back across the yard toward the open gate of the home paddock, almost bowling over Honk and sending the goose into a frenzy of trumpets.

Dolly immediately quietened and sank back to her belly, regarding Callie with her head tilted.

Silence settled back over Glenmore. Callie stared at the sky, swallowing hard to hold back frustrated tears. Her palm felt scorched, matching the prickly fire in her throat and eyes. She breathed hard through her mouth, fighting against a threatening sob and her conscience whispering to just give up, mining inner reserves of strength that had seen her survive the eight years since Hope's death. And would help her survive beyond.

Trembling but under control, she walked toward Wal. He'd set down his mug and was using a thick plait of rope to play fetch with Dash.

'Why?'

'You need to talk to the lad.'

'I have nothing to say to him.'

The pup dropped the rope into Wal's hand. A praise and a pat and Wal threw it again.

'He has plenty to say to you.'

'He can talk all he likes. I'm not staying.' She paused, then hit him with the deal-breaker: 'I've sold the farm.'

Wal waited for Dash to return and scoot off on another chase before speaking again. 'So I heard.'

Callie crossed her arms and placed the curl of her hand against her mouth. Why wasn't he berating her? Where was the lecture about Nanna?

'You don't seem very upset about the news.'

'Doesn't mean I'm happy about it.' His eyes turned watery. 'Poor bloody Maggie. She deserved better.'

She did. So did Poppy, but there was nothing Callie could do to change things now.

'Please, Wal. Let me take Morton to Kelso and then let me go. I don't want to be here anymore.'

No matter how she pleaded, Wal remained steadfast. Unless she was willing to call the police or crash the tractor though his blockade, Callie wasn't going anywhere.

Twenty-six

Matt rubbed his hand down the leg of his jeans and placed it back on the wheel as the little car shifted on the gravel. For the umpteenth time he wished he had his ute but the Amarok remained at Dargate airport where he'd left it yesterday, and he wasn't about to waste precious minutes driving to the other side of town to collect it.

He'd squandered too much time as it was. Perth, Adelaide and now—thanks to a delay that caused him to miss his connecting flight to Dargate and spend five hours on the road in the hatchback he'd rented at Adelaide Airport—he was nearly home.

Home. Glenmore might technically be his now but without Callie it was simply a property, a 'commercial interest' as his mother had so charmingly described it.

He wiped his other hand free of sweat. Matt couldn't remember the last time he'd been this nervous. Not even before his first patrol had his heart hammered this badly, but that was an adventure. This was his life.

Amberton's burgundy gates came and went. Paddocks gave way to forest. His foot turned leaden, accelerating the little car as anxiety shot his thoughts into chaos. Please let her be there. Please let Wal have kept her safe. Please let her listen, just enough for her to know the deal never existed, that his love wasn't conditional on anything, not even his biggest dream.

Forest cut back to farmland. Matt edged forward as Glenmore appeared, lonely against the backdrop of empty paddocks. He searched for Callie, for her golden hair and athletic body and blue-eyed smile, glimpsing instead only the bulky white of Wal's ute blocking the gate.

He braked and changed down a gear, frowning as he passed Dolly sitting in an opening in the fenceline. As the view opened up, Matt's focus shifted to the yard. A glimmer of bronze had him releasing a long, relieved breath. Callie's ute was backed up to the house. She was still here. He had a chance.

Mindful to leave room for Wal's departure, Matt parked to the side of the drive. His legs jittered with the urge to sprint straight to the house but he wasn't about to barge in and risk fucking this up. He'd learned a few things during his years in the army; preparation and good intelligence were never wasted. Callie had been upset enough to sell Glenmore, the place that meant so much to her, even if she couldn't reconcile that attachment with her guilt over Hope's death. What state she was in now he could only guess at. His heart squeezed at how crushed she must be.

'How is she?' he asked, sliding round Wal's ute to where his uncle had risen from his chair.

'In a mood.'

Matt nodded toward the broken fence. 'I take it that was an attempt to leave?'

'Would've if not for Dolly.' Wal shuffled and squinted at the house. 'Feel a bit bad about that. Scared the horse. Think the missy hurt her hand too.'

'Is she all right?'

'Dunno. Probably wouldn't tell me if she wasn't.' His face scrunched. 'Called me a horrible old man.'

'Fuck.' Matt rubbed his hand over his head and followed Wal's gaze to the house and then past it. A flash of colour made his breath hitch. Callie sat on a chair under the liquidambar, watching him intently. Matt half raised his hand and then let it drop when she deliberately turned her face away. The knot in his stomach twisted. This wasn't going to be easy.

Wal bent to pack up his chair. Matt helped, debating whether to ask Wal to stay, then quickly dismissing the idea. He wasn't going to trap her here. If Callie stayed it would be because she wanted to. Because she loved him. Instinct told him that she did but how could he deny her desperation to leave?

Her ute was backed up to the house and by the look of the tray's tilt, heavily packed. She'd cut a hole in the fence. And only a moment ago she'd turned her face away, dismissing him.

Matt glanced in her direction again as Wal manoeuvred the LandCruiser out of the gate. Her attention was back on them. At least she hadn't raced for her car, but he couldn't rule out that she was biding her time, waiting for Wal and Dolly to leave their posts and for Matt to return to his car. A short sprint to the Jumbuk and she could be shooting out through the hole in the fence as he was driving through the gate. The thought drenched in him sick panic.

Ready to leave, Wal pulled up and reached his arm out the ute window to clutch Matt on the shoulder. 'Good luck, lad.' He shook and let go.

The act was so fatherly, so unlike anything Matt had experienced in his life, he wanted to hug his great uncle. Instead he nodded. 'All I can do is explain. If she wants to leave . . .' He stopped and stared toward the liquidambar, his sick fear returning. Callie couldn't leave. He loved her. She meant everything.

'I'll be around if you need me.'

'Thanks, Wal. Appreciate it.'

Wal nodded, and put the car into gear, puttering up the road to Dolly. With a whistle, the collie left her post and vaulted into the ute. Dust swirled, greying the air until a gust left the road clear once more.

The way out of Glenmore was open.

Matt watched for a moment, muscles on alert, ready to sprint to stop her if he had to, but Callie made no move. Her face was turned away, her body hunched over her crossed arms.

He strode for the hatch and drove it to the house, resisting a compulsion to block her ute. This had to be her decision. Even if it broke his heart.

Taking two solid breaths, Matt stepped out of the car.

'Hey,' he said, walking into the shade, his tension easing a tiny notch when she finally turned to look at him.

Fatigue tugged at her eyes. Her clothes were filthy, her long golden plait a mess. Though her arms were tucked in tight to her belly, she held one hand open. She looked beautiful, fragile and so very, very hurt.

He knelt by her chair and gently took her hand, opening it to inspect the raw mark streaking her palm. 'Have you put anything on it?'

Mouth tight, she shook her head.

He rose, still holding her hand. 'Come on, we'll get this cleaned up properly.'

'Go away.' A tear slid from her eye. She jerked her head aside. 'Just go away.'

'I can't, angel.'

Fire flashed. She snatched her hand back. 'I am not your angel.'

He took a moment, trying to stay calm. Nothing was lost. Not yet. He crouched down again, hand on the chair arm, wishing it was on her instead.

'Callie, what Deb told you isn't true. Not all of it.'

Her lips parted but she said nothing.

'Wal did offer to leave me Amberton if I could get you to stay but I refused from the start. Told him he was being an idiot. I want my own place but I'm not the sort of bloke who'd sell their soul to get it.' He made a wry face as his own tightly held hurt leaked out. 'I kind of hoped you knew that.'

She bowed her head but remained silent. He wished he could hold her but her lack of response stalled him.

'Callie, I love you. I'd never do anything to hurt you.'

Suddenly she rose and paced toward the house. Dismayed, he let her go, praying that she'd stop. That'd she'd look up and see him and recognise the truth in his words.

As abruptly as she'd left, she halted and swirled to face him, chest rising and falling in rapid heaves, blue eyes wide and bright with tears. Matt waited but she seemed incapable of speech. She lifted her arms and then let them fall, her head dropping again. A broken sob had him striding for her.

'Don't, angel. Shh.' He cradled her against him, stroking her hair. 'It's okay, I promise. It's all going to be okay.'

She felt ragged in his arms, as if selling Glenmore had cost her spirit, the spark that made her so gorgeous. He pressed his cheek against her hair and closed his eyes, wishing he could bring his Callie back, the girl who'd caught him with her banter and sexy smile, her strength and determination.

When she began to move against his hold he let her pull away. She retreated a step, rubbing her eyes with the backs of her wrists, before letting out a resigned breath and regarding him.

'I know about Hope, Matt.'

Now it was his turn for silence. His gaze flicked to the west, toward Amberton, his fists clenching. Fucking Wal. Fucking, fucking Wal.

'I wish you'd told me. It would have been nice to remember Hope with someone who loved her.' She looked toward her ute. 'I have to go. I've a long drive ahead.'

'No.'

She turned her weary, sad gaze back his way.

'I wanted to tell you about her, I really did but the longer it went on the harder it became. And I wasn't sure how you'd feel about it. I was too scared I'd lose you. I'm still scared.'

'It's over, Matt. I've done everything I set out to do and now I have to leave.' She shifted her gaze past him to the farm, a hollow, thousand-mile stare. 'I can't stay. I have to let it go. It's the last step.'

'No.' He knew he was being unreasonable, that he was going against what he'd said he'd do if she wanted to leave, but his panic was making him insane. 'Fucking hell, Callie, I love you!'

She glanced back, her sad smile breaking his heart. He didn't understand her expression. He didn't understand anything except the sinking dread threatening to consume him.

'What? What is it?' He reached for her hand but she stepped away. 'Angel?'

'I really have to leave.'

He watched her reach the water tank. In a few steps she'd be on the path. A few steps more and at her car. This couldn't be happening, not after all he'd said. It just couldn't.

Resignation and failure washed cold through his veins. She didn't love him. He'd been wrong.

'Was it really that bad, you and me?'

She halted and looked over her shoulder at him. 'No.' She smiled a little. 'It was wonderful.'

'Then why? Is it because of Hope? We were kids. Teenagers full of hormones. I loved her but she started doing all that shit stuff. I hated it, told her she was being stupid, but she just thought I was the stupid one. Next thing she stops coming to Glenmore. Sends me some crap "Dear John" email like I didn't matter. Broke my fucking heart.'

He approached Callie and, mindful of her injured palm, grabbed her hands. 'She was special and I loved her, and I wished I could have done more to stop her taking the path she did. But I was a stupid kid and it was all a long time ago. And just because I once loved her doesn't mean I can't love you.' Matt gently squeezed the fingers of her unhurt hand. 'Don't leave. She's the past. You're my now and my future.' He ducked his head to smile at her. 'I can beg if you want.'

His heart leaped as she smiled tentatively back.

'This is where you belong, Callie. Here, at Glenmore.' He paused. 'With me.'

'I can't.'

'You can.'

She shook her head. 'I sold it, Matt.'

'I know. To MPK Holdings.'

'Then you'll understand why I can't stay.' Her gaze dragged toward the paddocks, her grief at Glenmore's loss palpable. 'I won't be able to bear seeing it ruined.'

'But that's the thing—it won't be.'

'You don't know that.'

'Actually, I do.' At her confused expression, he grinned. 'You see, I happen to know the intentions of the majority shareholder of MPK Holdings, and he has no plan of ever dividing it up for hobby farms. In fact, he has pretty big plans for it. It's me, Callie. I own Glenmore.' His grin slipped a little. 'Well, not quite all. Mum and Kieran own the rest, but I have control over it.'

Callie's mouth dropped in shock. 'How can that be? I thought . . .' She shook her head before regarding him again in astonishment. 'You?'

'Yeah, me. Mum broke the news to me yesterday. She's been looking for a property for weeks and suddenly Glenmore comes up. Couldn't have been more perfect timing as far as she was concerned, whereas I just felt like I'd gained one dream only to realise I was losing an even bigger one.' He cupped a hand around her jaw. 'I haven't, have I? Lost you?'

She shook her head, frowning. 'I—'

'Love you?'

Her gaze dropped, sinking his heart with it, only for it to lurch again when her mouth curled as her eyes sparkled from under her lashes. 'If I stay . . .'

'Yeah?'

'That would technically make you my landlord. I'm not sure loving is allowed.'

'Lots of kinky sex then?'

She laughed, a sound that made his heart tumble. Then she quieted again. 'I've made such a mess of things. I knew Deb's accusation wasn't right. I knew you weren't like that, but everything had gone so wrong. I was so happy, then it was like the world wanted me not to be.' She bit her lip. 'It was always so hard after Hope died. Like enjoying all the things that she never would was wrong somehow.'

'Everyone deserves happiness, Callie. Especially you.' He studied her, wondering which way she'd turn. 'Stay? There aren't many girls in the world who can make nurses' shoes look sexy.'

She took a good while to reply, but when she did, her voice was light.

'I suppose I'll have to now.'

His eyebrows shot up.

'You ruined me.'

'All that great sex?'

She shook her head. 'It was the scrambled eggs. There aren't many men in the world who can make eating scrambled eggs erotic.'

'So it's just my cooking skills you want me for then?'

'You do have other assets.'

'I do. I'm an attractive, capable man after all.'

'And a terrible romantic.'

'With a big farm.' He wiggled his eyebrows. 'What a catch.'

She broke into a grin and wrapped her arms around his neck. 'How can a girl refuse all that?'

'Exactly. So you'll stay?'

Callie held his gaze. 'Yes.'

Joy surged. He hoisted her up, relishing in her giggles. Strong legs wrapped tight around his waist. The feel of her against him, laughing with happiness, made him want to shout to the sky.

She pressed her forehead against his, blue eyes gorgeously alive. 'I love you.'

'Now that's my kind of tenant,' he said, kissing her.

Twenty-Seven

Old fishing hat tight on her head and the tail of her long-sleeved shirt flapping in the breeze, Callie cast out into the deep gutter. Cool seawater lapped around her ankles. In a few months, she'd have to swap shorts and her Dunlop Volleys for jeans and waders but for now she thrived in the last of summer. Not tropical heat by any means, but enough for her all the same.

As it had with every other cast, the line remained slack except for the ebb and tow of the tide. It didn't matter. She hadn't trekked to MacLeans Bay in the expectation of catching anything. Fishing was something to do while Matt was in town, finalising his part ownership of Glenmore.

Callie bit her lip. The last several days hadn't been easy. Regret over her actions still lingered. He kept telling her that it didn't matter, that the past was done and she needed to look ahead, but she found it hard to forgive herself for acting so rashly, for believing a series of stupid accidents instead of in a man who'd done nothing to warrant such lack of faith.

Well, not nothing. He hadn't told her about Hope, and though his reasoning for the lapse was sound, a twinge of hurt remained. Love was winning though, knitting them together in trust. Besides, her hurt over his non-disclosure was no different to his over her easy belief that he'd made a deal with Wal. She needed to get over it.

A tap on the line caught her attention. She concentrated on the feel of the nylon against her fingertip, waiting for another dart. It came, the rod tip bending as the hook embedded. Callie began to wind, assessing the fight, curious to see what had taken the bait.

A big-eyed Tommy rough emerged from the water. She crouched down and rubbed her fingertip over its coarse scales before checking where it had been hooked, gratified to see the barb through the fish's lip. Working quickly, she manoeuvred the hook out and let the fish dart back into the sea. Strong-flavoured Tommy roughs weren't her favourite eating, and summer's end was when they made their way westward to spawn. That little one could live another day.

She walked back up the sand and settled down by her tacklebox to change her rig. If one Tommy existed, there were bound to be more and she didn't want to keep tossing them back. Perhaps today she'd snag a coveted mulloway. She could bake it whole. Let Matt make a salad. Sit outside and eat in the cooling evening. Talk about Hope if he wanted to, although he never seemed keen to do so. She was his past, he kept saying. Callie was his now and forever.

How she loved him for that.

Rig changed to a lure, she padded back down the beach and cast out. The line was too light for mulloway, the risk of it snapping against the power of the fish high, but she didn't care. The likelihood one would even bite was minimal. She just wanted to fish, let the ocean smooth the last of her hurt away.

A car engine filtered through the sea noise. Her heart did a little flip when she turned to see a ute crawling along the edge of the high-tide mark, where the sand was firm. She followed its approach, unable to keep the smile from her face as Matt signalled a farmer-like raised finger salute through the windscreen at her.

'Catch anything?' he asked as he joined her, lifting the edge of her hat to kiss her temple.

'A Tommy rough. I threw it back. I'm trying for mulloway.' She fingered the rod. 'How was it?'

'Dull and exciting at the same time. Lots of papers. The solicitor looking traumatised from his dealings with Mum.' He rubbed at his scar. 'Bit sad because your name wasn't on the deed.'

'That's okay.'

'No, it's not. But we can always sort that out later.'

The way Matt made 'later' sound so full of promise, so full of a future together, left Callie wrapped in a feeling she'd never before experienced. A feeling like safety and tenderness and optimism all bundled into one blanket, its warmth dissolving the last of her doubt. Leaving only love.

He kissed her temple again. 'Are you done?'

'Why?'

He grinned. 'That fishing hat's given me ideas.'

'You always have ideas.'

'Yeah, it's one of the things you love about me.'

'It is.' She glanced at the ocean. Fishing had lost all allure. Nothing unusual there. Matt had a way of dragging her attention away from everything. She inspected him, noting the sparkle in his green eyes, the tilt of his mouth. He had ideas all right. Anticipation prickled like drying salt water across her skin. 'I thought you preferred nurses' shoes.'

'Can't a bloke develop a fishing hat fetish too?'

'He can. So, kinky boy, what's on your mind?'

He dug a toe into the sand and flicked a clod. 'Remember that sex in the sand thing?'

'I do. You've never done it.'

'Neither have you.'

'And?' As if she needed to ask, but it was all part of the game. One they'd been playing a lot lately.

'I thought we might test it out.'

Callie scanned the beach. It might be late morning on a Wednesday but MacLeans Bay was a popular place. 'Risky.'

'Yeah, I know.'

'I suppose we could make it quick.'

He raised an eyebrow.

'Okay, so we'll do it slow.'

'How about we just do it and see what happens?'

She lowered her lashes, mouth curling, heart racing as his eyes widened.

She loved the way he responded to her, like creatures in tune. 'You sure?'

He answered by tumbling her to the ground, snaking his hand up her shirt as he covered her face and mouth with feverish kisses.

'My rod,' she said, wriggling in protest. 'What if I hook something?'

'You already have. And it's a whopper.'

She broke into laughter, the sound so good to her ears. Happiness bubbled inside.

Matt rolled her over until she sat on top of him and gazed at her with lovesick dopiness. 'Fuck, I love you.'

She leaned forward to kiss him. 'And I love you, attractive, capable man.'

'You forgot horny.'

'I figured it didn't need saying.'

'You're right. It didn't. Now come here. I have sandy bits to explore.'

***

Honk signalled Matt's arrival home. Callie skipped to the back door. He'd snuck off an hour ago, refusing to reveal where he was going, calling it 'secret men's business'. Whatever he was up to, it left him smug.

Everything seemed to leave him smug lately. Making love on the beach at MacLeans Bay two days ago had left him grinning like an infatuated idiot. Moving his clothes and belongings into Glenmore the same. Callie had never seen a man look so happy, or so in love.

She wasn't much better. Deb had told her as much at the barbecue Callie and Matt attended at the Graneys', describing the pair of them as being like lottery winners. The description wasn't quite right—money could never make her feel the way she felt with Matt. It wasn't love alone either. She was finding peace. With Hope, with her parents, but most of all, with herself.

Every dawn brought with it a sense of renewal. That she was gradually becoming the person she'd always wanted to be, one who no longer hid behind a mask of stoicism. For the first time in years, Callie was free to laugh and cry, yell with anger and smile with contentment. She could love and be loved. Free.

The barbecue had been another step forward, for both of them. Tension remained between Matt and Tony, but thanks to Wal's revelation about his will, the cousins were attempting to reconnect. Apologies had been made and accepted. Knowing his children would inherit Amberton eased Tony's apprehension for his family. He still felt Amberton represented a lost opportunity, and said so, pointing out to Matt that Glenmore was the same, but the properties' fates were out of his hands. Nor could he complain too much after the commission he'd earned from Glenmore.

Callie let the screen door bang shut behind her and skipped up the path to the yard, halting at the end with her lips pursed when she spied Wal's battered horsefloat attached to the back of Matt's ute.

A horse. She should have known. The cycles in her life seemed to be endless.

Smiling and shaking her head, she strode across the yard to assist Wal from the Amarok's passenger seat. The driver's seat was already empty.

'Okay, what's going on?' she asked Wal, stepping aside as he waved her away.

'Surprise.'

'Might I remind you that the last surprise like this ended in disaster?'

'Not this time.'

A whinny sounded, the float rattling and bouncing as the horse inside stomped and shifted. Beyond the noise she could hear Matt making soothing sounds.

Callie crossed her arms.

'Place needs a horse,' said Wal.

'The place needs livestock.'

But even as she rebuked him, excitement tumbled through her belly. Glenmore hadn't been the same since Lyndall took Morton home to Kelso. Time and again, Callie caught herself scanning the home paddock, wishing he was back. Her memories of Glenmore were so tightly enmeshed with Phantom and her love for horses that not seeing one made the farm feel out of kilter.

Unable to pretend indifference any longer, she strode to the back of the float and peered inside. A glossy black rump faced her, dark tail flicking. Callie breathed in deeply, the scent of horse better than any perfume.

Matt's voice echoed from the float. 'Come on, fatso. Your mistress is waiting.'

Obedient, the horse began to back out. Black rump gave way to sleek but solid flank, then a wide chest and lovely sloped shoulders. Callie's hand went to her mouth, her heart thumping wildly. Two more steps and the bright-eyed black horse turned to regard her, ears twirling like radars. He stretched to give her a quick sniff before raising his head and releasing another high-pitched whinny.

'Get a move on,' said Matt, pushing the horse further backward. He grinned at Callie as he followed the horse down the ramp. 'Beauty, isn't he?'

She nodded, torn between wanting to laugh and cry. 'Literally.'

'Lucky accident.' Matt stroked the horse's regal nose. A thin white star marked the centre of his forehead, another strip of white on the point of his nose. 'But kind of fitting.'

'What's his name?' she asked, approaching and holding out her hand for the horse to sniff before stroking his lovely face. 'And please don't try to tell me it's Beauty because I won't believe you.'

He was a stunning-looking animal—glossy coated and fine boned despite the extra weight he carried. Another snip of white coloured the coronet of his off foreleg, just above his hoof, but otherwise the horse was a glorious shade of black. Her own nature-built china horse.

'Cannonball.'

'Out of Magic Missile,' said Wal, shuffling his way toward them. 'Didn't inherit his speed though. Jumps well. Mainly pony club. Lass who owned him is off to Melbourne for university. Been looking for a good home. Happened I knew of one.'

Matt handed Callie the lead. 'He's yours.'

Callie swallowed, thinking of her grandmother. Knowing Glenmore was safe with Matt had made coming to terms with her betrayal of Nanna's wishes easier, but guilt over Morton remained. Though she hadn't seen Callie in years, Maggie had known her heart better than Callie knew it herself. Time for Callie to honour her wishes.

'Maggie would have wanted it,' said Wal.

'I know.' She smiled at Wal and then at Matt. 'Thank you.'

'Anything to make you happy.' He touched her cheek, the caress tender, then dropped his hand and grinned. 'You do realise it's all part of my cunning plan.'

'Oh, yes?'

'Hard to find another landlord who'd take on all your animals. Mad goose, horse.'

'Next you'll be giving me a dog.'

Wal coughed

Callie shared a look with Matt and sighed in defeat. Matt had brought up Wal's spare pup last night. They'd need a dog for the farm. Dash would be perfect but not if he upset Callie with memories of Patch.

'Oh, all right.'

Wal's grin threatened to crack his walnut shell face.

She turned back to Cannonball, amazed at how like Beauty he was. Warmth flooded her as she stroked his silky neck and breathed in his delicious horsey smell. Memories of Phan clamoured. Of glorious days riding the paddocks, trails and beach. The life she'd thought lost.

A life she'd found again.

Matt sidled alongside and kissed her temple. 'Angel.'

'Attractive, capable man.'

He bent close to whisper. 'You should marry me then.'

'Do you think?'

'Yeah.'

She slid him a look from under her lashes and smiled. 'Well, in that case . . .'

The End

More from Cathryn Hein

A vivid, moving and passionate story of love and redemption set in the gloriously rich landscape of Australia's Hunter Valley.

Brooke Kingston is smart, capable and strong-willed, and runs her family's property with dedication and skill. More at home on horseback than in heels, her life revolves around her beloved 'boys' – showjumpers Poddy, Oddy and Sod.

Then a tragic accident leaves Brooke a mess. Newcomer Lachie Cambridge is hired to manage the farm, and Brooke finds herself out of a job and out of luck. But she won't go without a fight.

What she doesn't expect is Lachie himself – a handsome, gentle giant with a will to match her own. But with every day that Lachie stays, Brooke's future on the farm becomes more uncertain.

Will she be forced to choose between her home and the man she's falling for, or will the very things that brought them together tear them apart?

*

If you'd like to know when my next release comes available plus gain access to exclusive content, news and giveaways, and a couple of sweet short stories to enjoy over a cuppa, please sign up to my newsletter at cathrynhein.com.

Dear Reader

Thank you so much for buying and reading *Heartland*. I hope you enjoyed Callie and Matt's journey to love and happiness.

If you'd like to know when my next release comes available plus gain access to exclusive content, news and giveaways, please sign up to my newsletter. You can also connect via Facebook and Twitter using @CathrynHein. More information about me and my books, including the inspiration behind *Heartland*, along with plenty of other fun stuff, can be found at cathrynhein.com.

Help others find their next read by leaving a review of this novel on your favourite book website.

*

My other rural-set romances include:

Wayward Heart
Santa and the Saddler
April's Rainbow
Summer and the Groomsman
The Falls
Rocking Horse Hill
Heartland
Heart of the Valley
Promises

Romantic Adventure:
The French Prize